Message

from

the

past

Part-01

To my dear friend, Mr Victor Campbell MacDonald for your endless patience, support, guidelines and help. Without you I would never be able to finish it. Thank you very much!

Norbert Rafał Grenda,

Directory of Characters, London:

Danny Davis, Rachel Davis.

Declan O`Connor

George Bradley

Matthew Braddock Harry Green, Simon Edwards.

North Hill:

Susan McKane, John McKane, Nicole Denice McKane,

Nattaly Swanson,

Mark Brown,

Magda Richardson, Joanna Richardson,

David Robert, Carolin Roberts,

Oliver Wilson, Christopher Wilson Jessica Murphy, Aleksandra Murphy.

Second/third plan characters:

Noelle Kemp,

Pamela Stewart,

Ain Hailu, Angelina Hailu,

Diana Sallow,

Lucy Clarke,

Jack Johnson,

Katy Taylor,

Terry Smith, Andrew Harris and others.

'You must be strong with the power of love,

which is mightier than death...

You must be a love that is patient, is gracious...'

John Paul 2

Table of Contents

Prologue

Currently

18 August 2019, North Hill suburb, 10:10 pm.

The car slows down gradually, now bouncing and rocking from side to side. The road has become bumpy.

We are no longer driving on a level surface. Apparently, we have just left the motorway.

So, it must be some kind of unmade road, a clearing or a forest.

We glide slowly forward.

By my calculations, it should be approaching ten o'clock.

Because we couldn't have been on the road for more than forty minutes, the last time I looked at my watch, it was ten past nine. This was before I was attacked in my own home, then forcibly dragged out onto the street and shoved into the boot of a car.

Obviously, they're not in too much of a hurry - after all, why would they be in a hurry?

Everything has been carefully planned, so they probably still have a lot of saved time in reserve.

I'm lying in the boot, furious at myself for bouncing sideways under the turbulence caused by the obstacles the moving car encounters on the surface.

I can't believe I let myself be approached so easily. Fifteen years of police work, and they dealt with me like I was a rookie.

Do I regret having failed? Of course, I do, but not because of my own fate.

I find it hard to swallow the bitter taste of failure because I know that Susan McKane is waiting for me now, out there somewhere, hoping that together we will find her daughter, Nicole Denice.

Beyond that, I know that I was on the right track to explaining the mystery of the missing four from North Hill while also fulfilling the task assigned to me by the stray soul of Denise Randal.

My tormentors had ensured that I now had no tools with me which, possibly, I could have used to improve my situation, let alone even a mobile phone.

That my personal phone was left at home, I could foresee.

But why the hell wasn't I pulling out a tiny emergency phone that I additionally never part with and always carry with me mostly behind my trouser belt?

It may not be the best phone in the world, but it is easy to stow and has satellite tracking, which could help me now in trouble.

While I'm lying locked in the boot, being carted off to nowhere by two criminals, my emergency phone lies conveniently on the cupboard next to the bed where I left it.

I don't stand a chance because I've taken it from myself. I'm completely defenceless.

I already feel completely exhausted and can't move my hands as they are handcuffed behind my back.

I am now at the mercy of two guys who would sell their own mother for petty cash.

God damn it!!! I curse in my mind resignedly.

I am aware that these could be my last moments, but life does not pass before my eyes. It was the same when I was shot in the head a

2

year ago and miraculously avoided death, and I also did not see anything back then, either.

Instead, trying to recall fond memories, I thought back to my last meeting with Connor in London a few weeks ago when we met the banker Ain Hailu, followed by an evening dinner at the 'House of St. Barnabas' in London's Soho.

I could see my wife Rachel's face before she left home that afternoon to go see friends. I wish I had said a more affectionate goodbye to her then, but how could I have known then what awaited me later?

But there is something else: I am not alone here. I feel another presence in this cramped boot. She's here too, Denise Randal, she's back, she's beside me watching helplessly, I can sense her piercing gaze.

But I know she can't help me, and she probably doesn't even realise the gravity of the situation and the danger she's in.

I can't blame her for that because she's just a child, a stray soul who got me into all this trouble.

Since the day I first saw her, she has never left me alone and has followed me everywhere.

Now, at least, I know that from the very beginning, she had good intentions and only wanted to help.

Even though it might not have always indicated that, and from my point of view, it looked very different for a long time, it did.

It was not her fault that things turned out the way they did. In fact, I should blame myself for that because I am a professional police officer and should have foreseen the imminent danger.

However, my intuition and experience failed me at the last moment, and now I am where I am.

Fifteen fucking years on the force like it never happened!!! I am getting nervous.

The car slows down even more.

I think we are just getting to where we were supposed to get to.

I lie handcuffed and have no choice but to wait for events to unfold. I take deep breaths, trying to get my nerves under control, knowing full well that being nervous won't help me now.

Only calmness can give me a chance in this situation, a small hope that maybe, by some miracle, I will get through this.

I try to breathe calmly and steadily, retaining the remnants of my ability to think logically.

The car stops.

...PUM...PUM...

I hear the slamming of doors closing on both sides of the car, driver and passenger.

Then, muffled voices reach me, but I hear nothing of the conversation. Then the sound of branches cracking under the shoes of people taking the next steps, coming towards me.

- Just as I thought we were, we are in the forest.- I assess the situation.

...IS THAT HER???...NOOOO...NOOOO...IT'S NOT HER....

With each louder and louder sound of footsteps, my heart starts to beat faster.

The pressure in my bloodstream hits my head mercilessly, making me hot, and I can feel the veins in my temples begin to tighten.

Okay, the nerves are back, and logical thinking has decided to take a holiday. All that's left is fear and the panic that is slowly engulfing me.

"I can't let them know how scared I am. I won't give them that satisfaction." I say to myself quietly.

4

A moment later, the slamming sound of the boot lock being opened reaches my ears. Then the lid rushes upwards, and the light of the torch falls directly on my face, blinding me completely.

"This is where your journey ends." The first man speaks to me.

"Get out!" Adds the second.

Together, the two men grab me by the shoulders and drag me out of the boot onto the ground. They are clearly amused at this; it is obvious that this is not the first time they have done this.

When my sight returned, I realised that they no longer had their heads covered with hoods.

With this, I momentarily identified the other man who, had knocked me out in my house that evening.

Although I did not know their names, I now knew exactly where we had already met.

It was at the housing agency 'BnB Lettings.'

I remember Rachel and I passing them in the office, it was the first and last time I had seen their faces until now.

- You should be glad, Grandpa, that we were kind enough with a colleague to dig you a cosy hole! - Laughs the first one.

-Well, we were afraid you'd go down on your heart if you had to dig yourself and ruin all our fun!!! - Adds the second, and they both burst out laughing.

I look around slowly, ignoring the criminals, and experience enlightenment.

I know this place. I state in my mind.

I notice a small wooden tool shed that looks exactly like the one in my dreams, standing not far away, hidden among the trees.

Behind it, under the moonlight, water shimmers.

I think it is a river flowing through here.

But I cannot say for sure because it is night, and darkness reigns everywhere.

I also see unnatural bulges on the ground that are roughly two, maybe three metres apart. I counted four of them.

The missing four from North Hill. I say quietly to myself.

There may be more if something else is hiding beyond my sight. My mind prompts me.

There is also one hole, clearly recently dug.

I can easily tell because there is still a pile of fresh rubble lying next to it. I don't have to wonder for long what purpose it was dug for and who it is waiting for.

I recognise this forest. I have seen it in my nightmares, which have

tormented me for many nights, and now I know why.

Is this where I will die? - I allow myself the grim thought.

"We'll wait for one more person, so relax and enjoy the fresh air for as long as you can, you'll soon be smelling the flowers from underneath," says the first of the hijackers to me.

"I don't get it. Why did he insist on waiting here...?" says the second.

"...It's never been like this, bam bam mate in the sand, by now it would be

over, and so we're just wasting time." He added.

"I don't know, he told us to wait, so we wait. Do you have something better to do...?" asks the other rhetorically.

"Actually, so far, we haven't knocked grandpa yet. Maybe he's special or something and wants to talk to him before we'll send him on his way." As he says this, I notice the glint of a metal object in his hand, and it's a gun.

We continue to wait.

I'm sitting leaning against the back of the car with my hands immobilised behind my back, thinking about Rachel now.

Is she looking for me? Has she already realised what has happened? Does she still think I'm waiting for her at home? I am tormented by questions.

Denise Randal's soul is beside me. I can't see her, but I can clearly feel a presence that I have grown accustomed to and recognise.

...IS THAT HER...???...NOOOO...NOOOO...THAT'S NOT HER....

To my surprise, I find that I can sense other people, this is a very strange and new experience as it is the first time I have encountered this.

It's something that gives me the unmistakable impression of being in a crowded school room or corridor because I sense the presence of the souls of very young people or even children.

The only difference is that the young people around me are not calm. They are very agitated or irritated.

You can sense a great anger in the air with a sinister atmosphere. It is as if these young people feel as if someone has cruelly taken away a very valuable possession and now, they want to punish this person for it.

They want reparation, justice, revenge.

There are only three of us here, but it seems to me as if there are more people. The situation is becoming, with every passing minute, more and more tense, although not a trace of nervousness can be seen from these two guys.

They don't have a clue about anything. Explains my mind.

However, I know that something must be happening, something that they did not foresee and for which these souls, whose presence I sense, have been waiting impatiently for a long time.

Life, once taken from them cruelly, without mercy, prematurely, now they have a chance to take revenge for it, the missing four from North Hill. I say to myself in my mind.

But I can't explain how I have this certainty or the reason why I attract the souls of the dead to me. It's just the way it is, and I've managed to come to terms with it, although I must admit that it came with considerable difficulty.

Now I know that something sinister hangs in the air, and only I can feel it, but I am not the one threatened by this invisible force.

It is not that I will probably die in this gloomy place far from civilisation because I have already started to get used to it, but the aura of this place. It was almost saturated with hatred and despair,

Making myself have an illusory hope that someone would manage to come to my rescue was also pointless, as no one knew where I was at that moment, not even myself.

There is no chance that someone will come across my trail in time to come to my rescue, and I am aware of this.

They have left no clues behind where they are taking me against my will. My intuition prompts me.

The surroundings I am now observing also look as if they have been forgotten by humanity.

A complete wilderness far into the forest, a place where the devil says goodnight.

Another twenty minutes or so pass.

I see these men becoming increasingly impatient, their behaviour revealing.

One walks back and forth incessantly, nervously smoking a cigarette, while the other sits in the passenger seat of the car with the door open, glancing at his phone every few seconds or so.

A few seconds later, I hear a car approaching and, taking my eyes off my kidnappers, I notice car headlights approaching in the distance.

There he is. Says the one with the cigarette.

Only thirty minutes late. Adds the other one from the car.

...IS THAT HER...???...THATS HER...??...IS SHE HERE...????

The headlights of the car are already very close and seem to be pointing straight at me.

The impact of the strong, bright light, which falls directly on my face, causes me to experience temporary blindness again. I must close my eyes to protect them.

The vehicle stops, but the lights still fall towards me.

Even so, I notice the legs of the driver getting out of the vehicle, they have stiletto shoes.

Why am I not surprised by this? I ask myself sarcastically.

I am not particularly surprised; in fact, I was expecting a woman. Yes, I am furious that they managed to lead me astray so easily, but on the other hand, my suspicions are just now coming to fruition.

Fifteen years on the police force, and I've been fooled and damn it!!! I get angry in my mind while keeping a stony face.

"So? Shall we start the show?" the first one gets impatient.

"You've got ten minutes, and we're finishing it! I don't have all night!" shouts the second one from the car.

"Hello, Mr Davis." A woman speaks up, and a shock runs through my mind. *Oh shit! After all, I know that voice!* I say to myself in my mind while trying to see her face.

...THATS HEEEER...!!!!...SHE IS HEEEER...???? ...YEEEES... YEEEES...SHE'S HERE...!!!!!

I suddenly hear whispers coming from everywhere. I look around, confused.

In truth, I couldn't see the person exactly yet, but the look on her face started to draw itself in my mind and at that moment, it occurred to me who she was.

A sense of disbelief simultaneously displaced a strange feeling of relief, creating a disorientating mix.

What is she doing here, for Christ's sake?! I thought in despair.

I can honestly say that she was the last person I would have thought would be here.

"I thought we'd have a little chat." She speaks to me in a calm tone.

...*HEEEEER...THAT'S SHEEER...SHEEE IS HEEEERE...!!!!*

At that moment, a strong wind began to blow, which meant a storm was coming.

A storm that was an accumulation of the huge negative energy that prevailed in this place and only I knew it.

...*HEEEER...!!!... SHEEEE IS HERE...!!!*

Again, I heard voices coming from the side of the forest, which blurred slightly in the wind.

Only I could see what was really happening now, barely visible transparent figures, each standing next to their grave in the ground.

She is here!

The person who took away everything that was most important to young people and started this whole nightmare.

She has just appeared here, she is here!

Now, the lost souls are ready to take matters into their own hands and bring justice.

The long-awaited time of retribution has arrived.

The time for revenge has come...

1

Immortal Soul.

'If you know the eternal Love that created you, then you also know that within you dwells an immortal soul.'

Ten months earlier.

18 October 2018, Tottenham Court Road district, London, 05:30 pm.

It all started on the day my partner, Connor, and I received a notice to check on an alleged domestic violence incident involving a child.

As we thought at the time, it was to be another routine inspection.

I had been on field duty for years, getting hundreds of these calls a month. So, there was nothing to predict that after this intervention, my life would change completely and trigger a series of mysterious and sometimes even ghastly events that were yet to come.

At the time I was patrolling the streets of London with my long-time partner and friend Declan O`Connor, whom I called simply Connor.

As we were both very fond of the film Terminator 2, this nickname suited him very well and quickly caught on.

Declan was a 50-year-old Irishman from north Dublin.

His family moved to Birmingham in the midlands of England when he was ten years old.

He himself came to London when he turned eighteen to join the Peel Centre police academy, Hendon Police College and we met there. We became partners in 1998 and have now worked together for almost twenty years.

Because we both enjoyed spending time in the field working closely with the public neither I nor Connor ever considered further climbing the professional ladder.

Although we could easily have moved into the Investigations Branch and dealt with investigations, for which we had an aptitude as well as an open door.

Over the years of working together we formed a very close-knit team and worked well together. Declan was a great driver, and I was able to patrol the streets perfectly. Without boasting, I can say that I had eyes like a radar because even the slightest suspicious behaviour did not escape my attention.

That day, we were already getting ready to finish our eight-hour shift. It was just past 5:30 pm, and we had twenty-five minutes left to head back towards the base.

The day was going relatively smoothly.

We apprehended a couple of suspected drug dealers who we searched on the street, and as a result of which, we found only small amounts of cannabis in their possession.

Then, after writing down personal details, we let go with a warning. There was also one car collision in the street, thankfully, with no people injured. "So, how's Connor...?" I chatted to a colleague...another twenty minutes and, one of the smoothest patrols we've had for many months is over. "Are we going for a beer before we disperse home?" I asked.

"Don't say hop until you've skipped..." Connor replied..."Remember, there's something going on every minute in this town, and twenty minutes is an eternity." He added.

As soon as he finished saying this, our radio rang out.

The switchboard was talking about a report of domestic violence in one of the blocks of flats near Goodge Street tube station.

The victim was said to be a woman named Miriam Randal, living with her ten-year-old daughter, Denis Randal, in flat number 9 on the first floor. It turned out that our unit was closest to the scene, so we immediately took the call. We then turned on the police sirens and rushed to the address indicated at the signal.

"Yeah, and there is your one beer before home." Connor laughed. "Oh, you're exaggerating. There's probably a drunken brawl again…" I replied. "…Ten minutes and it's done, you'll see, we'll make it exactly by 6 pm, I'll bet you that," I added.

I couldn't know how wrong I was at the time because situations like the one we were about to face were impossible for anyone to predict. Well, unless you are "clairvoyant," or in this case, it would be more appropriate to say "pessimist."

Either way, I personally have never believed in such things.

I have always been a person for whom everything should be explainable in a rational way.

I am a police officer, and I look at facts, evidence and tangible things before I believe something completely.

So, I never even wanted to hear about paranormal activities, ghosts, life beyond the grave or other, as I called it at the time, nonsense.

But fate decided to teach me a lesson in such a way that I would feel for myself and realise once and for all that I was wrong. It wasn't long before I was to find out what reality really was.

Arriving at the Gower Street flats, not far from Goodge Street tube station. We were approaching the location of the address where the event given via the switchboard should take place, and we saw a woman standing in the street who started waving her arms at us.

I immediately thought that this was the person who had reported the whole incident.

So, we parked the police car, and then, after exiting the vehicle, I approached the woman.

After a short conversation, she explained to me that she was a neighbour and that she had called the police because there was terrible shouting and sounds of fighting coming from the flat next door.

In addition, a little girl who lives with her mother at this address was probably involved.

This made the neighbouring woman even more concerned about the incident out of concern for her child.

It also transpired that this was not the first incident of an altercation in this flat.

The neighbour explained that after previous incidents at this address, the woman living there had justified everything by talking about a "little misunderstanding with her partner."

At the time, she argued that it was no big deal and asked not to call the police.

Because she did not want her ten-year-old daughter Denise to witness any drastic scenes involving the police.

Which struck me as very suspicious from the outset.

Apparently, this time, things had gone too far, and the woman finally decided to notify the uniformed officers. I thought.

Following this line of thought, it was apparent that previously, the neighbour was not so concerned about the disturbing situations that were taking place there.

Because she had decided not to interfere until now.

Well, people react differently to such situations. I explained the woman's behaviour to myself.

"Officer, her boyfriend, is most likely drunk..." The neighbour confessed at one point. "It's none of my business, but I think he might be an alcoholic. I don't know if he's taking drugs..." she went on... "Many times, I have seen him standing in front of the house and behaving strangely. Normal people do not do that sometimes; he can knock on the flat for an hour, shouting and kicking at the door, and she is either not inside or she does not want to open the door for him." She added at the end.

"And the woman who lives there also abuses alcohol?" I asked. "But no, officer, Clare is a very calm person. She has lived there for a few years with her little daughter named Denise and there have never been any problems with them." She replied.

"I understand. Is the man you are talking about still in the flat?" I asked.

"Since I called for you, I haven't seen anyone come out of there." She replied.

"Thank you for your help. My colleague and I will now go and check it out. Kindly return to your home." I ended the conversation.

I turned my gaze towards Connor, who was standing not far from me and staring at flat number 9 on the first floor.

No sounds of a brawl or even any loud conversations could be heard coming from inside it.

Perhaps they saw that we had arrived and stopped. My intuition prompted me.

I approached my partner and poked him on the shoulder then we both started towards the stairs and further up to the first floor.

We arrived at door number 9.

There was no bell, so I knocked a few times with my fists.

"Hello, this is the police! Please open the door!" I called out through the letter hole in the door.

Nothing happened for a short while, so I knocked again.

Then suddenly, there was a rather loud slamming of the door on the first floor of the flat, followed by the unmistakable sound of quickly placed footsteps on the wooden stairs.

"Someone is coming down to us in a hurry," I said to Connor.

I still didn't see any reason to be alarmed and even the opposite.

It was quiet in the flat so whatever had been going on there earlier had now calmed down.

But I knocked again just to be sure and repeated that we were from the police.

In this way, I wanted to make the person who was now going to open the door for us feel even more pressure to hurry up.

At the same time, I did not have time to put together an explanation in my head and what she should say.

After a few seconds, I heard the key turning in the lock, and then the door gave way, and now a tall, slim and very well-groomed woman stood on the threshold in front of us.

She was dressed in a red strapless T-shirt and blue jeans.

On her feet were homemade slippers, and her long blonde hair was braided into a ponytail.

I momentarily noticed that the woman was visibly shaken, but she was trying to hide it.

Other than that, I did not notice any visible injuries on her face or body. Apart from slightly smudged make-up, which indicated that she had cried a moment ago she quickly wiped her face in a towel or something else before opening the door for us.

I didn't notice anything that might indicate domestic violence. *However, something must have been going on here recently. I wonder what she will tell us in a while.* It crossed my mind.

"Mrs Clare Randal?" I asked.

"That's right..." She replied. "How can I help you?" She added.

"I am PC Danny Davis, and this is my partner, PC Declan O'Connor. We have received a notification from your neighbours indicating a serious brawl in this flat..." I replied truthfully. "Reportedly hearing loud screams and noises indicative of a brawl, we have grounds to suspect domestic violence involving a child." I continued.

"We have a duty of care to make sure everything is okay for you and your daughter, so please cooperate with us," Connor added.

"Yes, I understand..." she replied in a slightly cracking, strained voice. Which in turn indicated that she had either been shouting for a long time or crying.

"It's all right, gentlemen. My partner drank a little too much alcohol and couldn't find his wallet in my house. He was irritated, hence the shouting, but he's gone now. I'm alone now because Denise hasn't come back from school yet." Clare replied.

"So, I know she is no longer telling the truth, just why is she lying?" I thought.

Connor and I both knew that the woman was now making up a story on the fly.

A neighbour had just testified that she had not seen anyone leaving the flat.

Admittedly, she also did not say that she knew one hundred per cent that the child was now in the house, but my intuition told me that this was the case.

Maybe she doesn't trust the police? No, that's not it. Intuition was prompting.

It was clear how Clare was trying to choose every word so as not to arouse my and Connor's suspicions.

Police officers with an experience like ours can smell a lie a mile away. Connor and I sometimes played a trick in such situations. Understanding each other without words, we decided to pretend for a while that we were not guessing anything and then just see what else she would tell us.

"How old is your daughter?" Connor asked.

"Ten." She answered immediately.

"Ma'am, it's seven-fifty. School classes end at sixteen." I replied, looking at her with suspicious eyes.

"Your daughter should have been home a long time ago; shouldn't you be the one to pick her up?" Connor echoed.

"Oh yes, you're right…" She replied, visibly embarrassed. "But she went to McDonald's with the other kids after school. My friend is supposed to walk her home. They should be here soon." She dragged on.

Connor was standing behind my back by now, and I noticed him peeking deep into the flat over my shoulder, then he said.

"Whose shoes are standing by the stairs? I see two pairs of small children's shoes and large men's sneakers." He asked.

The woman turned her head to look at which shoes Connor was talking about.

As she looked back at us and was just taking in air to answer something, we heard a noise upstairs.

It clearly sounded like something heavy had fallen to the floor.

"Someone is upstairs." Immediately, my intuition kicked in.

"Ma'am, who is up there?" I asked.

19

"No one...!" she replied quickly. "It's just a cat." She lied.

"Is it Denise?" Connor asked.

"Or is it your partner?" I added.

"Ma'am, we can't leave until we talk to your daughter…" I said.

"Can I go upstairs and check?" I added.

I did not receive an answer to this question; instead, the woman was clearly hesitant to let me in.

However, she eventually lowered her gaze and moved out of the way, and I decided to make my move.

I moved towards the stairs, bypassing Clare, who was now standing next to Connor, who had also stepped inside.

As I slowly climbed up the stairs, I heard another clatter, and after a moment, the quiet sounds of a struggle and the muffled squeal of a girl reached me.

Then, with a sudden silence, everything stopped.

I stopped halfway and looked at Connor with surprised eyes.

I could sense from his face that he, too, had heard what I had heard and was looking anxiously in my direction.

I reached the door on the first floor and then slowly and carefully pushed it open into the room.

When the gap in the door became wide enough for me to enter, I squeezed through it sideways.

Once I was inside, a chest of drawers with a TV, a wardrobe and two armchairs stood in front of me.

I slowly looked to my left, scanning the room, and ran my eyes over the large double bed and the bedside table.

Only after a while did I notice them, as the view of this side of the room was still obstructed by a half-open door.

So, I had to tilt my head more to see them as they were standing next to the bed in the very corner of the large room.

Then, momentarily, I felt the adrenaline levels surge into my head, and at the same time, my heart started beating like crazy.

For a moment, I couldn't believe my eyes, as it might have seemed like it wasn't really happening.

A man was holding a crying child in front of him and putting a gun to her temple.

He was blocking her mouth with one hand and holding the firearm in the other.

He was tall and well-built, so the petite girl had no chance to resist him. She stood in front of him sobbing, and tremors ran through her body. I could clearly see her shaking with fear.

I slowly put my right hand, which he had not yet seen hidden behind my body, on the Taser, preparing for the worst.

I didn't want the individual to get scared and pull the trigger on impulse. *Talk to him and convince him that he was making a huge mistake.* Intuition was sending signals.

My mind was now working at increased speed, trying to find a way out of a situation that looked surreal, to say the least.

When I looked at his face, I saw that the man had huge pupils and white, already dried remnants of saliva had collected at the corners of his mouth. Jesus, he is extremely high on drugs. My mind explained the man's condition.

About this, I had no doubt. During my police work, I dealt with hundreds, if not thousands, of people abusing psychoactive drugs.

I could clearly see him breathing fast, his hands shaking, and his jaw walking sideways under the influence of intoxicants.

This was the first such situation I had been in.

In the past, I had been fortunate enough to never face this kind of drama. Colleagues more experienced than me, who have taken part in such actions, told me that, first of all, you must not panic and then slowly and calmly start negotiations with the desperate person without making any sudden movements.

A man with a distorted perception of reality and a gun in his hand has nothing left to lose. From the point of view of the situation in which he finds himself, an extremely dangerous person is capable of doing anything. You can never predict how he will behave. You should withdraw and then call for support. I was reminded of the words of a lecturer from when I was still at the police academy.

I must try to appeal to his conscience and convince him that he is making the biggest mistake of his life so that he puts the gun down and lets the girl go so that no one gets hurt. A plan of action automatically formed in my head in those few seconds when we measured each other with our eyes.

Unfortunately, I didn't even have the chance to try to say anything because, from now on, everything moved at a dizzyingly fast pace.

The whole situation lasted a mere thirty seconds, so in such a short time, Connor wouldn't even have had time to step on the front step, let alone move to help.

Especially since, at that moment he couldn't even see what I was seeing, so he was completely unaware of what drama was unfolding right in front of my eyes at that moment.

Just as I was about to open my mouth to speak, the man pointed the gun at me in one movement and, without thinking, pulled the trigger.

First, I heard the shrill bang of the bullet leaving the chamber in the gun. The last thing I saw was the blinding light of the bullet flying towards me at high speed and the gunpowder spraying out.

It immediately went dark before my eyes, and the force of the impact pushed me a few steps backwards.

I probably would have landed much further back had it not been for the wall just behind me, which blocked my further fall. I bounced against it and then slid inertly to the floor.

As I lay on the ground helplessly, I heard two more shots fired just a few seconds later.

He was firing in my direction to pick me up. Instinct prompted. Despite the shock I had just experienced, however, I was conscious the whole time.

As a result, I could hear everything that was now happening around me, but I didn't notice any further shooting, which was kind of a relief.

"AAAAA...!!!" First, I heard Clare Randal's loud scream from the ground floor.

Then Connor ran up the stairs at the same time, shouting over the radio.

"Shots fired!!! I REPEAT!!! Shots fired!!! Officer down!!! An ambulance is needed immediately...!!!! ...Stay out of here...!!!!" ordered Connor to the woman, then added.

"...Hang in there, mate. Help is on the way." He said to me, kneeling by my side.

At that point, Clare lost control of herself. She was crying hysterically and incessantly screaming on the ground floor, "...Denise...!!! My god, my Denise!!!" she lamented.

As I lay on the floor at the entrance to the bedroom and the blood slowly oozed from my head, the realisation of what had just happened only began to come to me.

I could feel the right side of my head getting hotter and hotter and the blood pulsing intensely under the rapid beating of my heart, which was pounding like crazy in my chest all the time.

But all I could think about was this girl, I was very worried about her, with no regard for my own life.

Dear God, if you can hear me, make sure nothing happens to her. It was the first time in my life that I had turned to so-called higher powers.

I had never done this before.

No more than ten minutes passed when the area was overrun with police units and medics.

As I was carried down on a stretcher to the ambulance, with a blurry vision, I saw little Denise walking beside my stretcher.

At this sight, I breathed a sigh of relief.

Nothing had happened to her. My mind registered.

It would probably seem strange that she was allowed to move freely during chaos in the form of rapid response units after all this time.

But under the circumstances, I was unable to think logically.

I looked along the stretcher and saw the girl trying to grab my hand. However, when I wanted to reciprocate the hug for some reason, I was unable to grasp her hand.

No matter how hard I tried, it looked as if my hand was penetrating Denise's hand.

I furrowed my brow in surprise at this sight.

However, I was unable to ponder this for any length of time and quickly explained to myself that it must still be the fault of post-traumatic shock. Apparently, the feeling in that hand had not yet returned. Any doubts were cleared up by my mind.

On the way to the hospital, I fell asleep under the influence of anaesthetics, so from then on, I had a blank in my memory until I woke up in "St. Thomas Hospital" at "Westminster Bridge."

Could it be that it was all over? Nothing could be further from the truth; my journey was just beginning.

2

An oasis of peace.

'Let us guard against the appearance of love; let us not love in word and in tongue, but in deed and in truth.'

10 years earlier.

20 April 2008 The town of North Hill, north of England, 155 km from London.

Situated by the North Sea, North Hill is a quiet, peaceful and very picturesque place with a population of just under twenty thousand. The town's name comes from the fact that the first settlers who came to the area had to walk almost ten kilometres uphill to the north, which is why it came to be called North Hill, a name that eventually caught on. The beautiful landscape of the historic town is filled with many old architectural buildings. The diverse fauna and flora flourishing in the impassable forests surrounding the community created a unique charm and a kind of magic floating in the air.

All this meant that new settlers, for many years, simply fell in love with this town, almost at first sight, and decided to spend the rest of their days there.

The small, yet modern, town centre had everything that people needed most.

Many grocery and clothing shops, pubs, cafés, restaurants, a shopping centre, a cinema, a historic town hall in the heart of the town and a school. A fishing harbour was built by the sea, at which local craftsmen moored their boats for fishing in the appropriately designated seasons.

On the other hand, at the edge of the town, there was a football stadium for the local football club and volunteer fire brigade booths, and there was also a sewage treatment plant nearby.

The town was surrounded by many kilometres of wild woods and meadows where farm animals were kept.

The outskirts of the coastal village of North Hill were mostly pretty and well-kept detached houses with gardens.

A few of the more affluent residents built swimming pools for themselves, while others farmed or simply went about their daily business.

It was on one such farm that Susan Jankins grew up, taking her husband's surname, McKane, when she married.

Twenty-two years old at the time, slim with a shapely figure and of medium height, she had nice brown hair and eyes of a similar colour.

What characterised her most, however, was her face, which some people called a 'baby face.'

Susan Jankins/McKane was an extraordinarily friendly and approachable person, and her beauty gave off a positive vibe, which meant that people liked to talk to her or simply be in her company.

This made it easy for Susan to connect with new people and made her someone who was easy to open up to without fear of hurting or betraying their trust.

However, it was not only her personality traits and appearance that made Susan a unique person, as she was also known for her intelligence. From an early age, she stood out from her peers in terms of learning, and when an IQ test was carried out on her, it was found to be a whopping 139 points when Susan was only sixteen.

Despite her young age of twenty-two, she worked as a lady psychologist at a local NHS clinic.

She managed to get the job just a few months after graduating with her degree.

Susan's ambition pushed her further, so she educated herself in the field of psychology on her own and wanted to gain as much knowledge about the subject as possible, and the books on the shelves of her surgery were mostly inspired by the subject.

Ever since she was a child, she was fascinated by the subject.

She loved to learn more about how the human mind works and how it affects people's behaviour and emotions because, as she used to say:

"I want to know how I can best help other people."

Susan's foster parents were extremely proud of their daughter and delighted that she was growing into a decent and wise woman with a good heart.

Susan was surrendered to an orphanage as an infant in 1987. At the time, the only information about her was that she came from a broken family and that she had been given up for adoption by the girl's mother when she was just one year old.

Having not been given a name by her biological mother, she was baptised as Susan by the nuns of the "Order of Divine Mercy," named after St Paul, in Glasgow.

Adopted by a North Hill couple in 1990, Rita and James Jankins, when the girl turned two.

She met her biological mother only once, in 2004, as a young woman just after turning eighteen.

Then, a woman one day, for reasons known only to her, decided to find her daughter and succeeded.

The woman arrived in North Hill at the time and then contacted Susan's foster parents, who, after much persuasion, agreed to persuade their daughter to meet her. Susan did, yes, agree to meet her biological mother, but she did so reluctantly and only after careful consideration during a conversation with her foster parents.

During the meeting, Susan went alone.

The woman tried to explain her situation from eighteen years ago and justify why she could not leave with her.

Clearly driven by remorse, which had plagued her for a long time.

She said to Susan:

"I was a single mother at the time. I had no choice but to give you up for adoption."

She also argued that she was not in a position to provide her with the normal living conditions that a small child needs due to her mental health problems and her heavy dependence on alcohol and other drugs.

Susan listened to her mother's statements with a stone face, unmoved.

The woman said exactly what Susan had expected to hear from her. *She could have just said that she was a hopeless junkie and saved me this farce.* Thought Susan at that moment, looking at her mother with pity. *So, she left out all the details that were not convenient for her.* Summed up the meeting for the young woman.

However, Susan was one step ahead of her mother, who had no idea. Susan had previously found out information about her during an investigation she had carried out to find out more about the person who wanted to meet her before they saw each other.

She had no intention of going blind without any knowledge.

This was just after a woman had contacted her and suggested a meeting. It was then that Susan decided to speak to Mark Brown, the North Hill Police Chief and a friend of the Jankins family.

Susan was a remarkably intelligent young woman and knew well how to deal with unknown people.

She had studied psychology and was constantly learning new ins and outs of the human mind, so she found it easy to deal with different people. She could also tell by their body language what the other person was thinking at any given moment and what emotions were driving them.

Chief Superintendent Mark Brown suggested asking his friend, a private investigator, for help in finding information about the mother.

Due to being on active duty, he himself was not qualified to undertake this task.

Susan then turned to a recommended man who had been retired for some time and, but for the sake of killing time, was involved in private investigations.

The man had his contacts in the police and was excellent at finding personal details of missing or wanted persons.

Given that Susan had been given up for adoption in 1989 to the "Order of Divine Mercy," the private investigator had little problem finding information about Susan's biological mother.

Unfortunately, following the policy of the Order, the employees were not authorised to give him the woman's private data, i.e. name, surname and age.

But, thanks to a power of attorney from Susan, the detective was given a file with notes on the person of interest, and this is what he delivered to the Jankins' estate.

Of all the information the man provided, however, Susan's biggest point was that the woman admitted to using psychoactive substances.

Also, while she was still carrying it in her womb.

This was during a handwritten conversation before the order decided to take the infant into its care.

However, there was no mention of who her father was, so this issue remained a mystery to her at the time.

"How typical of pathological people," Susan stated at one point.

However, the meeting with her mother was not a complete waste of time, as Susan thought at the time, cause at one point, the woman told her something extremely important.

Susan did not know it at the time, but this something was about to change her life forever.

Throughout the years of growing up in a secluded atmosphere, Susan had become entrenched in the belief that it was a very good thing that her life had turned out this way.

Her foster parents, Rita and James, loved her very much.

They cared for her and provided her with everything a young person needs to grow up to be a law-abiding human being.

She grew up in a nice and safe home, which should make her life so far a happy one.

I'm eighteen, I have a loving boyfriend, I'm going to get married and have my own home and family soon. Susan's thoughts on her life on the way back, just after the end of a rather unpleasant encounter with her biological mother.

Like every young woman in the 1980s, Susan had dreamt since childhood of one day marrying happily and having her own family, career and child. This is what she had aspired to in the beginning, and now that she had succeeded in making her plans a reality, she did not feel entirely fulfilled.

Susan was not like many others of her age.

While her peers were still going to parties and meeting all sorts of people, she had already settled down.

From an early age, she surpassed other children in her maturity, both physically and mentally.

She was far from the assumed norm, which was very easy to see in her behaviour.

Some people, upon meeting Susan, could not believe that they were dealing with such a young person. She always seemed to be a few years older than her actual age.

Which also made her foster parents proud.

But Susan's ambition, never allowing her to build on what she already had, meant she always wanted more from life.

Even though she had fulfilled her dreams, she did not want to be seen only as a mother and wife.

Susan loved new challenges and the feeling of accomplishment when she reached her goal.

That is why she never stopped educating herself and continued to read dozens of books about the field of psychology.

When she started going to school as a child, it was the first time her teachers noticed that she was ahead of her peers in terms of intelligence. As it was quickly established that she was exceptionally gifted, she was allowed to move to a class two years ahead of her year in educational level.

No one doubted at the time that Susan would easily assimilate the material intended for children older than her, and she did.

After leaving school, Susan began her professional studies, which she also completed with distinction.

She then moved seamlessly into a job as a lady psychologist and got her own practice in a local NHS building, where she regularly saw her patients for the next few years.

So, she achieved another success in her young life because she always wanted to work with people.

To help them with their mental health problems, and this was now what she did professionally.

Susan was a very well-known person and was recognised by the people of North

Hill.

People respected and trusted her, both privately and professionally. She was seen as a professional and courageous woman, at the same time very friendly with a heart of gold.

A kind of auntie, she was sometimes made fun of.

Life was going well at the time then Susan, as well as her husband John, were looking forward to the arrival of their child, and both were happy that they would soon be parents.

John McKane was a man almost twelve years older than Susan, but they were a perfect match.

And she loved him with all her heart, and the difference in their ages didn't matter to her.

Susan's parents, as well as John's, were also looking forward to having a grandson or granddaughter when it was not yet known, as the parents only wanted to know the sex of the baby at birth and to keep secrets.

Life in the town of North Hill went on its own, sometimes monotonous and boring way, but that was about to change soon.

For a great danger was slowly approaching the town, one that was about to take root for good and change the course of the history of the place forever.

A place that until now had been considered peaceful and safe.

At that time, however, there was still nothing to foretell the tragedy that was to take place so soon.

The name "North Hill" which by now was attracting people and could charm anyone.

It was not long before it was about to make headlines across the country and in the worst context imaginable.

Later that year, the eyes of the whole of England were to turn to North Hill and the people who had so eagerly visited the area, were to start shunning the place.

All the coming events were to cause the affected residents to leave their family homes and travel as far away as they could in a panic.

And the others will begin to live in constant fear for the safety of their loved ones.

One tragedy in one's life can cause the whole world, so far arranged, to collapse, but a whole series of such events can drive people to panic and madness.

At the time, no one was able to prepare for what was about to happen. Nobody, or so it would seem, because there was one person who knew exactly what was going to happen.

Events that were to continue for the next ten years and terrorise the, until now peaceful, town called North Hill

Only one thing became clear to the residents at that time:

It all started when a young couple from Ethiopia moved into the town.

3

Partners.

"The reason for the existence of all politics is service to man."

Four years earlier,

10 January 2004, Canary Wharf district, London, office of the "Bradley and Brad Lettings" agency.

A small, fast-growing housing agency, "Bradley and Brad Lettings," or BnBL for short, is a thriving new business on the market.

A company involved in the letting, selling, and buying of flats and houses.

At the beginning, when the office started, the listings consisted mainly of properties in London, but over time, the agency began to expand its range of listings.

Increasingly, it was possible to find houses and flats to buy or rent in other cities in England.

The main investor and founder of the agency was George Bradley, who, together with his junior partner Matthiew Braddock, ran the estate agency. Before they opened the joint business, George had known Matthiew for many years but had never personally kept in touch with him.

At the time, he agreed to work together actually through the persuasion of Matthiew's parents.

Mr and Mrs Braddock were very wealthy people and good friends of George Bradley.

At one of the many parties George enjoyed attending.

During a conversation with George, they assured him that their son would be "...an excellent partner for him..." who already had a large amount of financial capital, which he wanted to invest well.

Matthiew's capital had quite an influence on George's decision to enter a partnership with him.

However, this was not the main reason why he decided to do so.

George realised that Matthiew was a brilliant negotiator and salesman.

He knew well how to make money, and this fact tipped the balance in his favour.

When they opened the business in early 2000, they only had ten flats and three houses to offer to interested parties.

However, in the four years of its existence, the business had undergone a rapid and rapid transformation.

This saw it evolve from a small housing agency to a player of increasing stature in the market and able to compete with the biggest names in the industry.

In 2004, George Bradley was a fifty-two-year-old man, tall and well-built for his age. He was very distinguished and handsome.

His white skin complexion, typical of a British man, and his blue eyes and white hair only added to his charm and seriousness.

George was attracted to the opposite sex, but he carefully chose only mature women and was not interested in "passing adventures" with girls. However, he never married, as the life of a free-spirited bachelor always suited him best.

George Bradley was, quite simply, a good and kind-hearted man who had to work hard for everything he had through years full of sacrifice.

Because he himself was brought up in a poor but honest and loving family, he understood people and never looked for a quick way to make money, certainly not at the expense of someone else's misfortune.

There were times when some of his tenants had financial problems or were late in paying for their accommodation.

In those cases, George always tried to compromise and find a peaceful way out of the situation.

In contrast, Matthiew Braddock, George's partner, was his complete opposite.

Forty-five years old in 2004, he was a man of medium height with chestnut and curly hair, brown eyes and quite overweight.

This outward appearance meant that he had never been a man attractive to women, either during his school days or as an adult.

So, too, he was a bachelor, but not by choice, as was the case with George Bradley.

Coming from a wealthy family, Matthiew had the character typical of a spoilt child.

Who had to have everything handed to him under his nose from an early age, always getting exactly what he demanded.

His explosive, sophisticated and unpredictable character did not make him any nicer to those around him over time, which is why people found it rather difficult to like the man.

Matthiew Braddock was simply an unscrupulous man, which meant that George more than once had to call him to order when it came to agency matters.

George often had differing opinions on various issues and many times disagreed with Matthiew in his way of running the agency.

Despite this, he agreed to be complicit with him.

Because there was something that set Matthiew apart from most of the people George knew, namely, Matthiew was a remarkably intelligent as well as imaginative man who spent half his life with his nose in books.

Which made him very well-read and who possessed, literally, an encyclopaedic knowledge of all sorts of subjects.

It was this fact about Matthiew's skills that ultimately prompted George Bradley to enter a business partnership with him and to continue to put up with his 'see me.'

George was aware of what Matthiew brought to the business; he could be remarkably effective at what he did, and quite simply, he knew his stuff. Despite this, George went on the assumption that he had to keep control. Because it was up to George to have the final say, as the main investor, as well as from the fact that he was the one who opened the "BnBL" agency, he was the "de facto" boss.

Therefore, Matthiew Braddock had no choice but to politely submit, which sometimes made him furious.

In the early years of the agency, George believed that by owning sixty per cent of the agency, which made him the rightful owner, he would be able to put the brakes on Matthiew's enthusiasm.

He set himself, at the time, the goal of controlling, with a firm hand, both situations in the office and with clients.

Therefore, it was mainly George who dealt with people who rented, bought or sold their flats or houses through the "BnBL" agency.

In short, he was the one who made all the most important decisions. For George, it was a matter of honour to be sure of good relations with those concerned.

So only he had direct contact with the agency's most important clients. Matthiew, in fact, had always remained in George's shadow and played only a supporting role in the business.

He didn't always like this, and slowly, over time, he began to get fed up with it.

Within four years of opening the office, thanks to some very good financial decisions, but above all, George Bradley's feel for the property market, the agency came into possession of three new houses in London in a short space of time.

They also managed to buy one large house in Luton, for a bagatelle of eight hundred thousand pounds, and five flats also in that town.

This was a tremendous success, as the agency's shares rose rapidly and almost doubled their previous value on the property market.

The main tasks of the employees of the "BnBL" agency were to constantly monitor the property market,

compare the prices of surrounding properties and look for opportunities to put money on the budget.

They then transferred the strictly verified documentation to the desk of the bosses.

George and Matthiew would then proceed to check the offers presented by the agents and discuss accepting the transfers together to decide the best. None of the staff at a lower level had access to company bank accounts or any money belonging to the agency "Bradley and Brad Lettings."

Even Matthiew had to consult George about any transfer made from these accounts.

Only George Bradley had access to them, and this was never allowed to change due to the security of the funds.

Although, at the time, the estimated value of the agency was over twenty million pounds, and Matthiew owned 40 per cent of the shares, he had no direct access to this fund.

The money was frozen and placed in the agency's investment budget. Matthiew was paid like any other employee every month, which he agreed to at the outset by entering a partnership with George and signing a contract.

Because George and Matthiew, even before the agency officially opened, decided to adopt a business policy of relentless growth.

In doing so, they imposed a very fast pace so that the work never really ended.

Some employees were forced to deal with paperwork outside of their paid hours in the office by doing it at home.

However, the hard and mobilised work paid off for everyone.

Because thanks to the joint efforts, the business was just undergoing rapid growth, and everyone involved started to earn better and better money because of it.

Saturday 23 March 2004.

That day, Matthiew did not come to the office.

He stayed in his flat because the day before, he had gone to the bar for a typically unsuccessful pick-up, after which he had traditionally drunk alcohol and was now curing his hangover at home.

It was a typically leisurely time out for him.

It was past 3 pm.

George was in his office. Apart from him, there was only a secretary with two estate agents still in the agency.

As every Friday and Saturday, they closed the agency two hours earlier at 4 pm and on Sundays, everyone took a break from their daily duties.

The afternoon in the office was going along quietly, and everything seemed to indicate that nothing interesting would happen again today. Then the phone rang on the desk of the secretary, who answered it immediately.

"Good afternoon, Bradley and Brad Lettings Housing Agency. How can I help you?" she said automatically into the receiver.

"Hello, I would like to speak to Mr George Bradley, please." The woman on the other end spoke up.

"Of course, do you have an appointment?" the secretary asked.

"No, unfortunately, I don't have an appointment, but I absolutely need to speak to this gentleman." The woman replied.

"I'm sorry, ma'am, but without an appointment, I can't put you through directly. If it's something important, I can put you through to an agent now. Would you like me to?" the secretary replied.

"Is there really no way that Mr Bradley can spare me two minutes?" The woman insisted.

"I'm afraid not..." burbled the secretary. "...Mr Bradley is a very busy man. I can't just put you through to his office. As I said, I'd be happy to find you a free date and set up an interview for you." She added.

"Is he in his office today?" the woman asked.

"He is." The secretary replied.

"So please do me a favour and tell him that Noelle Kemp is calling..." the woman said suddenly. "...It's a family matter. He'll know who it's about." She added after a moment.

There was a momentary silence on the line.

"Okay, I'll see what I can do..." The secretary finally replied. "...Please wait a moment." She added, then put the woman on the line on hold.

George was sitting at his desk going through documents when his landline rang.

So, he pressed the button to turn on the speakerphone option so that he didn't have to be disturbed. "Hello, Miss Katy?" he said.

"Sorry to disturb you, George..." the secretary spoke up uncertainly. "...There's a woman on the phone. She absolutely wants to talk." She added.

The employees were not afraid of George as a strict boss, and he even preferred it when they addressed him by his first name.

However, it was different with Matthiew, who always stood out from the rest of the agency's line-up and liked to exert himself.

At this point, the secretary simply didn't want to disturb George unnecessarily, especially as it seemed to her that she did.

However, she also could not have known that she was just in the wrong and that the person who wanted to talk to him would turn out to be extremely important to him.

"Did she have an appointment with me?" George asked.

"She doesn't have an appointment, but she says it's a family matter..." said the secretary unconvincingly.

Because she did not personally know anyone from George Bradley's family, and she sincerely doubted that the woman was telling the truth.

"...She says her name is Noelle Kemp." She added.

"Noelle Kemp?" said George under his breath, wrinkling his eyebrows in surprise.

How do I know that name? thought George and immersed himself in thought.

"Sir...?" The secretary admonished after a few seconds of silence. "Yes, Miss Katy, please wait five minutes and switch her to my office," George replied hurriedly.

"Okay, thank you." The secretary replied, then hung up.

George leaned back in his comfortable leather chair, his thoughts now tangled quickly and chaotically in his head in search of clues. He was completely surprised and knocked out of his flow by what the secretary had just told him.

"Noelle Kemp? How do I know that name?" he spoke quietly to himself, desperately trying to recall the answer in his head.

He could feel his heart begin to beat faster as, jolted out of his paperwork, he was suddenly overwhelmed with distraction.

How am I supposed to know this name? I know I know this person, just where? When? he couldn't remember.

At the age of fifty-two, there were times when he could not match the name to the face, previously met, of a person.

This was understandable, as he had met many people in his line of work. Over time it had become impossible to remember them all.

George was now completely confused, thinking intensely to the point where his head began to spin slightly.

After all, I don't have to torture myself like this. If I don't remember, I'll know who it is in a moment anyway. He thought and smiled under his breath.

Then, it suddenly dawned on him, just now, when he decided to let go of his failing memory.

Once he remembered who Noelle Kemp was to him, he automatically saw her face in his mind as well.

Then, another question popped into his head.

All right, but that still doesn't answer for what reason she is calling me now...? Suspicion arose. ...After all, it's been over eighteen years since I last saw her. What could she want from me now, after all these years? George tangled in his thoughts, trying to think of a reason that would explain this unexpected renewal of acquaintance.

Well, I don't suppose she's calling to ask me for money...? he said to himself ironically in his mind. "...she's had enough time to get her life together. After all, she's never been a stupid woman. Maybe her life has been a bit complicated and out of sorts for a while, but she's probably on the straight and narrow now..." George said to himself. "...Noelle, my god, it was twenty years ago, how young we were back then."

Memories of his young years came flooding back, which filled George with nostalgia and sentimentality.

For a moment, it made him feel better, but just as quickly, he remembered the circumstances under which he and this woman had separated. This occurred after she had chosen a path towards self-destruction. She slowly and irreversibly began to plunge into the dangerous world of drugs and addiction.

Not even all efforts on George's part to help her out of the trap helped, that's when he decided to leave, he had had enough.

He couldn't, just like that, watch helplessly as Noelle wasted her life. He had suffered too much through it and left her.

Tormented by remorse over the next few years, he wondered if he had done the right thing, if he should have stayed and kept trying, not given up. Over time, the doubts and troubled conscience slowly began to subside until, one day. He finally forgot all about it.

This episode in George's life was behind him, and it was finally time to focus on the coming future.

Despite everything, George was now excited.

He realised that, regardless of the unpleasant incidents of the past, it would be nice to catch up with the woman he, after all, loved twenty years ago.

At that moment, all his previous nervousness went away like a hand; instead, curiosity began to overtake him.

He wondered what the person he had fallen in love with when he was still a young man would say to him. He wanted to know how she went on with her life.

George straightened up comfortably in his chair and stared at the landline phone lying on his desk, impatiently waiting for it to finally ring.

I wondered how much her voice had changed. He still had time to say something to himself, and then the phone rang.

He looked at it and smiled broadly, took a deep, relaxing breath, grabbed the phone then put the receiver to his ear.

"This is George Bradley; how can I help you?" he said, smiling the whole time.

However, when he heard the voice on the phone, he furrowed his brow in confusion, and his eyes widened in surprise.

In a few seconds, his smile disappeared completely from his face, and its place was now taken by an expression of shock so strong that he almost dropped the phone receiver.

He sat in silence for a while and tried to listen carefully to the woman on the other end but could not understand a word of what she was saying to him at first.

The situation overwhelmed him because, for the second time that day, he felt completely baffled, which did not happen to him often.

Therefore, this was a new experience for George. He felt totally shattered. *I don't know how a voice can change after eighteen years, but it certainly shouldn't sound younger. Who the hell is this woman??* he was talking to himself in his mind.

Fifteen minutes later, George left his office just after he had finished speaking on the phone with the unknown woman.

He felt that he now had even more confusion in his head than before and needed to spend some time in isolation.

As he walked quickly through the office, he was visibly shaken and off balance, which his staff noticed.

He simply walked in a hurry, past the workers and their offices, straight to the front door. He closed it behind him without a word.

Without saying goodbye to anyone as he was accustomed to doing, without a "Have a good weekend" or "See you on Monday."

He left the building to continue to his car.

The employees sitting in front of their computers looked at each other bewildered, but no one dared to follow him and ask him if he was okay. His closest employees did not feel that they were in a good enough position in their relationship with their boss to ask him about his private affairs. So, all that was left for them to do was to wait until the agency's closing time and then go to their homes.

At the same time, they hoped that when they returned to work on Monday, everything would become clearer.

All of George's co-workers sincerely liked him and wished him the best, so this unusual behaviour from their boss was very worrying and gave them food for thought.

But they could only hope that George had not got himself into some serious trouble.

4

Illusion of normality.

'Suffering is also in the world in order to release love in us, that generous and selfless gift from our own self to those affected by suffering.'

Fourteen years later.

18 October 2018, Westminster Bridge, London, St Thomas Hospital, 10:15 pm.

When I woke up in the hospital, I was lying on a bed in a recovery room full of people who, like me, were just waking up from anaesthetic.

My head was throbbing with pain, and the all-encompassing, helpless moans of people that reached my ears filled me with anxiety and despondency.

I had never been operated on, so this was a new experience for me. However, I was often in hospitals, mostly in business, but there were also private cases.

Usually, I brought in people who had been arrested and injured in a brawl and needed medical attention.

But one time, my wife, Rachel, broke her arm, falling on the stairs, and we had to rush to the emergency room.

My beautiful wife, Rachel. My mind found a quiet haven to escape the pain.

We met in high school, where we attended parallel classes, and we instantly took a liking to each other.

At the time, I wondered what such a beautiful girl could see in a common boy like me.

I considered myself lucky in this respect, and I saw envy in the eyes of my classmates more than once.

My wife Rachel was a tall, forty-nine-year-old blonde with a slim body shape and blue eyes.

She possessed all the outward appearance traits I had always liked in women.

I, on the other hand, was a bit on the bony side in high school, but fortunately, over time, my fat had turned into muscle, thanks to hard physical work at the police academy.

I was also a bit taller than Rachel; I was 185cm tall, she was 179cm, and we were both born in the same year.

The only thing we both had in common, speaking of looks, was the colour of our hair, my dark blond and hers light.

We were still united by similar interests, as we both wanted to help other people.

At the time, my dream was to become a police officer, hers to become a doctor.

My intentions came true; however, Rachel went a little off course and eventually became a physiotherapist.

But she was happy with her work and that's what mattered most, and I supported her in everything she did all this time.

We have been married for nineteen wonderful years, and before that we were engaged for five.

We met when we were both nineteen, so I can safely say I've known Rachel almost all my life.

Although I was still feeling drowsy as the anaesthetic began to gradually pass upon waking, my bandaged head slowly began to hurt more and more. Lying on the bed at the time, surrounded by people who were also suffering fresh from their operations,

I needed to concentrate on something.

Therefore, I started to recall in my mind the memories of my wedding to Rachel, so I closed my eyes and returned with my imagination to those moments.

I felt it relaxing me with every passing second.

A small ceremony in a historic church with an incredibly beautiful interior in south London.

She was so wonderfully lovely and young in a lovely white wedding dress, and me the happiest man on earth at that moment.

I didn't want to start thinking about anything else.

There would be time to come back to reality later. I concluded

I felt that it was still too early for me to try to analyse what had happened that afternoon in the flat where I had been shot in the head.

All I knew at that moment was that nothing had happened to the girl and that was all I needed to know for that moment. So, I decided to dwell on pleasant memories.

As I lay like this, in my temporary hospital bed, immersed in my own thoughts, a nurse approached me.

"I see you've already had a good night's sleep." She said, smiling warmly. – "You know, I used to sleep better." I replied, however, reluctantly, when she shook me out of my thoughts.

"It's still a long way from a five-star hotel." I wanted to make a joke to make the atmosphere a little more pleasant.

The nurse smiled again at me, not lying to myself, rather poor joke.

"If you wish, we can already move you to a separate room." She said. "I would very much like that," I replied with great relief that I would no longer have to listen to the depressing moans of the other patients. "I would like to contact my wife; she must be very worried," I said quickly before she left.

"Oh yes, sorry, I was just about to say your wife is already at our hospital...." The nurse replied, clearly embarrassed that she had forgotten to tell me this earlier.

"...She came to us as soon as you were brought in and has been sitting in the waiting room for a good five hours now." She added, at the same time looking at the time on the clock that hung on the wall.

"Could I see her?" I asked.

"I think you'll have to see the doctors first..." She replied. "... But I think we will be able to make an exception for your officer..." she said, smiling at me in agreement. "...I guess how much you care about that." She added. "Thank you very much, ma'am," I said with relief, reciprocating her smile. "At your service, officer. She said jokingly at the end, then sent me a look and slowly walked away.

I felt then that I could finally fully calm down and relax. I wasn't even particularly surprised that Rachel was in hospital.

In my heart, I probably would have expected it, of course, if I had already been sobered enough for it to even cross my mind.

"So now the nurse will probably inform her that I'm fine, we won't see each other for a long time. In addition, my instincts were reassuring.

I waited ten minutes, watching the clock on the wall, when the same nurse came to me.

"I was just talking to your wife." She announced.

So, she did exactly as I expected, and Rachel already knew I was waiting for her. My mind had already worked out the rest, which did not change the fact that I felt immense gratitude for the sympathetic woman.

"Thank you very much indeed," I replied.

The young nurse gave me another charming smile, then returned to her duties.

As soon as she left, a nurse came in her place and started pushing my bed into another room.

Moments later, I was already in a separate room, which, in turn, I still shared with only one other man, which made no small difference.

I closed my eyes for a moment, anticipating the next events. Then, for the first time, I found myself in an environment to which my subconscious was later to take me repeatedly during the nights to come. I remember the first such dream as being very vague and unclear, even though I knew it was a forest.

I was walking alone, confused and lost, surrounded by trees and an all-encompassing darkness.

I was heading somewhere. I didn't yet know the destination at the time, but that too was to become clear in the course of time.

However, the most surprising sensation in this dream was that I knew I was there for a reason, almost as if I was in the right place at the right time.

Never, before or since, have I felt this way in a dream.

This was no ordinary nightmare; it was about much more than just a horrible product of my imagination, but the problem was that at the time, I had no idea what it could mean, not yet.

Maybe I would have found out more if it hadn't been for the fact that I was quickly woken up by two doctors who came in for individual consultations with each patient separately.

As I was closer to the entrance, they started with me, separated my space with a screen for privacy, and then set to work.

They were both tall and wore glasses, one of them had a brown skin colour by which I deduced that he might originally be of Asian origin, while the other was of a white complexion like mine.

European. My instinct explained.

Until now, however, I had been quietly hoping that Rachel would be the first to show up before I had to talk to a stranger.

"Well, you'll have to wait a little longer." He brought my mind back to order before the doctors approached my bed and greeted me.

"Good evening, Mr Davis. My name is Dr Richard Stanson, and this is my colleague Dr Anthony Kumari." Said the first of the doctors, indicating with a gesture to the man next to him.

"How are you feeling?" asked the second. Without raising his eyes, he was looking at the notes he had brought with him.

"As if I had been hit by a truck..." I replied, and a slight smile appeared on the doctors' faces. "...I have a terrible headache. - I added after a short while.

"No wonder, Mr Davis." Dr Stanson replied.

"What happened to you is comparable to being hit by a truck." Dr Kumari stated.

"But believe me, we can speak of rare luck here, if I may say so." Dr Richard added.

"Luck? Or would it be more appropriate to use the word "miracle"?" He revived at the sound of his colleague Dr Kumari's words.

Dr Stanson looked away from me and looked at his colleague, then silently nodded slightly in agreement.

After which he again fixed an attentive gaze on me and spoke:

"Indeed, do you realise what happened? Do you remember anything?"

"I remember being hit in the head," I replied, at the same time realising that it was a bullet from a gun.

But at that moment, it was as if I was pushing this fact out of my consciousness, and it was hard for me to come to terms with it.

Because deep down I was still secretly hoping that it was something else, maybe I had just missed something?

"You have been shot in the head, Mr. Davis..." said Dr Kumari in a serious tone, thus dispelling my last remnants of hope that, in a moment, I would hear that it was some unidentified object.

"...I'm going to be honest with you, Mr Davis, you are incredibly lucky to be able to talk here today..." Dr Kumari continued. "...The bullet literally rubbed against the right side of your skull, hence the discomfort you are feeling now. We had to stitch your head." He added, in conclusion. The second doctor, Dr Stanson, remained silent and kept looking at me with fear in his eyes.

If the bullet had hit a little closer, it would have ended tragically... began Dr Stanson. "... At best, if you had survived such a gunshot, you would most likely now be in a coma or a protracted paralysis...." He continued speaking, interrupting every now and then and looking at his notes. "...I don't suppose I need to tell you what would have happened if the bullet had hit you one centimetre away and then lodged in your head?" he finished with this theoretical question and looked at me in agreement. He knew perfectly well that I was aware he was talking about my immediate death.

"Yes, I know." I replied.

Despite everything I had just heard, I had to admit that I felt a little better. Admittedly, all the information I had just been given sounded very serious and grotesque, but I had managed to come out of it unscathed and was still alive, which was a success given the circumstances.

"As they say colloquially, luck in not luck." He quoted the parable to my mind.

"We will keep you under observation for a few more hours, as long as you are under the effects of a strong anaesthetic, but, apart from that, I see no counter-indication that you cannot still be discharged from the hospital today unless you have any objections?" Dr Stanson concluded and was now waiting for my answer.

"I have no objection, and I agree, thank you very much," I replied.

Excellent...!" delighted Dr Kumari with a smile on his face.

"... So, we will send your discharge from the hospital soon, along with the date of your next appointment to remove the stitches." He added. "Speaking privately, I would just like to add that we consider you a hero. I really admire the police officers serving this city, who often risk their own health and lives to help others." Dr Kumari said unexpectedly. "That is very kind. I also thank you very much, gentlemen..." I replied. I tried to be polite, but I could feel my head starting to hurt more and more. The anaesthesia was quickly wearing off.

"... Can I have some more pain pills, please?" I added.

"Of course, the nurse will bring you something right away, and we will also write you a prescription and add it to your hospital discharge." Dr Kumari replied.

"Would you like us to notify your family?" Dr Stanson asked me.

"There is no need for that. My wife is here in hospital..." I replied. "... The nurse has already spoken to her, and we should see her soon," I added and smiled.

"Okay, we'll check it again for you, Mr Davis..." Dr Stanson replied. "... Finally, I would like to say that you should consider yourself very lucky. Someone is watching over you. A very small percentage of people come out of this situation unscathed, especially after what happened to you. Take my word for it." Dr Kumari said at the end of his visit.

"Perhaps you should play the lotto?" Dr Stanson tried to joke.

But I saw Dr Kumari rebuke him discreetly with his eyes, letting him know that this was hardly the place or time for jokes.

"Goodbye, Mr Davis. I wish you much happiness in life." Said Dr Kumari, smiling warmly at me.

"Goodbye, gentlemen, thank you," I replied, unaware that now these were just wishful thinking and that I could indeed use the happiness the nice man had just mentioned.

Dr Stanson bowed gently in my direction as a farewell, after which they both slowly walked away to my temporary roommate.

When I was finally left alone, I leaned more comfortably against the bed, trying to ignore the pain and waited for Rachel.

Then slowly, the memories of a few hours before began to come back to me, making me necessarily interested in the state of little Denis Randal's health.

Which, in turn, led to a curiosity about what had happened to the psychopathic man who had shot at me.

In my mind, the triggered thought process itself created further nagging questions:

Did they manage to arrest him?

Did he fight the police officers to the end?

Did he survive the shooting?

Was anyone else injured?

Forget about him! You probably won't see him again anyway, at most once at the trial, if there is one at all. I was brought down to earth by my instincts.

I was reassured by the thought that the most important thing was that nothing happened to Denise Randal.

I was sure of this at that because I remembered well and clearly, how she had escorted me to the ambulance.

My head will heal, and everything will be fine. Why not take time off from work to go somewhere with Rachel? My mind was adding more pleasant ideas.

However, what I was to find out in the next couple of hours was going to completely undo my improving mood, as was my conviction that everything was going to be business as usual, which was also going to be soon and irrevocably lost in the chaos, that was going to take over my life that night. On top of that, it was all to come from the very first night that I was longing to spend back in my safe bed after returning home.

All the upcoming events were to simultaneously and completely change my view of the world and make me start questioning everything I had believed in up to that point.

Absolutely nothing is or will ever really be right, as I thought now while talking to the doctors.

Fortunately, at that moment, I was still able to enjoy not knowing anything about the near future,

Ignorance, however, is indeed sometimes bliss, as some people claim. But from now on, it was soon to come to me that things were happening that I could not control or even understand because fate had willed to put me in a situation where I would have to face something that I would not be able to see.

Just the other day, I found myself in the middle of a huge storm without even realising it yet.

I would have given a lot in that moment to know that someone's life would depend on how quickly I accepted the truth, and probably not just one person's life, but potentially many innocent young lives.

My hospital bed was positioned opposite the door at such an angle that I had a view of the whole corridor.

So, I crossed my arms over my chest and, to kill time, watched the people who went back and forth: doctors, nurses, other patients and so on.

When behind their backs, a familiar face emerged.

I squinted slightly to get a better look and saw that it was Rachel.

I smiled broadly and watched as she headed towards me with a quick step. As she entered my room, I noticed the tears in her eyes and the slightly smudged makeup on her face.

As she approached my bed, without a word sat down in the chair next to me and then took my hand thoughtfully.

She sat like that for a few seconds and stared at me intensely, with sadness in her eyes.

I could see her gaze alternately jumping from one of my eyes to the other. I loved it when she did that because I thought there was something incredibly charming about it.

At the same time, her facial expression said, "What have you done?" she always had that look on her face when I had, in her mind, "Done something wrong."

I didn't like it when she looked at me like that because then I felt like a kid who was about to be punished by his mum after having done something wrong, and not like a grown man and a police officer by profession.

As I silently stared into my wife's sad face, she finally spoke, bringing the inevitable conversation closer.

"Jesus Christ, Danny..." she said quietly. "... I thought I'd lost you...." she added and wiped away a tear that ran down her cheek. "... When Connor called and said, "They're bringing you here", I immediately dropped everything and ran out of the office...." she recounted. "... I left a patient, who is probably still wondering what happened. I cried all the way in the car driving here. I was so scared." She added.

She lowered her head for a moment and pulled her nose quietly, clearly shaken by the whole incident, I had to calm her down somehow.

"It's okay, honey..." I spoke in a calm voice, ignoring the headache. "...It's going to be fine; the doctors say that nothing serious has happened to me." I added.

The moment I said this Dr Stanson's words echoed in my head, and I saw him now in a few seconds' flashback.

As he stood facing my bed with the other doctor and spoke. *You should consider yourself lucky. There really is someone watching over you, a very small percentage of people come out alive with similar injuries.* I also remembered them explaining to me what distance "miraculously" saved my life.

That is, about the millimetres when the bullet rubbed against the edge of my skull.

In short, it was about all those factors that made up the "miracle," or as I would call it "luck in misfortune," that was on my side in that situation and prevailed for me not to leave this world yet.

However, there was no need to tell all of this to Rachel, as she clearly had enough to worry about for one day.

"When the nurse came to me and said you were awake, I called Connor straight away..." she said. "... He told me that immediately after the incident, he had to go to the police station to give an explanation and report, but he wanted me to let him know immediately what was going on with you. As soon as I found out anything..." she added all the time she was looking into my eyes and her gaze was alternating from one of my eyes to the other. Only Rachel did that, and I always felt it make my heart warm, so it was the same in this case, too.

"...I called him, and he should be here soon." She added.

As we talked, I noticed how Rachel was slowly calming down more and more, and I felt the same.

"Why don't I talk to him when I get home...?" I suggested. "... I don't have to stay in the hospital overnight. The doctors have decided that there is no need to keep me here. I will be discharged with a prescription for painkillers, and we can go home." I said.

"That is very good...." Rachel replied. "... If that is the doctors' opinion, then there is really no need to worry any further." She added, smiling at me. Rachel sat next to me and gently stroked a part of my head, wrapped in a bandage under which the wound was hidden.

"They put stitches in me. I don't know how many exactly. I wanted to ask about that, but somehow, I completely forgot..." I said, due to her interest in the bandage. "...In a few weeks, they should be gone. The hair will grow back and cover the wound. There should be no trace." I added, smiling at her in agreement.

"You always must get yourself into something." She replied, looking at me with pity.

And I see that look again as if she wanted to rebuke me with her very eyes, exactly as a mother looks at her child who has messed something up again and is now crying, seeking consolation. - My mind, for the sake of variety, decided to interject a scene from real life.

"Darling, after all, you know how dangerous my profession can be. This is not children playing with plastic guns somewhere in a park...." I said in a calm voice. "... Unfortunately, in real life, such things sometimes happen," I added, in a way trying to justify myself.

"Well, yes, you're absolutely right. It's much worse than children." Rachel replied and knowing exactly what she meant, I couldn't disagree with her at this point.

"Children, unlike adults, use toy guns with toy cartridges. They don't get intoxicated like some kind of pig to the point where they lose touch with reality." I said, completing what Rachel meant. "Exactly, that's what it looks like," Rachel replied.

"But a lot of people, they seem to have less sense in their heads than some children," I added and then looked back at my watch.

"And for goodness' sake, who even came up with the idea of toy guns and allowing a child to hold a gat in their hand from a young age?" My instincts suddenly interjected themselves into the conversation.

Some things remain unchanged in this world, little girls have their doll prams, and boys have their guns, soldiers or computer games, which also accustoms them to violence, is this where psychopaths come from? I continued the conversation with myself in my mind. Fortunately, I was the only one who heard it.

As I drifted off like this for a while, immersed in my own thoughts, I was brought down to earth by Rachel's phone ringing loudly at one point. The sound of music coming from a small speaker was loud enough in the quiet room to attract the attention of several people, who looked in our direction curiously.

Therefore, Rachel quickly and violently dived into her handbag to retrieve it.

When she had it in her hand after a few seconds, she quickly picked it up and then covered the microphone with her hand for a moment.

"Sorry, I forgot to turn it down." She said to me quietly, clearly embarrassed.

Then she moved her hand away, revealing the bottom of the camera and put it to her ear.

"Yes? Yes, Connor, we are here..." she said in a hushed voice. "... I don't know exactly how to explain to you. Ask at reception..." she spoke to my partner, pausing every now and then to listen to his answer. "... Ask about the post-operative ward...." she explained.

It seemed that Connor had apparently gotten lost somewhere again, which was very typical of him, as it was his lack of ability to navigate and find his way in unfamiliar territory that set him apart as a police officer. This trait soon became famous throughout the entire police station, causing some uniformed officers to jokingly refer to him as "GPS."

"...Well, then come up and ask, well we're here waiting for you, bye..." Rachel ended the call, put the phone back in her purse, and then took my hand again. "...Connor is already at the hospital; he should be here soon." She added with a smile on her face.

"I wouldn't say too soon..." I replied. "... After all, you know him, he couldn't find a McDonald's restaurant in London even if he drove an hour by car." I joked.

"Oh, come on, don't be mean." She replied.

"You think I'm joking? You'll see for yourself." I replied.

Rachel looked at me pityingly, still with a smile on her face.

However, she quickly realised that I wasn't wrong, as it took almost thirty minutes before Connor found us.

The fact was that the hospital wasn't one of the smallest, but no exaggeration.

But that's what happens when pride prevents you from asking someone for directions, and you try to look for a place by signs in a sizable building, like the hospital. My mind quickly visualised the actions of a friend I knew intimately.

When Connor finally reached us, he was visibly tired, catching air quickly and greedily with his mouth while trying to regulate his breathing in this way.

"There you are, at last." He choked out after a while.

"At last, you are here..." I joked... "We have been warming up the place for a good fifty minutes, I even much longer," I added, smiling in his direction. "No kidding." Said Connor further trying to steady his breathing.

"What's wrong with joking? The fear is gone, everything is fine, so it's okay to joke." I said, winking at Rachel, but she, in response, shook my hand tighter in protest.

"How are you feeling, mate?" Connor said, breathing normally.

"Well, you know how they say it could be better..." I replied. "... My head hurts, but other than that, it's not too bad." I added truthfully. At this point, a nurse approached us, bringing my tablets, which I had completely forgotten about through all this.

In fact, I had also stopped thinking about my headache since Rachel came to me, and I concentrated on her, so that I did not pay attention to the wound.

"These are for you, please swallow them." The nurse said.

Then she handed me two tablets in a tiny paper cup and some cold water to drink.

"Thank you." I replied.

I grabbed the cup and threw the pills into my mouth. I did it so awkwardly and greedily that two pills went almost to the bottom of my throat. This almost caused me to vomit, but I only choked and drank water. "Sorry, I'm clumsy." I said, embarrassed, and the nurse smiled at me with understanding.

"And just for good measure, almost an hour waiting for pain pills is quite a long time." My mind reeled, recalling the recorded time from talking to the doctors until the nurse arrived.

It would probably have upset me if Rachel and Connor hadn't been here and I hadn't had anything else to do.

Along with the pills, the nurse also brought my hospital discharge, which she placed on the mobile table next to my bed, along with the promised prescription for the next painkillers.

This meant that I could go home as soon as I was ready.

So, I decided not to waste any time and started to slowly crawl out of my temporary bed.

I was assisted in this by Rachel supporting me gently under my arm. I have no trouble walking, just a wound on my head. After all, I'm not going to fall over. My mind was irritated.

Even so, I didn't have the heart to reject Rachel's help, so I pretended to support myself on her arm.

"Maybe you'd like me to drive you in a wheelchair to the main front door?" Connor suggested.

When I heard that he wanted to push me in a wheelchair all the way through the hospital to the exit, I just measured him with a look of disapproval.

Connor quickly realised this and then compensated for his earlier gaze. "I've also brought you some clothes to change into." He said, pointing his finger at a plastic bag that I hadn't noticed until now.

"When Rachel called me and said you were awake, I thought you'd need to wear something fresh." Connor was clearly proud of himself.

"Well, thanks, mate, well thought out. I wouldn't have expected that from you." I joked.

"Don't get too excited. These are just things I was going to donate to charity, to help the homeless." Connor didn't remain indebted to me.

"It's okay, boys, play nice," Rachel interjected.

It amused me so much that, for a moment, I forgot that we were still in the hospital the whole time.

Momentarily, there was almost a family atmosphere, just like on the first day of Christmas.

When everyone is relaxed, joking and getting lost in the comfort of a cosy house.

I really needed this now. Such a respite, especially as the idyllic mood was not going to last very long.

Once we left the hospital, we decided, despite the late hour, that the three of us would go to mine and Rachel's flat. I agreed then, however reluctantly. There, Connor was to tell me, in detail, everything that had happened that afternoon, immediately after the shooting.

I had to admit that neither during my stay in hospital nor when I returned home was I in the least bit ready for what I was about to hear from him. In fact, nothing could have helped me prepare for the shock I was about to experience.

5

A woman is a variable.

'The family is itself if it is built on such reference, on mutual trust, on trusting each other. Only on such a foundation can also be built the process of education, which is the family's primary purpose and its primary task.'

10 years earlier,

04 May 2008, North Hill, home of Susan and John McKane, 11:35 am.

Susan was going into town at this time to do some shopping when her husband John had to go to check on work at a house site, that his private building/repair company was carrying out.

Before Susan left the house, John asked her to pick up a parcel that was waiting for him at the post office, as he did not have time to go there himself that day.

Susan was six months pregnant and was slowly growing tired of carrying out her husband's whims.

In truth, it was not an exorbitant request, according to John, but Susan felt as if he was trying to make her feel like a servant.

"After all, it won't take you long..." John argued. "... The parcel is not big. You can easily pick it up." He added.

"I really don't understand why this cousin of yours couldn't send it straight to your house." Susan replied.

"After all, he did send it, remember? I told you two days ago that a courier called me, but we weren't here at the time. You were looking after a patient, and I was on site...." John began to explain. "... So, they sent it back to the post office. It's hard, it's not a problem, you'll drive over and pick it up after all, you'll be in the area, and I can take care of business in the meantime." He added.

"It's not a problem for you. I'm tired of serving you." Susan replied under her breath, turning her back on her husband so that John could no longer hear her.

"Did you say something, darling?" he asked.

"No, nothing!" lied Susan and headed for the front door.

When she left the house, John was just starting to put on his shoes in the hallway, then a moment later he left the flat as well.

Once outside, he stood still for a moment and furrowed his brow in surprise.

John felt a little puzzled as he saw that by this time, Susan had managed to drive away from the driveway in front of the house.

Where is she going in such a hurry? She didn't even say goodbye to me. He said to himself, in his mind confused.

He then headed to his car, opened the door, sat behind the wheel and closed his eyes, sinking into a reverie.

Something not very good must be going on with Susan, just what is it...? He thought. *...I understand that she's struggling with hormones right now, mood changes, because of the pregnancy..."* John considered the reasons. *...However, it's as if her whole personality has changed. Previously, it didn't bother her so much when I asked for help with things. I know she has her patients who probably litter her head with their problems, but she's a professional, and she's* *never brought work home, certainly not to the extent that it affected our private lives, so why the constant resentment about everything...?* He wondered frantically, searching his head for the answer. John felt the sudden turn of mood and atmosphere in his private family life starting to overwhelm him more and more.

Particularly as he did not have the slightest idea where such behaviour in Susan could have come from, which at the same time entailed that he also did not know how he should react.

The feeling of powerlessness and hopelessness made John become depressed over time, as he couldn't find a way out of this situation. This was compounded by the fact that Susan did not broach the subject with him, so John became entrenched in a sense of helplessness.

Susan's attitude towards John began to gradually but radically change, since she returned from London.

It was at the end of April 2004 when Susan suddenly announced that she had to go to London for a week's holiday.

She went there alone at the time, leaving John behind at home for seven days.

When John asked why they couldn't go together, Susan argued by saying

"...I need to be alone for a few days to clear my mind and reboot myself." John then reluctantly acceded to his beloved's whim, for some time thinking it was not the best idea given her advanced pregnancy.

He tried to dissuade her from it, but Susan persisted and eventually stood her ground.

Things started to go from bad to worse after that. Yes, they stayed together and eventually got married, following pre-arranged plans, and started a family. However, John couldn't shake the feeling that

Susan was no longer the same person she had been before, but he couldn't pinpoint what had really changed.

*... She wasn't like this before she left for London, surely, it's just because she's pregnant, perhaps, that is why she is behaving like this? Women's moods change quickly when they are carrying a baby under the heart...*For the moment, John decided to accept the most fitting answer to justify his wife's behaviour or the one that hurt his feelings the least.

He smiled at the thought of his yet unborn child, then started the engine in the car and slowly backed it out onto the street.

Only now did he glance at his watch on his phone and realise that almost fifteen minutes had passed since he had got into the car.

Susan had already left a good twenty minutes earlier.

He quickly shook himself out of his reverie, then looked in the rear-view mirror, making sure he could safely join the traffic. "...time to get a grip." He said to himself motivationally.

John missed the affectionate kiss from Susan to prove it, and it used to be her habit to always do that before they parted ways before the day's chores. However, those beautiful times were gradually passing into history before his eyes.

John could clearly see something changing in his wife, and this "something" was very worrying.

But he was in no position to get to the bottom of this subject, so he placed all the blame on the pregnancy and the mood swings associated with it. That was the easiest way.

Fact, there was some truth in this, but not much, and the main reason was completely different.

John was never to discover the truth of what had happened to Susan and spent the last moments of his life wondering why his beloved wife had changed without return.

John McKane was a businessman and construction worker apprenticed to his father, Kevin McKane.

He owned and managed a private construction company, which he had taken over four years earlier from Kevin when he decided to retire. Although John was the type of man who is perpetually busy and, on the move, for his beloved wife Susan, he was always able to find time whenever she needed it.

When they married a year ago, the then thirty-four-year-old John was the model of the man Susan considered her ideal.

Tall, handsome, intelligent and ambitious, a grey-haired man with plans and a view of a bright future.

Susan fell in love with him almost at first sight when she was eighteen, and shortly afterwards, John proposed to her.

Then, after three years of engagement, they married and only a year later, they were expecting their first offspring.

John loved Susan very much and would do practically anything for her. The moment his wife announced to him that she had become pregnant, and they were going to have a child together, John was taken aback and could not believe his own happiness.

He knelt before her then and hugged her belly with tears in his eyes. John often recalled those moments with emotion as it was everything he wanted in his life, a beautiful wife, a child, a home and his own business. *My little happy world, full of happiness and love.* John liked to think of his fate in this way, it filled him with pride and fulfilment.

However, although John's world, which he had built on what might appear to be firm and solid foundations, was soon to become extremely fragile and unstable in its structure.

A world that was soon to collapse completely overnight.

All because of the unexpected and devastating news he was about to receive.

Susan, meanwhile, was driving towards town, still feeling cranky after her conversation with John.

"Bloody cocky..." said Susan to herself under her breath.

The nervousness that had shot through Susan translated into her paying less and less attention to caution when driving.

"... Who does he think he is! Honey, do this, honey do that...." she said, glancing in the rear view mirror every now and then, as if she expected someone to follow her.

"...He should be the one to serve me, he doesn't even know, who I am and what I can do..." She added nervously. "... Plus, I'm carrying his child." She added, now slowing the car down to the prescribed speed just before entering the centre.

As she drove slowly and carefully, her attention was drawn to three white delivery trucks that passed her, going one after the other in the opposite direction.

Susan closed her eyes slightly to look more closely at the vehicles. Then she read the name of the haulage company on the sides of the vehicles, which read "BnBL," and the contact details listed below. At that moment, she felt her heart start to beat faster as she momentarily recognised the name, which was familiar to her.

However, she quickly pushed the feeling away and shook herself momentarily.

Don't be ridiculous. Susan thought.

When she finally reached the town centre, she decided to go to the post office first to collect for John the unfortunate parcel that had caused so much controversy that day while getting the problem out of her head. So, she headed towards the town hall, where the post office was located. Then, as she drove past a couple of the shops she had intended to enter first, she felt her anger at John begin to take hold again.

If it hadn't been for that cocky man, I might have half the stuff sorted out by now... she thought with nerves. "...and so, I must drive all the way to the town hall, only to backtrack later..." she said to herself in a half-hearted voice. "...the queue will probably be huge, and I will have to wait at least thirty minutes."

Susan did not have an explosive temperament by nature and used to not react nervously in such situations.

But now, her thinking was completely different from before, which made her unrecognisable without even realising it.

She had turned into a haughty and arrogant person, and her ego had become more exuberant than ever before.

To an uninitiated person watching from the sidelines, it might seem that nothing has really changed in Susan McKane's life.

The same town, the same job, the same familiar people, the same house and, of course, John, also the same.

But everything had changed, and she felt that her surroundings were different to what they had been before: more depressing, mundane, boring, and, to put it mildly, unattractive.

This is what upset her most at the time and made her unhappy because she no longer wanted such a "normal," life.

Susan felt now that she was made for more important things, much more important.

She continued to drive slowly down the narrow one-way street and was already close to her destination. She looked around carefully, searching with her eyes for a free parking space where she could leave her vehicle. A few seconds later, she spotted an empty space next to the pavement and quickly occupied it.

She then stopped her car there, between the post office and the town hall, and stepped out into the street.

After walking a few steps, she remembered irritably that she had left her handbag in the passenger seat of the car, so she immediately went back for it.

"Because of this bloody situation, I'm starting to forget the most important things." She burbled under her breath, irritated.

She picked up the lost thing, then pushed the door of her car much harder than it needed to close, and it slammed shut with a bang.

She cast another angry glance at the blameless car, then took a quick step towards the post office.

As she climbed the stairs towards the door to the building, she greeted a few familiar people who passed her on their way out.

A moment later, she was already inside the small post office and saw that there were several more people in front of her.

She quickly counted them with her eyes and found that she was only thirteenth in line.

I knew it, I would have to stand here for an eternity, and on top of that, only one window opens out of four, how typical. She said to herself in her mind. However, the queue was moving at a rapid pace, so from Susan's estimated thirty minutes, it made ten when it was to be her turn.

But even ten minutes spent in the queue was far too long for Susan. Driven by the belief that by that time, she could have walked calmly around all the shops, done the most necessary shopping, and at that point, she would probably have already been driving back home.

These were, of course, severely stretched intentions because she needed a lot more time to complete it.

Susan was simply subconsciously looking for reasons to be upset, and she wanted to blame the execution of the request her husband had asked her to make. As she continued to stand in line, she felt another hot wave of indignation begin to pass through her mind.

Because then she remembered that she would still have to prepare dinner that evening.

Well, sure, that's all I need tonight, standing at the pots for that twit... she started cursing John in her mind again. *...He's probably chatting away with his mates on the building site right now, and I'm standing here picking up his stuff, then I'll still have to go shopping to finish cooking him dinner before he gets home.* She was stoking Susan's anger within herself.

But the truth was that it was John who mostly cooked at home. Even on days when he was working, he would come back and whip up something in the kitchen for them for dinner.

He never minded and was good at it, and Susan always enjoyed the food prepared by her husband.

Susan, on the other hand, cooked once or twice a week, at most, but now she did not remember or, rather, did not want to remember it.

The reality at the time was that Susan wanted to be angry with John and looked for pretexts to do so.

She wanted to get angry and to amplify her anger.

This was no longer the same Susan that John had met and then married, she was different now, she was changed.

When it was finally her turn to go to the window.

Although all the time she could feel herself almost boiling inside because of her nerves, she immediately put on her favourite mask, hiding her anger under an expression of satisfaction.

She then approached the saleswoman with a charming smile on her face. "Oooo...Hello Susan..." The woman on the other side of the glass greeted her cheerfully. "...O! Excuse me! Doctor Susan." The saleswoman corrected herself quickly.

Susan looked at her with a learned expression of kindness.

"Good afternoon, Carolin," Susan replied.

"What brings you to us?" the shopkeeper asked.

Having worked as a psychologist for quite a long time and having lived in North Hill all her life, Susan knew almost everyone in the town by name, most of them simply by sight.

It so happened that a cashier named Carolin Richardson, was one of the people Susan still worked with until recently.

At the time, she was helping a woman deal with her depression when she was having a hard time going through a nervous breakdown right after a difficult divorce and later separation from her husband of many years.

"I've come to collect a package for John," Susan said.

"Coming up, please wait a moment!" Carolin replied.

The woman nimbly turned with her back to the window in her swivel chair and a moment later, had already disappeared behind the door to the back room.

Carolin mostly reacted to meeting Susan with exaggerated joy, this was because she felt that she owed her a lot and always looked forward to meeting her.

Although Susan doubted Carolin's sincerity and appreciated her gratitude, but she tended not to share the woman's enthusiasm, which she felt was not necessarily excessive.

To Susan, Carolin was just one of many patients she had once cared for and supported emotionally.

Susan was a professional and never let any resentment towards other people show.

Whatever the situation she found herself in, it could have been a chance encounter on the street or a forced, not uncommon, conversation. The universally respected lady psychologist always behaved in such a way as never to offend anyone.

So, she smiled kindly at such moments and put on a good face, even when she didn't feel like it in the slightest.

A few seconds later, Carolin returned carrying a medium-sized package in her hands, smiling broadly.

"There it is...!" announced the woman in a joyful voice as if she had just found a precious treasure and was extremely proud of it. "... Go to the window next to you." Carolin pointed to a window with a metal parcel shelf.

"Thank you," Susan said.

She then collected the box from her side. When she was about to turn to leave then Carolin said quietly.

"Have you heard about the new neighbours?" She asked conspiratorially.

Oh, dear mother of God, not that! I don't have time for it! said Susan to herself in thought, rolling her eyes discreetly in annoyance.

Talking to Carolin was the last thing Susan wanted to waste her precious time on now.

However, at the same time, she felt curiosity sparked by intrigue that Carolin already knew something about the subject.

This was especially true since, at the same moment, she recognised three vans with the logo of the housing agency "BnBL" that she had passed on her way there.

Susan stopped in her tracks.

Instead of saying goodbye to the woman and leaving the building, she turned her head to look behind her and saw that there was now no one in the post office except her and Carolin.

Someone else was just shuffling around at the back of the back office, but other than that, they were alone.

So, this is the reason why Carolin decided to speak to me, she had received some news and had picked up some gossip. Susan understood what had prompted Carolin to talk.

"No, Carolin, I'm not aware of any new residents," Susan replied truthfully. "Aaaa... Because you see Susan..." Carolin began to say, encouraged by Susan's attention. "...this new couple bought the beautiful villa in front of the centre, you know, the one that has been standing unoccupied for a long time." She explained.

Big deal, people come and go, today they're new and tomorrow, they won't look any different from the other residents I pass on the street every day. Susan added ironically in her mind.

Nevertheless, she was lulled by a slight feeling of jealousy because the villa Carolin was now talking about was truly beautiful.

It is a huge property and the people who could afford to buy such a house had to be, at the very least, wealthy.

"It's a very nice house, Carolin. No wonder someone finally bought it." Susan replied briefly.

She wanted to put an end to this unnecessary conversation as soon as possible and get back to her other activities.

"It's true, Susan, but these people flew here straight from Africa, from Ethiopia, to be precise," Carolin added, her voice once again taking on a proud quality.

Apparently, she was pleased to have already found out where the new arrivals were coming from.

It is indeed a bit out of the ordinary, straight from Africa to North Hill to start a new life here? Susan wondered.

"It seems so..." Replied Carolin. "...We haven't had that situation here before of course there are black residents, but for a couple from Ethiopia to buy a house here for over a million pounds? It's the first time I've seen anything like that."

Susan listened to her further and no doubt, Carolin knew what she was talking about.

Firstly, due to the fact that her family had lived in North Hill for generations and she herself had never left the town.

Secondly, Carolin just liked to gossip and know everything about everyone. "Just don't get the wrong idea Susan, not that I have anything against people from Africa." The woman added unexpectedly.

It was as if she was afraid that Susan would accuse her of racism or something else in a moment.

"I know, Carolin..." Susan smiled at her. "...And how do you know they flew here from Africa?" Susan asked.

"Aaaa... well, you know Susan, North Hill is a small town..." replied Carolin quietly, again adopting a conspiratorial tone of voice. "... the delivery men for their stuff stopped for lunch at the 'Cafe Orbi,' Thomas was serving them, so he immediately asked a few questions, and they told him. I spoke to him, and he told me..."

Carolin went on, the satisfied smile not disappearing from her face, which was slowly starting to annoy Susan more and more. "...He was just here. If you'd come ten minutes earlier, you would still have bumped into him." She concluded.

Well, yes, of course, because stories like that are as important to me as they are to you, Carolin... she rebuked the woman Susan in her mind. *Soon, the entire city will be talking about them. They don't even know how famous they will be, even before getting here for good, all thanks to Carolin's big mouth and her friends.* Susan thought, then smiled under her breath, making herself laugh.

"Thank you, Carolin, it was nice to chat, but I really must go now. I still have

some important things to do today..." said Susan, fed up with the conversation. She was starting to get impatient. "...Goodbye." She added at the end.

"Goodbye," Carolin replied, clearly disappointed that she had failed to engage Susan in further gossip.

Susan left the building and took a quick step to her car. Trying to get her thoughts back to the day's agenda, she almost immediately downplayed the whole conversation with Carolin.

She walked over to the car, got in and put John's package on the passenger seat, then started the engine.

As she was about to turn the vehicle around and continue towards the shops where she intended to go next, however, she thought she would rather change her intentions.

"Since I'm already wasting time, I'll stop by the surgery for a while. I'm in no hurry to get home and get on with the cooking." Susan suddenly stated.

Her small surgery was located in an NHS building in the city centre, so from where she was now, the distance was really short.

She pointed the car in the opposite direction to the direction she had originally intended to go a while ago and moved slowly forward.

After less than seven minutes, she was already there.

As she was off work that day, she was not expecting any new messages, which were sometimes left by patients on her private landline. As she was already six months pregnant, she was going to look after her patients for another two months, after which she would go on a well-deserved maternity leave.

Until not long ago, Susan had still rejoiced at the thought of this, but now she felt that the whole situation was starting to bother her more and more. However, it was too late for her to change anything now.

In her sixth month of advanced pregnancy, she could not remove the baby, so there was nothing left for her to do but hold out until the birth and then see how things worked out.

Susan was a different person; she had changed a lot.

Moments later, she left her car in the staff-only car park in front of the NHS facility and walked quietly towards the building.

Once inside the room, a familiar woman working at the reception desk called out warmly at the sight of her.

"Oh, Susan, hi, you here? I thought you were off today?" Anna, the woman at the reception desk, spoke up, smiling broadly at Susan in the process. "Hey Anna, indeed..." Susan reciprocated the woman's smile. "... I'm just here for a minute. I forgot something from the office." She lied.

"Understood, so I won't keep you," Anna replied. "I'll be back in a minute, anyway," Susan replied.

"Certainly." Said Anna, then turned her gaze back to the computer screen and went back to her business.

Susan moved at a leisurely pace towards the corridor at the end of which was her office.

She decided that she had no intention of rushing any further, to get home as late as possible.

Within a few seconds, she had walked down the long corridor, past several other rooms where other doctors were seeing patients, and finally reached the room where her office was located.

Before entering, she stopped in front of the door for a moment, frowning her eyebrows as she looked at the badge attached to it. "Dr Psychology Susan McKane," she read quietly; however, she hadn't paid attention to it before.

"I don't like that name." She acknowledged, then opened the door with her key and stepped inside.

Once inside, slowly ran her eyes over the not-very-large room she knew very well.

By the window to the right of the entrance stood her desk, which contained a computer, a desk phone, several folders of notes and a set of pens. Next to it, against the wall, was an office chair standing exactly where she had previously left it.

To the left, a chest of books was set up, and everything was organised in such a way that there was room for a patient couch almost in the middle of it.

Until recently, Susan had been very proud of her small office, but now she was indifferent to it all. She had changed.

She walked over to the chair and slid it closer to the desk, then sat down on it and straightened up comfortably, closing her eyes for a moment.

She took a deep, relaxing breath as if starting a pleasant nap.

She was no longer in a hurry to get home, so why not sleep for a while?

At that moment her mobile phone rang.

She pulled it out of her bag and looked at the display, then gave a resigned gasp.

It was John calling.

Susan pondered for another moment whether to answer or pretend she had missed the call.

Even though she didn't want to talk to him now, after a couple of beeps, however, she pressed the green "answer" button.

"John?" she spoke up first.

"Hi honey, how are you doing?" he asked.

"Fine…" Susan replied. "…I'm busy shopping." She lied.

"Ah, that's good," John replied uncertainly.

"Why do you ask? You knew I went out to the shops." Susan furrowed her brow, sensing the hesitation in John's voice.

At the same time, supposing that he might be calling her for a completely different reason.

"Because I thought we could order something from the restaurant for tonight...?" John explained.

Susan momentarily liked the idea. As she didn't have the slightest desire to cook, she felt a sense of relief that she wouldn't have to do so.

"… But now that you've done the shopping, I think I'm calling a bit late, or I'll cook something myself. I don't want you to strain yourself in your condition."

John added out of concern for Susan and the still unborn baby. "I'm just looking around the shops now..." she lied again. "…I haven't bought anything specific for dinner yet." She added.

"Okay, so give yourself a break tonight. We'll order dinner from La nostra Famiglia," John replied.

Pronouncing the name of their favourite Italian restaurant, John tried to create an air of spontaneity and excitement.

But his voice did not sound enthusiastic at all, and Susan sensed this straight away.

She knew him intimately and immediately picked up anomalies in his manner of speech, if any.

Which only confirmed her earlier suspicion that perhaps, John was calling about something else.

"John, is something wrong?" she asked.

"Nah..." John answered again, without conviction. "... I'm not entirely sure."

He finished the sentence.

"What do you mean 'I'm not entirely sure?'" Susan was irritated by such an answer.

"Do you remember I was called in for a chest x-ray a few days ago? In connection with my notorious cough?" he asked.

"Yes." She replied.

"So, earlier, I got a message from the clinic Dr Clark Gable's clinic. He wants to see me at my next available appointment regarding the results." He explained.

"Oh yes, I understand…" Susan said. " …listen, John, it's probably best if you tell me everything when I get home. I should be there in half an hour or maybe even a bit sooner if it goes well."

"Actually, there's nothing else to tell..." John replied. "... just that I should go to a meeting tomorrow."

"Why don't you try calling Dr Clark again today and find out more?" Susan suggested.

"Do you think it's worth it?" John had his doubts.

"It certainly wouldn't hurt."

"Well, if you think so." John agreed.

"I'll come over soon, then we'll talk in private."

"Alright, I'll see you then." Added John in conclusion.

"See you."

Then she pressed the red button on her phone, placed it on the desk in front of her and leaned back on the chair.

For a moment, she stared at her phone thoughtfully.

I knew immediately he was clearly concerned about something, the dinner call was just a cover for the real reason to call me. she thought.

Yet she was absolutely right.

Because after receiving such disturbing and unexpected news, John sensed the worst and was then gripped by complete terror.

The uncertainty of what was going on and the helplessness of waiting until the next day, to find out only heightened the fear in John.

The phone call to Susan was supposed to be an escape for him from reality and the state of mind, he was in at that moment.

It was also supposed to make him feel a little better just to hear her friendly, loving voice that he adored so much.

However, what he couldn't know at the time was that Susan wasn't going to make anything easy for him, limiting herself to just listening to what he still wanted to tell her.

Susan was a different person; she had changed a lot.

Five minutes passed.

Susan was still sitting in her chair with her eyes closed instead of driving home as she had promised her husband at the time.

She had to admit to herself, however, that she was somewhat intrigued by what John had just said to her.

Although not in the sense that she was worried about him, it was simply curiosity about what his X-ray results might be about.

Having worked in a medical environment herself, she knew that such news never boded well.

For a while, she also still considered whether to go to the shop and buy some things so that it would look like she had been shopping and not give John any reason to suspect her of being untruthful or forget everything and go directly on her way back.

In the end, however, she decided to go straight home.

After all, she hadn't done anything wrong, so she didn't need to create the impression that she had something to hide from such an innocent lie.

Five minutes later.

Susan took her phone from her desk and her handbag and left her office, locking the door behind her.

As she crossed the corridor again and reached the front door, on her way out, she waved Anna to say goodbye.

"Bye, Susan!" Anna called out, covering the phone receiver with her hand as she was in the middle of the conversation.

"See you tomorrow!" Susan replied and went out into the street

She stood in front of the entrance for a moment and, taking a few breaths of fresh air through her nose, pulled out her phone to check exactly what time it was.

The electronic watch now showed 4:30 pm. Susan noticed that the sun was already slowly heading towards the west, even though it was still pleasantly warm.

She walked a few steps and got into her black BMW.

Then, without further ado, she started the engine, which thundered ominously with horsepower.

"A mighty beast." She smiled under her breath.

Her sports car filled her with pride, and she sincerely loved it. She was also never bothered by other people's opinions about how she should drive a safer family vehicle just because she was six months pregnant.

This was also the case when her parents, together with John, just before buying the car, tried to convince her that, as a respected psychologist, she should drive a vehicle more suited to that title.

Susan believed it was entirely her decision what kind of car she wanted to drive.

She had always liked sports cars. Therefore, she had absolutely no intention of compromising under family pressure.

And certainly to get rid of her current vehicle or replace it with another, less conspicuous model.

Manoeuvring carefully, she reached the main street and continued driving slowly and unhurriedly towards home.

Once she had left the city centre in the comfort of her car, she analysed the day's events one by one in her mind.

Thanks to which, she remembered her conversation with Carolin at the post office.

The timing was good, as she was about to drive past the villa with the new tenants that Carolin had spoken about with such great concern and interest.

Susan began to wonder if the lorries that passed her as she drove into the centre were just heading for the house that the irate woman had mentioned, or could it have been pure coincidence?

And if so, they should still be there. Maybe I could see someone? She thought.

Susan, at one point, caught herself involuntarily, hoping to spot someone with a dark skin colour.

Such a thought was subconscious since it was Carolin Richardson who, during the conversation, effectively planted the seed of conviction in Susan's mind about the appearance of the newcomers.

Under other circumstances, she would probably not have paid much attention.

If furniture has been brought in, then the owners should also be there. I would certainly supervise my move. She concluded.

When not quite ten minutes later, she was already driving past a large, elegant, but above all, very expensive house.

Then she saw that, indeed, there were still standing in front of it those three delivery trucks with the logo of the housing agency "BnBL" that she had seen earlier.

At that moment, Susan felt her heart start beating faster again. She slowed the car down to a suitable speed so that she could take a closer look at the people she had spotted from a distance.

It was then that she concluded that the workers from the agency had apparently managed to finish their assigned task because she saw three men standing next to the cars, talking to each other and smoking cigarettes.

She estimated there should have been six of them, three drivers and three helpers.

However, apart from the workers, she saw no one who could potentially look like the new owner of the property.

Slightly disappointed, Susan ignored this immediately, turned her gaze back to the roadway and then pressed harder on the accelerator.

"Since they've already moved in, I'll meet them sooner or later anyway." She acknowledged.

A few minutes later, she was driving her sports BMW into the garage of the house.

On the way, she passed John's car, which was parked in the driveway. She was slightly surprised to see it, as she hadn't expected him to return from work so soon.

John usually didn't get home until eight o'clock in the evening.

And I was hoping I would still have some time to myself before he arrived, damn it. she thought, and her irritation began to build again. She decided, however, that there was nothing left for her now but to pretend that nothing bad was happening.

She must be as charming to him as ever so that John could not guess anything.

At least, that's what she thought.

Susan left the car in the garage, then entered the house quietly through the door from this room.

She then made her way to the hallway, where she hung up her coat and removed her shoes.

Turning back towards the kitchen connected to the dining room, she slowly walked past John's piano.

When she entered the kitchen, she saw that John was already there waiting for her.

Susan and John McKane lived in a nice two-storey house with a large garden that included a swimming pool and an elegant patio. All this had been built by the company of Kevin McKane, John's father. In contrast, the land once belonged to John's parents, who bought it specifically for him when he was born, with the hope that one day he himself would want to build his own home on it and start a family. They gave him possession of the land as a gift on his sixteenth birthday, so officially, both the land and the house were owned by John.

Because even with the construction of the house, all costs were paid in part by Kevin McKane and the rest was paid by John.

Susan, at the time, was not yet earning her money, so John felt responsible for creating a cosy nest for his future family, where they could build a future together.

Thinking back to those days, John felt a sense of accomplishment and pride that he was able to provide Susan with everything she needed. In return, she supported him to the best of her ability and did her best to help design and, later, build the house they were both soon to live in.

A spacious and modern kitchen with dining area, two bathrooms, six bedrooms, a two-car garage with an elegantly laid out driveway, a garden with a patio and swimming pool.

At one time, Susan loved this house, especially as she and John witnessed it being built, brick by brick.

At the time, this project brought them even closer together, and they couldn't wait for it to be completed.

Such a property cost almost a million pounds on the property market, at the time impressive to Susan, but on the current day she didn't care much about that anymore.

Susan was a different person; she had changed.

"Oh, Susan! How good that you are home already." John was pleased to see her.

"Well, hello." She replied with a friendly smile on her face. She tried to keep up appearances.

"How did the shopping go?" John asked.

At the same time, looking in the direction of her hand looking out of the shopping bags.

"I didn't really buy anything..." she replied. "...I didn't feel like shopping. I turned back home as soon as you called." She added sitting down on a chair by the kitchen counter.

John furrowed his brow, slightly puzzled by this statement.

He knew Susan well, and there had yet to be a case where she came home completely empty-handed.

She always had to bring at least some sweets from the shop, but today she had bought absolutely nothing.

Again, John had reason to think that this was not like her at all.

"It's a shame because I know that chocolate always makes you feel better."

John replied after a while.

Then he walked over to Susan and embraced her around the waist. He bent his head to kiss his wife, but at the same moment, she reached for her handbag, avoiding his face while pretending not to have read his intentions.

Which made John confused, so he let her go and took two steps back.

"Something wrong?" he asked, looking at Susan with puzzlement.

"No, I'm fine…" she replied. "... I just smoked a cigarette in the car, and I know that you avoid the smell of tobacco." She lied.

Susan knew very well how to approach John, who had quit smoking less than a week ago and was struggling to stay away from the habit.

John had been a smoker for over twenty years.

At a time when his addiction was reaching its "peak," he could smoke up to two packets of cigarettes in one day.

Now, he tried to avoid anything that might remind him of his pleasurable addiction.

Susan, therefore, saw this as the perfect excuse when she did not want to be too close to her husband.

She would then say that she smoked a cigarette, which she did very occasionally for relaxation, but such an excuse always works on John, who would then quickly move away, no matter whether if he could smell any tobacco from Susan or not.

"Don't remind me..." John laughed. "...but I don't smell any smoke..." he said while sniffing with his nose. "...besides, you know you shouldn't smoke in this state." He added, having in mind her advanced pregnancy. "I smoked earlier on the way back, so the stench has already had time to air out..." Susan lied again. "...nothing will happen if I smoke one cigarette a week. Better tell me what about that message you told me on the phone? Have you tried calling Dr Clark?" she added quickly to change the subject. "Yes, I called..." he picked up the conversation. "... but I haven't been able to find out anything specific, Clark was unavailable, I spoke to the receptionist, and I have an appointment for one o'clock tomorrow." He added.

He certainly spoke to Anna; I wonder if he called while I was still there. Susan thought.

"Don't worry about it now, darling...." she said thoughtfully to her husband. "...we'll order some delicious dinner and have a nice evening together." She added.

"I'm sure you're right. There's no point in worrying too much..." John tried to smile. "... well, what would you like to do tonight?"

"Hmmm..." she wondered. " ...why don't we stick with favourites and call La Nostra Famiglia?" she suggested in flawless Italian.

"Agreed, I already know what I want to order." Replied John, more clearly already cheered up.

"Me too..." she replied. "... I'll just go and change quickly, and I'll be back in a minute." She added without waiting for her husband's answer, turned towards the stairs, and then set off ahead.

John followed her around with his eyes for a while, admiring her feminine curves.

Even at six months pregnant, she had an alluring effect on him, he wondered if tonight he may get lucky.

It had been a while since the last time they had been intimate with each other as husband and wife, and John sorely missed Susan's tenderness. Susan tended to say that her lack of interest in marital life was only because she was pregnant.

At the time, John did not want to put any pressure on her because he loved and respected her too much to insist.

She'll probably put me off again by saying she's not in the mood today, but at least I'll try. John thought.

In those days, John had not yet fully associated all the facts because if he had, he could put all the clues together then.

Unfortunately, many things easily slipped people's attention, mixed in with the events of everyday life.

Many times, it is impossible to know what is happening, why or for what reasons.

Some things seem too obvious to ponder or to look for some other hidden reason.

However, it is worth stopping, from time to time, for a moment and looking at even the smallest anomalies that appear in places where there was no trace of them before.

By questioning any doubts, we can learn so much more about the other person during an honest conversation.

Had John also followed this thought, he might have been able to get answers to the questions that plagued him at the time.

But he, all the while, was himself trying to justify all of Susan's strange behaviour.

Consequently, he had, or preferred not to have, no choice but to remain in a position where a misguided feeling of blissful ignorance overshadowed common sense and the desire to know the truth.

As Susan disappeared at the top of the stairs, John plunged his hand into the dresser drawer that stood in the hallway and retrieved from it the menu of their favourite Italian home delivery restaurant, "La Nostra Famiglia." Then, he made his way to the living room and sat down comfortably on the sofa, after which he began to flick through the familiar sheet of paper listing the dishes on offer, even though he already knew in advance what he wanted to order.

Thus, trying to occupy his thoughts with something until Susan returned to him.

When she came down to the lounge ten minutes later, dressed in her favourite, albeit somewhat flared, sweatpants and an oversized T-shirt. Admittedly, she didn't look very alluring in these clothes, but when John looked in her direction, he thought she was beautiful.

"So, what do you think...?" she asked, at the same time snapping him out of his reverie. "...have you chosen yet?" she added looking at the menu card in his hand.

"Aaaa... yes, sure." He replied quickly.

"So, what are you waiting for? Call them because I'm hungry..." Susan urged him. "... you know what to order for me, don't you?" she added with a knowing smile on her face because she always ordered the same thing from this restaurant: meat lasagne and coleslaw.

"Easy now, where's the fire...?" John replied and as he looked at Susan's grimaced face, who was staring at him with her arms crossed over her chest, he felt himself start to laugh. "...would you like something else to go with it? Or just ask for a double portion?" he asked when he finally managed to stifle his amusement.

"Hmmm... I'll have two pieces with a large coleslaw," Susan replied.
"I think our little one will like it too." Replied John with a smile, looking at Susan's swollen belly.

"So far, there's no other choice. Now it's up to me to decide what she's going to eat." Said Susan, stroking her belly.

"Hehehe... of course, that makes sense," John replied.

"Well then, make the call because I must go to the toilet." Replied Susan and walked out of the living room again leaving John alone.

As soon as she had gone, John fished his mobile phone out of his pocket and dialled the number for the restaurant.

After a few beeps, the woman's voice on the other end rang out.

"Good evening. This is the restaurant La Nostra Famiglia. How may I help you?" the woman with a heavily Italian accent asked politely.

"Good evening. I would like to place an order."

"Of course, I'm listening. What would you like?" she asked.

"So yes, I'll have a large pepperoni pizza, a large portion of chicken wings in Buffalo sauce, two pieces of meaty Lasagne and a large coleslaw salad and chips.

The lady at the restaurant repeated the whole order to herself once more, silently writing it down.

"I see you must have invited the family over for dinner tonight." She joked.

"No... Hehehe..." John laughed. "You see, my wife is pregnant." He added in an amused voice.

"Ah yes, I understand, hehehe... my apologies." The woman replied, also laughing quietly.

"It's alright."

"And what would you like to drink?" she asked while changing her tone of voice to a more appropriate one.

"A large Coke, no sugar, please," John replied.

"Okay, I've already sent your order to the kitchen, should be delivered in less than an hour. I'll have your name and address, please." The woman said.

"My name is John McKane I am a regular customer." He replied.

"Ah yes, of course! Hello Mr McKane, I knew from the start that your voice seemed familiar to me indeed. I already know the address..." she replied suddenly cheerfully. "...to pay on delivery as usual?"

"Yes, please, thank you, so I should expect the delivery man in less than an hour?" asked John for reassurance.

"I will tell you in confidence that we are having a very quiet evening at the restaurant tonight. As you are a regular customer, I think between thirty and forty minutes, you will have a delicious dinner delivered." She replied.

"Thank you very much, and have a good evening."

"You too, please give our regards to your wife, and I wish you much happiness with your newborn baby." The woman from the restaurant replied, significantly going beyond the typical boundary of the relationship between customer and service.

"Greetings, thank you very much, goodbye." Said John in conclusion.

"Goodbye." The woman replied and then disconnected the call. John put the phone down on the table in front of him and straightened up on the sofa. At the same moment Susan came back into the living room.

"Have you been talking that long?" she asked.

"A very nice woman, she sends her regards." Replied John, smiling at her in a friendly way.

"Oh, that's nice, thank you," Susan replied.

Less than forty minutes later, they were already sitting together in the living room, with the table set with all the delicacies.

When Susan saw the pizza, chicken wings, chips, two boxes of Lasagne and coleslaw in front of her, she didn't know what to start with.

She had momentarily forgotten; she had only ordered two dishes for herself out of everything that had been delivered to them and was treating herself to whatever she fancied.

John felt happy as he silently watched Susan eating her delicacies one by one, grabbing whatever she could find. After all, she was feeding two people at the same time.

To pass the time during the meal, he turned on the television, which was showing a film.

At the same time, he tried not to disturb Susan while she was eating.

An hour later, John thought it would be a good idea to go to bed early. It was only approaching ten-thirty when he announced to Susan that he was going to bed.

He was still silently hoping that Susan would go with him.

However, she only led John away with her eyes as he got up from the sofa and started towards their shared bedroom upstairs.

"I'm going to stay here for a bit longer, goodnight." She said.

"Good night."

Well, yes, another lonely night. he thought resignedly.

Sometimes, even when they lay together in the marital bed, John felt like he was alone in it, and that thought depressed him greatly.

As he climbed the stairs to the first floor and onto the bedroom, he stopped halfway for a moment and looked in Susan's direction.

She was invariably staring at the TV, nibbling on another chicken wing, not even noticing him.

"I wonder if all marriages go through a crisis like this when a baby is on the way?" he wondered, trying to seek comfort.

John relentlessly still hoped that once the baby arrived, their life together would return to the normality of their past.

They spent a pleasant evening together that day, allowing John to completely forget the suspicious and worrying visit that awaited him the next day at the doctor's.

Yes, it was a pleasant and peaceful evening.

Only three more months, then their baby would be born, and his beloved wife, would once again be the same Susan he had fallen in love with and married.

Moments later, John lay down in bed.

In some situations, ignorance is indeed bliss.

At the time, he had no way of knowing that this was the last such pleasant evening he would spend with his wife until the end of his days.

What he did not know that night was Susan would never be the same again and that his life, which had been so far arranged, would soon turn into a living hell.

But it was nice to spend the evening with his wife and go to bed, hoping that everything would soon be fine.

A false hope, but at least that night, he could still have it.

6

Mystery phone call.

'Look for this truth where it is actually to be found! If necessary, be determined to go against the tide of popular opinion and propagated slogans! Do not be afraid of Love, which makes demands on man'.

Four years earlier.

23 March 2004, Canary Wharf, London, on the ice of the "Bradley and Brad

Lettings," 03:40 pm.

A few minutes into an unexpected and surprising conversation with a female stranger, impersonating George Bradley's beloved from years gone by.

This one almost threw the landline phone that was on his desk, after which he literally ran out of the office of the housing agency "BnBL." At the same time, he felt the confused stares of the co-workers who witnessed this at the time.

He was well aware that it must have looked disconcerting, to say the least, from the perspective of those present.

However, he cared little at the time about what his employees might have thought. Since it was too late for him to do anything about it anyway, he didn't bother.

He had a tougher nut to crack at the time.

He was having a panic attack and lost control of himself.

George felt himself suffocating at one point and ran out of the building as he immediately needed to get some fresh air.

He was in shock and had to leave his office as soon as possible. "Let them think what they like. I don't have to explain myself to anyone." Said George to himself.

As he stepped out into the streets, he squinted a little under the glare of the sun's rays, which hit him painfully.

Thoughts tangled in his head at the speed of light through which he could feel himself starting to get weaker and weaker.

It was imperative that he sat down somewhere for a while before it got worse and he fell over.

So, with a quick step, he made his way to his car, parked in the private car park in front of the agency, and got in.

For a long moment he sat motionless with his eyes closed, leaning against the driver's seat, breathing deeply.

"I need to calm down. I can't drive like this after all." Said George to himself under his breath.

He waited a few more minutes, and when he decided he was ready to drive home, he started the engine and set off ahead.

George trusted his staff he knew they would close the agency safely in his absence.

But even if that were not to be the case, he was in no position to even think about it at the time.

For the moment, it was all the same to him.

On the way home, George thought it would be a good idea to have something stronger to soothe his shattered nerves.

As he was not used to drinking alcohol among strangers in some random bar, he decided that he would return to his flat, where a fine ten-year-old Whisky was waiting for him.

At the very thought of the refined drink, he cheered up a little. Rational thinking slowly began to return to him.

"It is imperative that I get my emotions under control and think about all this calmly..." he began to develop a plan of action. ... *I will analyse everything from start to finish, and maybe she is an imposter? But how does she know about Noelle and me? After all, the woman who called me couldn't be more than twenty years old...*he thought intensely.

George stopped the car in the traffic jam of vehicles that usually piled up on "Tower Bridge."

That was in the seventies; this woman wasn't even in the world yet. He pondered going back his memory to the time when he had formed a couple with Noelle.

Thus trying to unravel the mystery that had fallen on him unexpectedly like a bolt from the blue.

The vehicles on the bridge moved forward, along with them George's car headed for, "Old Kent Road."

Despite the shocking and unexpected news of the day, however, George was also a little lucky.

He felt a little relief when it didn't take him too long to tear his car through the town, as it usually did.

For a moment, he worried that he would be forced to be stuck in the car along with his exuberant thoughts.

However, the moderate traffic jams, just that day, on the often-crowded streets of London, did not cause that much of a problem.

As a result, after less than fifteen minutes, he arrived in front of one of the guarded blocks of flats in the "New Cross" district.

Here was his three-bedroom flat, which he rented.

He parked his car in the space reserved for him, right under the watchful eye of CCTV security cameras.

He got out of it and then pressed a small button next to his keys on his way into the building.

When he heard behind him:

"BIP!!! BIP!!!" he knew his vehicle was properly locked.

As he slowly approached the lift, he looked up and ran his eyes over the balconies above his head.

Then, a slight smile dawned on his face.

Because he remembered what he used to say when he sometimes joked about himself ...*I am a man who earns his living by renting flats to other people and I must pay for my own four walls....*

The fact was, however, that renting a private flat was very much in his favour.

Plus, the place he was currently living in was very tasteful and elegant, just the way he liked it.

However, George Bradley was just, deep down, a simple man. He earned well and wanted to let others earn.

At the time, with his current earnings, he didn't even feel the money he was spending paid for rent.

In addition, for any problems with the flat, he could always call the landlord when needed without taking any responsibility.

Even so, he sometimes thought it might have looked a bit lazy on his part.

But that was the deal. He pays, so he requires everything to run smoothly. Because George dealt in the same way with his tenants, who sometimes complained about things, he dealt with problems on the spot and did not put anything off so that everyone could be satisfied.

Therefore, in this situation, he felt that it was only right that his landlord should also make sure that he, as a tenant, had everything he needed, paying the right money for it, of course.

George walked over to the lift and summoned it with the button. When the doors opened a moment later, he got in and marked the fifth-highest floor of the building.

After a while, he was already walking slowly towards his flat, feeling exhausted both mentally and physically.

He couldn't wait to finally sit down in his favourite leather armchair with a glass of Whiskey, fire up a cigar and turn on some relaxing classical music. On weekdays, George wasn't used to drinking alcohol, mostly reaching for a glass only occasionally or for a celebration.

However, this was not one of those days that he could count as normal or common.

Therefore, he felt it justified him to break away a little from his worn-out routine and experience a moment of much-needed respite. George, too, had never been a fan of getting drunk to the point of unconsciousness, and even in his youth as a teenager, at countless parties, he had not done so.

He was always the type of person who knew his moderation and how to keep his cool.

That evening, George decided that he could no longer afford to let anyone or anything further disturb his desired tranquillity.

He had had enough excitement for one 24-hour period, so he switched off his private and work phone.

The day's work and problems were over the moment he stepped across the threshold of his flat.

Tomorrow is Sunday, I don't have to do anything now that can't wait until tomorrow... he thought as he pulled out his shoes in the hallway. *...fuck it, I'm putting everything o until tomorrow for the hell of it.* he concluded and smiled under his breath.

Nothing else mattered except a Whiskey, a cigar, a comfortable armchair and classical music.

Upon entering the flat, George sat comfortably in the armchair with a glass of Whiskey in hand.

He placed the half-drank bottle on the table next to him so that he wouldn't have to get up for it again and turned on the pleasant music. It was approaching 9 pm when George, sipping the luxurious drink with small sips, closed his eyes and was then overwhelmed by sleep.

He drifted off to dreamland, unaware.

He didn't wake up until eight o'clock the next morning, just as he was sitting up in his seat.

He had a slight headache from the alcohol he had consumed the previous evening.

George was already in his old age. As he had been too tired to go to bed the night before, he had fallen asleep to the accompaniment of classical music from his favourite vinyl record, as he also sometimes did.

He got up from his chair and stretched his arms high up to stretch his back. Then, with a slow step, he made his way to the bathroom to take a refreshing morning shower there and get himself in order.

He was in no hurry with anything.

The time spent in the shower and the general routine that accompanied it took him almost forty minutes.

When he had finished, he felt as if he had been born again.

However, he remembered the problem that had come up suddenly the previous day and the fact that he had promised himself, to deal with it today.

He felt, however, that he needed to talk to someone.

As George did not have many trusted friends to whom he could confide such a sensitive subject.

The matter was extremely personal.

After much consideration, the choice finally fell on Matthiew Braddock. He seemed to be the most suitable person for this at the moment, for several reasons.

"After all, this could have a negative impact on our mutual interests, so I should warn him beforehand," George stated.

He reached for the phone and dialled Matthiew; it was ten minutes past nine o'clock when George heard the call tone in the receiver.

Matthiew answered after a couple of beeps.

"Hallo?" said Matthiew in a still sleepy voice.

"Hi Matt, it's George. A matter has come up, and I need to see you as soon as possible." Got straight to the point.

"Man, do you know what time it is?" Matthiew muttered.

He was clearly not happy with the wake-up call George had given him. "It's now exactly ten past nine, so don't exaggerate. I'm not ringing the bell in the middle of the night." George replied.

"I'm tired. I was up all night, and it's Sunday, so is it really that urgent that you can't wait until Monday...?" explained Matthiew, blatantly trying to get rid of him. "...after all, we can have a quiet chat tomorrow when we meet at the office." He added.

"It can't wait until tomorrow, and we'll talk today..." George replied firmly. "...I know very well that last night you drank yourself into a stupor again, in some club of yours, like every Saturday anyway, and you believe me, I don't give a damn. It is solely your business..." he said, then took a short break to collect his thoughts.

...and you are probably, as always, curing a moral hangover after a failed hookup. Will you ever wise up? he added to himself, already in thought and smiled under his breath.

George was right on this point.

Because Matthiew was, in a way, just famous for liking the party lifestyle, so, when the weekend nights came, he mostly spent them in various nightclubs, then, for days on end, curing a murderous hangover.

Although he visibly stood out from the young people turning up at the club, both in appearance and age.

For he was an unattractive forty-five-year-old man who was quite overweight.

These were his favourite places to party.

He chose such clubs basically only because of the large numbers of young girls who came to the parties and often got drunk there to the point of unconsciousness.

Matthiew then saw the best chance for himself to take any of the heavily intoxicated with alcohol or psychedelic drugs, vulnerable girls to his flat. But even such a simple and un-sophisticated idea, which basically involved dragging the target away from the group of people he happened to be with, then buying a couple of drinks for the most drunk girl and trying to convince her to leave the place with him, was not working out.

In such cases, Matthiew tried a different tactic.

Namely, he would simply try to spot a single woman who had come there alone, or her friends had gone home early, and she had decided to stay in the club longer.

But such "hunting" was more reminiscent of a lecherous elderly freak looking for his next "victim" than any form of hookup.

In short, it looked unsavoury, to say the least, and was almost always unsuccessful.

"...Listen to me carefully. An emergency has arisen that requires immediate attention. Can you meet me at lunchtime?" George continued. "Well, fine, but in the afternoon, maybe after one or two o'clock?" Matthiew dragged out the meeting time as long as he could, not one bit happy with the idea.

"One o'clock…" George decided immediately. "…does Nandos on Elephant and Castle suit you?"

"Alright, I'll meet you there," Matthiew replied.

"Okay, see you."

George glanced at his watch; it was twenty past nine.

For this, he thought, he must somehow use his free time usefully.

Alright then, I've got another three hours or so before I'll leave the house. I need to eat something and then sit down and plan my course of action. He thought.

He then went to the kitchen to prepare himself some sort of easily digestible breakfast.

He didn't want to eat too much before he left, as he was worried how his stomach, fuelled by the night's Whiskey, would react to the meal. Besides, he was due to go to the restaurant in not too long anyway.

Elephant and Castle, London, 12:40 pm.

Matthiew arrived at the venue first, twenty minutes before the agreed meeting time.

On this day, he decided that his best bet was to use public transport. He did not want to drive because he had not yet sobered up completely, which made him feel dizzy.

Furthermore, he stated that this way, he would also avoid another problem.

For those living in the city, it is a well-known fact that the "Elephant and Castle district" in central "London" is not a place where it is easy to find a parking space for a private car.

Therefore, Matthiew felt that he had managed to avoid at least one problem for the day.

When he got to the 148 bus.

He walked through the streets, with a slow and still somewhat shaky step, through the roundabout in the centre of the district, which brought him to the "Nandos" restaurant.

He then went inside and, without waiting for anyone from the start, chose a table for himself, usually intended for several people.

He sat down at it and checked his watch; it was ten minutes to one o'clock. *Knowing George, I'd give my hand that he'd be here at one o'clock sharp.* Matthiew thought.

He had no appetite at all and didn't want to eat one bit.

Therefore, when the waiter approached him offering service, he disposed of it by quickly saying: "I'm waiting for someone."

All the time, he had the feeling that the remnants of the alcohol he had consumed the night before in the club were still floating in his stomach, which made the thought of food uncomfortable.

He sat at the table for a while before deciding that it would be a good idea to have a cold Coke on the rocks.

As he approached one of the cash registers to pay for a large cup, which he could then refill himself later without limit.

The smells coming from the grill, which was right behind the back of the woman who was serving him, reached his nostrils, making him barely suppress a vomit reflex.

"Oh, mother..." he said, covering his mouth with his hand. ...*On top of that, this fried chicken, I can't stand it...* he thought and went to fetch the drink he had paid for. "...I'm really going to make a mess here in a minute." He said quietly to himself, at the same time feeling his stomach acids rise to his throat.

As he stepped outside, he inhaled heavily a few times and felt it slowly start to pass.

He quickly found one free table in the concrete garden, sat down on a chair under an umbrella and checked the time again.

In a few seconds, it was going to strike one o'clock, at which point he heard someone calling his name.

"Matthiew!"

So, he turned in the direction from which the voice had come and saw that George was already only a few steps away.

I knew how he always had to turn up on time. What a fucking bureaucrat. he thought.

"Hi George…" he replied. "…welcome to my humble abode." He joked, at the same time indicating with his hand the vacant seat at the table opposite him.

"Don't be silly." Replied George in a slightly breathless voice.

"Did you come by car?"

"Yes, why do you ask?" he replied.

"Just chatting…" Matthiew said. "…sit down and tell me your story." He was trying to be funny again.

George just looked at him disapprovingly, then pushed his chair away from the table in one motion and sat down on it.

"I hope you've had time to sober up." Said George unexpectedly. In response, Matthiew sent him an angry look. He hated it when his partner pointed out his penchant for alcohol, and George knew it well.

"Don't try to patronise me…" he replied. "…don't forget that you're the one who called me here, so if you want to talk, then I expect a little more respect from you." He added in a serious voice. "Okay, sorry." George was slightly embarrassed.

Under the circumstances, he really needed his help and starting the conversation on the wrong foot did not play to George's advantage. "Fine, do you want to order something for yourself first? Or would you rather get straight to the point?" Matthiew asked out of politeness. "No, I won't be able to swallow anything right now. I think I'll just have a drink."

Matthiew furrowed his eyebrows in surprise.

He hadn't expected George to refuse his favourite rotisserie chicken in a medium spicy sauce, which he never failed to at least take away with him, if not consume on the spot.

At the same time, he realised that the matter must be extremely serious if it had taken George's appetite away so much.

However, it was, for the moment, extremely convenient for him. Luckily, he won't be eating anything. I'd probably puke if I had to look at him while he was eating. Matthiew thought.

"Okay, I'll get you some orange juice..." Matthiew suggested, knowing George's habits intimately. "...and you, in the meantime, think what do you want to tell me."

Matthiew headed once more into the restaurant, leaving George alone at the table for a while.

The man was immersed in his thoughts, watching the countless passers-by on the street.

Matthiew returned after a few minutes.

He placed a glass of orange juice in front of George with ice as he liked, thus snapping him out of his reverie, and then took his seat.

The man raised a still-preoccupied gaze at him.

At that moment, he looked completely as if he had not expected to see him here. "Thank you."

"No problem at all," Matthiew replied, pushing his chair closer to the table, not taking his eyes o George.

"So? What is it...?" said Matthiew. "... what could be so important that it can't wait until tomorrow?"

George took a deep breath and then slowly let it out, clearing his mind. "Yesterday, while I was in my office, I got a very strange phone call..." he began to narrate slowly. "...actually, I'm not one hundred per cent sure, but I think someone is trying to blackmail me."

Matthiew opened his eyes wider in surprise.

Not even for a moment had it crossed his mind that he would hear such words from George. He had completely not expected it.

He suspected that George would want to talk to him about a good offer to sell or buy some property that he had spotted.

He assumed, in advance, that he wanted to work out the details with him on a deal for a larger sum of money that they both had to agree to. However, at this point, he felt that the topic George wanted to talk to him about had begun to exceed Matthiew's competence from the very beginning.

"A blackmail...!?" Choked out Matthiew at last. " ...Where did something like that even come into your head, George?"

"I got a call from a woman who claims to know who and where my daughter is." He replied.

"Daughter? What do you mean, daughter?! After all, you don't have children, for fuck's sake." Matthiew still couldn't shake the feeling of shock. "Exactly! Do you think I don't know that? That's the problem..." George replied. " ...I'm sure that if I was expecting a child, the woman I was going to have it with would have told me."

"I'm more than sure of that too..." Matthiew replied. "...the women you see know that you are not poor. If you pollinated one of them, she would probably want to get something from you in such a situation."

"Don't be vulgar..." George was annoyed. "...it's not a question of whether any of them would want money from me. I would take care of my own child if the need arose."

"Of course," Matthiew replied, looking at him enviously.

For he knew perfectly well how successful George was with women and was morbidly jealous of it.

While he himself went around the clubs and bars every Friday and

Saturday, looking for so-called bargains, he usually went home alone. George, on the other hand, had several numbers in his phone for friendly women, willing to date him at any time.

"I probably wouldn't be so concerned about it if it weren't for the fact that the person I was talking to mention the name of a woman I knew almost thirty years ago..." George replied. You could sense the despair in his voice. " ...and even dared to use it to outwit the secretary by saying it was a family matter when she didn`t want to not connect her with me in my office." He added.

"Yes... it is, indeed, not an everyday situation..." Matthiew replied. "...she said something more when you spoke to her? In what way does she want to blackmail you?"

"She only said that she knows my daughter and knows where she is, also that she wants to meet me..." George replied. "...but the person I was talking to can't be more than twenty years old!? How the hell can she know about a woman I was in a relationship with, thirty years ago!" George's head was reeling.

"Do you have any leads on her?" Matthiew asked.

"No, she didn't leave me any information about herself. At the end she just hung up." George replied.

"If she called from a regular phone, then we will be able to find the number in the list of calls received in our office. Alright, but why?" George was surprised.

"What do you mean? You're not thinking rationally George, listen carefully, if this woman knows you and has some information about you, then we need to take a closer look at her, before any problems arise..." Matthiew replied. "...It is imperative that you get in touch with her to clarify the situation and find out, what she is after."

"Ah yes, you are indeed right..." nodded George. "...Keep your friends close, but your enemies even closer."

"That's right..." Matthiew replied. "...When we get back to the office tomorrow, we'll go through the call list from Saturday and I'm sure we'll find her number there, but until then, keep it to yourself."

"You don't have to tell me that, I'm not a fool, I've only told you that and it will stay that way." George replied.

"That's good, so breathe easy, I won't breathe a word, you can count on me." Matthiew assured him.

"Thank you, Matt." George smiled and a feeling of relief was painted on his face.

"You're welcome, let's get out of this place, I'm getting depressed by this neighbourhood." Matthiew said. "Do you need a lift somewhere?"

"Actually, I'd be happy to, I'll get home faster, I don't want to drag myself on buses again." He accepted Matthiew's invitation.

"Then let's go." George added.

After which they both set off to where George's parked Jaguar was waiting. "Also go home now, or wherever you want to go and don't worry about it anymore today George..." Matthiew lifted his spirits. "...Tomorrow we will come back to this matter, and everything will be explained." They had to walk quite a bit more before they finally reached the car. By this time, George felt more relaxed and calmer thanks to this conversation.

Tomorrow everything will be explained. He repeated in his mind. But through this whole situation, George had forgotten for a moment how cunning and sophisticated Matthiew was. People like him never do anything selflessly.

George did not realise at the time, how big a mistake he had made by confiding in him a secret that he could, after all, have tried to solve himself. Although Matthiew agreed to help him, at the same time he was already wondering, what he could gain from it for himself.

Because for a long time now, he had been considering the possibilities of how he could jump into his partner's place and take control of the agency.

Now, the opportunity practically knocked on his door by itself.

A question immediately popped into Matthiew's head:

Could George's supposedly unmarried daughter, be a good enough asset to win him off the stool?

However, he did not have to think about this question for too long, because the answer came virtually by itself.

To Matthiew's delight, in a relatively short space of time, everything was about to go exactly his way.

7

A shake-up of reality.

'You must demand of yourselves, even if others would not demand of you'.

Four years later.

18 October 2018, Camberwell Green, London, Rachel and Danny Davis's flat, 11.30pm.

After getting out of hospital, the three of us went back to mine and Rachel's flat that night.

Connor insisted on going along with us. He wanted to make sure I was okay. I felt terribly tired and didn't have the slightest desire to host him that day. I would have preferred him to come the next day, but I still couldn't say no to him.

I knew that he was worried about me all the time.

I was indebted to him for this and really appreciated his dedication.

Be that as it may, he also went through a nightmare that day.

However, I found it difficult to put myself in his shoes.

I thought about it, and I had no idea how I would have felt if I had been the one to witness the moment when, almost before my eyes, some drug addict almost sent him off into the other world.

I could only assume that he was as exhausted as I was, maybe even more so.

I tried to understand him, that's why I agreed to spend some more time with him, that awful day.

Of the three of us, only Rachel seemed not so tired at the time.

I could see from her now that she had stopped worrying and her good mood had returned.

I was happy about this because I didn't want her to continue to worry about me.

After entering our two-room flat, I went with Connor to make myself comfortable in the living room.

Rachel, meanwhile, headed for the kitchen.

"Anyone fancy a cup of tea?" She asked sticking her head out of the kitchen.

"Yes, I'll have one, please" Connor spoke up.

"I'll have a drink too." I said after a moment's thought.

"Coffee is not suggested at this late hour, we all deserve to get a reasonably normal night's sleep." Rachel added.

Holy words, there's nothing I want more at this moment, than to lie down in my bed and end this nightmare. I said to myself in my mind.

However, what I didn't realise at that moment was that the real nightmare, was yet to begin.

I looked at Connor, who was staring at me intensely the whole time.

Then I saw something in his eyes that I had never seen before.

Apart from the extreme tiredness, there was something else in them. It was only after a while that I realised that my partner looked devastated and that the something expressed in his gaze was nothing but immense sadness.

I felt a little uncomfortable at this sight.

"Oh man..." Connor started uncertainly. " …What a tragedy."

"Yeah, what can you do?" I said, not really knowing how I should react to that.

"Well, just what kind of people are they...?" Connor replied. "…If they were just killing themselves, that's fine, but taking the lives of innocent people?" He said it as if he was thinking aloud more than talking to me.

His gaze hung on the ground and for a while, I got the impression that he was temporarily absent.

I was very tired, nevertheless I thought he was right.

But at the same time, I had the feeling that he was nevertheless exaggerating a bit and over-dramatizing, after all, I came out of it in one piece.

"Do you know anything more about this man? Did you get any information about him in the meantime?" I asked.

"According to our data, he is an alcoholic and a drug addict, he spent some time in treatment at several times, but as you can see, without success..." He replied. "...He was also convicted of burglary, three years ago he was given a year's imprisonment, because in court he was not proven to have been in the looted flat, his defence argued that he was only driving for companions, besides, he has a record of stealing money from an elderly woman, he was supposed to take care of once." He completed the report after a while.

"What a twat... - I cursed under my breath. "... I don't understand how this woman, what was her name?"

"Clare Randal," Connor helped me out.

"Yes, Clare, I don't understand, how she could end up with an individual like him, on top of that having a daughter to look after." I wondered aloud.

"You know what they say, the bully loves the most, but some women have an unhealthy attraction to mentally twisted men." Connor laughed.

"Well yes, perfect, a drug addict, alcoholic and criminal, nothing to do but get married and start a happy family." I said half-jokingly, half seriously.

A few minutes later, Rachel returned, carrying a tray of hot drink in her hands, which she set down on the table.

She then placed an empty cup in front of Connor and immediately afterwards another one, right in front of me.

"Help yourselves." She said and turned back to the kitchen.

After a while she returned to the living room

Walking slowly and slurping carefully the hot chocolate from the cup so as not to burn herself, which she selfishly made just for herself.

I looked at her and wanted to laugh, but then Connor said something that started the biggest shock I've ever, experienced in my life.

"But the thing I feel most sorry for is that little girl, she still had her whole life ahead of her, it's a huge tragedy." He said and lowered his gaze again. These words hit me like a thunderbolt, and I didn't know how to interpret them.

At first, I thought he was being over-dramatic again.

Because as much as I could understand the fact that a traumatic situation would probably leave a mark on Denise Randal's psyche, no doubt, for many years to come.

But after all, nothing more serious had happened to her, so why such consternation?

At the time, I didn't know what had happened to the man who had put a gun to her head, although at the time, I didn't much care.

I was sure, however, that the girl was alright.

Because I saw her walking beside me when I was carried to the ambulance and she even held my hand then, at least, I thought so.

I could only guess that since the man was shooting at me, it was quite possible that he could have done so, towards the other police officers. If this was indeed the case, it certainly did not end well for him.

At this point, I thought the time was right to ask about Denise Randal. In truth, I should still be resting, and I was also aware that such a topic might be too difficult for me at that time.

Although I did not want to download more thoughts on my head on the same day.

I decided that since we were already here and talking anyway, so it was as good a time as any.

"Where is she now?" I asked Connor, who looked at me visibly confused.

"What do you mean, where? In the hospital." He replied.

"Have you seen her? Do you know how she's feeling?" I inquired.

Connor had a look of shock painted on his face, but he kept it quiet.

Rachel also squinted her eyes and watched me in silence with curiosity. I realised they were both looking at me as if I were asking some hopelessly stupid question.

What the hell is wrong with them? Why doesn't anyone want to answer me? My mind started to get irritated.

I tried to approach the subject from a different angle.

"Then maybe at least, one of you can tell me what happened to this guy?" I asked again.

The expression on Connor's face seemed to 'say mate, are you messing around or are you serious?'

"Death on the spot." Connor replied shortly.

"Well at last, some progress." Interjected my mind.

"Did our guys shoot him?" I asked again.

"He shot himself..." Connor was visibly disturbed by this conversational situation. " ...Listen man, I don't know what else you were able to see after you fell to the ground, all I know is that you were conscious the whole time after I got to you." ...He added after which he paused for a few seconds; I could see him putting thoughts together in his head. "...This guy fired three shots overall..." He continued. " ...The first one to you, the second one to Denise and the third one, he put in his head." He concluded.

What Connor had just said literally made me freeze.

I was now sitting with my mouth wide open, my eyes widened to maximum size, it wouldn't have surprised me at all if they resembled, in shape and size, the medals that Olympic athletes get on the podium.

I was unable to move for a moment, I could feel the thoughts boiling in my head, trying to process this information.

Injured then, was Denise walking me to the ambulance? How was she able to walk beside the gurney with a gunshot wound? After all, the paramedics would have taken her to the ambulance first and then come back for me, those are the procedures... My mind was working at full speed and only after a while, I realised what complete rubbish I was now thinking about. *...No, the whole thing didn't even make the slightest sense.* Summed up my instinct at last.

120

Even though I was already beginning to have an idea of where this was all going, I didn't want to allow it into my consciousness just yet.

My subconscious was trying to push it out with all its might, so I had to keep asking.

"But will she come out of it?" I choked out.

The question was as pointless as watching the movie "Titanic" for the umpteenth time, hoping that this time it wouldn't sink.

But people who want to remain in denial have it in common, not to accept reality.

"Who!" Angered Connor.

"What do you mean who? Not that son of a bitch, for sure! Denise, damn it!!" I shouted as my nerves finally let go.

The consequence of being nervous was an immediate migraine attack, I leaned against the sofa and closed my eyes to withstand the pain. "Danny please, just no nerves, calm down already." Whispered in my ear Rachel who was sitting next to me.

With that the anger started to slowly pass, she always had a calming effect on me.

"Danny..." Connor took up the subject once the atmosphere was conducive to it. "... Denise, she's dead, that fucker shot her in the head before he took his own life, she didn't have the slightest chance of coming out of it..." He paused for a moment. "... I'm extremely sorry to inform you of this Danny, I swear, I thought you knew." He finished staring at me with tears in his eyes.

Rachel reached out and put her hand behind my back, pulling me close so that I was hugging her.

My head landed on Rachel's shoulder.

Despite this gesture of sympathy, I could not now calmly let go of the thoughts that once again began to fill my head, bursting it painfully from the inside.

I wanted so badly for this not to be true.

Denise is dead, but what do you mean she's dead? After all, I had seen her... she was next to me, walking right by the stretcher, could it be just a delusion? No, no, that's not possible! My senses went crazy with disbelief. I felt faint again, not having had the slightest opportunity to breathe that evening, every now and then visited by new reports.

I could feel my thoughts accumulating into one great abyss, which was now humming in my head and fuelling the pain of bitterness.

As I pulled myself out of Rachel's embrace, I saw them both staring at me anxiously.

I didn't know how to act.

I had to explain all this to them, but how?

I wanted to say something, but I couldn't get a sentence out.

So, I took a breath and counted to ten in my mind.

Then I tried again.

"But she..." I started slowly and uncertainly. "She was walking, next to my stretcher..." I tried to go on, but words came with difficulty.

"Excuse me?" Rachel straightened up in her seat and opened her eyes wider.

They stared at me intensely together with Connor, waiting patiently to see that I was trying to tell them something important.

"Denise..." I replied. "... I saw her walking beside my stretcher when I was carried to the ambulance." I went on.

"Danny..." Connor began. "... I don't know what you saw, but I assure you, it couldn't have been her..." He added "... Maybe because you were in posttraumatic shock something happened to you? I'm sorry to say, but she and the man were dead, before I could run up the stairs."

"I swear Connor, I saw her, just like I'm seeing you and Rachel now, she was holding my hand." I replied.

Then I remembered that I didn't feel her handshake at the time, I only saw her hand reach for mine.

"Alright now, I think that's enough for one evening, Danny, take your pills and go to bed..." I was suddenly interrupted by Rachel. "...Connor, it's time for you to go home, tomorrow is another day, we'll come back to this next time, today we all deserve a decent rest." She decided.

"That's fine..." Connor replied. "... You're right Rachel, I'm off, keep it up and I'll see you tomorrow." He said goodbye to us.

Then he got up from the couch and headed for the door, Rachel went to walk him out.

I was too tired to get up, so I remained in my seat.

As Connor put on his shoes in the hallway and they both stood outside the front door, the mu led sounds of conversation came to me.

But they were talking too quietly, for me to understand anything of it.

I only managed to catch the moment when Rachel spoke to him saying:

"He's still in shock, give him some time."

As I sat, I leaned back on the sofa to get a better view of that side of the flat.

The moment I made eye contact with Connor.

"Drive carefully." I said.

This was my way of letting him know that I didn't like the fact that he was talking about me to my wife, especially, behind my back.

"Don't worry about that." He replied, then grabbed the door handle and left the flat.

Rachel returned to the living room with a slow step and approached me. "Come on..." She said. " ...Get up, I'll help you get ready for bed." She added and grabbed me under the arm.

"My head is damaged, not my legs, after all I can walk alone." My mind rebelled again, but I obediently let myself be led.

If I wanted to sleep that night, I had to try not to think about what Connor had said to me that bleak evening.

But the sight of little Denise, walking by my side on the way to the ambulance, kept me awake the whole time.

"I could see her, she was there, I could see her as clearly as you can see the sun..." My mind was arguing with the facts. "...Or was it another child? Maybe I had mistaken her for someone else? No, that was out of the question."

Another explanation slipped through my fingers.

The police and paramedics would never allow a child, just like that, to walk under the tapes securing the street. Let alone, walk freely around a crime scene.

I had to admit to myself, at the time I didn't have the slightest idea, what had happened there.

"After all, there must be a rational explanation, or maybe the shock was indeed to blame." I began to lean towards Connor's version.

There was no choice but to accept such an answer as true, however much of a stretch it might be.

It was always a better explanation, than having someone mention ghosts. At the time, I would probably have laughed, but now, I would take it as seriously as possible.

Anyway, I needed to explain it to myself somehow.

Because otherwise, it wouldn't have stopped bothering me and I could have said goodbye to the hope of falling asleep that night.

Let it be shock, guilt, some kind of delusion, whatever. - I thought. I was ready to agree to anything, like a KGB interrogation, just to make it stop bothering me.

The truth, however, was quite different.

No explanation I would have considered at the time, was even close to explaining what was really happening.

But later that night, I was to find that potentially the most exuberant theory would turn out to be the answer, and the consequences would exceed my wildest imaginings.

I took painkillers and, following Rachel's advice, went to bed, but I couldn't sleep for a long time.

My head wound was bothering me and, on top of that, my thoughts were tormenting me.

I lay patiently and waited for sleep to come over me or for the pills to take effect, which should also daze me.

I couldn't wait to finally feel the blissful feeling of oblivion and drift off , into the world of dreams.

Rachel, unlike me, fell asleep quickly.

When she turned off the light in the room and lay down next to me, after only a few minutes I heard her asleep breathing deeply.

Eventually, I too managed to fall asleep.

Then, without knowing when, my subconscious took me back to the earlier events of that day.

Before I knew it, I found myself again in the flat in Tottenham Court Road with Connor.

I saw him standing next to Clare Randal as I walked past them.

Exactly as it had happened in real life.

But this time they were both motionless, frozen in time with no life, like mannequins displaying new clothes in a shop window for potential customers.

I couldn't even see their faces, and no matter from which angle I looked, I just couldn't see them.

It was as if, their heads were completely covered with hair, with no room for a face, or they were able to turn them, so evenly to my movements that in the end, all I could see was their backs.

My subconscious was telling me that it was in fact, Connor and Clare, they were dressed in the same way and on top of that I could feel a familiar aura about them, I had no doubt.

"Goooo up." A quiet voice told me, that I needed to go up the stairs, as I had done the first time.

My intuition was silent on this point, because it was a flashback in which I simply had to recreate everything, step by step, exactly as it had happened before.

It was a memory and there was nothing I could change.

I didn't want to go there, because I knew what would happen to me in a moment.

Nevertheless, my legs carried me on their own, step by step, I could not put up even the slightest resistance.

When I reached the top of the stairs, breathing heavily in my sleep, I pushed open the door and entered the now familiar bedroom.

126

All the time I was aware of what was about to be revealed to my eyes. Without knowing why, I didn't feel any fear or even anxiety until now, as is usually the case in sleepy nightmares.

At least not yet, at this moment.

Once I was inside the bedroom, past the threshold of the door, I took two steps and looked to the left, where a large double bed was set up.

I expected to see Denise there with the man who had brutally taken her life, right on that spot.

However, he wasn't there, Denise herself was standing alone.

She looked exactly as I remembered her, but the difference was that in my dream, her back was turned to me.

I stared at her for a moment, unable to make a move.

I wanted to approach her, but I stood still, immobile.

"Please help."

I heard a girl's voice and realised it was Denise's.

It came directly to my ear, but not from where she was standing.

The voice seemed to come from someone much closer to me.

A quiet whisper from behind me, it was so close and so clear, that I got the impression that she was standing right behind me, at the level of my head and speaking directly into my ear.

I twitched slightly in surprise at this.

Then, at once, a terribly piercing shriek rang out from the ground floor:

"HELP HER!!!!"

I momentarily looked down the stairs as my heart went up to my throat.

There I saw something I originally recognised as Connor and Clare, staring at me quizzically.

Their mouths weren't open, they were literally stretched and bent in such an inhuman way, that my heart thumped in horror.

It was from within them that the terrible screams came out.

I would probably describe the appearance of their faces as cadaverous skulls, if it were not for the way they were deformed.

However, the lack of skin, hair and eyes matched the description.

When I looked at them, the noise had stopped, they were both standing still, slowly and inertly tilting their heads into a horizontal line, looking at me.

I let them out of my sight for two seconds to glance at Denise, but she was gone.

When I turned my gaze back, to the figures on the ground floor, I discovered that they were already standing next to me and, panting deeply, bringing their cadaverous faces closer and closer to mine.

I woke up instantly, through an excess of adrenaline.

Still breathing deeply, I propped myself up on my elbows and reflexively looked towards the foot of the bed.

It was then that I saw Denise Randal standing there.

She was faintly visible through the prevailing darkness in the room, but I was able to recognise her posture, clothes and figure.

Also subconsciously, my intuition said it was her, even if I could not see her face obscured by the darkness.

Over the course of a few seconds, she gradually faded away more and more until she finally vanished into thin air against the backdrop of the bedroom, the trace of her disappeared.

Afterwards, I had to pat myself firmly on the cheek with my hand.

I wanted to make sure somehow that this was not, still, just a dream. For a brief moment I still had a small hope that I was asleep and what I had seen a few seconds ago, wasn't really happening.

But when I heard Rachel's breathing next to me, then glanced at her and saw her continuing to sleep hard unmoving, I realised two things, one, I was already awake and my cheek hurt, and two, I wouldn't sleep a wink until morning.

The next day, I decided not to tell Rachel anything.

I thought there was no point in bothering her with such nonsense, as night dreams.

But I had to admit, the sight of corpse faces, or rather something that was where Connor's face should have been, and Clare Randal's face, twisted in such a grotesque way, sank deep into my memory.

I got goosebumps every time I involuntarily recalled them and knew, without a doubt, that the sight would stay with me for a very long time. However, I was convinced that this was just an isolated incident of this kind, that would not happen again.

In fact, even then, I firmly believed it.

It was nearing ten o'clock when we finished eating breakfast together. There was a pleasant atmosphere in the kitchen accompanied by music from the radio.

A sleepless night and a sore head did not make me eager to talk that morning.

Rachel went about her typical daily chores and was understanding enough not to pressure me into unnecessary chat, which I clearly didn't feel like engaging at the time.

When we had finished our meal, she came over to me and took my bowl of cornflakes.

She then scooped up two coffee cups, her plate from which she had eaten her toast, and went to put everything in the dishwasher.

"I'm wondering, if you'll be able to do anything today?" She asked, turning the dishwasher on at the same time.

As I heard the water inside start to run, my attention seemed to focus all its energies on just that.

I registered Rachel's question, but I had the impression that her words were coming from behind the wall of waterfall, being drowned out and barely reaching me.

Before I could answer, I listened to the hypnotic sound of the rushing water which seemed to be several times louder than usual.

…SSSSSSHHHHHH...!!!!!

"DANNY!" Now her voice was strong and blunt, thanks to which, it broke through the overwhelming sound of the water and hit me straight on. "Actually..." I choked out, snapping out of my trance. "...I haven't thought about it yet, I think I'll stay at home, call Connor later, ask if he's coming." I added more clearly already.

"That's good, you need to rest..." she replied "...If you're hungry there's food in the fridge, I should be back by four o'clock, then I'll cook something fresh for dinner." She added, smiling kindly at me.

"Sure."

"Just please, do one thing for me." She said unexpectedly.

"What's that?" I asked surprised.

"I know you can't help yourself, but when Connor arrives, try not to pursue the matter too much, agree?" she said looking at me with pleading eyes. "Okay, I can try…" I nodded. "…I'm going to go lie down in the living room for a while," I feel exhausted.

"Go on, I must go too, it's getting late."

130

I left the kitchen and went into the living room, got comfortable on the sofa and turned on the TV.

A little while later, Rachel came over to give me a kiss goodbye.

It was just like every other time we parted ways.

Just as she was about to go to put on her shoes, I decided to raise one more point.

"We will have to go there." I said.

Rachel stopped in her tracks, then she turned towards me, and I could see her waiting for me to develop the thought.

"Where dear?" she asked.

"To Denise's funeral..." I replied. "... It is imperative that we are there, I want to say goodbye to her." I added.

"Sure, we can go if you care so much."

"I care Rachel, I care a lot." I replied.

She then nodded as a sign that she agreed with me, put on her shoes and left the flat.

I watched for a while longer as she closed the door behind her. When I was left alone, I turned my gaze to the television, which was showing the news, but I was unable to concentrate on it.

Every word, it sounded like one big nonsense, and I could not see any coherence in what the reporters were saying.

I felt awful.

I was sleep deprived, tired, my head hurt, and my nerves were ragged. At that point, I decided it would be a good idea to drink some alcohol, 1 to numb and soothe me.

"After all, I'm supposed to spend the whole day at home anyway, so there was nothing stopping me from finally relaxing a little." My mind was justifying the resolve.

The clock was now showing ten-thirty.

I had never had an alcoholic drink at such an early hour, so I took a moment to consider whether to wait until at least midday.

However, I quickly decided that time was not playing in my favour. I needed relief from the pain, I needed it immediately, there was no point in delaying.

After all, I was going to be sitting at home all day anyway, it wouldn't hurt to drink something stronger. My mind repeated the decision I had accepted earlier.

I got up from the sofa and with an uncertain step walked over to the bar where Rachel and I kept various drinks, for special occasions. Rachel liked to have one glass of refined red wine in the evening, with dinner for, as she used to say, "Good health."

I, on the other hand, when it came to uplifting drinks. simply put, I preferred beer.

When I opened the bar, I found a bottle of Rachel's wine in it, almost half empty already.

Apart from it, there were other coloured spirits that I would never have touched in my life, because I never liked to experiment.

To my surprise, I noticed that behind all these bottles was a large Smirnoff . Since I rarely looked there until now, I didn't even know that there was one in the back.

I then momentarily realised that, combined with the cold orange juice from the fridge, it would make the perfect concoction for me.

I also remembered that it had been brought by Connor, last New Year's Eve. At the time, none of the assembled guests felt like getting drunk to excess, so there was half of bottle left.

Without thinking any longer, I grabbed the bottle and poured myself a third of the vodka into a 500-millilitre glass that was already standing in the bar. After which, I made my way to the kitchen to top it off completely with orange juice.

I took a solid sip, then returned to my seat in front of the TV, where, lazily flipping through programmes, I continued to sip my drink.

The alcohol quickly made me feel pleasantly relaxed.

"Oh yes, just what I needed." It confirmed the right decision with my mind. Before I had time to realise it, an hour had passed, and I was already approaching the bar for the third time for a refill.

It was coming up to twelve in the afternoon.

I took out of my dressing gown, my small spare phone and placed it in front of me on the table where it lay quietly.

It was a mini smartphone I had received for my fiftieth birthday from Rachel.

At one time this phone was hailed as the smallest mobile phone in the world, as it measured just under nine centimetres in length and could be hidden literally anywhere.

Rachel bought it for me as a playful gift, that she thought I would feel safe with anytime, anywhere.

The spare phone quickly became an integral part of my wardrobe, and I never parted with it, I always had it somewhere with me.

Clipped or tucked into the pocket of whatever trousers I was wearing that day, behind my belt, in my jacket, jeans, next to my uniform, wherever. I found a place to hide it everywhere, it became as routine for me as putting on socks, for example.

By design, this phone was intended to keep me safe if I found myself in an extremely dangerous situation.

In truth, it did little to help me in my confrontation with the stoned psychopath, who nearly sent me o into the other world, but after all, that was not its purpose.

Both Rachel and Connor were at times amused at the fact that I never parted with my little friend, whom I diminutively called "mini".

However, I got used to it in time and thought it was a good idea, I cared little for their banter about it.

The day I came into possession of it, I decided that I would only give the number for that phone to Rachel and Connor, no one else, it remained that way.

They were the only ones who had a number on it and their numbers, were the only ones, I had saved in my contacts list.

I believed it would be enough if only the two people closest to me knew it. I also used a second phone, which was already known to a more extended circle of people.

Through my morning routine, I put the "mini" in my dressing gown pocket and completely forgot about it.

At some point, however, I felt it start to pinch my stomach a little as I lay down more comfortably on the sofa and it got underneath me.

So, I decided, for a while, to get rid of it for my own comfort.

This procedure made me realise that, after all, my other phone was left on the bedroom floor.

It would probably be appropriate to go for it, perhaps someone had called me. My intuition suggested, while at the same time trying to motivate me, to finally get up from the sofa.

The alcohol injected into my bloodstream was already working at full force, so I was extremely comfortable and didn't even feel like moving.

But I already knew, from the moment I registered the absence of the second phone, decision been made and sooner or later, I would have to go for it.

So, I decided I'd rather get it over with as soon as I could.

That way I could get back to lazing around and enjoying another drink. I slid off the sofa and then, slowly and reluctantly, set off for the bedroom to get my everyday phone.

As I climbed the stairs, I heard the "mini" begin to ring and vibrate, left on the table.

It was the third time in his career, that someone had made a call on that number.

As it had only been Rachel and Connor before, so I was quicker to save their contacts, in my memory.

I immediately stopped and turned my head in his direction surprised. But surprise turned to fear after a moment later, it was a delayed reaction due to the alcohol stun.

The thought struck me that something very bad must have happened. Because both Connor and Rachel, knew to only call this number as a last resort or in cases, of emergency.

In the over a year that I've had it, it hasn't rung once, until now.

Therefore, with this thought in mind, the fact that it was ringing could not bode well.

I ran down the stairs at breakneck speed and got to it as quickly as I could. Then, without looking at the display, I pressed the green button and put it to my ear.

"Hello!!!" I shouted into the receiver.

But all I heard in reply was a dragging network signal:

"TUUUUUUU..." Indicating that there was no one on the other end anymore.

So, I moved it away from my ear and looked at the small display, then started snooping in the "menu", I wanted to check the calls. There was nothing in there, no calls received or missed, incoming, outgoing, absolutely nothing.

135

There were two numbers in the contacts, Rachel and Connor, but neither of them had called just now.

I stood for a moment with the "mini" in my hand, stunned.

But alcoholic intoxication had once again taken control of me and dimmed my intuition.

I therefore trivialised the situation, thinking that there was no cause for alarm.

As I put the "mini" back on the table, another phone ringing came from upstairs.

This time, it was the one I had left in the bedroom.

"What the hell!"

I grabbed the glass with my still undrinkable drink, then set o again with a quick step, up the stairs.

I made it to my bedroom just in time as my phone was still ringing, slowly shifting under the vibration on the bedside table.

I took it in my hand and looked at the display, it was Connor calling, I answered.

"Hello." I said slightly drowsily.

"Well, hello there partner...!" Connor replied cheerfully, clearly, he was in a good mood. "...How are we feeling today? How's your head?"

"It's fine..." I lied. "...Listen, did you call me a minute ago?"

"I'm calling you now." He laughed.

"Well, yes, but a minute ago on my emergency phone, it was you?" I asked. "The little one you carry around in your underpants all the time?" He replied jokingly.

"Yes, that one." I was getting a little irritated.

"No, I didn't call that number, why do you ask?" He asked.

"Because it rang…" I replied. "... Rachel left an hour ago, but she never contacts me on that number."

"Did you check in the calls list? Maybe you gave the number to someone else and don't remember?" Connor suggested solutions.

"I remember that, only you and Rachel have it."

"It doesn't matter, sometimes they call from the net, or someone accidentally dialled the number, don't worry about it..." He replied. "...What are you doing today? Are you at home?" He added changing the subject.

"Yes, I am, I'll be here all day."

"Okay, I'll drop by in half an hour..." He replied. "...Buy you something on the way in town? Maybe you fancy something to eat?"

"No thanks, come if you want." I said.

"Sure, I'll see you in thirty minutes." He replied in conclusion and hung up.

"See you then." I replied already to myself.

I tucked my phone into the pocket of my dressing gown and finished my drink in one gulp.

What a fucking day.

Just as I was about to take myself out of the bedroom, to make my way down to the living room and on to the bar for another refill, I again heard a tune barely reaching me from the ground floor.

It was the sound of the "mini" ringing again.

8

New residents.

'In illness or in any kind of suffering, it is necessary to entrust God's love, like a child who entrusts everything he holds most dear to those who love him, especially his parents.
We need, then, this childlike capacity to entrust ourselves to Him who is Love.'

10 years earlier,

05 May 2008, North Hill township, home of Susan and John McKane.

John left the house before ten o'clock in a hurry.

True, he didn't have a doctor's appointment until 3 pm and still had plenty of free time, but he couldn't sit still at home.

Even after waking up, he felt that he was too irritated to wait idly, so he decided, before his appointment, to go to the building site where his company was currently working.

He wanted, as a way of killing time, to meet with his workers and, in the process, look at whether any major progress had been made since the previous day.

Susan's first client appointment that day wasn't until two o'clock and she was relaxing at home while John headed into town.

She tried to reassure her husband first thing in the morning as he paced back and forth nervously around the house.

She tried to show him empathy and that she shared his irritation until she was left home alone.

In reality, she was also taking the situation hard.

Matters were further complicated by her pregnancy and Susan preferred to focus more on her own wellbeing rather than worry about John's personal problems.

One o'clock had just passed, when Susan decided that it was high time to set o for work.

She dressed slowly and carefully; took all the things she needed and left the house.

When she got into her sporty BMW, her watch showed half past one. She had driven the route from her home to the surgery hundreds, if not thousands, of times, so she knew full well that she would easily reach the NHS building, at around one forty-five.

Fifteen minutes ahead of schedule.

Exactly as much as she needed for herself before her first appointment, to buy a take-away coffee in the popular "Café Orbi" nearby and, without rushing, get ready for her appointment. John was also in the NHS building at the time.

So, Susan assumed that even if she happened to meet him, a few minutes would be enough to listen to him.

She also considered the circumstance that John would come to see her after his appointment was over, then she could simply tell him that she had no time now.

Due to the tightened schedule of the day, she had left virtually no slots free so that she wouldn't have to stuff something else into it. *Perfectly set up.* She thought, contentedly.

Susan had no desire to see John in the coming hours.

She was sure that he would then immediately want to share with her what the doctor had told him earlier, she did not want to deal with it.

At the same time, she felt that there was no rush and whatever it was could wait until the evening, such a last piece of information to sum up the day.

On the way to the city centre, she again turned her attention to the beautiful villa standing near the main highway.

It already belonged to a newly arrived couple from Ethiopia, and it looked like they had managed to settle in.

As Susan drove past the property, she slowed the vehicle down a little to get a better look at the grounds, then she was able to see inside the tasteful, purple curtains on the windows, the pots of fresh flowers on the windowsills shimmering in different colours added to the charm of the whole view.

And in the driveway, there was a luxurious "Mercedes" car.

Maybe they have a second one in the garage. She thought.

Suddenly, the phone rang from her handbag, which was lying on the passenger seat.

She pulled it out carefully, without taking her eyes off the road. She quickly glanced at the display and, although the number was not stored in her contacts, she quickly recognised it in her memory.

She picked up after a few beeps and switched the call to speakerphone. "What do you want?"

"Oooo hehehe... Why so unpleasant...?" Laughed the man on the other end of the handset. "...I'm calling to ask how the pregnancy is going?"

"It's none of your business."

"Well, have you met your new neighbours?" The man asked. Susan momentarily guessed that he was talking about the Ethiopian couple, whose house she had just observed.

"No, why do you ask?"

"We were the ones who sold them the house, quite an investment for people from such a poor country, I can't hide the fact that although I had them on the hook for a long time, it took me a good few months of negotiation until I finally succeeded..." He said. "...One million two hundred thousand pounds, pure profit." He added.

Susan felt her heartbeat faster, the news of such a large sum of money was very impressive and worked on her imagination.

"If I had that now, that much money in my account." She thought subconsciously.

"Congratulations." She replied.

Without letting it be known that she was overwhelmed by jealousy, fortunately on the phone it was not difficult.

"In our agency, only a small percentage of such an amount is left..." The man continued. "...However, your town is very popular nowadays, more and more people are asking about it, ready to invest good money, unfortunately, this was the only house we had on offer there, which is a pity, you could make a lot of money." He added.

"Why the hell are you telling me all this?" Angered Susan.

"Relax, I'm just trying to keep the conversation going." The man lied. "...I just wanted to warn you Susan, supposedly, these people are dangerous."

141

"Dangerous...?!" She was surprised. "...What do you mean?"

"Well, you know, Africa is a huge continent, divided into fifty-two countries with a population of over a trillion people, some of whom are not as civilised as we are here."

"Don't bother me now with some stupidity...!" She replied angrily. "...And for the record, don't ever call me again, we have nothing to talk about, goodbye!" She wanted to end the conversation.

"Yes, we do, and lots of it, I'll be in touch." The man replied and then hung up without saying goodbye.

Susan had no intention of discussing anything with this individual. From the very first day she met him, he got on her nerves and irritated her terribly.

However, she knew that she would not be able to float him away so easily and would probably hear from him, more than once.

The worst part of it all, though, was that Susan realised that the man was right, when he said they had something to talk about.

Especially at this point, she felt herself starting to convince herself to give him a chance after all.

So that he could say what she did not want to hear, the last time she saw him personally.

Undoubtedly, the scales of bitterness had been tipped by the said amount, that had been paid for the beautiful villa in North Hill that Susan had heard about.

Like any human being, she immediately began to see the state of her account with so many zeros and from the spot, she could list thousands of things she would like to own at that very moment.

"What a rake, who does he even think he is...!" She said to herself, continuing to drive. "...I don't need to be in contact with him at all,

I know as much as I need to know, I can check the rest occasionally, without him being involved." She added, trying to convince herself that this was for the best.

Despite her efforts to explain to herself how she should proceed, in her heart, she already knew very well what decision she had made.

Soon, she would have to call the annoying man back, albeit reluctantly, and have a longer conversation with him.

Moments later she arrived in front of the NHS building.

She parked her car in the specially designated staff car park.

The time was 01:43pm.

Before she got out of the vehicle, she looked carefully around the area, searching with her eyes for John's car.

It was standing parked on the opposite side of the street, a few dozen metres away.

So, he's still inside, far too long for a routine visit. She concluded intrigued.

Without thinking any longer, she grabbed her handbag and got out of the car, locking it behind her with the button next to the keys.

BIP! BIP!

As she stood on the pavement, she glanced at the signboard of the café "Café Orbi" that protruded from around the corner.

However, she decided that she would skip the next coffee of the day and walked calmly towards the main entrance of the building. At the reception desk, her colleague Anna was once again on duty. Susan approached her immediately, without even looking around the waiting room.

"Hi Anna." She chatted.

"Oh, hello Susan, how are you?" The receptionist took her eyes off the computer screen and greeted her with a smile.

"Everything's fine, have you seen John, by any chance?" Susan asked. Yes, he's in Dr Clark Gable's office, he arrived after one o'clock, and he was a bit late, they're not finished yet." Anna recounted. "...It's taking quite a long time." She added, virtually unnecessarily.

"Oh yes, I understand, thank you Anna." Susan replied.

"Dr McKane." She heard someone calling her name behind her back. As she turned her gaze towards the familiar voice reaching her from the depths of the waiting room, she saw Christopher Wilson, the patient with whom she had an appointment at two o'clock.

"Hello Christopher…" She replied warmly. "... You are welcome to see me in ten minutes, you obviously know the way." She added kindly.

"Yes of course, thank you." Christopher replied.

Susan focused her gaze for a moment on the people, who sat a few seats away from her patient.

They were a black couple she had never seen before.

They were sitting and filling in a form of some sort, presumably the clinic registrations.

Susan momentarily identified them as new residents in North Hill. *Apparently, they had come straight to register at the clinic, a smart move, I'd do that too if I were them.* She said to herself.

The newly arrived settlers were indeed very different in appearance from the rest of the townspeople.

Even the black people, who also made up a sizable population in the city.

Because the skin colour of these people was a shade of Jet black.

Susan looked at them for a few more seconds, then looked away and moved slowly ahead along the corridor. Fortunately for her, the couple did not notice.

As they were busy now writing out their personal details on a piece of paper, supported by a plastic plate, she managed to avoid an awkward situation.

Susan headed towards her office.

Walking down the corridor, as she passed one of the offices on the way, she stopped for a moment.

She looked at the door with a badge, bearing the name of the doctor who was seeing his patients there that day:

"Dr Clark Gable,"

Suddenly she heard the quiet sounds of conversation coming from inside.

As she strained her hearing, she managed to recognise John's voice. However, they were talking too quietly for her to catch anything specific from the conversation.

So, she ignored it.

She immediately reached the end of the corridor where her office was. *I wonder what they are talking about...?* She said to herself thoughtfully, then added. *...Well, whatever it is I'm sure John will tell me everything, later at home.*

She opened the study door with her key and went inside.

She only had time to hang up her coat and put her handbag on the desk, next to the computer screen.

Her movements were to some extent very restricted, thanks to the heavily developed o spring she was carrying under her heart.

Moments later, two o'clock struck and a knock sounded on her door. "Come in, Christopher!" She called out.

A therapy session with a patient took only forty-five minutes of the scheduled hour.

Mr Christopher Wilson leaving the office, as always, thanked Susan warmly for his visit.

He also assured her that he would greatly miss seeing her in her absence once she became a mum.

"That's very kind indeed, Christopher…" She replied with a smile. "…But don't worry, I will be here for two more months and then we can talk on the phone."

"Thank you again." Christopher added finally and left the office, closing the door behind him.

Susan sat motionless in her chair for a short while longer, then booted up her computer.

She logged on to her work email address to check if she had received any new messages, while talking to a client.

There was one succinct letter sent from reception, a few minutes earlier. The message said only that her next appointment with a woman called Diana Sallow, had just been cancelled by her.

Susan glanced at her watch; it read two forty-seven.

Given that she had no more appointments scheduled, she thought she would go to the "Café Orbi" for a meal.

She was now eating for two and was notoriously hungry.

She took her things from the desk and before closing the door behind her, she turned around still on the threshold to scan the room with her eyes, to make sure she hadn't forgotten anything.

Once she was sure she could leave in peace, she locked the door. She then headed back down the corridor towards the waiting room, connected to the reception area.

Anna continued to sit in her seat behind the desk, busy with her duties, she did not notice her.

While the waiting room was almost, completely empty.

Once there, she automatically looked around her.

Subconsciously, she was looking for the unfamiliar pair of newcomers she had seen earlier.

Naturally, these people had long since left the clinic and instead she saw John, sitting next to the front door.

Apparently, he was waiting for her.

Is he still here? She wondered in her mind.

"Were you waiting for me?" She asked walking up to her husband.

"Yes, we need to talk." John replied, in an uncertain voice

When she looked at his face, she saw that he seemed very pale, you could say he was white as a sheet.

Susan furrowed her brow, wondering why John had chosen to wait there for her, instead of going home.

At the time, she wasn't sure if his appearance meant he was unwell or perhaps it was due to something else entirely.

It might as well have been both.

Then, it occurred to her that John must have received some very worrying news from the doctor.

There was no other explanation.

"Okay, but not here, though..." She said grabbing his arm. "...We'll go and get something to eat and a cup of coffee."

John looked at her with sad eyes, but did not answer.

He only nodded his head obediently as a sign of agreement.

"See you later Anna." Called Susan towards the reception desk. "See you!" She replied cheerfully.

Susan and John left the building.

As they walked slowly along the pavement, Susan took him under the arm, to which John responded with a slight twitch.

He needed this, she had no idea how much, he needed it just now.

John felt terrible, devastated and powerless.

His only relief was the support of the person closest to him, Susan. Apart from her, he only had his parents, who lived in London, but she was always the most important.

Only you and me, against the world.

Susan used to think of him that way, too, until she received unexpected news that completely changed her life and her attitude to everything around her until then.

Just then, her transformation began.

They walked one block away and arrived at Susan's favourite café. As they went inside, then sat down at a two-seater table next to a window, overlooking the city centre and the beautiful historic town hall.

"What would you like me to order for you?" John suggested.

"I'll have an English breakfast with an extra poached egg, a double avocado and a medium latte."

John confirmed with a nod that he understood the order.

He turned his back to her and moved to the till, placing his order.

Susan watched him as he moved away, feeling her curiosity begin to grow as to what was on his mind now.

When he returned, he sat in his seat in silence, and Susan didn't take her eyes off him.

He rested his gaze on his knees for a moment.

Then he took a deep breath, raised his head and looked Susan in the eye. At the same time, he grabbed her hand, affectionately covering it with his own.

Then, his spouse saw the terror in his eyes and twitched at the sight.

"John..." she said quietly. "...What happened?"

"Ah, a lot darling, I don't know how to tell you." John started to say. But his voice was breaking, so he quickly interrupted and bowed his head again.

"Just tell me." Susan insisted.

John raised his gaze again and it straight into his wife's eyes.

Clasping his hands a little tighter at the same time, around her arm.

"I'm, I'm sick, Susan..." he choked out slowly. "... very sick." He added.

Susan felt herself begin to grow impatient.

She wanted him to tell her everything immediately in detail, exactly as he had heard it from the doctor.

But she could see his face now. She knew he was in a terrible state, so she could not rush him.

She understood it wasn't that easy for him, so she didn't push and let him get to the bottom of his statement himself.

"I... I have lung cancer." He finally announced with an effort.

A state of devastation was taking over John.

His voice was clearly breaking, thanks to the sudden influx of tears to his eyes as he uttered these words.

His gaze went to his lap again, a failed attempt to hide his weeping face.

Susan was stunned, completely unsure of what to say.

She only stared at the top of John's hanging head because she couldn't see his face.

Then the waitress approached them with their order.

She set down two cups of coffee and a plate of breakfast for Susan, but she didn't even pay attention to it.

After a short while, John raised his head and let go of Susan's hand. He clumsily rubbed his hand over his face, wiping away the tears that were now streaming down his cheeks.

"It appears that I became ill over fifteen years ago..." he said in a shaky voice. "...But this type of cancer, it develops without symptoms, that is why, it was not detected earlier." He added.

Susan had already guessed what John was about to tell her.

She had dealt with people with lung cancer in the past and knew, that the chances of beating the disease were virtually nil.

God, is he really going to say what I think he will? She asked herself in her mind.

"I'm dying, Susan." He added despairingly.

9

Call me Nattaly.

'Conscience is a matter of fundamental importance for every human being. It is his inner guide and is also the judge of his actions'.

Four years earlier.

25 March 2004, Canary Wharf, London, the office of the "BnBL" agency.

George arrived at the office at eight-fifty in the morning, as always ten minutes before the scheduled opening.

He was only warned by his new secretary Lucy Clarke, who was already in place and waiting for him outside the building.

"Good morning, Lucy." George greeted her.

"Good morning boss." She replied.

The kind-hearted George Bradley was not fond of being addressed in such a formal way.

He preferred it when employees simply addressed him by his first name. Because then he felt he was one of them, part of the team they formed together.

Today, however, he did not have the heart to correct the newcomer. The girl had only just started working for them, so she might not yet know what the customs of the agency were.

George had more important matters to attend to as priorities than playing with polite phrases.

His most important item of the day suffered no delay, and he had to get straight to the point, using the secretary's help to do so.

"Miss Lucy..." he addressed her politely as soon as they entered the building. "...Your first task this morning, will be to get a list for me of the numbers who called the agency on Friday, from two thirty to three thirty." He added in a serious, official tone.

At the same time, he was aware that this assignment would not be at all easy or quick to carry out.

It was the perfect moment to test the young secretary's abilities in practice. Because in this situation, she will be forced to demonstrate great patience, persistence and meticulousness.

Like a private detective, she must track down, obtain and follow up the necessary information and finally report back.

When Lucy Clarke heard what George was asking her to do, she instantly realised what an uninteresting task she had.

You could see on her face as she counted in her mind, how long it would all take her.

The office did not have an automated number register for her to use.

There were no incoming or outgoing calls from the landline.

Which meant, that the secretary would have to contact the operator of the telecommunications network that handled their calls on the ground and provided internet access.

In practice, this almost always meant sitting with the phone receiver to her ear for an undefined period, often exceeding one hour.

On top of this, she was not relieved of the rest of her standard work duties while carrying out the order.

She was now completely alone with everything.

At least until the other employees, who should arrive at ten o'clock, showed up at work. Lucy swallowed her saliva.

She really had no idea how long it would take her to get the numbers or if she would even succeed.

However, with no other option, she broke through within herself, clenched her fists and said with a stony face: "Yes sir, I'll get on with it immediately."

"Excellent..." He replied pleased. "...Please also bear in mind, I am mainly concerned with numbers with incoming calls, once you have this list, I would very much ask that you separate these numbers for me with a red marker.

"Fine, as you wish." The secretary replied.

She sat down at her desk, booted up her computer and got straight to work. "Thank you, Miss Lucy, please let me know when you are ready. I will be in my office." George said in conclusion.

"By all means."

"Attagirl..." Praised her in thought George. "...She could use a little test, I'm curious to see how she'll handle it." He added, opening the door to his office.

He entered the room and hung his jacket on a small hook by the door then, with a slow step he crossed the room and sat down at his desk.

He straightened up in his chair and hung his gaze on what was happening outside the window.

He was a little calmer that morning, but he was still plagued by an unpleasant feeling of uncertainty.

Therefore, he decided, exceptionally, that he did not feel like starting the working day as he was used to.

He decided to take time o and not take any more thoughts into his head, at least until, the mystery with the mysterious girl who had called him on Friday, was cleared up.

He pulled out his phone and dialled the number for Matthiew.

However, after waiting a while for an answer with the phone to his ear, George realised that he couldn't count on his partner, who was apparently indisposed again.

Just as he was about to hang up bitterly, he heard a voice on the receiver.

"Hello?" A clearly sleepy Matthiew spoke up.

"Just don't tell me you were drinking again last night." George was annoyed.

"Who said I was drinking? A couple of beers is not drinking."

"Don't annoy me, Matthiew…!" George was furious. "…You know I need you here today! What time will you be here?"

"And what the time is now...?" Asked a confused Matthiew. "... It's only fifteen past nine, what are you fretting about?"

"You know what? Don't come here at all! Stay at home, sleep, or whatever it is you do, I don't want to see you today! I don't need your help!" George had to let his emotions out.

"Alright, alright, calm down, why the nerves?"

Matthiew was holding his tongue, making George realise that he hadn't yet managed to sober up since last night.

George disconnected the call without saying goodbye, he was fuming. "Bloody alcoholic, to hell with him...!" He cursed under his breath. "...I don't need him, I'll sort this one out myself, I needlessly initiated him into the details in the first place." George was only now beginning to realise that he had made a mistake, but it was too late to undo it somehow. Matthiew already knew about the woman, who claimed to know George's daughter.

George pondered the situation at the same time, trying to calm his nerves.

In truth, he didn't know anything concrete yet, but in his heart, he sensed that he should keep Matthiew out of it.

He knew him all too well and realised what the man could be capable of. On the other hand, however, this woman might want to harm the agency they ran together, after all.

In that respect, though, he should tell Matthiew if he found out anything about her.

"Damn, there is not a right answer here, is it?" George thought, analysing the facts.

Then his landline phone, set up on the desk next to his computer, rang. When he looked at the small display, he saw it was Lucy calling him from reception.

George picked up the phone and before he could say anything he heard:

"I have this call list for you sir." The receptionist spoke up immediately, in a proud voice.

"Oh, that's great...!" Delighted George. "...Please bring it to me."

"I'll be there in a minute." She announced.

She managed to get through it so quickly? That's really, amazing! I'm impressed. George thought.

But when he looked at his watch he was stunned, because it was just reaching ten o'clock in the morning.

"I had no idea that a whole hour could have passed so quickly, after all, I just sat here." He said to himself in astonishment.

He was so deep in thought that he lost track of time.

A knock at the door sounded.

"Yes Miss Lucy! Please come in!" He called out towards the door.

The secretary entered uncertainly.

Clutching nervously in her hand, a sheet of printed numbers.

When George saw her, he smiled warmly.

"Excellent Miss Lucy...!" He said excitedly. "...Truly, excellent work." He added contentedly.

The woman approached his desk with an outstretched hand in which she held a paper with the telephone numbers he had asked for.

As she got closer George could see a slight blush appear on her cheeks. "Thank you, sir, please, I've highlighted the incoming numbers in red as you requested." She said shyly.

"Outstanding, thank you very much."

Lucy nodded obediently, then turned on her heel and headed for the door.

Suddenly she heard George's voice behind her:

"There is one more thing, Miss Lucy!"

The girl stopped immediately and turned to face him.

Then, she straightened up stiffly like a soldier, ready to accept the next task.

"I beg your pardon, sir?"

"Please, address me by my first name..." He smiled kindly at her. "...I`m George."

The surprised secretary reciprocated his smile.

"Of course..." She replied. "...Is there anything else I can do for you sir..." She interrupted her sentence for a moment. "...George?" quickly corrected what she wanted to say.

Smiling even wider at George in the process.

"Yes, please keep this to yourself..." He replied, showing her the piece of paper she had brought. "...I will be obliged."

"Of course." Lucy nodded, then turned and left the office.

The girl felt proud of herself for the praise from her boss on top of that, she had gone informal with him.

The other staff knew that it was basically nothing, but she felt singled out in that moment.

George, sitting further back in his chair, slowly and in concentration reviewed with his eyes, all the numbers highlighted in red.

She even used a red marker, just as I asked her to. He thought and smiled slightly to himself.

He ran his finger over the sheet of paper, line by line

Looking carefully at the hours of calls coming into the office from Saturday. *There it is, fifteen zero two, she managed to get through to my office at about fifteen, it took her about ten minutes to get the secretary through.* George thought.

He checked the number again, it started with 020... so it was a landline.

For a moment he hesitated, whether he was sure to call it.

Or maybe it wasn't this one? No, it must be that number. He convinced himself in his mind.

Eventually, he decided, he absolutely had to check it out. He grabbed the handset and nimbly tapped the number, after a few seconds he heard the call tone.

When the phone on the other end was answered by a woman, George realised that this was not the same person he had hoped to contact at the time, she was clearly much older than the previous one.

"Hallo?" The stranger asked in a serious, mature tone.

George was a little taken aback, but nevertheless had to try to strike up a conversation.

"Good morning, madam, could I speak to Noelle Kemp, please?" He asked politely.

At this point, there seemed to be some sort of interference on the line, as the woman apparently missed his question completely.

"Hello? Who is this?" She said more loudly.

"Good morning, ma'am, my name is George Bradley, could I speak to Noelle Kemp, please?!" He said, this time slowly and clearly.

"I'm sorry, I don't know anyone by that name, there's a Nattaly Swanson who lives not far from here, but she's probably still out of town, is this about her?" Asked the confused woman, whose memory was obviously failing by now.

"No ma'am, Noelle is French for Nattaly in English."

"I think you have the wrong number, sorry." She replied and then immediately hung up, not even giving him a chance to add anything else.

George heard a protracted beep signifying that the call had just ended.

He hung up the phone and looked at it for a moment.

"God damn it…!" he cursed nervously. *...And what now, the end? Is that it? There are no other numbers from this hour, maybe I got the time wrong?*

He wondered intensely.

He looked at the call statement again.

But no other number, not even close to the hour he had spoken to the mystery woman on Saturday.

All the other calls had been made way too early or too late, when he was no longer even in the office.

He remembered that it was after three o'clock and only that one number rang at that hour.

At three forty I was already in the car; I remember because I was checking my phone... George replayed the sequence of events in his mind. *...Damn, I'm in a bit of a fix.* He added resignedly.

Suddenly then his landline rang, it came from reception.

"Hello Miss Lucy?"

"Sorry to bother you, there's a woman on the phone called Noelle, she says she has an appointment for an interview..." said the secretary. "...Shall I put her through to your office?"

George was stunned.

At that moment, he felt his heart begin to pound like a hammer, almost tearing through his chest.

It must have taken a good few seconds before he managed to shake himself out of it.

"George...?" His secretary urged him.

"Aaaa... Yes, of course, put her through." He choked out.

"I'm on it."

"What the hell!? How did she know? Coincidence...?" He thought quickly. "...Calm down George, you need to talk to her, preferably arrange a face-to-face meeting." He was hinting at a plan for the conversation.

He didn't have much time to do this as the phone had just rung.

George took a breath and answered it immediately.

But he didn't even have time to say hello when he heard a shout: "Who told you that you could call me back!!!!" The young woman on the other end was truly distraught.

10

She`s here.

'You don't live, you don't love, you don't die - on trial.'

Fourteen years later,

19 October 2018, Camberwell Green, London, Danny and Rachel Davis's flat.

I was sitting tired in the living room, and Rachel was slowly getting ready to leave.

Last night I slept badly again, had another nightmare, woke up in the middle of the night and couldn't get back to sleep again until morning. This time I dreamt that I was alone in some dark and gloomy forest. I was walking among the trees in complete darkness, looking for any sign of where I should go.

From everywhere I heard whispering, mu led voices calling for help.

They were the voices of young people, boys and girls.

That is all I managed to remember of it.

I woke up at the point in my dream where I had fallen into some pit in the ground.

Waking up, I again thought I saw Denise at the foot of our marriage bed, just as I had the previous time.

Immediately after, I went to the ground floor to the bar, pouring myself a drink to soothe my nerves.

After drinking some alcohol, I returned to bed and continued to lie still until sunrise, when the hour came to start the next day.

Since yesterday, I had almost emptied the large bottle of Smirnoff vodka. Fortunately, Rachel didn't realise that I had drunk that much, as she would no doubt have resented me for it.

She thought at the time that I'd only had a couple of beers the day before when Connor came to visit.

That was the case.

Only the difference was that those few beers were only going to make me finally fizz, because I was already quite heavily intoxicated, consumed with vodka, even before Connor showed up.

I had only had one drink last night and wanted to go on sleeping.

However, the feeling that someone was watching me kept me awake.

I constantly sensed someone's presence wherever I went.

As a police officer, I am sensitive to such stimuli.

Years of service have taught me to have eyes around my head and to be alert in different situations.

It is like a sixth sense.

I may not be able to see or hear something, but I can sense that it is there, somewhere.

For that too, I knew I wasn't wrong.

Even though it was ludicrous to say at the least and passed by common logic.

As I sat in the living room and Rachel was not yet ready to leave, I could feel myself getting more and more impatient.

I was desperately thirsty for a drink.

I surreptitiously looked towards the bar longingly, I felt like walking over there and pouring myself a decent drink.

But I couldn't do that with Rachel walking behind my back, because she wouldn't leave it unsaid, and I didn't want to listen to her complains, so I kept waiting.

"Connor said he's coming to see you later." She spoke up suddenly from the kitchen.

"Oh, well, that's good." I replied reluctantly.

"Just don't drink today, I saw how those three beers messed with your head yesterday..." She called out. "...Connor was fine, but you were clearly drunk, you don't have a head for alcohol sweetheart, so save it." *Three beers and half a bottle of vodka.* My mind summed up the actual amount of alcohol I had consumed.

"Honey, I'm not a child..." I said irritably. "...Don't forget, I'm 52 years old and a police officer." I added, and it only took me a moment to realise how childish that must have just sounded.

"Oh yes." She said and came up to me to give me a kiss goodbye.

She kissed me on the cheek and immediately wiped off the lipstick marks on it with her hand.

"My dear law enforcement officer."

She moved towards the exit, stopped in front of the door and, putting on her shoes, said:

"I'll be here before 4pm, lunch..."

"Lunch is in the fridge..." I finished the sentence for her. "...Take care and see you at 4pm" I added with a smilc, Rachel reciprocated it and left, closing the door behind her.

The moment I heard the slam of the door lock closing, I jumped up from the sofa as if burned and walked quickly to the bar.

I pulled out the bottle and saw that there was only a third of its contents left.

I poured myself a drink and went back to the TV, sipping it slowly.

"I think I should buy another bottle just like it..." An idea was forming in my head. "...Just in case it occurs to Rachel to open the bar and see that this New Year's Eve one is almost empty, besides, I could use some fresh air." I justified my intentions.

Resolved.

I swigged the glass to the end and momentarily felt a wonderful sense of bliss.

"Oh yes, exactly what I needed."

I got up from the sofa a little too quickly and my head spun.

"What a departure hehehe!" I laughed silly under my breath.

I started getting myself together to go out to the shop.

Wallet, one phone, another "mini" phone, keys.

I put on my shoes and was just about to pick up my flat keys, which had awkwardly fallen on the floor in the front room, when a loud crash came from the living room.

It sounded as if two wooden objects had bumped into each other with great force.

I stared for a few seconds in front of me in stillness, listening.

Then I went to check it out.

I walked quietly into the living room and looked around slowly and carefully. However, everything looked normal as it was, nothing was out of the ordinary.

I tried to scan everything carefully, but the alcohol had already slightly started to disturb my senses.

Only after a while did I notice that the door on the wooden bar was now open.

I furrowed my brow wonderingly.

I was inclined to think that I had left them open after pouring the last drink, although, I wouldn't guarantee that.

I wrestled with my thoughts for a moment before I managed to ignore it. *Big deal, you probably forgot to lock them, let's go, no time to waste on silly things.* My instincts urged me on.

Before I left, I grasped the handles on the wooden doors that opened in opposite directions and closed them in one motion.

I wanted to be sure that this time nothing would not be open, when I returned.

"Any minute Connor could be here; I don't want him to see me walking around with a bottle of vodka in my hand." I stated self-consciously.

I moved towards the door again, ready to leave the flat.

When I grabbed the handle and was about to pull it towards me, I froze in place for a few seconds, pierced by a momentary paralysis.

Because the feeling that someone was standing behind me got to me. Even out of the corner of my eye, I thought I saw movement behind me, but I didn't turn around, choosing to ignore it.

I left quickly, inattentively slamming the door loudly behind me.

It was past 10am.

On the way to the shop, I breathed deeply, relishing the fresh air and the nice weather.

The alcohol only added to the feeling of bliss.

I watched people heading somewhere in a hurry, busy with their business. *Probably most of them are in a hurry to get to work, after all, it's only ten o'clock in the morning...* My intuition told me. *...They're off to work and I'm off to get a bottle of almost two litres of vodka, like some kind of alcoholic.* I commented on my trip to the shop and laughed to myself under my breath.

It was then that I realised I had said it out loud.

I was at the pedestrian crossing at the time, waiting for the green light and a strange woman was standing next to me, holding the hand of, I estimated, an eight-year-old girl.

The child was staring at me, with curious eyes.

No wonder, no doubt I must have looked like a madman.

Most likely her mother, also heard what I said, because she looked at me with disapproval written on her face.

I felt terribly stupid.

Wanting to justify myself somehow, without knowing why, all I managed to get out of myself was thoughtless:

"Excuse me, ma'am, I'm a police officer."

The woman immediately looked away from me.

She then moved swiftly ahead as soon as the green light came on, nervously tugging on the child's arm to make her hurry too.

Jesus... I thought embarrassedly ...*To get a two-litre bottle of vodka? Like an alcoholic? I'm a police officer...?* I repeated my own monologue in my head. *...What a shame.* I reprimanded myself in my mind.

I crossed to the other side of the street, with a slow step.

The woman and the girl were still on the near horizon, and I wanted them to get as far ahead of me as possible.

Let's just hope they weren't going where I was. My mind was making fun of me.

I arrived at a local shop where I was going to get a "supply."

I was already about to go inside, but my phone rang.

I pulled it out and checked the display, it was Connor calling, I answered.

166

"Hello." I said putting the receiver to my ear.

"Well, hello, how are you holding up there today?"

"I'm okay, I went out to the shop to get some groceries."

"I spoke to Rachel a while ago, she chastised me for having a beer last night, I hear you've been getting nicely riled up." He laughed into the receiver.

"Come on, she's exaggerating..." I replied. "...I'm still weak and have a headache, I guess it's better to have a drink occasionally instead of stuffing myself with painkillers?" I tried to justify myself.

"Well, I wouldn't say that, but I think you know what's best for you, yourself."

He declared.

I immediately liked that statement:

"I know what's best for me myself." I registered the quote with my mind as the perfect guiding thought for the day.

"That's right." I nodded.

"How long will you be home in...?" He asked. "...I'm in the area and I could drop by your place in fifteen, twenty minutes."

"Make it twenty, just to be sure." I replied.

I had to give myself enough time to get home, have a quick drink and hide the alcohol.

"Okay, then I'll see you in twenty." He said and ended the conversation.

I felt a sense of relief.

Not only had I successfully convinced myself that reaching for alcohol instead of pills, was the result of knowing what was best for me.

On top of that, I still had a few minutes to spare to get home and get ready before Connor arrived.

So, with no rush, I walked into the shop and asked for what I had come here for.

The clerk put the bottle of alcohol in a blue disposable plastic bag. However, it was of considerable size and did not fit completely into the small capacity plastic bag.

As a result, the red neck of the bottle with the seal and cap was sticking out clearly at the level of the ears by which I was supposed to hold it. This created quite an embarrassing problem, as it gave away too clearly what I was carrying inside, and I had no other way of hiding it.

I felt simply embarrassed, marching down the street carrying a large bottle of vodka in broad daylight and that, early in the morning. Me, a respected police officer with many years of seniority.

For a moment, I felt like a regular alcoholic who can't wait for his next dose of addictive liquor.

But I needed it and no matter what the neighbours would say, I didn't want to stu myself with pills, I know what's best for me myself.

By the time I reached my building, I saw Connor's car parked in the street.

He had arrived earlier and was already waiting for me, at my door. I had no choice but to approach him, at the same time I tried to hide the alcohol behind my body

"Oh, there you are." He said when he saw me.

"I am."

"I arrived a few minutes faster, I guess it's not a problem?" He asked.

"No, not at all." I replied.

I positioned myself to his right, holding a bottle behind me in my right hand.

I pulled out my keys.

"You were going to buy something?" he asked, searching with his eyes for the shopping bags.

"I had thought about it on the way, I had only gone for a walk." I lied.

"Hm, okay." He replied.

I saw out of the corner of my eye, as he looked at my right hand the one, I was trying to hide. Connor was no fool.

We had worked together for many years, and I knew what a great cop he was.

My poor trick of hiding my hand behind me didn't impress him.

I was well aware that he could see I was trying to hide something from him.

I ignored it, however.

"I know what is best for me." I recalled his words in my mind.

I opened the door and together we went inside.

However, I did not let him through the door as custom demands.

I squeezed in first and pulled o my shoes in a quick motion, helping myself to my feet.

After which I set o for the lounge, now carrying the alcohol in front of me at stomach level, Connor following behind me.

When we reached the lounge room, my gaze immediately went to the wooden bar, more specifically its door.

That's when I saw that they were once again open wide.

What the fuck! I shuddered in thought.

I was a bit confused at the sight, because from a distance I could see a 1.5l bottle of vodka, almost fully drunk by me already.

I looked at it and felt a sting in my stomach.

Again, I had an overwhelming desire to drink.

With a calm step I moved to the bar so that Connor wouldn't see anything, I put my new purchase inside and closed the door

"Sit down, make yourself comfortable…" I offered already confidently. "…Would you like something stronger to drink?"I asked, pointing with my hand to the piece of furniture I was standing by.

"I hope he'll be tempted, then I won't feel guilty about drinking alone." He suggested a positive scenario to my mind.

"It's not too early for alcohol…?" He replied, however, looking at me suspiciously. "…I would prefer coffee." He added.

I was slightly disappointed, but I wasn't about to give up my drink. "Coffee, fine…" I said. "…I think I'll have a drink, it's good for my head." I added, feigning indifference while trying to justify myself again.

Connor looked at me disapprovingly but made no comment.

I pulled out the almost-finished bottle of alcohol and set it on the dresser next to me.

There was no glass, however.

I had forgotten that the last one I drank from, had been left in the kitchen before I left for the shop, so I had nothing to pour vodka into now. - I'll put the cattle on for coffee. - I said and headed for the kitchen. I put the water on and pulled out a glass for my drink, threw in two office cubes from the freezer and went back into the living room.

I'll have a drink before the water is ready. I thought contentedly.

Connor was looking at the news on the TV at the time, preoccupied. I walked over to the dresser where I'd left the part-drank bottle earlier and reached out to grab it.

But this, without rationale, ran the full length of the piece of furniture up to the edge and shattered against the floorboards with a bang.

Splashing everything around it and scattering thousands of pieces of tiny glass on the ground.

Connor's gaze immediately landed on me startled, as I stood stiff as a post, in front of the dresser with my hand still, outstretched.

I couldn't believe my eyes.

The bottle, which had been standing at least fifty centimetres away from the edge from which it had fallen, had literally slid across the length of the table, as if by an invisible thread and shattered. There couldn't even be a question that it was my fault.

I didn't snag the piece of furniture with my foot or cause some kind of major turbulence so that, for example, it fell to the side and rolled further away. It just rolled away in the opposite direction from me as it stood, and it didn't last more than one second.

"Well, now you're going to hear from Rachel..." Connor laughed. "...You'd better go quickly and get a mop and wipe it off, before the stench seeps in. God damn it!" I said furiously and reached for the new bottle I'd brought from the shop.

It was all the same to me then. Whether Connor was looking at me or not, I needed to calm my nerves.

I made myself a drink and took a few sips greedily, then set the glass far and safe on a small dresser to make sure it didn't fall.

I was starting to get oversensitive.

This was no longer a joke.

The spilt alcohol stank more and more, so I went to get some cleaning utensils to counteract as soon as possible.

When I returned, I started to pick up every larger piece of glass at first. The rest I carefully swept up, wiped with a mop and finally sprayed with a spray that kills odour and bacteria.

Completely in the process, I forgot about coffee for Connor, who had been sitting quietly watching the news the whole time.

I got rid of the rubbish in the kitchen and put away the cleaning utensils.

I made my friend an instant coffee and brought it into the living room. Then, I set the cup down, in front of Connor who waited there patiently for me.

"Thanks a lot." He said.

Before I sat down next to him on the sofa, I walked over to the dresser where my drink stood.

When I was close enough to reach for my glass, I did so, then this one moved too.

Admittedly slightly, and if I hadn't been looking at it at that moment I probably wouldn't have even noticed.

But I did notice, the fucking glass moved, first the bottle now this.

"What the hell is going on here!" My instincts were going crazy, confused. I glanced surreptitiously at Connor; I was curious if he had also witnessed this.

He, however, kept his eyes on the TV, sipping his coffee to do so.

"Denise will have a burial after tomorrow..." he spoke up suddenly. "...You said you wanted to go?"

"Oh yes, of course I want to." He shook me out of my stupor.

Man, you've got to shake yourself up at last. - My mind reprimanded me. - The funeral will be at twelve o'clock, in the cemetery at St Paul's Church. - He announced.

"Yes, I know where it is..." I replied. "...You will be going?"

I walked away from the dresser to take my comfortable resting place.

Thus, setting aside the question of self-moving things in my flat for later.

"I'm on duty, but I'll swap with someone, I'll come."

"Great, it will be good to have you there with me." I said and sat down.

Connor smiled kindly at me then we both suspended our gaze on the TV. Our attention was drawn to a reporter who was then talking about the helplessness of the police in a case, the disappearance of four children aged between twelve and fifteen.

The situation took place in a town called North Hill, north of London. The reporter was going back to 2008, the time when the first disappearance was recorded.

The investigation was to remain open, but over the following few years, there were three further disappearances of young people.

The reporter spoke briefly about the clique of clues, and the evidence the police had at the time.

Among other things, about Voodoo dolls that parents were finding, not long before their children went missing.

The reportage was concluded, with an official request from the Police to residents for help in the case.

This was to culminate in a substantial cash reward of £100,000, for the person who provided information that could help solve the investigation.

"I've heard of this before, a hundred thousand quid, they must be desperate..." Connor spoke up. "...I remember in 2008, it was all over the country for a while, then it went quiet, now they're back at it again, if they haven't found them by now, there's no chance those kids are still alive."

I listened to what he was saying, but I couldn't speak.

I stared at the television screen as if hypnotised, unable to take my eyes o it.

I had also heard it once, and I knew it subconsciously.

But at that moment, I felt strangely connected to the case, almost as if it were something personal.

But after all, I had no reason to do so, because I had absolutely nothing to do with it.

At the time, I didn't know if it was the instinct of a police officer that had such an effect on me, or if it was something else entirely.

I just watched and felt that I had to follow the developments in this case more closely.

"Time for me to go..." Connor announced.

He set his empty cup down on the table for me to wash, then picked himself up from the couch.

"...I'm still going to the bank and in the evening, I have an appointment with my lady, we're going to dinner together and then to my place." He added.

Winking at me with a mocking smile on his face.

He amused me with this.

"I understand, so, have fun." I replied.

"You too, and don't overdo it with..." He didn't finish speaking, just pointed to the bottle in the bar.

"I know what's best for me myself." My mind replied.

"Don't worry about me, I can take care of myself." I assured him and walked him to the door.

Connor left and I was alone in the flat again.

I returned to the living room and poured myself another drink.

I wondered for a moment if, indeed, I was going a little overboard with the alcohol.

But I quickly concluded that I knew myself well enough, to know my limits. Especially as the alcohol relieved my headache and relaxed my nerves at the same time.

It was everything I needed most at the time.

Even more as now, the strange things were happening in my house and nightmares plagued me at night.

These arguments were good enough, to make me feel justified.

I sat down in front of my computer and typed the name North Hill into Google.

The basic information came up first.

Geographical location, population, pictures of landmarks, town hall, houses, harbour and so on.

It was only below that I found the first articles I was interested in.

One of them was from 2008 and described the first disappearance.

It was a girl named Magda Richardson; she was 14 years old.

It was at this point that my memory gradually began to clear up.

"...Prior to her disappearance, the girl lived in a single-family home with her single mother of Polish origin, Joanna Zielinski, after her marriage, Richardson...' It read.

...Her father, a professional soldier in the British Army, Kevin Richardson, 49, was shot dead in Iraq in 2000 while carrying out one of his military operations when the girl was 11..."

"...The child's devastated mother, Joanna Richardson, aged 45 at the time, lost her mind a few months after the girl went missing and, as a result, was forced to return to her family in Poland...'

"...To this day, it remains unclear what happened to the child. Initially, the woman claimed that the misfortune was caused by a Voodoo doll..." "...The accusation fell on a newly arrived couple from Ethiopia..." "...They were then accused of practising black magic. The couple had moved to North Hill just six months before, missing a child..."

"... The couple were quickly cleared of the allegations, however, after the

incident, they left the town and never returned...'" I felt very sorry for Joanna Richardson.

The woman first lost her husband, only to later lose her daughter as well.

To top it all off , such a young one.

I then saw the character of Denise Randal in the person of Magda Richardson.

Because when tragedy struck, they were both just, innocent children. I could not imagine the nightmare their mothers must have been going through.

It drove Joanna Richardson to such a state that she could no longer bear the burden of despair and eventually, she mentally broke down.

Although I had no new information about Clare Randal, I presumed that she was not in the best mental health either.

I felt very depressed by the information I had just absorbed.

At the bottom of the article, I found the accompanying photographs.

The first photograph showed Joanna and Kevin Richardson, between them stood Magda, thirteen years old at the time, with her hands joyfully stretched upwards.

I inferred from this view that the girl was trying to show o her new jewellery, a bracelet, on her hand that reflected the sun's rays nicely.

Magda was proudly displaying it, which was immediately striking.

Did you get a present? My mind was interested.

The photo had evidently been taken in front of their house in the garden on some celebration, for, they were all elegantly dressed and smiling broadly at the camera, looking very happy together.

The next image belonged to Angelina and Ain Hailu; the young couple originally wrongly accused of being involved in the disappearance of a child.

And only at the very end was a large photo, of the lovely face of Magda Richardson herself.

As I looked at it, I got the impression that something flashed slightly on my laptop monitor.

On the computer screen, right where Magda's eye was, a single drop appeared.

I touched it with my finger and indeed, the screen was wet in that spot.

I furrowed my brow, puzzled.

I smeared the droplet between my fingers after which, I wiped it on my trousers.

At that moment, I felt the phone start to vibrate in my trouser pocket. For a moment, I waited for the familiar music from my mobile phone to reach my ears.

But to my surprise, instead, I heard a melody from a "mini."

A phone that, in my opinion, should rather be silent.

The music sounded and it seemed louder than before, almost, it filled the entire living room with sound.

I rummaged around awkwardly, diving my hand into my trouser pocket.

However, the phone stopped ringing the moment I reached it.

I pulled it out, looked at the display and froze.

I felt the blood drain from my head and cold chills run through my entire body.

This time, there was one missed call, signed: Magda Richardson.

11

We'll meet on Wednesday.

'Man seeks love because deep down he knows that only love can make him happy'.

Fourteen years earlier,

25 March 2004, Canary Wharf, London, "Bradley and Brad Lettings", 10:15am.

"...I'm warning you!!" Thundered a young woman on the phone. "...if you call this number again, I will start spreading rumours about you, on your agency's website, and wherever I can, I will tell that you have not only one illegitimate daughter but several! That you are a seducer and abandon women who are pregnant with you, without financial help!!" she added furiously at the end.

George listened to this irritated.

He knew perfectly well that if the woman followed through with her threats, then the agency's reputation, as well as his own, would be in great decline.

People are over-sensitive to such topics and very vindictive. All it takes is one person to believe such rumours, and then the news will spread rapidly, with potentially disastrous consequences.

Most likely even bankrupting both George and Matthiew.

"Please calm down..." George tried to defuse the situation. "...you didn't leave any lead on yourself; I was just trying to contact you somehow on my own..." He explained. "...I think we need to talk."

"Why do you think I did call you on Friday...?Because I want to buy a house?!" she replied, still exasperated, but slowly, her voice calmed down. "Ma'am..." George began. "...the situation is delicate, and we shouldn't talk about it over the phone."

"Are you suggesting something?" she asked.

"You are claiming to know my daughter..." George said. "...you introduced yourself as Noelle Kemp. These are facts I cannot ignore, I would like to propose a meeting."

"Well, I agree..." she replied without a moment's thought. "...I'll come to London in two days, but it's all at your expense. I'll let you know by Wednesday which hotel I want you to book me a room in."

The situation had obviously improved for her.

The woman knew that George could afford a five-star hotel and whatever else, she could think of by then.

She was going to make the most of it with sophistication.

At the mere thought of a sponsored trip to the capital, the nervousness that had made her red in the face only five minutes ago passed.

She had long dreamed of getting away from the people and surroundings of the city she knew too well.

On top of that, she'd be going to London to live in luxury for a while, to sample the lives of unimaginably wealthy people and all at a rich man's expense.

All this made her look forward to the trip and nervousness, was now replaced by a feeling of excitement. George was also jumping to his conclusions.

So, she doesn't live in London, in which case, I'll absolutely have to find out where she's from, but one step at a time. He spoke to himself in his mind.

"Okay, I accept your terms." George replied.

"Great, I'm starting to pack."

"I'll need your phone number." Added George.

"No way...!" The woman quickly called him to order. "...I'll contact you myself, if you don't want me to call through reception, then you give me your phone number." She replied.

"Then how do I buy you a ticket? I need to know where you live, so I know where to order it from and for what time." George tried to approach her.

He was anxious for the woman to reveal any information about herself.

But she didn't let him outsmart her this time either.

"Don't worry about the ticket..." She said shortly. " ...I'll buy it myself; your job is to pay for my hotel room in advance from Wednesday to Wednesday."

"Fine, as you wish." George replied politely.

He now had to dance as she played him and not provoke her. At least until she proved that she was stalking him unfounded, and he could, once and for all, get rid of the intruder.

Nevertheless, he was intrigued and wanted to meet her in person.

If only to ask her how she knew Noelle.

George was not a vindictive person.

But he also considered the option of charging her with libel and blackmail.

Before that was to happen, he had to meet her first, face-to-face.

So, he gave his phone number to her.

"Great, I'll be in touch." She said finally and hung up.

George straightened up in his chair and took a deep breath.

He had to analyse the conversation in his head.

"I couldn't have done otherwise..." He concluded. ...*At least there is the certainty that she will be in town on Wednesday and here I can keep an eye on her, find out who she really is.* He summarised in his mind.

He looked at his watch, it was coming up to eleven o'clock.

At that moment, the door to his office opened and Matthiew walked in.

George measured him up with his eyes, from head to toe.

He looked as if he had come straight back from a nightclub.

Unshaven with bloodshot eyes in a rumpled suit.

He could most likely still smell the alcohol, but he was too far away for George to tell.

"Jesus, Matt." He spoke back to him.

"Did I miss something?" He asked.

You didn't miss it, you just couldn`t be bother, again. George thought. "You haven't missed anything..." George replied maliciously. "...And certainly nothing that concerns you."

"Did you find this woman's number?" Matthiew tried further.

"I found it." He told George off-handedly.

He didn't want to read any more into it, but he knew there was no other way.

The girl had clearly threatened them by saying she would start writing comments on the agency's official website.

George was sure she would start doing this, if something went wrong or she got very upset.

So, he had to tell him everything, whether he wanted to or not.

"And when are you going to call...?" Matthiew continued. "...Or would you prefer me to do it?"

"Why would I want you to handle things for me, when it's my business." Replied an irritated George.

"I don't know. Maybe you're scared or something?"

"I've already spoken to her."

"So, how did it go?" Matthiew immediately picked up.

"She's coming to London on Wednesday."

"Oh, she's coming here, which means you don't know her, you don't stick your nose out of this city." Said Matthiew, proud of his detective thinking Matthiew.

Jesus Matthiew, sober up... George was clearly irritated by this conversation. "...And does it only work one way? After all, she's the one who could leave here."

"Right, then where are we going to meet her?"

"What do you mean we...!" A bewildered George replied. "...It's my business and I'll meet her."

"Come on George, after all, she could be some nutcase, you'll need support."

"Matthiew, I'm not going to meet the leader of ISIS, I'm going to meet a young woman who is under 20 years old...." George argued. " ...I'm a grown man, I can deal with some barking mad shit myself, I don't need you."

"Okay, don't get so annoyed, I just want to help." Matthiew replied.

"Thank you, but there is no need..." George assured him. "...Now go to the bathroom and make yourself look presentable somehow, we have an appointment with a client at twelve o'clock, you will talk to him."

Matthiew lowered his head to look at his clothes

He didn't know what George was clinging to in his mind, he looked not too bad.

"Buying or selling."

"Buying, you know them, I think they're determined to make an offer, for that villa in North Hill." George replied.

"Well, yes! The one for one million two hundred."

"You're not wrong, indeed, the same one."

"Oh, that's nice. I knew I had them on the hook...!" Matthiew replied. "...More and more people are starting to ask about this town, and we only have this one house there..." He added after a while. "...A good deal for rich Londoners, peace and quiet, sea, forests and monuments."

"It just so happens that this couple are from Ethiopia, you should already know that." He was interrupted by George.

"But settled in the U.K?"

"You missed it again, they happen to still be living in Ethiopia, wealthy people set on moving to England." George replied.

"Wealthy is an understatement, if they want to buy a house for such a huge amount of money..." Replied Matt. "...They must be millionaires."

"Maybe they are, none of your business. George brought him down to earth, again."

Matthiew looked at him with a dismissive gaze.

"North Hill, a gluttonous morsel for stu y people..." He mused.

"...And we've only got that one house there, if you had several or a dozen houses like that for sale, you could make a fortune!" Matthiew thought.

"Millionaires from Ethiopia, good one, hehehe..." George slapped him with an angry look.

"Matthiew! I already told you once, it's none of your business!"

"It kind of is, don`t you think?" Matthiew tried to calm him down. "Your job is to present this house to them in the best possible light, in a friendly, pleasant but above all professional atmosphere, do you understand?" George continued angrily.

"Chill out a bit, after all, I haven't been doing this since yesterday!" Matthiew," tried to bite back.

"Looking at you today, I could have sworn that I probably would though, yes...." George replied. "...In addition, if you'd come to work like that on your first day, no one would probably even let you into the building, you're lucky we're partners, otherwise I'd have thrown you   out."
He added seriously, leaving no stone unturned.

Matthiew wasn't bothered by George's comment.

The fact was that he could only talk and he, anyway, was untouchable.

Instead, something completely different was going through his mind. "Yes... North Hill is a beautiful town." Said Matthiew suddenly thoughtfully, completely changing the subject.

George knew he wasn't listening to him.

He rarely did, which got even more on his nerves.

And this time he was not surprised that Matthiew ignored his remarks and starts to drivel about something completely different.

"A beautiful city, so what?" George asked.

"It's a shame we don't have more properties for sale there." Matthiew swept his gaze somewhere outside the window, focused, he seemed to be putting together a plan in his mind.

"People are happy there and don't want to sell their houses, what's so strange about that...?" George replied. "...You just said yourself that more and more people are asking for this town, which means more and more people want to move there than to move out."

"Well, yes, that's the trouble."

"Come back down to earth, think about your task today..." George insisted. "...You need to focus on what we have and not what we don't, get this deal completed and signed."

"Will do." He told Matthiew briefly, then left and went to his office.

George just led him away with his eyes.

"What a man..." He said resignedly. "...The devil has tempted me to enter partnership with him, fortunately I rule the roost here, so he must continue to listen to me." He added to reassure himself.

Matthiew knew that George could still, after all, order him around, and there was little he could do about it at the time.

However, he was an intelligent, possessive and sophisticated man with an exuberant ego.

He planned to take control of the agency and only waited for opportunities to do so.

Now, when a woman appeared to blackmail George, he saw his chance.

Immediately then, he thought it was imperative that he met her.

He silently hoped to woo or persuade her and form a team together.

He wanted her to come to his side so that they could, together, join forces.

So, he began to put together a plan.

A plan to bring her to the top of the hierarchy.

He knew that without George's supervision, he would be able to lead the agencies to big money.

At the same time, he make himself disgustingly rich.

Things are slowly starting to fall into place. He thought as he sat down at his desk in his office.

Of course, he didn't listen to George and did not go to bring himself up to a neat appearance, as he'd been advised earlier.

He didn't like the old man ordering him around, so he decided to completely ignore his advice.

He switched on his computer and started looking at information about North Hill.

Then, he looked at pictures of neat and pretty properties.

And in his mind, he counted the percentages of the profits that could potentially fall into his pockets, after completing so many deals.

"Oh yes..." he said to himself contentedly. "...This town is a gold mine, if I could only make these people want to sell their houses more willingly."

He thought aloud.

Matthiew let his imagination run wild, languidly not expecting then how quickly his wish would come true because he was about to come up with a brilliant idea, that would soon make him a very rich man.

And it was all thanks to the millionaires from Ethiopia who at the exact time, were just travelling to meet him.

12

What's going on in this town!?

'There are times when we are confronted with truths for which there are no words'.

Fourteen year later,

4 November 2018, Camberwell Green, London, Danny and Rachel Davis's flat, 11am.

It had been two weeks since Denise Randal's funeral.

It was a small ceremony attended mainly by family, friends and peers from school.

Of the strangers, it was just me, Rachel, Connor and two strange-looking men who were standing too close to Clare Randal for my liking.

There was a depressing atmosphere in the air.

Everyone was dressed in the traditional black, with most people weeping, especially the children.

They were united in their pain with the mother of the murdered ten-year-old girl.

This sight tore my heart to pieces.

But the saddest picture, however, was the coffin, which was closed because of the way the child had lost her life.

Apparently, the damage to the head was in such a terrible state that it had not been possible to prepare the corpse sufficiently to make it suitable for public display.

All of this left me unable to control my emotions, and I also let my eyes expel the liquid that had accumulated in them to create an outlet for the overwhelming sadness and despair.

I learnt from Connor that Clare Randal had been in a locked ward at Lewisham Hospital called Ladywell Unit since the tragedy. *So, these men next to her must have been the paramedics who were keeping an eye on her to make sure she didn't do anything inappropriate at her own daughter's funeral.* Said my instincts.

When Connor mentioned the closed ward to me, my thoughts went back to the article I had read earlier.

Because it was about a woman, of Polish descent from North Hill, Joanna Richardson, who also found herself in such a place after the disappearance of her 14-year-old daughter.

At the time, it crossed my mind that such a fate might await me, too. Since the shooting, I also felt that something was seriously messing with my head.

I haven't had a normal night's sleep since the incident.

I've had strange nightmares. I couldn't shake the feeling that someone was watching me, I saw things shifting without any logical explanation right before my eyes.

And the emergency phone, whose number only two people on the planet had, rang a couple of times for no reason.

As if that wasn't already disturbing enough, one of the missed calls shows Magda Richardson, the name of the girl who went missing in North Hill ten years ago.

And there's no number given under that name, and it's just a blank. If all this wasn't a sign of some kind of paranoia, then I don't know what could be.

At times, I thought I was losing my mind.

Only alcohol was able to soothe the pain I felt in my psyche and bring as such, balance to my life.

So that I could still function somehow, every day.

That also started to be a problem and a reason for more and more frequent arguments between me and Rachel.

Ever since she found out about my "self-medication," she never stopped urging me to stop it immediately.

She claimed that I should start attending therapy with a psychologist as soon as possible.

However, I was not 100% convinced about this.

Because I believed that there was nothing wrong with me and that I could deal with it myself.

At the same time, I saw alcohol as the only relief that I simply did not want to give up.

It was easier to live in denial than to try to do something about it.

Yet, at times, I had doubts about the truthfulness of my own words.

I think I was too proud to admit defeat.

My self-confidence did not allow me to accept that I might lose. Not for a moment did I consider myself defeated, and therefore, I had no intention of asking for help from third parties.

Although that day, I could forget about returning to duty.

Even if my superiors did not know what was really going on with me.

I was only supposed to remain on leave for four more weeks. But even then, I sincerely doubted that this amount of time would be enough for me to put myself back together.

Especially since, from the time I read the first article on North Hill, the case had completely absorbed me.

As a result, I often felt like I was in some kind of trance.

I couldn't stop thinking about those events and the people involved. I would read articles, check the news, check the actions of the police, and look at pictures, evidence, and everything I could access on the Internet. This was becoming my obsession and my reason for wanting to get out of bed in the morning, apart from the alcohol.

I memorised literally every detail about it.

The last person went missing five months ago, 05 March 2018.

The first, 04 October 2008, almost ten years ago.

The modus operandi seemed to be the same.

Which pointed to the same character or perpetrators.

Single parents were the most vulnerable, never married couples. The mysterious Voodoo doll would appear in the house out of nowhere. A few weeks later, the child would disappear.

No prints, apart from one in the garden. It was a shoe print, but nothing further could be done about it.

Other than that, zero witnesses, zero fingerprints or any other clues.

Only dolls associated with black magic.

The children simply vanished into thin air.

The perpetrator or perpetrators seemed to be very familiar with every place they entered, even though it should have been completely foreign to them to move freely in unfamiliar territory without fear of being noticed.

They knew how they were supposed to find their way around it.

They also had to know the exact time and place when the victim was alone so that they would strike precisely at that moment.

From experience, I know that to develop such knowledge about someone, they would have to observe that person every day for months.

Only then would they be able to work out his or her exact daily schedule. Following this line of thought, they either had unprecedented luck or, they had information from someone who knew each of these people intimately, which was also unlikely.

However, if I had to accept either version, it would probably be the second one.

At one time, people were horrified by the situation and in mid-2017, the media gave a nickname to the case by calling it:

"The missing North Hill four."

Passed from mouth to mouth, the colourful rumours quickly turned into a tale of a curse cast on the town by visitors from the Horn region of Africa.

And it was all due to, the black magic of Voodoo.

Of course, at one time I would have said that this was complete nonsense and there was no such thing as a curse or black magic.

But in the current situation, I didn't know what to believe anymore. Some people, especially single parents with children, as the panic grew, decided to take the desperate step of leaving the city.

They sold their homes and wanted nothing to do with the city, or to put it more simply, they were afraid to stay there.

In one article I read:

"...Suspicion fell on a newly arrived couple from Ethiopia who moved into the city in May 2008..."

"...Exasperated residents took matters into their own hands..."

"...Local police struggle to prevent self-immolation..." and:

"...Police arrest the couple after, a respected businessman obstructs the performance of their duties. However, soon after, they are released from custody, thanks to a lack of evidence..."

It may seem suspicious that after these incidents, they no longer return to their home and leave the city for good, which is described at the end of the article.

But it seemed to me that they simply decided there was no future for them there anymore.

Because, even if they were innocent and cleared of all charges, they undoubtedly faced finger-pointing or even fear for their lives from other residents.

Over the course of the next few months, another child disappears, and the process is repeated until 2017.

In between, there were also many reports to the police about mysterious dolls from various residents.

To recap.

I have divided all the information about each of the missing children separately.

One folder for one person.

After which, I started to write down all the facts and my thoughts in them.

I sorted and organised them neatly on my computer screen.

Using the date of disappearance as the name of the folder, so that the title itself did not indicate what was inside.

Only when opened would the information stored in it appear.

As a result, I now had four separate windows signed in front of me:

04/11/08 - Magda Richardson.

29/04/09 - David Roberts.

15/06/13 - Oliver Wilson.

05/03/17 - Jessica Murphy.

I calculated at the time that the average interval for disappearances was 29 months, per person.

Just to start with, the first two children disappeared six months apart. Adding the next and the last five months ago gives an average of one child per 29 months.

This could still change, of course, if someone else disappears again.

I analysed it all again and again without rest.

As soon as Rachel left for work, I would turn on my computer and, read the same articles repeatedly and wait for new information.

Sometimes, I found myself turning to God in my mind, praying that no new information would emerge about another victim.

It gave me no peace of mind; I felt I had to unravel this mystery. It took up most of my free time at home, sipping drinks and browsing the internet.

I did it surreptitiously so that Rachel wouldn't know anything.

I didn't want her to worry about me abusing alcohol and agonising over a case that, after all, I was unable to solve.

However, my police instinct, or something else entirely, wouldn't let me stop.

I had the feeling that this case was made for me and that I was personally responsible for the fate of these children.

Of course, this was not the case.

After all, I didn't personally know these people or, even less, the victims themselves.

But it was a huge tragedy.

And I, since the tragic circumstances in which Denise Randal died, had changed a lot, and I wasn't sure if it was for the better.

But the plight of the children of the town of North Hill had become close to me, and I could not move past it.

I loved the children with all my heart.

Even though Rachel and I did not have any of our own.

At one time, Rachel was very sad that she could not have children, yet we never decided to adopt.

However, I have always loved children very much, and I knew then that I had to do everything in my power to explain what happened to the missing North Hill four.

And who was behind it all.

Terrible things were happening in the north of the country from the town where I lived, and the police there were virtually helpless.

I could not have known at the time that my personal involvement and my attempt to help, would put me in a situation where my own life was hanging on the edge.

13

A new life.

'The future starts today, not tomorrow...'

Ten years earlier,

05 August 2008, North Hill, City Hospital, 03:30pm

Susan was lying in bed in the postnatal ward and John was sitting at her side.

He held her newborn daughter in his arms and looked at her with tears in his eyes.

"She's perfect..." He whispered with a shrug. "...She has your eyes." He added, lifting his happy gaze to his wife.

Susan was exhausted.

The labour had started in the early hours of the morning and had lasted eight, long, hours.

John was not feeling well either.

As a result of his rapidly progressing illness, he was very weak and looked miserable.

Despite his condition, he managed to help his wife out of the house and drove her to the hospital as soon as the birth started, taking great care. Everything went very smoothly for which Susan was immensely grateful to him.

She now looked at John, holding the infant in his arms.

A feeling ran through her mind that John looked like a shadow of the man she had married.

She had long urged him to opt for chemotherapy.

But he categorically refused, claiming that he had managed to come to terms with his destiny.

John said he was ready to leave this world.

Because in his life to the fullness of happiness, the only thing missing was an o spring.

And now, as he held his daughter in his arms, he could feel his happiness coming to completion, which only strengthened his conviction that he would soon be able to leave in peace.

Susan was aware that John's days were numbered and that chemotherapy would only prolong his suffering.

Despite this, she insisted that he take the treatment after all.

Maybe now he would decide to be with his child, if only for a few months longer. She thought as she saw John cradling the infant in his arms.

The baby girl was sleeping heavily when John handed her over to Susan.

He was clearly tired.

"Go to your mother." He said.

"I'd like to name her Nicole." Said Susan suddenly, cuddling the baby gently to her breast.

"I like it." John replied.

Susan smiled kindly at him.

At this point, the little girl began to make indistinct sounds, which meant that she was just waking up.

On cue, Susan carefully uncovered her face before the infant had time to cry for good.

"I think it's time for the first meal." John said.

He was moved by the sight and remembered every detail.

He recorded everything in his memory, like a television camera, so that he could replay the footage in his mind later.

Nothing but this moment mattered to him.

There was no illness, no worries and no problems. There was only them.

The three of them, in the hospital room, together, happy.

John wished with all his heart that this moment could last forever.

Susan slid her left breast under the girl's mouth, and the girl naturally, greedily began to suck her mother's food.

"AAA... It tickles me..." Susan laughed. "...She's hungry." She added.

"Denice." Said John quietly.

"I beg your pardon."

"Let's give her the middle name Denice, after my beloved grandmother..." he replied. "... Nicole Denice McKane." He added.

Susan nodded her head in agreement with him.

"AAAHAHAHAHA... You tickle me!" Laughed Susan.

"I'd be hungry too if I ate leftovers from someone else's dinner for nine months." Joked John.

"Oh, I beg your pardon. She was getting everything she needed. Look how healthy and plump she looks." She looked at John and realised what a silly thing she had just said.

"I shouldn't say that when he's losing weight every day and looking worse and worse." She complained in her mind.

But John did not feel offended. This subject did not exist for him at that time.

"Indeed, she looks very healthy. Excellent job..." He replied, not drawing attention to her earlier words. "...Really, I am sure she will grow up to be a very beautiful woman one day." He added with a smile pierced with bitterness.

Just then, the nurse who had earlier helped deliver the baby entered the room.

She fawned over the newborn parents and the baby girl, who was still greedily eating from her mother's breast.

While making a loud smacking sound.

"Oooo... What a beautiful picture..." she said with a tender smile on her face. "...How are you feeling?"

"Fine, thank you," Susan replied.

"Excellent, Mr and Mrs Rita and James Jankins are here..." She announced formally. "...They would like to say hello. Can I invite them?"

"Of course...!" delighted Susan "...They are my parents, please call them." "Certainly, I wasn't sure if I could keep them in the waiting room any longer..." joked the nurse. "...They are very excited." She added, after which she turned on her heel and left the room.

Susan covered herself up more and looked at John.

"Have you spoken to your parents yet?" She asked.

"Yes, they should be on their way now..." he replied. "...When I called them, they told me that they would catch the earliest train from London and get here as soon as possible."

Just then, Susan's parents, Rita and James Jankins, entered the room.

Momentarily disturbing the tranquillity that John had by now savoured.

Rita, Susan's foster mother, was a loud and chatty seventy-year-old. And her stepfather, James, a year older than his wife, was a man of small talk who was characterised by the fact that he liked to express himself in a few but blunt words.

"Aaaa, where is our baby!?" Rita called out from the threshold.

Her voice echoed around the room, bouncing off the walls and filling every nook and cranny of the room.

"Here, mum..." Susan replied, pointing with her head to her hands. She gently uncovered the baby "...She's eating her afternoon meal."

Rita walked over to Susan's bed with a quick step to see the little girl up close.

She then uncovered the baby's face, still slightly obscured by the pink blanket.

Paying no attention to the fact that Susan was just breastfeeding her. Which caused James to feel the need to look away. He didn't want to see his own daughter's breasts.

"She's gorgeous!" exclaimed Rita in delight.

James, meanwhile, approached John with a serious face, stood beside him and patted him on the back as a reward.

"My congratulations, son." He said.

That was all James said that day during the hospital visit.

"Thank you." Replied John and walked closer to his wife and child to form a set.

There was a blissful atmosphere of happiness in the room, which even James shared.

John could swear that even for a moment, he noticed a smile on his father-in-law's face.

Which was unusual for this hardened pessimist.

"Our darling granddaughter...!" rejoiced Rita without taking her eyes off the infant.

"...You don't even know how happy we are."

Rita's make-up began to melt a little through the tears of joy invading her eyes.

"So are we," Susan replied, grabbing John's hand.

"And what is our name?" Rita turned to the newborn as if the child was about to answer her.

She took the child's right hand and waved it gently from side to side.

"Nicole." Susan replied.

"Hi Nicole, I'm Rita, your grandmother...." She said in a diminutive voice. ...And the sullen man standing there is your grandfather, James." She added, pointing at James with little Nicole's hand.

James then stood still and impassive, looking out of the window for something, not responding to Rita's taunts. "Nicole Denice." Added John after a moment.

"Oooo... How pretty..." said Rita and turned to the child again.

"...Well, we have two names. I wonder which one you will like better, once you can decide."

At this point the now friendly nurse entered the room again.

John hoped that she was here to say that his parents were also already in the waiting room.

"The family complete?" she asked.

"Not quite. My parents are still missing." Replied a disappointed John.

"They will probably still make it..." said the nurse, trying to comfort John when she saw his expression. "...I came to tell you that according to the regulations, you will have to stay with us in hospital for at least two days...." She addressed Susan directly. "...The birth went naturally without any complications, but this is standard procedure, and there is no need to worry."

"Yes, of course." Susan replied.

"Excellent, visiting hours end at 5 pm, and at 6 pm, we serve dinner, please, here is your menu..." She handed Susan a laminated sheet of paper. "...I will be back in a moment to take your order, you still have less than an hour to complete your visit, but feel free to join us tomorrow from 3 pm." She announced finally and returned to her duties.

John pulled out his phone.

Which had been muted all this time so as not to disturb anyone.

But there were no missed calls on it.

"I'll check on my parents." He said to Susan and left the room. He then went into the corridor to make a call; he was sorry they hadn't arrived yet, and it was imperative that he made sure where they happened to be.

Leaving Susan alone, at the mercy of Rita, who was excited to the extreme. And James, a man who wouldn't even have realised if Rita had decided to kidnap the baby and run out of the hospital with him

John's parents, Judy and Kevin McKane retired over two years ago and left North Hill to live in one of the wealthiest areas in west London, Knightsbridge.

They were very wealthy people who owned several luxury flats in European countries and Asia.

As a result, money never posed a problem for them.

Unlike Susan's adoptive parents, Rita and James Jankins.

Who, at one time, were involved in farming.

Rita also worked as a part-time childminder at a nursery school.

They lived in a small but nice house in the suburb of North Hill.

In this family, what they lacked in luxuries and a great deal of money for all kinds of whims, they made up for with domesticity and love for each other. In this respect, they stood out.

In contrast, in John's family home, there was a very strict atmosphere.

When he turned thirty, he decided to move away from his parents.

At the time, he used the cover of studying as a reason.

But as time went on Kevin found out that John wasted the next five years of his life mainly on parties, achieving absolutely nothing.

Their son's attitude was very disappointing to Kevin and Judy, who had hoped that their son had decided to pick himself up and take his studies seriously.

John was their only child, and they knew they couldn't give up on him. But he had never been interested in books or science. In this respect, he was very different from Susan.

While she was an outstanding student.

Assimilating new knowledge without difficulty, she was able to think and calculate several years ahead.

She also skipped two grades quickly at school and easily passed her psychology degree at the age of 22.

She was fascinated by the human mind, mentality and psyche.

She had always wanted to know how different people perceive the world and what makes them make their decisions the way they do and not otherwise.

It was a broad subject for her, and she never stopped exploring, all the time continuing her education.

John, on the other hand, never had an enthusiasm for learning.

He took up a degree in economics but never finished it.

When he moved in alone at the age of thirty, the flat was paid for by his parents, of course.

He partied a lot, went to clubs, met new people and abused alcohol and drugs, which often got him into trouble.

Then, his father finally decided that he had to save his son from himself. Therefore, he gave him a job at his construction company.

He did this to bind him to the company he was going to inherit from him one day.

At the same time keeping him in his sights.

John, however, was a quick learner, and it was easy for him to find his way in the construction business.

A few years later, when Kevin McKane was confident that he could rely on his son, he decided to retire.

Thus entrusting the management of the company to John.

It was then that he and Judy, also a now-retired English teacher, decided to sell their North Hill property and move to a luxury area in the UK capital. From there, they were able to travel and enjoy the fruits of their hard work in their old age.

Kevin McKane trained his son well.

When John was born, his parents bought a sizable plot of land for him on which they hoped he would one day build his own home. John didn't get down to it until he met Susan when he turned 39. By then, he was a settled man and knew he was ready to start his own family.

Then, together, they started work on building which was to become their home in the future.

Susan, excited at the time, detailed all her ideas for the rooms, including the patio and heated pool.

Then John, as much as possible, would fulfil her whims.

It was to be their dream home.

And it was, until a certain point.

John stood in the hallway with his phone in his hand.

He hesitated to call his parents, who should have just been heading their way.

He was a little afraid of meeting them.

Because they had only recently known about his illness, and he was aware of how nightmarish he already looked.

Kevin was 78, and Judy was 76, and precisely because of their age, he feared that seeing him might come as a huge shock to them.

Welcoming a new life into the world, always means, saying goodbye to an old one.... He thought. *...At least they will have something left of me. A part of me will remain.* John consoled himself in his thoughts.

He held the phone but delayed making the call.

"My parents are old people. Who knows how much more time they have left? I know mine is not much anymore." He said to himself despondently, then glanced, through the ajar door, at Susan and little Nicole Denice.

The sight brought a smile to his face.

"At least my two greatest loves, they still have many wonderful years of life ahead of them." He lifted his spirits.

14

This young lady is my daughter.

'It is not he who loves who proclaims love, but he who is silent and carries it in his heart.'

Four years earlier,

27 March 2004, New Cross, London, George Bradley's flat, 12.30 pm.

George was waiting in his flat for a call from Matthiew with whom he had an appointment.

The day before, he had agreed to let Matthiew go with him to meet a female stranger who had started harassing him a few days ago.

For some reason known only to him, the man insisted that his help would be essential to George.

After a long conversation with him and thinking through all the pros and cons, he finally decided to let go and agreed to let the man accompany him.

So, the three of them were to meet in the restaurant of the "Hilton London Metropole Hotel", by the, "Hyde Park."

Since George's last conversation with the stranger on Monday, she latter had called him twice more.

The first time, to announced to him that she wished for a week's room booking at the Hilton Hotel in the name of Noelle Kemp.

Starting on Wednesday, she had, of course, indicated in advance that her stay could be extended, thus leaving herself the option to change her mind just in case.

A second time, to declare to George where and at what time she would like to meet him.

After this second conversation, George was under the impression that he was seeking an audience with the Queen of England herself. The stranger had exorbitant tastes and quite a nerve, like a spoilt noblewoman.

When George asked if she would be okay with him coming to meet his partner.

He heard her burst out laughing in his earpiece, thereby infuriating him. Her reaction was because she had seen Matthiew's picture on the agency's website and knew he was talking about him.

She then calls him a "fat fart", but she replied that he could come if he wanted to so badly.

George, of course, did not repeat this in his conversation with Matthiew, as he did not want to make him uncomfortable.

He merely confirmed that the woman had agreed to meet them, to which the man replied enthusiastically:

"I knew she was going soft up. Don't worry about anything. We'll deal with her."

George didn't think the phrase "deal with" was the right expression in this context.

Nor did he think it would be so easy to "deal with her".

For this person, right from the start, gave the impression of being very intelligent and cunning.

She seemed like the type of individual, who always has a backup plan in case of need.

George's intuition told him that he should be extremely careful in the way he approached the stranger.

He had to handle the conversation skilfully and think everything through carefully.

Before deciding what was the right next step to take.

The phone rang, and George looked at the display. It was Matthiew calling.

"Hello, Matthiew."

"Hi, so where do you want to meet? Come to pick you up, and we'll go together?"

"No, I'll meet you there. Go directly to the hotel," George replied.

"Are you sure...?" Matthiew quipped. "...Maybe it would be better if we met earlier and discussed everything again?" he suggested, "There is no need for that."

"Suit yourself, so I'll see you at the Hilton." Matthiew ended the conversation and hung up.

There was a reason why George did not want to go with him at the agreed time.

Namely, he decided that he would drive there a little earlier and try to meet the stranger alone before Matthiew showed up.

He wanted to start with a one-to-one conversation without any third parties.

Dressed in a smart suit, George put on his black coat.

He took the keys to the flat and the car, which lay on a cabinet by the front door.

He closed the door behind him and made his way to his luxury "Jaguar".

It was 12:30 pm when he started the engine in the car.

If I'm lucky, with no traffic jams on the roads, I should get there at about 1 pm. He planned in his mind.

Officially, they were not due to meet until 2 pm.

He drove the car and found, to his surprise, that he felt no mental discomfort.

Earlier, he had thought he would be irritated to say the least, maybe even stressed.

When the time would come to find out who the person was who was talking about the woman, he had fallen in love with thirty years ago and the alleged daughter.

Now, however, he felt as if this was the most normal thing under the sun.

Little by little, he was poised and relaxed.

Almost as if he was going to meet an old acquaintance with whom he had not been in contact for many years.

At times, he was overwhelmed with curiosity and excitement.

Heading towards the "Hyde Park", at which the "Hilton" hotel stood. Minute by minute, he was getting closer and closer to his destination, and then he began to wonder who he would soon meet.

He had no idea what he should expect.

He wondered what the woman, who had turned his well-ordered life upside down, looked like.

Does beauty go hand in hand with intelligence, which she apparently does not lack?

He arrived at 13:15 pm, fifteen minutes later than planned.

Not bad... He thought, looking at his watch. *...It's still at least thirty minutes before Matthiew gets here. It's not work, so he'll be on time or a bit quicker.* He added in his mind.

He walked into the building where, after all, he was now renting a room, even if he wasn't staying in it himself at the time.

Then he walked towards the reception desk.

"Welcome to the Hilton London Hotel..." The receptionist recited quickly, with a fake smile on her face. "...How can I help you?"

"Good afternoon, I'm renting a room where a friend of mine is currently staying..." George began. "...I would like to inform her that I have already arrived and am waiting."

"Of course. Can I ask for her name and room number?"

"Yes, my friend's name is Noelle Kemp, she is staying in room 737." Replied George.

"Your name?" she asked formally.

"George Bradley."

"Thank you. Please wait a moment, I will know in a moment if our guest is expecting you." She said automatically.

George walked over to the beautiful purple armchairs that stood against the wall of the large lobby near the reception desk and settled comfortably in one of them.

He waited for the receptionist to make the call.

Not two minutes had passed when she let him know with her hand that she was ready.

"Mrs Kemp asks you to go to our restaurant and wait for her there..." she announced and showed him the way. "...She will meet you in a few minutes."

"Thank you," George replied, then set off in the direction indicated.

He walked up to the bar and ordered an orange juice with ice.

When the barman asked £7.99 payment from him, George looked at him puzzled and handed over a £10 note, of which he immediately received change.

He had never been to a Hilton hotel and didn't know what the cosmic prices were here.

At least now I know why I haven't set foot in here before... he thought. *...£7.99 for a juice on top of that £356 a night for a room I'm also paying for a week, and that's on top of it being the cheapest I've been able to book...* he was annoyed. *...Really, it gets better and better.* He added to himself in conclusion.

He sat down at a table and began to look around nervously, looking out for a female stranger.

After a while, however, he decided that there was no point.

After all, I don't know what she looks like anyway. He realised.

He picked up the menu to occupy his thoughts for a while.

Of course, next to the dishes ordered on the menu, there were no prices listed, which is typical in places for wealthy clientele.

They don't care what they pay, so why list prices? I for one, will not be ordering anything here. He decided.

He looked at his watch. It was just passing one thirty-five.

Damn, if this keeps up, any minute now, Matthiew will show up, and we'll have no more one-on-one conversation. He cursed under his breath.

At that moment, a person approached his table.

When George raised his eyes to see who it was, his heart went up to his throat.

For a moment, he had the impression that he was looking at a ghost. It wasn't until the person spoke that George realised she was as real as flesh and blood.

Jesus, I know her, after all. He thought stunned.

He didn't know. He just thought he did.

Matthiew, meanwhile, was rushing at breakneck speed, knowing full well that he was already late.

He looked at his watch, embedded in the car's upholstery, and saw it was passing 2 pm.

And he wasn't even halfway there yet.

On top of that, the traffic jam that George had managed to avoid earlier was spreading.

Matthiew had the feeling that they were now on every street deliberately, just to make him angry. There was no way around them.

When he finally managed to get there, he left the car outside the building and moved quickly towards it.

His lack of fitness and unhealthy lifestyle made him tire quickly, so he rushed inside, out of breath, only twenty minutes after the appointed time. His physical fitness was also exacerbated by the fact that the previous night, like most nights he had been out, had been heavily fuelled with alcohol.

Because of this, Matthiew's appearance, too, left much to be desired. A rumpled suit, a sweaty forehead and curly hair that was now spilling out of order towards all sides of the world.

A sizable belly peeking out slightly from under the once-white shirt by way of two buttons that were undone.

He looked more like a poor private detective/alcoholic than a serious real estate businessman.

He walked briskly up to the reception desk.

The receptionist, at the sight of him, lowered her gaze and made a face that said:

"I need to do something/anything on my desk right now."

Just then, she heard a loud:

"Excuse me!"

She had no other choice but to look at him with an elaborate smile.

"How can I help you, sir?" she asked.

"Which way, to the restaurant?" Matthiew replied while breathing deeply. The woman pointed the way with her hand, just as she had done with George.

Matthiew turned around without thanking her and, with a rush, went on his way.

The receptionist only shook her head disapprovingly.

After a moment, he got into the restaurant and almost collided with a woman in the doorway who was just coming out of there.

"Excuse me!" He called out behind him without turning around.

He stood at the entrance and scanned his surroundings for a familiar face. "There he is!" He caught sight of George, who was sitting in the company of some woman and smiling benevolently at her, sipping his juice. He could see George's mouth moving contentedly; he was apparently chatting with the woman and was in a good mood.

The woman was sitting with her back turned to the entrance.

This made it impossible for Matthiew to see her face, to determine whether he liked her or not.

This was typical behaviour for him. He always judged women by their appearance, first the body, then the face.

Although he himself was not a tasty morsel for the opposite sex, however, he assumed that it was the woman who had to please the man and that he should have the right to choose, not the other way around. With this attitude, he was a single man, but not by choice.

He ran his eyes slowly over the long brown hair of an unfamiliar woman. *She could be quite a good one.* He thought and bared his teeth in an unsavoury smile.

He corrected his suit and hair a little and moved to the table where they were sitting.

George spotted him emerging from among the people in the restaurant. More and more guests were coming into the room, and it had become quite crowded by this time.

Jesus Christ, Matthiew. George thought.

It was partly a reaction to his appearance and partly from the fact that he had managed to completely forget about him at some point.

Matthiew approached the table and held out his hand in greeting towards George, at the same time looking at the unfamiliar woman.

When she turned her eyes on him, she burst out laughing slightly, choking on the water she had just been drinking.

At the first moment, she almost spit it out on Matthiew, but she quickly lowered her head down to control the unpleasant reflex.

"I would like to introduce you to my partner..." George began formally. "...This is Matthiew...."

"Matthiew Braddock." He interjected and shook her hand.

"That's right," George added.

The woman reciprocated his gesture.

But when Matthiew tried to be gallant and kiss her hand, she quickly pulled it back, leaving him in an awkward position.

She's pretending to be difficult to get. That's the way I like it. He explained to himself in his mind and smiled mockingly.

His exuberant ego and his difficulty in interpreting reality often allowed him to live in a fantasy world.

"Sit down, Matthiew. Would you like a drink?" George tried to be polite. "I'll have a beer, please." He replied but clearly had no intention of getting up and going for his drink himself. He settled himself comfortably in a chair.

He followed the waitresses with his eyes for a moment as they paced back and forth through the crowded restaurant at lunchtime.

At the same time, he did not take his eyes off the unfamiliar woman, who was now sitting opposite him at the table, for more than a few seconds.

Which made her feel uncomfortable.

The discomfort, however, did not make her fear him in any respect. To her, he was just an orangutan that she could easily lock in a cage and feed, whenever she felt like it.

He posed no threat.

After a while, she also started looking at him curiously, but for completely different reasons than Matthiew looked at her.

He was wondering what colour her underwear was.

She, on the other hand, what he could be used for and how to use him.

Matthiew mistakenly perceived this prolonged eye contact as flirtation.

He decided that he had obviously caught her eye.

A momentary awkward silence fell.

Eventually, George felt uncomfortable during this exchange of glances between them.

So, he ordered to go to the bar for drinks.

After more than half an hour of talking to the woman alone, George became convinced that Matthiew was not able to force her to confess something George would not like.

He could safely leave them alone for a few minutes.

"Excuse me, but I don't think I heard your name." Said Matthiew.

"Because I didn't introduce myself to you." She replied sharply.

"Indeed, and so, what is your name?" He asked.

"You'll find out in due course." She sharply curbed his urges. "I'll insist. I suppose I should know how to address you." Matthiew continued.

"With all due respect, I'm here to meet George. I don't feel obliged to put my name forward to someone I don't know. Didn't George tell you who called him?" she replied, leaning boldly towards him.

The tense atmosphere was making itself felt to Matthiew. He was getting hot and slowly losing confidence.

He could already see that the person he was talking had a razor-sharp character.

It wasn't going to be as easy as he thought.

"He told me it was a woman called Noelle Kemp, but that would make you over 55 now."

"I understand. That's how you can address me..." She replied firmly. "...Nattaly."

Matthiew looked at her, confused.

He had completely forgotten how curious he was about her underwear just a moment ago.

"Excuse me, how old are you?" he kept on asking.

"How old do I look?" she replied.

"Twenty, I think."

"Close enough, and you are 45." She said, driving a devious look into him that said. Exactly as you think, you're not wrong, I know you.

"Yes, that's right, how do you know that?" he furrowed his brow perplexed.

"I know a lot, Mr Braddock." She summed up the conversation.

Thus causing his investigation into unravelling her identity to crumble like a house of cards.

Matthiew felt awkwardly embarrassed.

The unknown woman was, to say the least, several steps ahead of him.

She had obviously traced his biography, while he, didn't even know her name.

But she was not going to say anything more or, in any way, make his task easier.

Let him tire himself out. This could be fun. She thought, watching Matthiew almost brimming with curiosity.

She knew him, and that was enough. This acquaintance was to remain one-sided, at least for now.

They sat in silence for a while and measured each other's eyes as they waited for George with their drinks, observing their surroundings in the meantime.

However, Matthiew couldn't stand the tension any longer and once again tried to start a dialogue.

"Excuse me, ma'am..." He started; the woman immediately caught his eye. "...With all due respect, I need to know who is blackmailing my partner?" He asked firmly.

"Mr Braddock, I really don't know where you got the idea...?" she bounced the ball. "...But I would advise you not to speak on subjects you don't know anything about." She added and gave him a mocking wink.

Matthiew straightened up in his seat, indignant.

He felt the blood rush to his head and turned red in the face with anger.

The woman saw this, too and smiled at him dismissively.

At that moment, George returned.

He put a drink in front of everyone and hadn't even had time to sit down yet when Matthiew immediately spoke to him angrily.

He didn't want to wait a moment longer; he had to know immediately what was going on here.

"George...!" he started in a combative mood. "...Who is this woman!"

But George belittled his explosive tone.

He smiled communicatively at the woman, and she reciprocated his smile.

Which infuriated Matthiew even more.

"Why...?" George began calmly. "...Didn't you two have a chat while I was away?"

"NO!" he replied.

The woman sat in silence and watched the events unfold.

"Matthiew..." George was composed. "... This young lady is my daughter."

This answer did not calm a nervous Matthiew, who was not about to give up. "How can you be so sure? You've known her for less than an hour, and you've had time to do DNA tests in that time, dammit...?!" he thundered angrily. "...Don't be naive, you believe her because she told you so? After all, she could be anyone. You

218

don't know her. How do you know she's not a fraud!" he added while exhaling the last air from his lungs.

At this, he pointed his finger at the woman in an accusatory gesture.

"Matthiew, sometimes you can tell more from a face than a DNA test..." George commented. "...As soon as I saw her, I knew immediately that my blood flowed in her veins. She looks exactly like her mother, only, a younger version." He added, smiling at the woman, who looked him straight in the eye and continued to remain silent.

Matthiew was breathing hard, his nervousness never leaving him. "After all, she claims to be Noelle, you said yourself you knew her thirty years ago!" He attacked again.

"It's true, I said I met Noelle thirty years ago, but we parted before twenty, and this young lady, she's nineteen now..." George replied. :...You're good at maths. You can count it yourself now."

Matthiew looked at George and then at the woman, furious, but they completely ignored him.

They looked at each other, and with the naked eye, you could see there was a family bond between them.

Reunited after years, father and daughter.

Matthiew was confused and for a moment, it seemed to him that the ground beneath his feet was beginning to be collapsing.

Because, at the time, he couldn't imagine the impact that finding his daughter might make George have on the agency.

Nor whether it would affect him personally.

He was too upset to think rationally at the time.

This would have to be analysed later in a calm manner. He decided. "Alright..." He began in a composed voice. "...In that case, can I at least know the name of your daughter?" He turned to George.

He knew that, after the way she had brushed him off earlier, he had no chance of finding out from her.

That's why he tried with George.

"If she wants to, she'll tell you herself." George replied.

Matthiew looked at the woman with an expectant expression on his face.

"Just call me Nattaly."

After these words, he boiled with anger again.

15

Black magic.

'We must overcome our fear of the future. But we cannot fully overcome it, except together.'

Four years later,

12 September 2008, North Hill, home of Joanna and Kevin Richardson, 10.30 am.

Joanna was in her bedroom, getting ready for a meeting with Susan McKane.

Every Saturday, she would go at 12 pm for an hour-long therapy session to help her unload the negative emotions that had built up after a week of normal life.

She treated these meetings as a break from reality.

During them, she could allow herself to completely switch off her consciousness and lose herself in a world without concerns.

Susan was very good at what she did.

She was excellent at putting people into a state of undisturbed relaxation.

Joanna really enjoyed these therapy sessions.

She felt charged with new positive energy after them, which made her ready to face the week ahead.

There was nothing she was afraid to say to Susan.

She had been through several severe nervous breakdowns since her husband Richard was killed in Iraq in 2000.

However, she knew she had to be strong for their 14-year-old daughter Magda.

So, she took advantage of every available help for women in her situation that was offered.

She would then rummage around the marital bedroom that she and Richard had once shared.

She would select from the wardrobe some pretty dresses to go out in. Every now and then, she would avoid the large double bed that stood against the wall, almost in the middle of the room.

Joanna also kept a lot of joint photos and memorabilia there.

They stood everywhere.

On every shelf, vacant spaces, windowsills next to fresh flowers.

She loved flowers, as you could see by walking through her garden behind the house.

The sun was shining strongly that day, and when it came through the windows, it lit up the flowers, the pictures and the rest of the stuff nicely.

It really looked very positive.

Regarding her time spent at the house, Susan had advised Joanna to try not to surround herself with mementoes.

Because they can have a bad effect on her and can be negative and depressing rather than uplifting.

However, Joanna ignored her advice and was happy with her choice. She wanted to have souvenir photos reminding her of when her family was still together, happy.

Magda did not waste the nice weather; she had already been playing alone in the garden since the morning.

The girl loved playing football, which made her father very proud. He used to say to her that when she grew up, she would become a professional footballer.

Magda would then jump up and down joyfully excited.

Joanna was not particularly thrilled at the thought that her daughter would take up running after a ball as a real career in her life.

She was a realist.

That's why she preferred Magda to focus more on her studies than on kicking a ball.

But if it made her happy, she didn't mind.

As a form of entertainment, of course.

Joanna finally found for herself, a suitable dress.

She wore it, then went to the bathroom to put on her make-up.

When she had finished getting ready, she went down to the ground floor to call Magda there, who was continually running around the courtyard.

When she looked at her watch, it was 11:10 am.

"Sandra should be arriving in a moment." She stated.

Sandra Jones was a fifty-nine-year-old widow.

An African neighbour, she lived alone, in the house next door.

Her husband had died a few years ago, and her two grown-up sons, had left home long ago to start their own families.

Therefore, she was a rather lonely person, and it gave her pleasure to be able to, at least once a week, spend time with a comforting child.

She stayed with Magda every Saturday when Joanna left home. An elderly woman from the neighbourhood, she was very fond of Magda and was always happy to visit her.

Joanna walked up to the transparent sliding door on the garden side and opened it in one movement.

"Magda!"

The girl stopped running on the other side of the spacious courtyard and looked towards her mother.

"Come here." Joanna made a motion with her hand, beckoning the child towards her

Magda bent down to pick up her ball before moving towards her.

But her attention, was caught by something else that was on the ground at this point.

Without thinking long, the girl grabbed the strange-looking toy and then ran towards Joanna, who was waiting for her.

"Sandra's coming in a minute. I want you to be good to her. I should be back as usual at two." Joanna tenderly corrected the child's long and tangled hair.

Magda smiled happily. At the same time, she held out her hand to her, in which she held a small, funny-looking rag doll. "Mummy, look what I found!" she called out excitedly.

Joanna took a fleeting glance but could not now look more closely at the child's find.

Because the front doorbell had just rung.

The woman turned quickly and immediately set off to see who had come in.

Magda followed her, all the while holding the doll in her hand.

Joanna opened the door, Sandra stood in the threshold.

"Hello dear ladies..." Sandra greeted them kindly. "...I'm sorry I'm late, I got too chatty on the phone and lost track of time."

"It's alright, thank you for coming." Joanna replied with a smile. "And how is my pretty little flower today?" Sandra turned to Magda, who was standing a few steps behind her mother.

"Very well, thank you..." The girl said. "...And you, Sandra?"

Joanna rebuked her daughter with her eyes. She did not approve when Magda socialised too much.

She considered it inappropriate when a child addressed an older person by name.

"Sandra was almost sixty years old, and Magda should be spoken to with due respect, not as a peer." Joanna assumed.

Sandra, however, did not mind at all.

They had been calling each other by their first names since the first day Joanna asked her if she could watch Magda for a few hours.

They did so until now, whenever they stayed home alone, Joanna didn't even know it.

"I'll be going then..." Joanna said. "...Have fun. I'll be back around two o'clock," she added as she left the house.

As Joanna closed the door behind her, Sandra looked at Magda and noticed that the child was holding something in her hand.

"And what do you have there, dear?" She asked.

"I found it in the garden," Magda replied and showed a doll.

Sandra took it in her hand and was stunned; she knew exactly what it was.

She also knew that nothing good could come of it.

In the woman's mind, memories of when she was fifteen came flooding back.

That was when her family had their first experience with black magic. The doll she now held in her hand was shaped like a woman in a dress and a headscarf.

She could have represented both an adult and a young person's form.

It did not have a face.

It was made of cotton strings tangled together.

Sandra had seen dolls like this before, and as a result, she immediately felt a sense of dread begin to grip her.

The last time she had looked at one of them, not long after, a person close to her had lost their life.

And all those horrible memories just came back to her from the depths of a past she hoped never to look into again.

Sandra stood motionless for a moment, staring at the doll.

Magda was in front of her, waiting for the return of her new toy.

"Honey, where did you get this?" She finally asked Magda.

"I already told you; I found it in the garden."

"Dear, I'm very sorry, but you can't keep it."

Magda made an exasperated face.

She clasped her hands together on her stomach and looked at Sandra with anger in her eyes. "But why can't I?"

"Darling you won't understand. These dolls are bad, very bad." Sandra tried to explain.

"I like it!"

"Darling, it's not about that. They bring bad luck on people. You don't want something bad to happen to you or your mum, do you?"

The child was silent on this last sentence from the sitter, but she was not convinced by it.

Sandra did not expect the girl to be able to understand what she meant.

To her, it was simply a rag doll.

What could be so bad about a toy?

But Sandra tried to protect the house because she was convinced that whoever had tossed the doll into her garden could not have good intentions.

"This is how it starts, first the Voodoo dolls, then the blood on the porch and the remains of dead animals, and finally, it will come to a real tragedy." She spoke to herself in her mind.

She alternated between looking at the doll and looking at Magda.

"Whoever this person is, I only hope it ends there." She concluded. "Alright now..." Sandra said after a while. "...Or are you hungry? Shall we go make pancakes?" she added, cleverly changing the subject. Magda loved pancakes, so this was the best way to distract her from her doll.

The girl immediately became animated.

The grimace disappeared, and in its place, there was now a wide, satisfied smile.

Magda looked at Sandra with greedy, sparkling eyes.

"Yes...!" she replied without hesitation. "...Let's go!"

She added and moved towards the kitchen, leaving Sandra behind. At that point, the woman took advantage of the child's moment of inattention and quickly hid the doll in her carry-on bag, hoping that the girl would forget about it in time.

At first, she wanted to throw it away immediately.

But she decided that she absolutely had to show her find to Joanna and have a serious conversation with her about all the dangers it might entail.

So, she left her bag with the doll inside in the front room.

She then followed Magda into the kitchen, where Magda was already taking the necessary products out of the fridge to get down to frying the pancakes as quickly as possible.

01:07pm, Joanna left Susan McKane's office, a few minutes after one o'clock.

She was feeling great.

Because of the early hour, she decided she would go to the café and have some more coffee.

She knew Magda was in good hands, so she was in no hurry to go straight home.

Sandra, too, had always told her to make good use of her time away from home as long as she wanted.

She never minded when Joanna returned later than announced.

So, she went quietly to the "Café Orbi" where she ordered a large latte. Afterwards, she sat down comfortably on one of the large leather armchairs.

To sip her coffee and, incidentally, catch up on a few pages from the book she had just been reading during her breaks.

When she had finished, she only had to stop at one grocery shop on her way home.

Less than fifteen minutes later, she was leaving the supermarket with her purchases.

Once she was sure she had bought everything she needed to cook dinner that evening, she decided she could go home.

She arrived home twenty minutes after two.

As she pulled into her driveway in front of the house, Sandra heard her car and looked out of the window.

After making sure it was Joanna, she told Magda to go play in her room.

She wanted to talk to Joanna in peace, alone.

Joanna entered the house and, already on the threshold, announced that she was back.

"I'm back!" she called out, at the same time leaving her belongings in the front room.

She picked up her shopping bags and headed for the kitchen to unpack them.

Sandra moved towards her; they met in the hallway.

"Oh, here you are, Sandra…" She said on seeing her. "...And where is Magda?" "She's playing in her room..." Sandra replied and added. "...Wait a minute, I must show you something."

She said, after which she went to get her bag.

When she came back, she was holding a rag doll in her hand.

"Will you stay for dinner? I'll cook spaghetti." Joanna suggested. "I'd love to…" she replied. "... But first, I'd like to have a serious talk with you.

Joanna stood still, stopped pulling products out of her bag and looked at Sandra, intrigued.

"Did something happen?" she asked.

"Yes, but not yet," Sandra replied, somewhat unclearly.

"I don't understand, is it about Magda? Has she done something wrong?"

"She didn't do anything, it's about something else." Sandra said.

She was still wondering what the best way would be to explain the subject to Joanna.

She held the doll in her hand the whole time, but low enough that Joanna couldn't see it.

"Okay, so now, officially, I do not understand anything." Said a confused Joanna, half-jokingly and half seriously.

"Let's go sit down in the living room. I'll tell you everything in a moment. "Sure, I'm coming, I'm just going to make myself another coffee. I have a feeling I'm going to need it..." Joanna agreed. "...Would you like a drink too?" Please. "Answered Sandra and went to the living room to wait for her friend there.

She put the doll on the table and sat down on the sofa, intertwined the fingers of her hands on her stomach, waiting for Joanna.

She wondered how to begin talking about her experiences with black magic.

Whether to get straight to the point or try to convince her first that such things really exist.

Some people believe in such phenomena, while others, categorically deny them.

Sandra wasn't quite sure in which category to place Joanna, in this respect. After a while, Joanna came into the living room, holding two cups of coffee in her hands.

She placed them on the table, at the same time, her attention was drawn to the doll lying there, over which she quickly ran her eyes.

She sat down next to Sandra and asked immediately:

"Isn't that something Magda showed me this morning? Before I left the house?"

"Yes, that's what I want to talk to you about." Sandra replied seriously. Actually, what is there to debate...? Joan smiled. " ...Just some abandoned old doll."

"It's not what you think..." replied Sandra. "...This doll was not abandoned or lost, by anyone, by accident. Joanna sipped her coffee, looking at it curiously.

At the same time, she tried to search her mind for reasons why Sandra would want to talk to her seriously about children's toys.

The only thing that came to her mind was that it must be something serious.

Because Sandra wouldn't bother her, with trivialities.

She also noticed that her neighbour looked very concerned and worried. – "Now listen to me carefully..." Sandra began firmly. "...This is a Voodoo doll, they represent black magic, if Magda found it in the garden, it means that someone dropped it there, so that, she would find it..." She pointed her finger at the doll.

Joanna just stared at her friend in silence, she didn't know what she was getting at yet.

So, she continued to listen patiently.

"…Whoever left it there, knew that Magda would find it, which means they must also know that the little one likes to run after the ball in the garden, it follows that they know you both very well. - Sandra continued. "Well..." She was interrupted by Joanna. "...But what exactly is all this supposed to mean?"

"I don't quite know yet, darling, what it could mean, I can only hope it doesn't mean anything... - Sandra replied. "...Because, you see, these dolls, they are created to bring misfortune on people, to cast curses and do evil, in general, it's a very disturbing omen, as you can see, this one here, looks like a woman or a young girl..." Sandra said. "…She could be, equally well, made to look like you or Magda."

"You're beginning to frighten me." Joanna interjected suddenly.

"Believe me darling, I felt terrified myself, as soon as I saw what Magda was playing with…" She replied. "…I took it away from her immediately, but she, she wants it back."

"Are you sure it's a Voodoo doll? Maybe it just looks like one?" Joanna tried to find another explanation.

"Joanna, let me tell you something…" the woman sipped her coffee, collecting her thoughts. "…Do you know that I originally come from Congo, from Africa?" of course I know.

"Okay, so, when I was ten years old and I was living with my parents, then my biological father, he abandoned me and my mother, he left for another woman…" She recounted. "…My mother, she went through a lot and for a long time after that, she couldn't recover, but, when I turned fifteen, she met another man, named Bob…" Sandra spoke and Joanna listened to her with curiosity. "…Bob was a good and honest man, he cared a lot about her and me, and we were eternally grateful to him, not only because he helped us the best he could to cope with our everyday difficulties, so that we wouldn't end up in poverty, but also because, in a way, he saved my mother and it was thanks to him, that we had the strength to put our lives together and just get on with life…" Sandra was visibly moved. "…We loved him with all our hearts for that…." She added with tears in her eyes and took a short pause, to calm her emotions. "…Then, a few months later, my biological father turned up, things didn't work out in his life, and he wanted to come back to us, after five years, can you imagine…?" Asked rhetorically Joanne who just, shook her head negatively. "…Anyway, my mother categorically refused him and told him to get out of our house, my father was furious, he started a fight, he almost threw his fists at her, I had to intervene so that he wouldn't hurt her, he was convinced that he had the right to demand whatever he wanted from us, that we were his property, in the end, he threatened my mother and Bob who had just come home, my father then said that he would kill him…" again, she took a break to drink her coffee. …A few days after this incident, I found on the veranda in front of the house, two such puppets..." she pointed with her finger to the doll. "...They looked like a man and a woman, but when I showed them to Bob, he didn't care about them at all, but my mother, she ordered me to burn them immediately, she knew what they meant..." She told me excitedly; Joanna could see how much she was going through it. "... But, by some strange coincidence, one of the puppets, the one that looked like a man, got lost somewhere, I left it for a while, but then I couldn't find it anywhere, as if it had sunk into the ground, I thought someone must have taken it, there was no other explanation, so I only burned the one I had, which was a woman, a few days passed, then again I found evidence on the porch that someone was trying to use black Voodoo magic against my family, unfortunately, only now I know for sure, I went out of the house and saw something tied to a support beam that looked like a bird's nest, only much bigger and inside were the remains of a dead raven and blood, lots of blood..." She took another pause. "...I was terribly frightened then; I didn't know why someone was doing such horrors to us? My mother was also very angry, only Bob seemed to downplay the situation, after a short time, in the house, strange things started to happen: the bulb in the bedside lamp would turn on and off, of its own accord, even when it was not plugged in, sometimes during sunny days, water would trickle down from the ceiling in places where there was no pipe, and where it shouldn't have been, in my bedroom, out of nowhere, flocks of black flies would appear and then disappear suddenly, even when the windows were closed, there was no logical explanation for this, how could they get in? On the veranda we found hundreds, if not thousands, of thin little worms..." She took in a breath. "...Honestly, they were everywhere, thousands of them, as far as the eye could see, once swept up or splashed with water, the next day, they were there again! And so it went, for several days in a row! Then, one day, it all ended, just as suddenly as it had started, my mum and I thought it was the end of the nightmare, a short time later we found out that Bob was missing, three days had passed and no one had seen him or, had no idea where he might be, then days, weeks and months passed, Bob was gone, I saw something die in my mum at that time, never again after that, could she be happy. - She concluded with sadness in her voice Sandra.

"My god Sandra, I am so sorry. Did your mum, at least, ever find out what happened to him?"

"No, but I knew he was dead. Bob would never leave us like that without an explanation, I don't know how, or what happened to him, I just knew he died, can't explain it..." She replied. "...Of course I didn't tell my mum, although now sometimes I think I should have done, but there was no evidence of that, and she, for the rest of her days, had to live with that burden and never found out where he went and what, really, happened back then.

"It's a very sad story. It's awful that these things happen." Joan said quietly. "Joanna, I want you to understand. I'm not telling you this to make you feel sorry for me. I'm just trying to warn you..." Sandra declared, overcoming her despondency. "...Although I still hope I'm wrong, and it's nothing, but you must know how serious this can be. Black magic is really dangerous and there's no room for jokes.

"I understand. Thank you for telling me." Joanna replied.

Sandra did not react to her words. Instead, she pointed her finger at the doll lying on the table in front of them.

"That's where it starts..." she declared. "...You must absolutely, immediately get rid of it, preferably burn it in the garden."

"Okay, that's what I'll do." Joanna agreed.

Sandra smiled at her expression of gratitude.

The caregiver carelessly wanted to pick up her coffee cup from the table, but she did it so awkwardly that it slipped out of her hand, dousing her skirt with the already cold liquid.

"Oh!!!" Sandra sprang to her feet.

Joanna immediately grabbed her handbag, which was lying next to her, pulled out tissues from it and started to wipe Sandra's skirt.

"Sorry, clumsy of me, at least it's a good thing it's cooled down now..." Sandra said. "...All I need is a burn." She added, already with a slight smile. "Why don't you go and change? I, in the meantime, will start preparing dinner."

"Yes, I think that's a good idea." The sitter replied, then slowly moved towards the front door.

Before she stepped outside, she still turned her face to Joanna and said: - Hide this doll from Magda, under no circumstances, do not let her play with it.

After these words, Joanna reflexively looked in the direction of the stairs to make sure the girl wasn`t somewhere nearby.

Once positive that she was still in her room, she nodded her head in agreement.

Sandra left, closing the door behind her. She stood on the threshold and leaned against it for a moment.

She needed to take a few deep breaths to calm herself before moving on.

At the same time, Joanna was very concerned about what Sandra had told her.

She felt sorry for her friend.

But most of all, her mum, who had lost a loved one in such strange circumstances.

To make matters worse, she never found out what had happened to him at the time.

Poor woman. She thought.

Joanna quickly set the dirty cups down in the kitchen sink, grabbed a cloth, then returned to the living room.

It only took her a few seconds.

A feeling of despondency accompanied her, but she decided she had to do something.

She walked over to the sofa and coffee table to see where she needed to wipe the traces of spilt coffee from the floor.

Focusing all her attention on this.

She stood next to the sofa, and at first, her mind did not register the appearance of the table in the restroom.

However, when she wanted to pick up the doll, which in her mind had been lying in the same place the whole time.

With the intention of hiding it so that, later, she could deal with it.

She stretched her hand in that direction and froze in stillness.

The doll was no longer there.

A cold shiver ran through the woman's entire body.

Joanna began to look frantically around her, gradually panicking.

She picked up a few cushions from the sofa, hoping that by some miracle it was somewhere there, wedged into the sofa.

She found nothing, however.

Then she crouched down, checked the floor carefully, piece by piece.

And nothing, it had disappeared.

A doll, dissolved into thin air.

But how the hell could that be? She was here just two minutes ago... She thought in confusion. *...Or maybe, Magda?!*

"Magda!" She shouted towards the stairs.

"Yes mum!?" The little girl spoke up.

Her voice came from the room upstairs.

16

My privet investigation.

'To be a man of conscience means to demand of oneself, to rise from one's own failings and to be converted again and again.'

Ten years later,

15 December 2018, Camberwell Green, London, Danny and Rachel Davis's flat, 02:30pm,

Rachel took a long time to convince me to start therapy sessions. She was worried about my behaviour and was convinced I was suffering from post-traumatic stress disorder.

In truth, I had thought all along that I could cope on my own, but I decided to step down for the sake of sanity.

At this stage, I didn't yet see a problem with alcohol, which was, however, growing quite rapidly.

I preferred to focus on my psyche.

I limited myself at that time to having only a couple of drinks in the evening, and I also tried not to start early in the afternoon.

Which, unfortunately, still happened to me sometimes.

A week ago, I had my first appointment with a psychologist.

At that time, I talked about my nightmares and the constant feeling that someone was watching me, even when I was completely alone.

I didn't need a psychologist to draw the conclusions that came to me on my own.

As for the nightmares, I interpreted them as evidence of guilt and a nagging conscience.

Because I could not save Denise from a tragic death.

In truth, I still could not understand the origin of the feeling of unease that haunted me almost all the time.

As for this, I had no logical explanation.

My new psychologist, at my first meeting, was also unable to answer why the feeling that I was sensing someone's presence did not leave me. When I asked him about it, I noticed how he got a little confused while searching in his head for a sensible explanation, which absolutely did not prevent him from stating that it was undoubtedly post-traumatic stress disorder.

In the end, the issue had to be left for another conversation, as the session time had just ended.

I wasn't really counting on him unexpectedly dazzling me with his knowledge of the subject at one of the meetings and saying something that could explain the whole phenomenon.

But it was worth a try, at least to go for a visit once a week.

In a way, it was also a good reason to leave the house for a more specific purpose than just, to go to the shop for a bottle of vodka.

Given that this was only the first such meeting, I had even yet to mention the shifting objects and my "Mini" phone ringing off the hook for no reason. I thought I would leave that for future meetings. I didn't want to end up in a mental hospital on the very first day.

As a police officer injured in the line of duty (now apparently, also with post-traumatic stress disorder), I could have benefited from government support in the form of free treatment at a centre for police officers with similar injuries to mine.

It was a closed centre, somewhere outside London.

I had been offered to stay there before, but the problem was that I would have to live there for several months.

I didn't want to leave Rachel alone.

Plus, I wouldn't have as much freedom as I do now, but it wasn't about alcohol, which I didn't want to give up yet, either.

The main reason was my private investigation into the missing four from North Hill.

Which I had been conducting on a freelance basis for most of my time. At the centre, I would not have had access to any information about it.

In fact, as far as specific files or data from the case were concerned, I didn't have access to them now either.

As I was a temporarily suspended police officer, I could not even apply for such.

So, I relied on what I could find out from articles on the Internet.

But in such a place, I would undoubtedly not have been able to do that.

At the time, it was the only activity for me that made me feel muted. It was the only time I was deprived of the feeling that someone's eyes were watching me.

Something made me not want, for anything in the world, to walk away from this.

I knew it was something I should do, and I absolutely had to continue doing it.

At the time, I felt that it was still too early to talk to Connor about it and possibly ask him for help.

I preferred to save that option for later, as I knew the day would come, when I would need his help.

Connor, as a police officer on active duty, could check for me, one way or another, for information.

Or even if there was a possibility of contacting North Hill Police Station to get more of the data he could gather from them.

I didn't want to do that yet because I realised how complicated it would be. Firstly, I had been on sick leave the whole time, and secondly, Connor knew that my health was not at its best.

I expected him to try to convince me to let it go, rather than putting his hand in the deterioration of my current condition.

The next problem was that criminal investigators were not allowed to share information with anyone.

Not even with other officers, without first presenting the appropriate authorisation.

Everything had to be considered by superiors before a decision could be made on whether such authorisation should be given.

Connor, therefore, would have to go directly to the commandant with this and have very good reasons for doing so.

Which were simply not there at the time.

All this made it impossible for me to get any closer to the case, at least by a little.

In fact, I had no new or unknown information on the subject.

Consequently, no reason to go any further with it.

I was wandering in the dark.

Relying on descriptions from newspapers and articles that everyone already knew.

Far too little, of course, to gather concrete clues that could help North Hill police find the missing four.

But I knew that the law enforcement agencies there would not have disdained any help with their situation.

When I heard while watching TV with Connor that a hefty cash reward had been set for providing information, I immediately thought of the hopeless position they must be in.

Journalists did not spare criticism of the local police.

Every article, in at least a few words, described the helplessness of the police.

The case was further complicated by the fact that there were only a handful of CCTV cameras in the town, which were only in the town centre and along the main highway.

In contrast, there were no devices to record activity in the vicinity of private properties.

Therefore, it was possible to forget about capturing the image of anyone who might have had anything to do with the events.

Admittedly, two people were arrested, as it soon turned out, wrongly suspected, in 2008.

Ain and Angelina Hailu coming from Ethiopia.

However, the lack of evidence was unequivocal, and the couple were released immediately after questioning.

It was the first and the last arrest the police made in the case.

Years went by and more people went missing, and the police held up their arms in frustration.

When, probably for the hundredth time, I looked up the same articles on the Internet, I felt sleepy.

The headaches, which until recently had come out of nowhere and knocked me off my feet, were becoming less frequent.

The gunshot wound, too, was healing nicely and slowly began to disappear completely under the regrowing hair.

In short, I was recovering.

That afternoon, I felt ordinary, sleepy.

My eyes were tired already from staring at the laptop screen.

I decided to rest a bit and go for a nap.

I turned off the computer and pulled the monitor down.

I didn't want to lie on the couch, from which my back would ache later, so I opted for the bed.

I lay down, and before I closed my eyes, I checked the time on my watch some more. It was 15:10 pm.

I've got roughly 50 minutes before Rachel comes back, enough perfectly. I thought and squinted my eyes.

I must have fallen asleep instantly because I didn't even feel myself drifting off to dreamland once I was there.

Before I knew it, I was in that spooky forest again.

And just like always in this scenario, I was walking ahead in the darkness, surrounded by bushes.

I could see the trees and bushes bending and dancing in an invisible wind that I couldn't feel.

This time, I seemed to subconsciously know where I was going.

I didn't feel lost like in my previous dreams.

Perhaps this was due precisely to the fact that this was not the first such dream.

Either way, it brought me considerable relief.

Then, from a distance, I saw a wooden fishing shed.

It was something new. I had never seen it before.

Each of these dreams had the quality of always revealing something new. Like pieces of a jigsaw puzzle, no doubt they had to eventually come together.

I was convinced of this.

The fishing shed, I felt, was where I was heading.

Or at least, I was supposed to be heading that way.

Suddenly, I heard, mu led by the wind, the laughter of children.

I had the impression that it was coming from everywhere. From the depths of the forest, the ever-present bushes, the air and generally the whole area I was in.

Some were louder and others quieter and alternated.

Although I couldn't see anyone, something became obvious to me then, they were surrounding me.

I came to a shed that only a moment ago seemed at least a hundred metres away, but now I was standing at arm's length from it.

I stopped and looked at a sizable empty area among the trees.

It was then that I noticed black, almost transparent figures.

They were moving quite fast back and forth.

They were blurry, and I could not see any faces or even specific body figures.

Shadows they were flying above the ground, and I realised that it was their laughter that I heard.

I was snapped out of my reverie by the desperate scream of a girl coming from somewhere deep in the forest.

"HELP!!!"

I looked in that direction, frightened.

"Denise!?" automatically, that name came to my mind.

I felt my heart start pounding like a hammer, and adrenaline hit my head.

At that moment, the figures stopped.

Each in a place where they happened to be.

Their laughter turned into a whisper, which I heard right next to my ears:

"HEEEEEELP, HEEEEELP…"

After that, I dashed, running ahead.

Of course, as in every dream, running is impossible.

Therefore, I had not even covered a few metres when I fell into a pit in the ground.

The pit, imagined in my mind, also appeared out of nowhere.

However, it was supposed to look like it had been there all this time, only that I did not see it.

I landed face down and then quickly flipped onto my back to stand up. When I looked up, I saw debris falling on me, and at that moment, I felt I couldn't move.

The earth, created in my dream, was so heavy that it immobilised me completely.

I tried to scream, terrified.

But I couldn't make a sound.

In this nightmare, sand was getting into my throat, making me start to choke.

My subconscious was telling me that it was the end.

"My grave!!" I shouted in my sleep at full throat and straightened up on the bed at the same time.

I propped myself up with my elbows, droplets of sweat running down my forehead.

Catching my breath greedily, I looked towards the door where Rachel was standing.

She was watching me with tears in her eyes.

It's past four o'clock I thought.

17

Magda Richardson.

'A human being must be measured by the measure of the heart'.

Ten years earlier,

04 November 2008, North Hill, Susan McKane's office, 11:50am.

Susan arrived at her office and was waiting for Joanna Richardson. Traditionally, as every Saturday, she was her first client of the day's appointment and should arrive at 12 pm. The last few days Joanna had been very cranky.

On her last visit, the week before, she had mentioned a strange doll that her daughter, Magda, was supposed to have found in the garden.

She also mentioned a terrible story that had happened to the child's carer, Sandra.

She briefly recounted the events she had heard, claiming that it was alleged proof of the existence of black magic or of Voodoo.

As well as the supernatural forces contained in the cursed dolls, which are supposed to represent the charm cast.

That is, the very same one that had appeared in her house.

Joanna felt greatly disturbed by the situation and could not be at peace about it.

Especially since the doll, according to her story, had disappeared from the table where she had left it.

Initially, she suspected Magda of taking the grim toy.

Because she expected that she might have heard her say that she was going to burn it.

However, during the confrontation, the girl denied everything.

She firmly claimed that she did not leave her room during the time Joanna was in the living room with her guardian, Sandra.

Either way, the doll was missing, and Joanna was, very concerned about this fact.

Susan tried to find a way to relieve the woman of her worries.

But she couldn't get through to her, as she was still distressed.

Susan's attempts to put her into a meditative state of relaxation, were also unsuccessful.

Joanna thoughts were elsewhere.

Susan, too, had not yet returned to her form since the birth of her daughter Nicole Denice.

She tried to behave professionally, but the situation at home, was taking its toll on her professional work and affecting her negatively.

Which, in turn, translated into her work and clients.

In addition, her husband John's illness was rapidly draining his strength.

Little by little, Susan had to help him more and more with everything. And at the same time, practically on her own, taking care of the then almost two-month-old Nicole Denice, running the house and going to work. At times, she even felt like she was looking after two children and not, just one.

Just a few weeks after giving birth, she felt it starting to overwhelm her. For this reason, she decided to return to the practice and her patients just a month later.

She was much more comfortable away from home.

She also thought that when she took care of other people, then her own problems would stop weighing so heavily on her, at least for a while. It was a strategy that initially worked well, although it did not have the right to last forever.

John McKane was still able to cope with Nicole Denice.

He was able to stay home alone with her for a few hours once a week.

This was also the assumption Susan was making.

John was in the habit of putting the infant next to him and playing the piano for her.

The new father quickly realised that the sound of the piano keys had a calming effect on the baby girl. John was overjoyed at this fact.

When he played for her, the child would fall peacefully asleep, but she would wake up just as quickly when he stopped.

This unusual behaviour of the girls was the reason for many happy and funny moments in his life.

John relished every second of them.

He wished that every moment spent with his daughter could last forever.

Because he knew very well that there were not many of them left.

That is why he loved to play the piano for her and watch her sleep sweetly. It was his favourite pastime.

When he was no longer able to drive to work, he had to entrust the supervision of the company to a manager he had hired specifically for this purpose.

From then on, he stayed at home, all day.

Susan finally managed to convince him to undergo chemotherapy, which was due to start in a few days, at their home.

John knew that chemotherapy would only prolong his time in this world but not significantly, but for the sake of his daughter, he decided to give it a try. Given a choice, hospital or an expensive home fit-out to suit his needs, he chose the second option.

Money didn't make much of a difference to him anymore, especially since he was only doing it because he wanted to stay longer with his child. This would defeat the purpose if he had to spend that time in hospital.

Susan decided, not to think about her family at least, for the next hour. Joanna was due to arrive in a moment, and she wanted to set herself up, for this session professionally.

Her goal for this afternoon was to reach her client's subconscious.

That is, what had not been accomplished the week before.

Joanna needed her help, perhaps even more than ever before. And Susan was aware of this.

She sat in front of her desk and stared at the computer screen. She furrowed her brow as she looked at her watch; it was past twelve o'clock.

"Strange, she had never been late before..." She said to herself in thought. "...I wonder what could be the reason, traffic jams or maybe the situation at home? She considered the reasons for Joanna's lateness.

For the time being, she decided that she would wait another five minutes, after which she would try to call her.

At that moment, a knock sounded at the door.

"Please come in!" Susan called out.

Joanna entered the office, slightly out of breath.

"Sorry I'm late." She said on the doorstep and started to pull on her coat. "It's alright. I'm glad you're here already Joanna..." Susan replied. "...I was starting to get a bit worried, just a moment more and I wanted to call you."

"I've had a bit of a headache these last few days, Susan." A visibly shaken Joanna replied.

"Please sit down." Susan pointed to her couch.

Joanna walked over to it but did not lie down comfortably as she always did.

Instead, she sat down opposite Susan and tried to even out her breathing.

"What's going on?" asked a concerned Susan.

"Do you remember me telling you about that doll a week ago?"

"Of course I remember." Susan replied.

"So, after we last met on Saturday, late one evening I found it, in Magda's room...." Joanna was still breathing fast, so she took short pauses. "...I was cleaning her room while Magda was eating dinner, I found the doll in the wardrobe. I was furious because it made lie to Sandra..." She explained. "...I felt terribly stupid, Sandra confided in me, she told me about her life to help me, and I had to lie to her when she asked what I did with the nasty thing..." When she said this, she meant the doll. "...I shouted at Magda, and she cried, then I felt bad about it, after all, she's just a child and doesn't understand such things..." Joanna needed to get rid of her accumulated emotions. "...To be honest, I can't really understand it all myself, black magic, Voodoo dolls and the like I can't imagine." She paused for a moment, but Susan knew this was not the end of the story. She stared at Joanna and waited for her to continue.

"Tell me, now that you know where the doll is, does it make you feel, at least partially, back to normal? Absolutely not!" she raised her voice.

Susan understood perfectly well that she was cranky, which often happened to her clients.

Outbursts of anger came with the job it was nothing personal, so Susan let the little incident go.

"I'm sorry..." Joanna corrected herself. "...I didn't mean to shout." She added with humility in her voice.

"Nothing happened..." said Susan calmly. "...Please tell me, what thoughts are going through your mind right now. I want to understand what emotional state you are in now."

"I don't know what's happening to me. I can't put it into words. It's as if, subconsciously, I know that something terrible is about to happen, something I can't do anything about. At times, I feel a sense of dread that quickly turns into an overwhelming panic."

Susan listened carefully, at the same time, reading her body language and facial expressions.

At one point, she noticed that the woman was still not telling her something and whatever it was, it was tormenting Joanna acutely.

"Joanna, but there's something else, isn't there...?" Susan began. "...Remember, please, you can tell me anything. This is your safe space, and you know very well that nothing you say will leave this office. Be honest with me because I can see from looking at you that it's not just about Magda and that doll. What are you really afraid of and don't want to reveal?"

252

Joanna looked at her perplexed, then lowered a confused gaze. She could see she was beating herself up with her own thoughts to say nothing.

However, she had to confide in someone eventually.

And who better person to do that than her private psychologist? "Yes, you're right, there is something else..." she began slowly and uncertainly. "...I couldn't tell Sandra this. I was afraid of her reaction, and I didn't want her to blame me for letting it happen because, from her story, it seems that the same thing happened at her home when she was still very young. Now, she is an older woman, and I wasn't sure how she would react. I didn't want to worry her unnecessarily because it could be just a coincidence..." she went on. "...Well, on Monday, I found in front of the entrance to the house a dead crow." She took in a breath again.

Susan noticed how her hands were shaking.

She is on the verge of despair. thought psychologist.

"I don't know if there's a connection...?" Joanna continued. ...*Maybe it's just a coincidence? Sandra was talking about how she found a nest on the veranda of her house, inside there were the remains of a raven and blood. I don't know if it's the same thing, maybe this crow died of old age in front of my house, maybe nobody dropped it off there, I don't know, I can't say for sure.* She wondered frantically.

Susan decided that she had to try to calm her down, so she advised her to lie down along the couch. Joanna did as she was asked.

"Close your eyes..." She began to say, in Susan's reassuring tone. "...Take a deep breath in, and now, exhale."

She spoke quietly to her, the psychologist's voice having a relaxing effect on her.

Susan's voice was warm and friendly.

Accompanied by sounds recorded in the rainforest, it perfectly formed a single unit, which always made it possible for Joanna to quietly switch off her consciousness and let herself enter a relaxing trance.

This time, however, this technique did not work.

Joanna was unable to control her inner emotions, as she had done during every previous encounter.

The mysterious situation at home tormented her too much, and she could not get rid of the premonition that something bad was about to happen. No matter how much she wanted to accept that nothing was going on and that, everything was going to be just fine.

In this situation, there was nothing Susan could do.

Joanna's intuition told her that a great misfortune was coming.

The woman was sure of it.

Especially as she remembered when the same feeling had gripped her on the day her husband, Kevin Richardson, died.

At the time, she knew he had passed away before she had even received information from the British Army regarding his death in Iraq eight years ago.

That day, a feeling of dread overwhelmed her at one point in time. And a day later, she received a call from his superiors with the news that Kevin had died.

Now she felt almost identical, lying safely on the couch in Susan's office, listening to her voice.

It couldn't help, not in this situation.

You can't push instinct out of your mind, or even try to silence it.

Susan stared into Joanna's closed eyelids.

She could see her eyes moving rapidly underneath, back and forth. She spoke to her, tried to put her into a trance, but couldn't.

When fifteen minutes remained until the session ended.

Susan heard the vibration of Joanna's phone, coming from her handbag, which she hung on a hanger next to her coat.

The phone rang again and again, without pause.

It stopped for a few seconds, then started again.

As always, Joanna muted it completely before the meeting so as not to disturb the quiet.

Susan looked at her handbag and thought someone was desperately trying to contact her now.

Then she hung her gaze on Joanna again, the woman not yet aware of anything.

The phone stopped vibrating.

This meant that the person on the other end had given up after yet another unsuccessful attempt.

Not three minutes had passed when Susan heard a knock on her door.

Before she had time to react, it swung open, and then into the office popped the receptionist's head.

Susan cast an angry glance in her direction.

"I'm sorry to disturb you..." The woman began shyly. "...There's a phone call for Mrs Joanna Richardson. A woman called Sandra says she needs to speak to her immediately." She explained.

Joanna, as soon as she heard the name of Magda's carer, instantly leapt up from the couch.

She then quickly stood up and walked over to her handbag to pull out her phone.

She switched it on, then ten missed calls appeared to her eyes.

They were all from Sandra.

Her heartbeat instantly sped up, and a cold shiver ran through her body. Without thinking, she pressed the "connect" button and waited, with her heart in her throat, for Sandra to answer the phone.

"Hallo! Sandra! What in God's name has happened!?" She shouted into the receiver as soon as she heard the sitter's voice.

For the next few seconds, she stood rigidly motionless, emotionless, holding the phone to her ear, listening to the Sandra's words.

Her face had turned completely pale and petrified, resembling a statue in this position with her mouth slightly open.

She stared mindlessly out of the window, paralysed by shock, as Sandra shouted something into the receiver.

The babysitter was speaking quickly and loudly, making the room audible with choppy words taken out of context.

Clearly, the matter was serious which made for a tense atmosphere in Susan's office.

Joanna stood with the phone to her ear while Susan and the receptionist waited impatiently and anxiously for her to finish.

Ready to rush to her aid if necessary.

It wasn't quite clear yet what had happened, but whatever it was, it couldn't bode well.

An ominous atmosphere, one could almost sense, hovering in the air. Susan continued to sit in her seat, as before, watching Joanna with a look of consternation on her face.

The receptionist was also stunned by the situation, and instead of leaving, she continued to stand in the doorway, intrigued by the incident.

Not a minute passed.

Then Joanna rolled her eyeballs in such a way that they showed only their white side for a moment.

She lost consciousness and slumped inertly to the floor.

"Mother of God!!" screamed the terrified receptionist.

Then, she quickly knelt beside her, at the same time lifting her head gently upwards.

Susan also immediately rose from her seat and rushed to the woman.

"Call an ambulance immediately!" she ordered her colleague.

Susan took over Joanna's head, placed it on her lap and tried to revive the woman by cautiously but firmly, running her hand over her cheeks. At that moment she heard someone else's voice coming from Joanna's phone, which was now lying next to her. So, she picked it up and put it to her ear.

"Hello, this is Susan McKane...!" she called out into the receiver. "...Please tell me what happened!"

"It's Magda! Magda has disappeared!" shouted a panicked Sandra.

18
Keep it in secret.

'Caring for the child is the first and fundamental test of a person's relationship with a human being.'

Three years earlier,

15 November 2005, Canary Wharf, London, agency office "Bradley and Brad Lettings", 02:20 pm.

It has been nine months since George Bradley met his biological daughter, whom he had no idea existed.

Since their first meeting, he had spoken to her on average once a week, on the phone.

George was happy to have met her.

In truth, he had never planned to have children, but she was already 19 and not a child but a grown woman.

George regretted a little that he had not had the chance to meet her earlier. However, he had no way of knowing that Noelle Kemp, whom he had split up with 20 years ago, was pregnant by him at the time.

These were also times when the woman was abusing drugs and alcohol, which made him decide to end the acquaintance.

Although George, in his time, also liked to party.

But Noelle had lost herself too much in the world of psychoactive substances, which quickly overcame the bitterness.

When after many attempts by George, during which he tried to break her out of her addiction and help her to start repairing her life, the day of separation came.

It was an extremely difficult time in his life, but no arguments were getting through to Noelle, and he had no other choice.

At some point, he simply ran out of strength to continue this toxic relationship.

He loved her but decided that he had to leave for his own good.

Now, he could look back on those years and reminisce about the days that were very close to his heart.

It was then that he remembered when he had made love to Noelle for the last time.

To his surprise, he already knew when his daughter had been conceived.

He had wondered many times over the years how Noelle was coping.

But he had no way of finding her at the time.

Now, George Bradley had a new purpose in life.

He had decided that he now needed to focus on taking care of his daughter. From his point of view, she was still a very young person, and he wanted to guide and support her as best he could, during this extremely difficult journey that we commonly call, life.

Even at the very beginning of their acquaintance, George was positively surprised to find that the girl, had no intention of greedily extracting money from him, just as Matthiew had suggested, which also made him feel that way, initially.

This became clear when she announced that she only wanted George to help her pay for her education, which was very expensive.

She could not afford to pay for the course she wanted to study.

George agreed without a second thought.

He then guaranteed her that he would pay for school, for as long as she needed it.

That remained the arrangement between them.

George sponsors her education, and she does not ask for more money.

Which also came out through her initiative.

In fact, George did not mind, from time to time, sending her some money on account.

However, she politely refused.

She did not want him to contact her first, letting him know that she herself would call him from time to time.

She was a very ambitious young person, which was very much like George's character, to the point that, at times, he felt like he was looking in a mirror. She reminded him of himself when he was that age.

So, she called once, sometimes twice a week, and they talked for hours.

Their conversations could stretch up to three hours.

George would reminisce to her about times spent together with her mother, and she, would tell him about her academic achievements.

The man was very proud of his daughter.

At the beginning of their reconciliation, however, he could not understand why she necessarily wanted to remain anonymous.

There were times when he wanted to introduce her informally to his friends, to boast about his beautiful and clever daughter.

But over time, he respected her request until it finally stopped bothering him.

The same could not be said for Matthiew, whose curiosity burned to know the girl's identity.

For some obvious reason, only to himself, he insisted that he had to know it.

But George ignored him.

He made no bones about the fact that he cared so much.

For weeks there was not a day, spent in the office, when he did not try to approach George so that he would talk it out.

This one, however, was unbending and resistant to his tricks.

Which annoyed and urged Matthiew even more to keep trying.

Many times, George had had enough of his games.

At the same time, he sincerely regretted that he had let himself be persuaded that day, to let Matthiew go with him to the Hilton Hotel, to meet a girl.

He realised after time how big a mistake he had made.

It couldn't be rectified anymore.

So, he had to put up with Matthiew's humours, which went from invoking camaraderie to invading his conscience to arguing, his reasons why it was necessary for him to know the name of George's daughter.

He went from calm conversations to outbursts of anger and vice versa.

George would then dispose of him with one sentence:

"Call her Nattaly."

Then Matthiew, usually gave way and walked away with a sullen face.

After which George, at last, had the peace he craved.

But one day Matthiew, decided to try a different tactic.

It was past 02:35 pm when he suddenly came into George's office and announced:

"We should open an office there."

"I beg your pardon." George tore his gaze away from the computer and looked at him, over his glasses.

"We should open an office in North Hill..." he explained. "...We need to have an outpost there; it would be a great investment."

George immediately guessed what was really on his mind.

Here we go, another gamble. He thought.

"Explain to me please, for what reasons, it seems like a great investment to you?" He bounced the ball without conviction.

"You can't be serious, as in for what reasons...!" Matthiew replied in disbelief. "...After all, you know yourself how many people are interested in property in this town!"

In his logic, this argument was going to explain everything. It was about business, which should have been the most obvious thing under the sun.

George shook his head.

He didn't even bother to comment on it, he slid his glasses up his nose and stared back at the computer screen.

Matthiew cast an angry glance at him in response, a sign of ignorance that George no longer saw for reasons he knew.

His partner, however, had no intention of giving up so easily.

"The idea, George..." He tried further. "...It's a beautiful city, people are interested in it, they want to live there, how can you not see it as an opportunity...?"

But for George, these were not convincing arguments.

He knew very well that everything Matthiew was coming up with now was baseless and only meant to serve his personal whims.

"...If we opened an office there you could give job to your daughter." He added.

George looked at him again, this time menacingly, in the face.

I knew he'd mention her sooner or later, it was only a matter of time. He thought.

"Matthiew..." George started to speak calmly. He didn't let his temper get the better of him. "...You are co-owner of this agency, but don't forget, I'm the one who has the final say here, and I'm not going to let you spend that much money to open an office just for the sake of your whim!"

Matthiew gave him an angry look.

He hated it when George reminded him who was the real boss. But there was nothing he could do about it; it was the reality of the situation, and he had to submit.

"What do you mean? After all, it's not about me. I just think we could make a lot of money out of it."

"That is for me to decide." George cut him short.

"You could also help your daughter that way, she'd get a job, start earning money on her own." He tried to go on.

"Matthiew, I've already told you..." George was getting more and more annoyed. "...Don't drag her into this! Espccially in your machinations! I don't know why you care so much about it and frankly, I don't care, not one bit! I forbid you, ever to mention her again, do you understand!"

George, once again, called his partner to order; for him, both the subject of North Hill and his daughter were over at this point.

Nor was he concerned that Matthiew would spread rumours among the "BnBL" staff, about him.

Because he knew that, basically, nobody really liked Matthiew at the agency. "Even if he wants to, set them against me, with nothing concrete to say, they will quickly get bored with his gossip and start ignoring it too." He was of the opinion.

"You know that, sooner or later, you will have to tell me what her name is." Matthiew did not give up.

"Her name is Nattaly."

"Her real name."

"I will tell you this for the last time and never again; do not come back to me with this subject..." George could barely control his nerves. "...Her name is Nattaly, after her mum, Noelle. In case you don't know, it's a variation of that name. If you want to be sure, check for yourself, and now goodbye, you're wasting my time!" Matthiew knew something wasn't right here.

He felt that this story was made up, and he was infuriated by the fact that George was not telling him the whole truth.

He was convinced that he was lying but was unable to prove anything. For some reason, it seemed highly unlikely to him that a mother would give her daughter a derivative of her name.

"I'm going to find out everything anyway..." He replied through his teeth, "...And this office will be opened, whether you like it or not."

"Over my dead body!"

Matthiew turned around and started walking towards the door.

"As you wish." He added in a half-hearted voice.

"Did you say something!"

"Goodbye!" Matthiew replied and closed the door behind him.

"What a cheeky bugger..." George said to himself once he was left alone. "...I dread to think what will happen if I am not here one day." He added worriedly in his mind.

George's fears were well-founded.

Matthiew was an unscrupulous person who would stop at nothing to achieve his goal.

On top of this, his nasty character deteriorated in parallel with his advancing age.

He dreamt of big money and, as time went on, he cared less and less about the means he would have to use to get there.

In truth, on paper, he was a wealthy man.

Because the shares in the "BnBL" agency he owned were worth almost two million pounds.

On top of that, he owned a three-bedroom flat in a good neighbourhood and two sports cars, both Mercedes.

But in his bank account, mostly, he only had a few hundred, at most. And the money quickly dissipated in nightclubs on alcohol, drugs and prostitutes.

Which meant he had to live from paycheck to paycheck like the average citizen.

He led an expensive lifestyle and wanted to have at his disposal an account with six-figure capital.

He was prepared to go to any lengths, which was about to become a reality soon, just to fulfil this dream.

19

We must help him.

'Happiness is achieved through sacrifice'.

Thirteen years later,

20 December 2018, Oxford Street, London, 01:10 pm.

On the day I went to my next psychologist appointment, Rachel made an appointment with Connor without my knowledge.

I then started attending appointments with another psychologist who had been specifically appointed for me by the Metropolitan Police HQ. The lady I had spoken to up to that point considered my case too complicated, beyond the limits of her competence.

After I recounted, in detail, my nightmares and feelings of relentless persecution, I was referred to a higher level of treatment. In those days, Rachel was becoming increasingly desperate. Unable to do anything about my behaviour, she was also looking for somewhere to seek advice on how to help me return to normality.

While I was in therapy, Rachel decided to take advantage of some free time and made an appointment with Connor at "Cafe Nero" in "Oxford Street". It was 01:10 pm, and I was usually home by 3 pm when nothing else stopped me in town.

This gave her a two-hour window in the day that she wanted to make the most of.

She chose to go there by bus.

Given that the famous London Street is not only known for its countless shops.

But also, the traffic jams and the lack of parking spaces for cars.

When she spoke to Connor on the phone the day before, she explained her reasons for wanting to meet him.

Connor expressed his willingness, without hesitation, to cooperate immediately.

Especially when she told him it was about my health problems.

She did this against my will.

I had firmly forbidden her to tell anyone about what was going on with me, even Connor.

I was embarrassed and didn't want anyone else to know about it except her. Rachel initially agreed to my request, particularly as she knew I had undertaken treatment and wanted to, help myself.

However, the fact that I was drinking alcohol daily, she was not yet fully aware of.

Because I hid it very well, or at least, that's what I thought at the time. Eventually, Rachel, under the influence of her emotions, decided to break our agreement of silence and confide everything to Connor.

But I had no right to hold a grudge against her.

After all, Connor was a long-time friend, both to me and to Rachel. He was not a stranger to me or someone who would want to use the private information he had acquired against me.

I know now that I acted very selfishly.

At the time, I only looked at what was good for me, I never even thought to put myself in the position, even for a moment, of my wife.

Maybe if I had done so, I would have known what a nightmare she must have been going through at the time, thanks to me.

Rachel arrived at the café that had been arranged.

She went inside and looked around the tables, but Connor wasn't there yet. She wasn't too bothered by this fact; she figured that he would probably come soon.

Until then, she ordered her favourite caramel latte for herself and then took a seat at a table near the front door.

Alright, but where would one start...? She began to think. "...How about night terrors? No, I'd better leave that for last, but what can Connor know about dreams? After all, he's not a psychiatrist but a police officer, so maybe he'll be able to tell, from a professional perspective, what a premonition that someone is watching him might mean for a police officer?" She was putting together, in her head, a plan for a conversation. She didn't want to bombard him at once with too many questions to which he might not know the answer anyway.

She had to conduct the conversation sensibly, concretely and as calmly as she could.

She counted on Connor's common sense and years of experience in the profession.

Rachel sat comfortably and watched the crowds of people strolling past the window while sipping her caramel latte.

She felt relaxed.

At home, she couldn't experience such a feeling due to the constant stress I put her under.

Both in her work as a physiotherapist, she dealt with people who were going through rehabilitation for various reasons.

Also, there was no room for relaxation there.

Not ten minutes had passed when Rachel saw Connor walk past the window with a quick step.

She had chosen this place specifically because of him.

Because Connor, although he was a police officer, was always lost somewhere.

Even though he should be well-oriented in the area.

He had trouble getting anywhere without a GPS navigation system.

But this place he knew well enough, and Rachel was aware of it.

He entered the café and nervously began to look around.

Rachel waved her hand at him to get his attention.

Once he spotted her, he smiled and moved towards her.

"Hello Declan." Rachel got up from her seat.

"Hi Rachel." He replied and exchanged with her, a friendly kiss on the cheek.

Rachel mostly called him by his first name, and the nickname "Connor," was more my speciality.

Although she did use it, occasionally.

Connor took off his coat and hung it on a vacant chair.

"I'm going to order myself a coffee..." He announced. "...Get something for you too?"

"Can you order for me another medium caramel latte..." Rachel replied and pointed her finger at her, almost empty, cup. "...It'll be useful for conversation; we could be here for a while.

Connor nodded his head in agreement, then turned and moved to stand in line.

We could be here for a while... He recalled her words in his mind. *...Something must really be bothering her a lot, not good.* He stated.

Connor waited his turn, and all sorts of thoughts ran through his head.

For example, he only now realised that this was his first meeting with Rachel, alone.

On top of that, she was the one who had called to ask him out.

He had never met her socially before, without a third party.

Mostly he had seen her for a reason in some festive circumstances, or on occasions when he was visiting Danny.

However, there had not been a single occasion when they had spoken face-to-face.

At the time, this made him realise how complicated the situation could be.

That it had prompted Rachel to call him to that place.

Connor had no doubt that she'd done it to make sure, none of their mutual friends saw them.

She needed privacy without witnesses who might disturb them. Following this line of thinking, for reasons that were already obvious, he decided that he would respect her wishes and do his best, to be as helpful as possible.

He adopted a serious attitude and put silly jokes aside.

When he looked at Rachel, she was staring out of the window, clearly looking anxious and deep in thought. After a few minutes, he took his order.

Before returning to the table, he stopped for a moment to take a deep breath.

Only then, did he return to where Rachel was waiting for him.

He was ready for whatever she might be about to tell him.

But even with this approach, he couldn't avoid being surprised by what she had just been preparing to tell him.

He walked over to the table and placed the coffee in front of Rachel.

At the same time, he set the already empty cup more to the side.

In contrast, he held his takeaway cup in his hand as he sat down opposite her.

"Your second coffee in the row..." He declared. "...Aren't you worried that your blood pressure will be too high?" He added, smiling suggestively. Rachel reciprocated his smile, then pulled the cup closer to her, catching it by the handle.

"Now that's the least of my problems. For the last few weeks, I've been feeling like my blood pressure is too high, most of the time..." she replied.

"...And it's not because of, over-drinking coffee."

Connor could clearly see that she was not at her best.

She looked very tired; you could even say she looked miserable.

Now that he got a better look at her up close, he became seriously concerned about what might be going on in her house.

He decided not to wait for her to start a conversation and asked her straight away.

"Rachel, what's going on?"

She looked at him, and her gaze said, "I knew I could count on you".

"Things are very bad with Danny." She replied.

Connor furrowed his brow, puzzled.

Personally, he hadn't noticed anything to indicate that things were that dire. Maybe apart from the fact that, in his opinion, Danny was reaching for the glass too often, but apart from that, nothing else bothered him. "I don't understand, I talk to him almost every day..." He replied concentratedly.

"...I didn't notice anything, I would have guessed, we have known each other for many years."

"He hides it well..." Rachel replied. "...And he can't know I've been talking to you, also don't talk about it sometimes. I promised him I wouldn't say anything to anyone, he wanted this matter to stay just between me and him.

Connor nodded as a sign of agreement.

He waited for her to tell him what Danny's big secret was all about.

"Declan, Danny claims to be seeing this girl.

Rachel's face turned serious. She spoke quietly as if she feared someone was eavesdropping on her.

Connor sat patiently in silence.

He looked at her and knew that this was only the beginning of the story. - She insists that he sees Denise Randal in our flat, on top of that, he has some terrible nightmares, screams at night, talks in his sleep, about a grave..." She recounted. "...He falls asleep only thanks to strong sleeping pills, and on top of that he drinks, more and more, he thinks I don't notice it, but I know everything. - And where is he now?

"He's having a therapy session, with a police psychologist, his previous one gave up, too complicated a case, now he's going to a specially assigned psychologist, this one is supposedly, more experienced in this type of case.

"Do you want me to talk to him?"

"I don't want him to find out that I told you about it..." She replied. " ...But yes, I would like you to try to find out from him what he sees in these dreams, he won't tell me."

"Don't worry. I know how to approach him so that he doesn't guess anything."

"Judging by what I've observed so far, I think he's slipping into schizophrenia," Rachel said, and her voice began to crack.

Connor saw tears gather in her eyes, so he grabbed her hand tenderly as a comfort.

She looked up at him and forced a slight smile.

"Don't worry..." He said. "...He has already received professional support; in time everything will work out." He tried to comfort her.

"Connor..." She wanted to ask one more question. "...Tell me, what can it mean for a police officer, when he has the feeling that someone is watching him all the time?"

"You want me to be completely honest with you, don't you?"

"Of course, this question has been bothering me for a while now. Tell me, what do you think?"

"Okay, I don't want this to sound cruel, but..." He started.

"...If a police officer on active duty has this kind of phobia, it practically rules him out completely from being able to practice this profession."

Rachel had already guessed that Danny would not be able to return to work.

However, she still secretly hoped that he would eventually be able to recover from this in time.

She hoped that, with the help of specialists, he would overcome his mental trauma.

But she also had to be realistic.

Especially as she saw how day by day her husband's condition deteriorated, more and more.

She also considered that Danny's behaviour could have become unpredictable because he abused alcohol.

Also, at times, she secretly watched him.

She would then see him listening to check if there were any third-party noises coming from the flat.

At other times, he would motionlessly watch someplace and wait.

It was as if he expected, in a moment, to suddenly see something there. It could be, for example, the corridor, the staircase or even the bar in the living room.

And his spare "mini" phone, which he had almost never left off before, was now lying switched o in the bedside table.

Danny was relentlessly on standby mode, ready to fend off a surprise attack.

Even if such a threat existed only in his imagination.

Rachel knew this and was terrified because of it.

The feeling of dread was often mixed with a sense of annoyance. Especially when she had to stuff him with sleeping pills that made him literally knocked out, after a few minutes.

But this was the only way she could be sure, that he would fall asleep quickly.

So that she, too, would be able to sleep through the night without fear of being woken up by screams in the middle of the night or having to throw herself panic-stricken on the bed again.

Her heart ached when she had to watch him suffer.

She wanted to help him, but didn't know how she should do it.

She was left to rely on specialists, who, however, also seemed not to know what they should do.

"Danny is going to have to leave the job he was fulfilled in and loved doing, all because of some finished drug addict who decided to end his life and the life of an innocent girl, a child before whom the whole world was still open, this man also killed a part of my husband and me." She stated sadly. Rachel had no doubt Danny's soul had partly died immediately after the events at Clare Randal's flat in "Tottenham Court Road."

And the consequences in the form of remorse were still there, terribly felt in Danny's subconscious.

A proud man and a dedicated police officer, who vowed to guard and protect those who would need his help.

And he'd failed.

He couldn't prevent a tragedy from happening and it didn't matter that he couldn't really do anything about it at the time.

That was no excuse for him.

He couldn't look at himself in the mirror and say, "it wasn't your fault".

He felt guilty and Rachel suffered with him.

More than once, she asked herself at the time:

"Is it possible that their life together, will ever again have a chance of returning to normality?"

Or perhaps, the awful feeling of anguish would remain, until the end of their days?

But one thing was certain, No matter what the future brought, and no matter what else might happen, Rachel was going to stick by Danny until the very end, for as long as he needed her to.

She vowed to "till death do us part." And she intended to keep, her word.

She loved her husband too much to even think that the result of all this could be the break-up of their marriage.

So, she decided that if the need arose, she would be prepared to take radical steps.

If nothing changed in the next few weeks, the only option left would be to pull him out of his current environment. She arranged, in her mind, a contingency plan.

Slowly, she began to consider moving to some quieter city, preferably somewhere on the outskirts of England.

Rachel was very fond of London; it was her hometown, and she felt very connected to it. She was reluctant to consider leaving.

She had grown up in London, had friends and family, and led her life both professionally and privately there.

The same was true for Danny.

But in the present situation, she put sentimentality aside and decided that all this no longer mattered.

What was at stake was her husband's well-being, and if it would help him, she was determined to take that step.

Over time, she gradually began to budget for such an eventuality, in secret from Danny, of course.

Then her train of thought, too, changed.

She began to see it as preparation for her impending, premature retirement.

Once she had settled on this decision, she felt how it gave her pleasure. The very thought that they would live somewhere together in peace and quiet, filled Rachel with optimism.

"Now is, as good a time as any to do it." She was reassured.

It was past 03:20 pm when I finally got home.

I was exhausted, both physically and mentally.

That afternoon, I had absolutely no desire to do anything else. The whole way home, all I dreamt of was making myself a drink, lying comfortably on the sofa and staring at the TV until the sun went down. When I entered the flat, I noticed that Rachel's shoes were already standing in the hallway.

This was a bit out of character for her, as I expected her not to be home yet. Then I could have a quiet drink, without feeling remorseful that I was doing something secret from her again.

Even so, I didn't want to give up the pre-arranged plan in my head, that I had managed to set myself up for when I drove here.

"After all, I know myself what is best for me".

In this case, I had to have a drink and that was out of the question. Quickly and silently, I left my belongings in the hallway, then just as silently continued towards the living room, where the liquor bar was.

On the way, I glanced towards the kitchen, but Rachel wasn't there.

She must be upstairs in the bedroom. Intuition prompted.

I decided that before letting her know I was back, I would first have a quick drink or two.

If she was unaware of my presence, I could have a drink with a clear conscience and only talk to her afterwards. I approached the bar with a quick but cautious step.

At the same time, I was careful not to make any accidental noise in the process.

I quietly opened the door to the bar and took out a bottle of vodka.

However, there was no juice to add to the alcohol.

I had no time to waste, because, for fear that Rachel might show up any minute and corner me.

I decided that I would drink pure vodka.

I didn't want to drink straight from the bottle like a desperate alcoholic. So, I poured, a third of a medium-sized glass and tilted it with a quick movement.

Drinking it all in one gulp.

The taste of the alcohol made me wince slightly, but it was not as bad as I thought.

So, I repeated the procedure.

After just a few seconds, I felt a relaxing sense of relief.

"Oh yes, just what I needed." I said to myself, under my breath.

Just as I was about to put the glass down along with the bottle on the bar, my phone rang.

Completely startling me, so much so that my first instinct was to almost drop the glass out of my hand.

The flat was completely silent, and the phone was terribly loud. There was no way Rachel couldn't have heard it upstairs and I wasn't wrong.

For a few seconds the sound of the phone dispelled the all-encompassing silence, I noticed Rachel's feet emerging on the stairs.

She was coming down in a hurry, most likely frightened by the unexpected event.

I only had a few seconds left before she reached the bottom of the stairs, which were to my right as I stood in the living room.

Luckily for me the whole time, I was next to the bar and managed to quickly place the bottle into it along with the glass.

I closed the bar and took my phone out of my pocket, the whole situation didn't last more than ten seconds.

"She almost caught me, because of that stupid phone." I said to myself nervously.

I had to remain calm, as if nothing had happened.

This was helped by a double dose of vodka, which made me pleasantly relaxed.

By the time I was holding my mobile phone in my hand, the melody had spread in earnest throughout the flat, which until recently had been plunged into silence.

Rachel made her way down to the living room and stopped in the doorway, looking at me with a surprised expression on her face.

To avoid an immediate confrontation, I lifted the phone towards her. In a gesture suggesting that "I need to answer," I then opened it and put it to my ear.

"This is PC Danny Davis; how can I help you?" I mouthed, stiffly into the receiver.

"What's so official?" Connor's voice rang out.

In fact, I never introduced myself like that when he called me.

From others yes, but not to him, so he had a right to be surprised. Although, in this case, there were several factors that contributed to me being a little off balance.

Firstly, I didn't take the time to look at the phone screen so, I didn't know who was calling.

Secondly, the alcohol had gone to my head a bit.

Thirdly, Rachel was standing not far away and watching me.

And I was just trying to, like, act normal.

"Och yes, sorry mate, I didn't see it was you." I was making excuses.

"It's okay..." He replied. ...Listen, do you have any plans tonight?

"Not really, no. I could sense in his voice that he was up to something."

"So, I suppose you could be talked into a game of pool?"

He hit my weak spot straight away, I loved playing pool and Connor knew it.

The nibbler knows how to approach me. He summed up my mind.

Look, Connor... I started. ...I feel tired and want to stay home, watch a movie with Rachel or something.

I said and looked at Rachel, all the while she was standing watching me.

She's been waiting for me to finish talking so she could ask me what the creeping around the flat meant, I'm sure I scared her with that. My mind left no illusions.

"Come on, don't be an old fart...!" He laughed. "...You're not going to say no to a old friend, are you?"

"I'll talk to Rachel and let you know, okay?"

"Fine, agreed, as long as you think about my invitation and call me back within the hour?"

"Yes, I'll think about it and let you know, stay tuned." I added at the end and closed the phone.

I put it back in my pocket and looked at Rachel.

Who, without waiting for me to collect my thoughts, immediately went on the attack.

"Danny, do you know how much you scared me...?" She began. "...I thought a stranger was walking around our house."

"Sorry, I didn't mean to frighten you, I just wanted to plug my phone into the charger before I called you." I lied awkwardly.

"It's okay, what was Declan calling for?"

"He's trying to drag me out to play pool but, I don't really feel like it." "Why not? Go with him." She replied, suspiciously too quickly in my opinion.

I found this additionally strange because she was never happy when I went out to the pub with Connor.

Mostly, she would try to arrange the circumstances so that he would come to us, or if we were all going out together, it would be to a cinema, a restaurant or somewhere quiet. I sensed some kind of ruse in this.

However, this feeling quickly passed, particularly when I realised that, after all, a game of pool equals a pub and alcohol. A green light was lit in my head for this thought.

For the rest of the day, I would be free to drink alcohol, with my wife's permission. I stated in my mind. However, appearances had to be kept up.

I decided that I would pretend for a while longer, how much I didn't feel like it, and then I would call Connor to make an appointment.

"You should have a bit of a blast..." Rachel continued. "...The last few weeks you've only been going to therapy and sitting alone at home. What she didn't know was that most of the time I spent at home, I spent ninety percent of it online in front of the computer."

I was hiding it from her.

No doubt, she would only have been more concerned about the fact of how deeply I was drawn in, the case of the missing North Hill four.

Rachel thought I was probably dozing o in front of the TV, making up for my lack of sleep at night.

And she didn't hold it against me, she cared about improving my health.

"Well, if you insist..." I replied feigning disinterest.

But deep down I was already happy, at the thought of the few beers I'd be pouring into myself before long.

"I'll call Connor, could you while I'm at it, get me some trousers to change into? These are a bit dirty." I asked.

Rachel smiled at me and, not immediately, set o towards the bedroom.

In fact, I didn't need to change my trousers at all, it was just a ruse to be left alone in the living room again, for a few minutes. I used this time to quickly tip another drink, for the road.

After that, any suspicion that made Rachel's agreement to go to the pub seem strange to me was gone.

I also ignored the fact that she too eagerly agreed to bring me a change of clothes.

Under normal circumstances, it certainly wouldn't have gone so easily.

At that point, all of this, no longer mattered.

All that mattered was that I would soon be able to drink, as much alcohol as I wanted.

Completely unaware of how dangerous drink had become, it had dimmed my normal view of reality.

Those were the times when all I could think about was when I would finally be able to drink.

But after all, I know what's best for me myself, don't I?

Less than an hour later, I was already outside a pool bar near "Vauxhall" station in south-west London, where I had arranged to meet Connor.

He wasn't there yet, so I phoned him to find out, how long it would take.

When he stated, "around ten minutes", I decided not to wait outside.

On the pretext of booking a table, I told him I would be inside.

Then, wasting no more time, I headed for the entrance.

The truth was, however, that I immediately needed to consume, another drink.

Because I could feel my body starting to sober up slowly, and was sending me signals that it was time to replenish before I got weak.

It was past 5pm.

Being already inside I looked around, checking my surroundings. I then directed my steps towards the bar, which attracted me with its treasures, like the California gold rush in the first half of the 18th century attracted wealth seekers.

To my surprise, the place seemed almost completely empty.

At this hour there were a maximum of ten people in a space, that could have accommodated at least a couple of hundred.

Satisfied that I wouldn't have to wait in line, I approached the bar. I ordered two paints of beer and started checking which pool table to occupy.

I thought it would be most convenient, to position myself between the bar and the toilets.

I knew that after a diuretic beer I would have to go to the bathroom, every so often.

I had no intention of running from the other end of the room.

I stood next to the table and took a solid sip of beer.

Next, I tossed a one-pound coin into the mechanism to get the balls out and, just to warm up, began spontaneously smashing them across the surface.

A few minutes passed and Connor continued not to appear.

I was under the impression that he was already at least thirty minutes late, but in reality, it hadn't even been ten yet.

I topped up my beer and proceeded to empty the pint, initially intended for Connor.

After a few more sips, I felt that I was already quite heavily inebriated.

However, I quickly ignored this detail.

I am a sizable man, weighing in at over a hundred kilograms.

"A couple of beers with a low alcohol content won't do me any harm." I concluded.

It wasn't until I saw Connor walking into the bar, then I realised how drunk I really was.

I called out to him, in greeting.

By design, I wanted to say something like, "Hey Connor."

However, my lack of control over my tone of voice caused me to let out an embarrassing shout, loud enough for the whole room, "HEY CONNOR!!!."

I realised from the spot then how foolish I had been.

Instantly I felt the gaze of all the people present, who just happened to have the dubious pleasure of being in the same bar with me that evening, including the bartender.

I turned red in the face and even the alcohol anaesthetic didn't help.

Connor walked up to me.

And I, stood stiff as a spike hammered into the ground, next to the pool table I had occupied, paralysed by the embarrassment.

"You don't have to shout. - He said.

"I know, sorry..." I replied embarrassed. "...It's this, loud music." I tried to justify myself.

The only thing I was able to come up with at the time, blaming it on the music.

After all, I couldn't say that I'd managed to get drunk before he arrived. I wanted to save face at the same time and shook his hand in greeting, Connor shook mine.

"It's good to see you out." He said.

"I spend most of my time away from home, you just don't know it." I replied.

I wasn't entirely sure, why I thought it would be a good idea to lie.

Apparently, the alcohol had lulled my ability to think rationally.

Otherwise, I would have known that Connor wouldn't believe a word I said, if I tried to push such nonsense on him

"Sure..." He replied and looked at the two beer mugs next to me, one empty and the other half drunk. "...I'm going to get a beer; I'm not taking one for you because I see you still haven't finished yours." He added on the sly.

I followed him away with my eyes and went back to hitting the ball with a cue.

I owed it to myself, by my uncontrollable outcry at the sight of him, it was not surprising that he guessed just how much, I was already intoxicated. Probably under different circumstances Connor would have offered me another round.

But he wanted to talk, and the pool outing was just an excuse to do so. To do that, he needed to be sure that I was still able to talk normally. Excessive alcohol would surely make this very complicated, if not impossible.

I tapped my cue balls aimlessly and watched them roll in different directions.

That evening I didn't want to think about anything.

I needed a break from reality and a chance to have a beer with a friend. My mind translated.

But the reality was that I just wanted to get drunk in an environment other than home.

At the time, I didn't realise it yet or simply, I didn't want to think about it in those terms.

Either way, I had a growing problem, and I downplayed it by repeating to myself, "I know what's best for me," constantly lying to myself.

But after all, I had to somehow fight the paranoia that had invaded my life, since leaving hospital.

I didn't agree with the argument that strong sleeping and psychotropic pills, should be the best solution in my case.

I found it easier to live anaesthetised with a glass of vodka diluted with orange juice, at my side.

At the time, I didn't recognise it as a problem or, most simply, my subconscious put the fact out of my head on its own.

When I saw Connor come back towards me, I began to evenly rack the game balls.

"Do you want to start?" I asked once he had put his beer down. I tried to maintain a semblance of sobriety as best I could. It took more effort than I expected.

It's hard to control your movements, especially when you're seeing double.

"Nah, you go for it." Connor replied.

I could see he was watching me, trying to pick out what state I was in. *I'm not going to give you the satisfaction...* I thought. *...I'm still going to have a couple of beers tonight and the evening, it's just starting.* I thought. I walked slowly to the top of the table, got into a shooting position and unleashed the cue in my hand to smash the balls.

With a quick movement, I hit the white one, and that, smashed the other balls, which scattered all over the table in every direction.

A nice hit, even if none of them fell into the pockets, I was proud of myself. Unfortunately, that was the first and last good hit I made that evening. After that it only got worse.

"Not bad...!" Laughed Connor. "...I can see you're in good shape."

"Like riding a bike." I looked at my friend with dominance.

I hadn't pocketed any of the balls, so it was Connor's turn.

He walked over to the rack of cues and picked one out.

He took a sip of his beer, after which, he started pocketing one ball after another, not actually giving me the slightest chance of winning.

I wasn't particularly upset about it.

Yes, I don't like to lose, and it annoyed me a little that I was getting beaten by him in a game.

But I was sitting comfortably, drinking a beer, my head was spinning and basically, I didn't care what happened around me. When he finally made a mistake, I had a chance to play.

I set the now empty mug down on the table and stood up, a little too quickly.

I felt dizzy, which made me need to lean on the table with my hands to keep from falling over.

Connor saw this from where he stood.

"Are you alright?" He asked concerned.

"I'm fine...'" I replied. "... I just, I got up too fast." I added, regaining my upright position.

I had already approached the game more confidently to make my move, Connor not taking his eyes off me.

With the grace of a professional pool player, I slowly and carefully checked the alignment of all the balls.

There it was an easy point! I looked out for an opportunity.

The whole yellow ball was standing right next to the edge, the left centre pocket.

No way to miss a shot. Recognised my instinct.

In concentration I tried on the shot, then I hit the white ball hard and decisively and the white ball didn't even touch the one I was aiming at.

"Fuck." I cursed under my breath.

"Bad luck." Connor said.

I looked at him angrily.

"You could call it bad luck if I was sober, I wonder if you'd be acting like you are if you see double, like I do." My mind was irritated. I turned my back on him and headed for the table, to drink.

It was only when I picked up my pint that I remembered that I had, after all, just finished it.

I looked at Connor's glass, which was also almost empty.

Great, I won't look as desperate as if I only bought one, for myself. My mind quickly assessed the situation.

Connor, meanwhile, was watching the balls and getting ready to continue playing.

"I'm going to get another round..." I said, walking up to him. "...What are you drinking?"

"Stella." He replied briefly, without turning his eyes from the table.

"Okay, I'll be right back." I said and headed for the bar.

Picking up my two empty pints and the glass Connor was drinking from.

In truth he still had some drinkable beer, but I took it anyway.

I'll get you a fresh one. I thought.

Of course, once again, I was getting it wrong.

Because I was only justifying the fact that I wasn't going to wait for Connor to finish drinking his beer.

It was mainly that my beer was already gone, and I needed to have another one.

But with too many glasses around me, it wouldn't be obvious that I was consuming alcohol unusually fast, while my friend was lagging and having to catch up with me.

I didn't even notice when more and more people started coming into the bar.

It became crowded.

With one bartender serving everyone, it became a queue.

I was not happy about the fact that I now had to line up behind people and wait politely, for my turn.

As I waited to be served, I could feel myself starting to get more and more annoyed.

I had the feeling that the whole thing was taking an awfully long time, and I was standing there for not ten minutes, but at least half an hour. When the bartender finally asked me what to serve, I ordered two large "Stella" beers and, unbeknownst to me shot of vodka, which I drank straight away, as soon as the man managed to place a filled glass in front of me.

It seemed as if I couldn't even wait.

Because, I hadn't even handed over the money yet, I just grabbed the glass and poured the contents into my mouth.

The barman measured me with a strange look, as if he thought I wanted a free drink without paying.

At this sight, I took a twenty pound note out of my wallet and solemnly, waved it in front of his face after which, I placed it on the bar. I did not even give him the money in my hand, which was generally accepted as an act of kindness and good manners.

I was indifferent to everything.

I felt upset that I had to wait though, which was getting me a hangover. But the shot of vodka I'd just consumed got me back on my feet, and I was ready to get back into the game.

Connor had, however, other plans at that time.

I guess he thought it was time to take me aside before it was too late. For, as soon as I returned to the table with our drinks, he was waiting for me sitting in a chair.

I placed one pint in front of him and held the other in my hand, he thanked me with a nod.

"Are we not playing?" I asked, pointing with my head towards the pool table.

"In a minute…" He replied. "…Sit down, I want to talk to you." He added in a serious tone.

I might have expected it, and, in fact, I would have expected it if I wasn't drunk.

Anyway, I had a feeling somewhere in the back of my head, that this was not just a spontaneous trip to a bar for fun.

I took a sip of beer and sat down opposite Connor, who was now looking at me intently.

"Mate..." He started. "...We've been friends for over fifteen years now."

"Yes, and we've known each other since, police school." I interrupted him rudely.

"Exactly..." He recounted. "...I would like to know why; you are not being honest with me?"

Even though I started to slowly guess what he was getting at, I decided to play dumb.

"What are you talking about? After all, I'm always honest with you." I lied.

Connor nodded his head contradictorily with disapproval.

I thought then that he must have been talking to Rachel.

I even tried for a moment to be angry with her about it.

We had a deal, and she talked herself out of it. It summed up my instinct. But I couldn't bring myself to intensify my anger at her, it wasn't her fault, and I knew it.

She had a right to talk to Connor when she needed to vent to someone, and I couldn't resent her for that.

Therefore, I quickly forgot that detail.

I looked at my friend with eyes blurred by alcohol.

I waited for him to say something else, but he remained silent.

He expected me to bring up the subject, I owed it to him.

"Do you want to know something specific?" I asked, breaking the awkward silence.

"I want to know, what's going on with you...?" He replied. "...What's bothering you?"

"And what am I supposed to tell you, huh?" I felt myself start to shake inside; the stress returned.

I paused for a moment and rested my gaze on the beer mug, then reached for it and took a solid sip.

Connor clearly had no intention of pressurising me, so he waited patiently.

"You know you can tell me anything…" He finally said, in a calm tone. "…I'm your friend and I want to help you, anything you say will stay strictly between us."

I tore my gaze away from the pint and looked at him, I could feel myself slowly starting to unravel.

The alcohol only intensified the feeling of being out of control of my emotions.

Eventually I couldn't stand it and decided to tell him everything in detail, just like I did in therapy.

"I know this will sound ridiculous but, I am haunted by the soul of Denise Randal…." I began uncertainly. "…Sometimes it manifests itself to me at night, sometimes during the day, but even when I can't see it, I know it is somewhere near me, all the time…" I said. "…I can't explain why, but I feel her presence and I know it's her…" I added and I felt tears spontaneously drip from my eyes, Connor was looking at me with a look of sympathy on his face.

"…It all started right after the shooting, when I was being carried to the ambulance, that's when I saw her for the first time, she was walking next to my stretcher, not long after that in the flat, I started to meet her shadow, she appears in dark and barely visible places, she was watching me from hiding…." I recounted further. "…I have nightmares in which, I'm walking through some woods in the middle of the night, I hear children's voices around me, but no one is there, then I fall into a pit and when the ground falls on me I feel myself dying."

Connor listened intently to me; he could see the tears running down my cheeks.

I knew that if he could, he would take some of my pain on his shoulders.

It was impossible though, there was nothing he could do.

"I believe you Danny, I really do, but after all, you know that alcohol won't solve your problems." He said.

"I HAVE NO IDEA WHAT THE FUCK ELSE I CAN DO!!!" An uncontrollable scream erupted from me, causing me to leap up from my seat. I did so spectacularly enough that people around me looked in our direction with interest.

I noticed that even the man behind the bar, leaned his head out to see if a fight was brewing.

"Relax Danny, have a seat." Connor said.

I felt terribly stupid for losing control of myself again, I lowered my gaze to my knees and started sobbing like a little child.

"Damn it Danny, get yourself together." My mind reprimanded me. Not five minutes had passed, when Connor suggested we go outside, get some air.

With the sounds coming from the crowded streets of the big city and the fresh air, I felt a little better, even sobered up a bit.

Connor didn't let me, finish the last of my beer and I was grateful to him for that.

If I had been there alone, I certainly wouldn't have been able to get out of that bar, on my own.

I did, however regret, leaving whole beer on the table, but I realised it was for my own good.

We stood in the street for a few minutes, then decided it was time to get the hell out of there.

Taking public transport was out of the question, it was quicker to get a taxi.

At that point Connor insisted on driving home with me.

Although I said it wasn't necessary, he didn't want to leave me on my own, seeing the sorry state I was in.

So, we got into a black "London" taxi together, at "Vauxhall" tube station, and headed for my flat and Rachel's flat in "New Cross."

When I got into the car I was overwhelmed by sleep, defending myself against it by looking out of the window all the way, watching the streets. My head ached progressively more from the moment I stopped pouring alcohol into myself.

A murderous hangover was beginning.

Which seemed ridiculous, because I had finished drinking less than half an hour ago and right now the alcohol should be hitting my head harder, not the other way around.

But I was as drunk at the time as any other person would have been in my position, only my brain was playing tricks on me.

It was putting pressure on me in this way, the illusion that I was feeling bad because I had run out of more alcohol in my blood, making me feel like I should keep drinking to keep feeling good.

Fifteen minutes later, we were already arriving at our destination.

By this time, the consumed alcohol had done its job.

My head was bursting at the seams, and I had to go to bed without delay, despite the early hour, as it wasn`t even ten o'clock yet.

Only Rachel was still standing in my way before I could finally reach my bed.

But Connor was willing to help me.

He walked me to my flat supporting me the whole way, holding me firmly under his arm.

When he saw that I was having trouble opening the door, he took the key from me then did it for me.

When we got inside, Rachel was sitting in the living room watching something on the TV.

The moment she heard us enter she turned her head, while leaning back slightly so that she could look in our direction.

Since the living room was at the end of a short corridor, all she had to do was lean back slightly from the sofa to the right, to have a view of the hallway.

From this part of the flat, I had to move down a few more steps to reach the stairs and continue upstairs to the bedroom.

Which seemed unfeasible at this point.

I couldn't walk on my own, yet I had to at least try to stay evenly on my feet, so Rachel wouldn't see me stagger.

The moment I realised that she had already spotted us, I straightened up with a quick movement.

The distance between us helped me, at least a little, to maintain a semblance of sobriety.

If she comes any closer, she'll figure me out in a blink of an eye, I won't be able to hide anything. My instinct said gibberish. "Why did you come back so quickly?" She asked.

I wasn't quite sure what she meant, because on the one hand, it didn't sound like she was surprised...

...Or you're too drunk to recognise it. My mind was prompting.

But I also didn't want to say too much, for fear that she would expose me.

"I didn't expect to see you here before eleven o'clock." She added.

"I felt bad." I replied, truthfully, after all.

"You haven't had too much to drink, have you?" She asked me, but I noticed she was looking at Connor.

"No way, Rach...!" he rushed to my rescue.

"...He didn't even finish his second round and started whining about feeling unwell." Saying this, he patted me on the back in agreement.

"Oh, that's not good..." she replied. "...Maybe you want to lie down?" she added after a while, as if she had read my mind.

"Yes, that's a good idea, that's what I'll do." I said and a weight dropped from my heart.

Rachel got up from her seat and made her way to the kitchen, at which time Connor walked with me to the stairs, from where I made the further journey alone.

"You made it, you can go safely to bed, this time there were no hard feelings..." my instinct summed up the evening. "...If you had gone to her in the living room, the whole fairy tale of two beers would have popped like a soap bubble."

At this thought, I nodded to myself as a sign of agreement, at the same time carefully overcoming the next obstacle to my goal in the form of steps. I could still hear from the ground floor as Rachel asked Connor if he would stay for tea, but he politely declined saying he had to go home now. Moments later there was a loud, distinctive, slamming of the front door closing.

Or at least, that's how it was supposed to look from my perspective at the time.

However, it had all been pre-arranged.

Since Connor wanted to talk to Rachel without my knowledge, they initiated this little show to further lull my suspicions.

In truth, Connor did indeed leave the flat, but only to wait outside for a while until I was asleep and then come back inside to share his thoughts with her.

He probably didn't have to wait that long, because from what I remember, I fell asleep almost as soon as my face touched the pillow.

Then Rachel quietly checked to see, if I was already asleep and let him back in.

"And, what happened? Did you guys have a talk...?" An impatient Rachel began. "...Did he tell you something?"

"Yes..." He replied. "...It's a lot more complicated than I expected, it's hard for me to interpret what I'm thinking right now, I need time to come up with some concrete conclusions." Connor thought aloud. "I'm begging you, don't keep me waiting, don't scare me."

"Basically, he hasn't told me anything new that you don't already know, the nightmares, the Denise soul, the feeling of being cornered, stalked and so on...." He explained. "...At first, I thought it was post-traumatic stress and remorse, that he felt guilty about this tragedy, but when I saw how much he was experiencing it, I realised, he really believes it, I think he really, sees the ghost of this girl."

"Do you have any idea how he can be helped?"

"I think I do, but I doubt he would like it."

"Meaning?"

"I know he's not keen on this sort of thing, but I think in this situation, he'll be persuaded to see a medium." He explained.

Rachel measured him with an investigative gaze, as if she didn't quite believe what she was hearing.

"A medium you say." She repeated quietly after him, clearly considering the idea.

I personally believe in these things, life beyond the grave and so on. "I understand Declan..." She replied. "...Yes, it could work. Will you be able to organise someone?"

Connor smiled as a sign of agreement.

"I'll see what I can do."

"I'll look around too, maybe from an ad? We're having a Christmas party on the 24th of December, I'll try to arrange a meeting by then..." Rachel thought aloud. "...Feel invited."

"Thank you, I'll come, but you know, spiritualist séances like this, they're held in a small group, a Christmas party might not be suitable."

"You know a lot about this stuff." She looked at him intrigued.

Connor replied with a quiet laugh.

"I've seen this and that."

"I was thinking more of the Christmas period than the party itself, say, the first day of Christmas."

"Sure, alright then, we're set..." He replied. "...Will you mention it to Danny?" He asked at the end.

"No, we'll put him on the spot, that way he won't have the opportunity to refuse."

"Okay, I won't say anything to him either, I'm running off now, I'll hear from you." Connor said and exchanged a friendly kiss on the cheek with Rachel. When he had finally left, she locked the door behind him and headed back into the living room, continuing to watch TV.

By the time Rachel and Connor were making plans, behind my back, about meeting a medium and having a spiritualist séance, I was exactly where such an attempt to contact the world of the dead, was going to take us. Despite the amount of alcohol I had consumed, and the fact that I didn't fall asleep like a normal person, I just blacked out as soon as I went to bed.

My mind was sober enough to take me on another dreamy adventure. Although, it was not the same nightmare as the previous ones about being buried in the ground as I lay in a pit or voices, whose origin I could not locate.

It was, however, the same forest and surroundings, only this time there was a slightly calmer atmosphere.

The strangest thing that distinguished this dream from the others, was that Denise was right next to me.

In other nightmares I also knew she was somewhere close by, but I never dreamt I could see her.

This time she was, leading me by the hand.

Bringing back the memory of the circumstances of 18 October 2018, when she was also by my side on the way to the ambulance, and now, as at that time, I could not feel the touch of her hand.

The only thing that remained the same was that I again could not see her face.

I looked down at her as she walked on my right, but I couldn't put my head at such an angle as to see her face.

We walked ahead through the forest, and I watched the trees swaying in the wind.

Then I noticed the now familiar old wooden fishing shed, appear in the distance.

It seemed still very far away, but we were approaching it at an unnaturally fast pace.

When we were a few steps away from the door, Denise let go of my hand, and I continued walking alone.

I tried to turn around to look at her, but I couldn't do it, I felt my legs driving me forward on their own, and I couldn't stop.

I only stood facing the entrance and heard quiet sounds coming from inside, they sounded like the sobbing of a small child.

I felt no fear, in fact I was overwhelmed by an inner peace that gave me strength and motivation.

Being at arm's length to the door and I pushed it slightly and it slowly opened ajar, creaking quietly in the process.

I was about to see who was inside, but at that moment a blindingly bright light fell upon me.

At that moment I realised that I had just woken up.

And the light pointing straight at my face was from the sun, because Rachel had just pulled back the curtains at the windows.

I contorted my face and looked at her, through the crevices in my eyelids.

"Good morning..." She said. "...Did you sleep well?"

All indications are that I did. I thought.

It was easy to tell.

Since I did not see on Rachel's face, an expression of deep concern.

As was sometimes the case when I woke up from the nightmares I was having.

This time I must have been lying still, as she didn't notice anything strange.

"What time is it?" I asked sleepily.

"10:30 in the morning..." She replied. "...You've slept more than twelve hours, so I thought it was high time you ate something." She explained.

She was right; my stomach was growling, and it was time to get up.

I got out of bed and found, to my surprise, that I felt pretty good.

I didn't even have as big a hangover as I expected to have.

But that was as far as feeling good went because the state of my psyche still left a lot to be desired.

Not long after waking up, I began to be plagued by last night's dream. I was curious as to what I would have found in the shed had Rachel not woken me up so quickly.

Even so, the notion remained in my mind that Denise was trying to tell me something, and with each subsequent dream, it became more and more obvious.

She wants to tell you something, only how do we find out what it is? My instincts prompted.

20

Priorities.

'People can be spotted by closing eyes.'

Ten years earlier,

10 November 2008, North Hill township.

News of the disappearance of fourteen-year-old Magda Richardson, spread throughout the town at a rapid pace.

The very next day, after the child's disappearance, the town was already buzzing with rumours.

Nobody knew any details about it, but that didn't stop people from speculating and making the incident a major topic of conversation. Which was perfectly legitimate, however, as people were downright terrified about it.

North Hill was one of the most peaceful and safe towns in the UK.

Never had such terrible circumstances taken place there.

Crime was at a record low, so much so that residents were not even afraid to leave the doors to their homes open at night.

Due to the small number of CCTV cameras, located only in the centre and the outskirts, Police Chief Mark Brown ordered the mobilisation of all officers and those willing to help, as soon as the "child missing" report was received.

In order to organise and carry out the search as quickly as possible, a time-consuming and traditional search was carried out in groups, around the immediate area of the Richardson family home.

For the first two days there were group searches of the nearby area. Uniformed services and dozens of volunteers scoured every nook and cranny, metre by metre.

Unfortunately, even with the help of tracking dogs, the venture ultimately failed.

People lamented the fate of both Magda and her mother, Joanna

Richardson, who remained under the watchful eye of Susan McKane and nurses, at the local hospital during this time.

Conversations on the subject never left the lips of residents, not even for a moment.

At one time, you couldn't walk down the street without hearing conversations, in which someone uttered sentences like:

"...I hope Magda is found..." Or "...That poor woman, I wonder how she is holding up..."

It was also natural that the gaze of the public, and not just those in North Hill, fell on further police proceedings.

The case quickly became extremely heated as it was first reported in the newspapers.

Then, it was talked about in the latest news, which circulated around the country for the next few days, before the subject was dropped.

The immense pressure on law enforcement in such a short period of time only made things more difficult for the officers, who did the best they could with their hands full and no experience, in this type of situation. Sticking to the rules and regulations, they started by questioning all the people who were in the area at the time.

This was to see if anyone had noticed anyone or anything suspicious, as no person had come forward so far, voluntarily to the police station as a witness.

The painstaking process of eliminating suspects began.

Initially, the prime suspect became 59-year-old Sandra Jones, Magda's carer and neighbour of Joanna Richardson.

The only reason for this was that she was staying with the girl at the time of her disappearance.

The woman was interviewed and released home, thanks to the lack of grounds for arrest.

Investigators had no reason to suspect that she was making false statements.

On top of that, she agreed to undergo tests to clear her of any suspicion once and for all.

She then had to return the next day to the police station to be tested with a polygraph, which had to be brought in specially for this purpose.

All officers, led by Chief Constable Mark Brown, placed great emphasis on the immediate resolution of this case, which became a priority from the outset.

It was extremely important to act as quickly and efficiently as possible. At this stage of the proceedings, the police were not yet able to give an official, statement to the public.

But slowly, it was becoming clear and most of the people involved believed without a doubt, that Magda had been abducted.

Nevertheless, without confirming these facts, police spokesmen decided not to release the abduction ruling to the world yet, as they did not want the residents to panic.

To prevent chaos, the police representative also made a request to journalists.

They were asked to refrain from using phrases such as "kidnapping" or "abduction" in their articles.

It was then that the press started to write about the "disappearance of Magda Richardson."

The case handlers were unanimous in their view, that such reports in the press would only cause some residents to start behaving paranoid. This was to dampen the feeling in people's nature of wanting to see in every person a kidnapper or in any other way, something suspicious.

Thus, hundreds of calls to the police station, for every little reason, were avoided.

Which could have been disastrous in its consequences and seriously hampered the work, which was already complicated enough.

At the same time, the investigators reckoned that people would speculate on what had happened to Magda Richardson, there would be rumours and stories it was certain.

Every attempt was made, however, to keep the peace.

At that point there was nothing left to do but to try, by all means, to keep the situation under control.

Inexperienced police officers, in circumstances new to them, frantically followed the procedures learnt at the academy, meticulously carrying out their successive tasks.

Unfortunately, it was a fact that with each passing hour, from the moment of the kidnapping, the chances of finding the girl whole and healthy, were drastically decreasing.

This had also been discussed in the police school classes.

Statistically, when it came to child abductions, the first three hours are crucial for the police to pick up the trail, after that time, the likelihood of rescuing the child, gets smaller and smaller.

From the moment Magda Richardson was reported missing, the sixth day passed.

Despite countless hours of searching, questioning neighbours of the Richardson family, thoroughly checking the garden where Magda was last seen, the police have been unable to establish anything concrete.

Nothing was found in the area, nor did any witnesses turn up.

Only in the garden behind the house, were shoe prints found in the ground, which were believed to belong to a man.

In addition, police officers were in possession of a rag doll that Magda had found three weeks ago and which, Joanna had not managed to burn at the time.

As well as Sandra Jones' statement about the mysterious toy.

The carer told police about the black magic and the moment when the girl went missing, when the landline in the flat rang and when she answered it, it turned out to be dead.

This was the only time the woman let Magda out of her sight, just when she went into the house to answer the phone.

Sandra claimed that whoever was calling at the time hung up as soon as she picked up the phone, and when she returned to the garden, the girl was no longer there.

Investigators quickly traced the phone number used to make the call at the time according to the woman's testimony, but this lead also ended in a dead end.

Because it had to be, an old mobile phone with a regular "Pay Us You Go" SIM card, of which there were literally millions in the UK.

Naturally no longer available, with no way of tracing it.

Attempts were also made to speak to Joanna about the incident, but this led nowhere.

There was almost no contact with the woman, she was in hospital and unresponsive to the reality around her.

It was as if her consciousness, was almost completely switched off and her mind, stopped functioning.

As Susan had been the woman's psychologist for a long time and knew her well, it was hoped that she would eventually be able to get through to the victim.

Susan, without prompting, agreed to help and promised to visit Joanna as often as she was able.

As the psychologist, she had also been given instructions in advance in case Joanna was fit to talk.

She was then to try to find out, if Joanna could name any person who had a grudge against her about something, even from the distant past, or someone who might wish her or Magda harm.

This was to see if anyone from the woman's immediate circle, could have anything to do with the case.

Susan, of course, agreed to all the conditions and pledged to contact the uniformed officers, immediately as soon as Joanna started talking. The first few approaches, however, proved unsuccessful.

Susan and John McKane's house, 01:20pm

That day, Susan also wanted to go to hospital, to visit Joanna and see if her condition had improved at least a little.

She was happy to have another activity to do in town.

It was a good reason for her to get out of the house for a couple of hours, where she felt increasingly depressed.

It was hard for her to see John going through home chemotherapy. According to Susan, he looked nightmarish, had lost a lot of weight, was balding and had to walk everywhere with an IV.

She found it difficult to spend time with him at home.

On top of that there was also, a four-month-old daughter, Nicole Denice.

As the time progressed, Susan increasingly left the infant in John's care. However, he, despite his illness and lack of strength, was able to take good care of the baby.

Only occasionally did he call for Susan's mother, Rita, who, living not far away, always willingly came to look after her granddaughter.

But even Rita noticed Susan's behaviour and was concerned about her indifference, towards her sick husband and her little daughter.

The woman also pointed out that Susan, spent most of her time at home on the phone.

And when she confronted her daughter regarding talking for so long, the daughter mostly answered:

"I have my patients."

On the days when Susan was mostly away from home, she explained this by saying that she was working intensively with the police on the investigation of Magda's disappearance, which was not even remotely true. Since her task was only to try to reach Joanna, who was in a state of shock all the time and had not managed to talk until now, however, Susan's constant presence was not required.

But for her it was a good enough reason to disappear from the house for a few hours.

Both Rita and John, surreptitiously watched Susan's behaviour with annoyance.

John, in particular, regretted it and resented it greatly.

It seemed to him that his wife had no sympathy for him, even at a time when he probably only had a few more, months to live. Just when he needed her support the most, she was absent.

For a long time, John couldn't understand why Susan had become so distant.

Of course, he considered the circumstances and the fact that the volume of work might have simply overwhelmed her at some point.

Still, he tried not to think about it and worry unnecessarily. All the man wanted was to enjoy every moment he had with his dear daughter, Nicole Denice.

There were moments when Rita watched as John, proud of himself, showed her how the child responded to the sounds of the piano. She was moved by the sight, and tears welled up in her eyes.

When the baby was crying, John would plant her on his lap and start playing and she, after a few minutes would fall peacefully asleep.

It was truly, a beautiful sight.

But Susan was never there, she missed the kind of relationship that should be building up, between child and the parent.

That afternoon, John sat with Nicole Denice in the living room and watched Susan walking hurriedly around the house, getting ready to leave. At one point, he noticed that she, apparently ready, moved towards the front door, clearly not intending to say goodbye.

So, he decided to stop her.

"Are you leaving already?" he spoke to her.

"Oh yes, sorry, I'm in a hurry." She replied, shaken out of her thoughts.

"Where are you going?"

"To the hospital..." she replied.

"...I must meet Joanna; I'll see if I can get something out of her today."

"Can't the police send someone to her, instead of you?"

"Well, you know, I'm her psychologist. Once she starts talking to someone, it will be me." She replied with a hint of pride in her voice.

"Don't worry darling, I'll be back soon, after all you know how serious the situation is." She said in conclusion and hurriedly closed the door behind her.

Yes, I know, and we are left alone again. John thought bitterly and looked sadly at the child, who had just been woken up by the slamming of the door.

"Good morning sunshine..." he whispered with a smile. "...Mummy woke you up, did she...?" he asked as if the infant was about to answer him. "...Do you want to listen to daddy play the piano? Come on, I'll play for you, your favourite tune." He added and struggled to get up from the sofa. With one hand he held the drip and with the other he picked up, the baby carrier.

Then with a slow step, he headed towards his favourite instrument. When he reached it, he placed the baby on the small sofa in front of the piano, sat down beside her and drew the drip closer to his left.

He investigated the carrier and saw the little girl watching him with big blue eyes.

He knew it was ridiculous, as she was still too small, but for a moment, it seemed to him that Nicole Denice recognised her place in front of the instrument and now looked as if, she was waiting for him to play for her. John felt emotion sweep over him, and his heart, filled with a warm feeling of love.

"Would you like daddy to play your favourite tune Denice?" he asked again and, as before, received no answer.

John always referred to his daughter as "Denice" in his wife's absence. As this always reminded him of his beloved grandmother, who had died several years earlier.

He felt that this name was more suitable for the little girl than Nicole, which Susan had chosen for her at the hospital.

John regretted at times that he had agreed without protest and went along with his wife's idea straight away. However, it did not really matter now.

Since he was the one who spent the most time with the baby, he could call her whatever suited him best, and he preferred to call her Denice. "We'll play the lion king." Said John and slowly began, tapping out a tune on the piano.

Suggesting, of course, the Elton John song "Can You Feel the Love Tonight," it was his and Susan's, favourite song and now also, Nicole Denice's. John felt a great affection for this song because it reminded him of the moment he danced together with Susan at their wedding, so he chose it for little Nicole Denice.

At the time, the child would very quickly calm down whenever she was out of humour by listening to the music.

Afterwards, she would either fall sweetly asleep to the sounds of the melody or lie quietly and with interest, absorb the sounds that were new to her, slowly getting used to them.

By this time, Susan, had reached the town.

It was approaching two o'clock when she decided to pop over to her favourite café first, instead of heading straight to the hospital.

She didn't feel she had to rush and didn't want to; she had no reason to.

She relished every moment of freedom.

Without any obligations or depressing and unpleasant sights.

For that is how she perceived John's anaemic figure with a drip by his side. Unfortunately, this is exactly how her sick husband acted on her in those days, and even if, she couldn't bear the sensation, she didn't know how she could cope with it.

But when she was completely alone, she felt that she could breathe fully and freely.

This option suited her very much, without a crutch or someone to slow her down.

It suited her to be alone.

However, this afternoon, she knew that her time alone was limited, so she wanted to make the most of every minute that followed.

She entered the small but tasteful café "Café Orbi" and was relieved to find that the usually crowded establishment, was virtually empty.

She ordered a large latte and moved to a table by the window, next to which stood a comfortable sofa, facing the street. She set down her coffee and was relieved to sit down.

From there, she had a view of the beautiful, historic town hall and almost the entire market area.

She watched the people walking down the street for a while longer, then reached into her handbag and pulled out a book.

She placed it on the table along with her mobile phone, which had been previously muted, so that no one could disturb her.

She opened the book, Stephen King's "Pet Cemetery," where she had left off last time and delved into the reading.

In some strange way, she was fascinated by this horror novel.

A story about a magical gloomy graveyard, the posthumous return of the dead to the world of the living, mystery, conspiracy and a deep love for loved ones.

It captivated Susan so much, that she even began to identify to some extent with the characters described by the distinguished author, of supernatural fiction novels, although she was not quite sure why.

She read attentively and avidly, turning page after page, absorbed in her imaginary world without even noticing that it had been over an hour since she had started.

Finally, she glanced at the clock, on the town hall which immediately brought her back to earth.

It was already past three o'clock, and she had to get moving right away, if she didn't want to be late.

She would have liked to stay longer to read on, but at the same time, she did not want her absence from home to drag on for several hours.

I still must, after all, go to the hospital. She thought.

Before she stood up, she took a deep and relaxing breath while stretching her arms, high up.

She had to be careful with her sense of time, as she didn't want to be seen to be neglecting her family or avoiding, being together with them. John was not a stupid person, he guessed that she was specifically leaving the house for spurious, sometimes not real, reasons.

Susan preferred not to provide him with any more reasons that might make him wonder, why she hadn't been back for so long, or worse, ask her what she had been doing all that time, out on the town.

Therefore, she decided that it would be best if she dropped by the hospital for a while and then, go straight home.

She packed her book and phone and was ready to leave, when she noticed a woman, she knew walking quickly past the window.

Susan recognised her instantly.

However, this came as no small surprise to her, as she had not expected to see her here.

The bell attached to the café door rang, signalling to the staff that a new customer had just arrived.

At this signal Susan turned and looked towards the entrance.

"Well, I don't believe it." She said, quietly under her breath. Given that Susan was close to the front door, the woman heard her immediately.

At these words she looked at her and bestowed a big, happy smile.

"Hello Susan!" The woman called out at the sight of her, coming closer. "Hello, what are you doing here...?" Susan replied. "...I thought you had moved to London."

"Oh yes, but I came back, three months ago...." The woman replied. "...Fact, I lived in London for a while, but you know how it is, I have a small child now, so I decided to go back to my roots, anywhere is good, but home is best!" She laughed.

"Oh, congratulations then..." Susan forced herself to compliment her. "...Listen, I've got to run now, I'm in a hurry, here's my card, give me a call, we'll make an appointment sometime." She added quickly so as not to get into any further discussion with the woman, then pressed into her hand, a piece of paper with the data on it.

The woman took it and lifted it higher to read curiously.

"Susan McKane, Doctor of Psychology..." She said aloud. "...So, you've made it, you've earned your PhD." She added.

Susan sensed a hint of jealousy in the woman's voice, but she had no intention of continuing the conversation now.

"I'm off, call me and we'll make an appointment, bye!" Susan said goodbye to her and left the café.

The woman followed her away with envious eyes, as she crossed the street and was just about to get into her car.

It was only then that Susan realised how astonished she was, by the unexpected encounter.

She sat down in the car and needed to wait a moment before starting the car engine and driving off.

On the way to the hospital, she began to recall in her mind memories of the woman she had just spoken to.

She was Nattaly Swanson, a peer and former rival of Susan's from school. The two ladies had known each other since they were children, as their parents were good friends.

But Susan had never liked the girl, considering her a conceited, mean, haughty and self-obsessed person.

They studied almost equally well, although Susan proved many times that she surpassed her in intellect.

Nattaly never stopped competing for grades at school and social status. In addition, she also wanted to become a psychologist so, like Susan, she studied in that direction.

Which apparently didn't work out for her, judging by the expression on her face when she saw the business card.

Susan rejoiced greatly at the thought.

Despite their mutual dislike, they were similar, both physically and intellectually.

Very beautiful and smart women who had one unusual fact in common.

Namely, they were both adopted and grew up in foster families. They had a similar story since their parents, through a mutual decision, decided to adopt two children from the "Order of Divine Mercy" named after St Paul.

The main reason was that neither Melissa Swanson, Nattaly's mother, nor Rita Jankins could have children of their own.

Therefore, fate made them grow up in the same town, side by side. But the difference between the two families, was also reflected in the shaping of these young women's personalities.

While Susan's parents were middle class, Nattaly's parents were very wealthy.

Which was also, for many years, a salt in Susan's eye, especially during the time when they both attended the same school.

Nattaly was in the habit of flaunting her new things and wearing different clothes every day, whereas Susan's parents, could not afford to buy her new things every now and then and spoil her.

Susan was the kind of person who wanted to achieve something in life by her own efforts, while Nattaly was always handed everything under her nose on a silver platter.

When, three years ago, Nattaly finally left North Hill to study in London, Susan was glad she would never have to see her again.

But now all the signs were that Nattaly had failed at university and was forced to return, back to her hometown.

Susan thought she would love to meet her, as she had a feeling that she would tell her how her plans had failed and wanted to hear her, talk about her failure.

Just the thought of it brought a smile to her face.

At the same time, she imagined how she would wipe the sneer o her pretty face when she revealed secrets about her successes, both professionally and in her private life.

Over the years, Susan had also undergone a metamorphosis. Not so long ago, she was able to enjoy what she had, but now she had become a person who was missing something all the time.

She didn't even know herself, how she should define it.

Ambition, possessiveness, greed, jealousy?

Whatever it was, she felt she wanted more from life.

Deep down she realised that this was not the right approach to life, but there was nothing she could do about it.

On the way to the hospital, she felt herself start to regret not taking Nattaly's phone number first.

Her rival may or may not call her, and Susan wanted to arrange a met up for a coffee with her, to hear how she had wasted her life.

That's what her intuition was telling her all along.

Oh well, I'll wait for her to call me herself, if not, I could drive over to her house one day. She thought as she drove up to the hospital, looking for a parking space.

The clock struck twenty minutes past three, when she finally managed to park the vehicle.

A few minutes later, she left the car in front of the building and with a quick step, set off for the main hospital entrance.

The weather was slowly starting to deteriorate, and a light rain was now falling, so Susan hurriedly wanted to take shelter inside.

Once inside, she immediately headed towards the ward where Joanna was currently staying.

She walked through the long corridor and arrived shortly afterwards; she had travelled this route many times, so she knew it by heart.

As she approached the reception desk to report the purpose of her visit to the ward nurse, she noticed that sitting in one of the seats in the waiting room was, Carolin Roberts.

A former patient of Susan's, an employee of the town post office.

She furrowed her brow, wondering what she might be doing there. Carolin's presence was now very much out of her hands, as she knew that as soon as Carolin saw her, she would immediately attach herself, like Velcro, forcing a conversation and would be hard to get rid of.

However, Carolin was not aware of Susan's presence, so she was able to talk calmly to the nurse at reception.

At that point, the latter announced that she could not come in yet, because the police were talking to Joanna at the time.

When Susan inquired about the patient's state of health to establish a temporary dialogue, the woman in the blue apron only replied that there had been a slight improvement, and then added, that she would have to wait at reception until the police officers had finished their visit. For a moment Susan hoped that she would be able to sneak inside unnoticed, but at that moment she realised that an encounter with Carolin Roberts would be, after all, inevitable.

True, the woman had not yet noticed her, as the corridor was crowded with people, but it was only a matter of time. Susan thought it was better to get it over with.

On the one hand, she really didn't want to talk to Clare, but on the other hand she thought it was a good opportunity, to find out what was being said around town now.

Maybe it won't be a total waste of time. She concluded.

Carolin Roberts was literally a walking database, if you wanted to know who with whom where and why, you could find out anything from her. Here, Susan decided, to break in herself and see what rumours had been circulating among the locals lately.

She clenched her teeth and, with a learned smile, directed her steps towards Carolin.

Then the woman finally spotted her at which, she almost jumped up from her seat with joy, at the sight of her.

"Hello, Carolin."

"Susan! Hi! How good to see you...!" She was genuinely pleased. "...I was just thinking I could use someone's company, it's sad to sit alone like this, especially in these circumstances."

"What are you doing here? Have you come to see Joanna?" Susan asked. – "Yes, I was hoping to see her and maybe, somehow, comfort her, if I could talk to her of course, those police officers have been there for more than an hour!

Carolin had a good heart, and Susan did not doubt her sincere intentions. But personally, she thought of her as the last person she would have chosen, as her comforter in such circumstances."

But I'm not the one in Joanna's shoes. She summed up in her mind.

"I didn't know you two were friends." Susan confessed after a while. "Our children go to school together; we sometimes talk at class assemblies and at the post office..." Replied Carolin. "...But we haven't really met on a social level, but I thought she could use any friendship now, which is why I came.

You're right..." Susan nodded.

"...Only she's still in a state of shock, I don't suppose she'll be able to talk to you."

"It's okay, she just needs to see me and feel that people are supporting her."

Carolin smiled.

"Actually, no one knows what really happened." Susan dropped the hint. It was a good time to start this topic and see, if Carolin knew anything more about it."

"It's true, nobody knows anything..." The woman admitted. "...People are talking about the kidnapping, others, about her running away, my friends who have young children feel threatened, everyone is waiting for the police to finally declare that they have found her or, that they have made some kind of arrest in the case, for the time being, many, people are terrified and are being extra cautious."

"Obviously it's an extremely difficult situation, it's no wonder they are reacting this way. I am also afraid of what will happen next, we must be of good cheer." Susan confessed.

At the same time, she realised that both the police and the residents, have no idea who did it or how it happened.

"I left my son David with my family today before I got here too..." Carolin replied. "...This is madness!

"I agree..." confirmed Susan. "...In my opinion, the most incredible and disturbing thing is this Voodoo doll, how did it get there..." Susan stopped speaking in mid-sentence.

She bit her tongue, realising at that moment she had just said too much. At the same time, she had broken her oath, which obliged her to keep this information confidential, as anything one of the patients said to her should remain exclusively between them and the psychologist.

Susan, however, was now repeating what Joanna had told her about in therapy, and it was too late to back out of it.

Although she had stopped talking so as not to delve further into the subject, Carolin had already managed to become curious about the new news.

The woman's eyes momentarily opened wide, intrigued.

"Voodoo doll...?" She repeated. "...You mean black magic?" She wanted to know more, but Susan had absolutely no intention of continuing. "I've acted stupidly, Carolin..." she replied. "...I shouldn't have said that. Please swear to me that you won't repeat it to anyone." She asked.

"Okay, I promised."

Even so, Susan knew immediately that she had acceded too quickly to her request and her promise, was worthless.

Because she noticed how her eyes almost lit up with excitement, of new idea to gossip about.

At one point she even felt that she would have run out of the hospital if she could, to share this information with someone immediately.

"I'm serious...!" Said Susan firmly, as soon as she saw Carolin, starting to squirm restlessly in her chair. "...If it comes out, it could be very damaging to the investigation!" She added, emphasising the seriousness of the situation.

The woman gave her an arrogant look that said, "Who do you think I am?" "I see..." She replied after a while, at the same time you could see her thinking intensely. "...Just, where does this kind of doll, could come from?" She added, more to herself than to Susan.

"Leave that in the hands of the police, it's their job to find out." Susan tried to end the conversation.

But Carolin, was just starting to get the hang of it.

"But just think, Susan..." Carolin started to say. "...Where does black magic come from? From Africa, yes? In our town, no one had ever even heard of it before, until now, as soon as this couple from Ethiopia got here, they've been living here, how long? Six months? And already such things are happening! Think about it and tell me, don't you find it suspicious?

"Carolin for God's sake! Come on!"

"I'm not suggesting anything, I'm just stating the facts."

She said it as if Susan didn't know it was the other way round.

"Oh, really?" Susan replied, thus letting her know that she knew exactly what was on her mind.

Carolin again sent an arrogant look in her direction.

"What if it could be a lead, for the police...?" She continued.

Susan was silent on this thread, she had no intention of participating in this conversation, she sat quietly and watched the people walking down the corridor.

But Carolin, continued her monologue.

"...I think we need to report this to the uniformed people, so they can investigate it, maybe these Africans are behind it? And little Magda is somewhere in their house? Most likely in the basement, tied up, crying, hungry, maybe they are even performing some kind of witchcraft on her?" She went on, completely letting her imagination run wild.

"Carolin, what the hell are you talking about...!?" finally, Carolin became unbearable. - ...Come to think of it, they flew in from Africa, bought a house worth a small fortune, why? To kidnap children here! Susan could no longer contain her irritation, after listening to all the silly things, Carolin was saying.

"You never know, anything is possible...." the woman did not give up. ...Remember, Magda has disappeared, and no one knows where she is, so all eventualities must be considered.

This is where I must agree with her, partly... Susan thought. "...But only partly, because someone knows what happened to her and where she is now." She added in her mind.

Susan pulled out her phone to check what time it was, completely ignoring Carolin, who continued to say something to her.

It was 04:25 pm.

At this point, she decided that she had already wasted enough time on a pointless conversation with Carolin, who was increasingly starting to get on her nerves.

From her next monologue, she didn't hear a word of it, completely stopping listening to her.

She got up and moved towards the locked ward where Joanna was staying, leaving the annoying woman behind without saying goodbye.

In fact, she should have waited further, but the limit of her patience had been exceeded.

As Ms Joanna Richardson's psychologist, she felt she should have priority to meet her, apart from the police of course.

Without asking permission, she entered the room where visitors were received.

As she looked around her, she found that she couldn't see officers, who should now be talking to Joanna.

She walked slowly through the large room and connected the dining rooms to a makeshift kitchen and a TV room, separated by thick glass. On the way through the corridor at the sides, there were three other smaller, more private rooms with closed doors that could be glimpsed through a small security window.

Susan approached the first of these to see if anyone was inside, but found it empty.

It was only in the third and final room that she found Joanna.

Seated in a deep armchair, she was looking out of the window with absentminded eyes; with her were two men, dressed in suits.

The first was a little further away, sitting to the woman's left, holding a notepad with one hand and a pen in the other, ready to write down a statement.

The second man, facing her with his elbows resting on his knees and leaning slightly forward was moving his lips, clearly trying to get her to talk.

Susan could hear nothing through the thick, soundproof door.

She couldn't read his lips, but it appeared that the policeman was speaking very calmly and patiently to Joanna.

As she looked at Joanna in turn, she could easily guess that the woman was saying little, if anything.

This was evident from the expression on her face, which gave the impression of being completely devoid of any emotion, completely motionless and petrified like a statue.

She watched them until she was startled by an orderly, thus jolting her out of her thoughts.

The man spotted Susan, standing by the door and peering inside, as he returned from his rounds to his seat behind the desk in the small reception area at the end of the corridor.

He decided to approach her.

"Is there anything I can help you with?" he asked Susan.

"Oh, I'm sorry..." she was embarrassed. "...I'm Mrs Joanna Richardson's psychologist, I'm here to visit."

"I understand, as you can see, there are officers with her now...." The paramedic replied. "...Would you like to wait outside?" he asked politely. "You know, I've been waiting for quite a long time, I think all the indications are that they won't be finished soon." Saying this Susan pointed with her head to the room, they were standing by.

She felt embarrassed that she had been caught peeping, so she decided to clear the atmosphere a little.

"Excuse me..." She began. "...I didn't mean to spy." She added smiling in agreement.

"Everything's all right, but unfortunately, I'm going to have to insist that you wait outside, this is a closed ward, and you can't be in here alone." The man replied in a friendly yet firm manner.

"Okay, actually I just wanted to ask you a few questions, about her current condition, perhaps, you could be so kind as to answer them for me...?" Susan replied. "...it would save a lot of valuable time that way."

"I'm sorry, but I'm not authorised to do that."

"Please, it's only a matter of concern, over her mental state..." She didn't give up. "...She has been my patient for a long time, I am concerned about her health." Saying this, she pulled out a business card as proof of the truth of her words.

The man took it in his hand and read it carefully.

"You know..." He began uncertainly. "...I'm new here, I wouldn't want to get in trouble." He added, clearly embarrassed by the situation.

"Please, don't worry about anything..." She encouraged him. "...I'm not going to ask for any confidential information, I just want to know if there has been any marked improvement with her mental state, in short, is she feeling better now?"

"All right, so as far as I know, Mrs Richardson has gone through a severe mental breakdown, brought on by a huge shock...." He began, reciting the definition from the textbook. "...There was no interaction with her for the first couple of days when she came to us, she didn't want to take food, so she was fed intravenously..." he said what Susan had known for a long time, but she listened to him patiently, because, after all, he was doing her a favour. "...As of today, the patient's condition has improved somewhat, although she is still severely depressed and rarely speaks, but she is feeding herself and making more and more contact with her surroundings. He finished speaking stressed, as if he were passing an oral test, in front of a professor."

"Thank you very much, I am extremely grateful."

"Now, I don't want to be rude, but would you like to sit in the waiting room?" "Actually, you've told me everything I wanted to know today, so I can go now, thank you." She moved towards the exit.

The paramedic watched her for a moment longer, before she reached the end of the corridor and disappeared behind a door, then returned to his post.

Susan walked out of the locked ward and reflexively looked towards the waiting room, where Carolin had been sitting just a few minutes ago, but she was no longer there.

She paused for a moment, then moved ahead to the main entrance. She wondered where Carolin, who was supposedly waiting to see Joanna, had gone.

"I'm wondering what had made her give up her visit? I guess she's not stupid enough to immediately start telling people, about this doll and her thoughts. Or maybe, just maybe, she went to the bathroom and continues to be in hospital?" Susan pondered, marching down the corridor then she stepped outside.

Let her do as she pleases, I don't care. She added in her mind, then headed in the direction where she had parked her car.

After walking a few dozen metres, she arrived at the vehicle, dug the keys out of her handbag, opened it and got in.

She took her phone out of her handbag and placed it on the passenger seat.

It was 04:47pm.

"Probably the right time to go home, by the time I get there it will be past five." She concluded.

She plugged her phone into the radio, eased into the upholstery of the car, to put on some music to make the journey more pleasant.

She started the engine and carefully merged into the traffic, but only drove a dozen metres or so, and found herself in a traffic jam.

In the distance, she could see two police cars, standing with their lights flashing red or blue.

Nearby on the street, parts of a vehicle were lying scattered about, it looked like a serious car crash.

"Damn it." She cursed under her breath.

Sitting idly, she turned on her favourite relaxing album, by a German group called "Enigma."

As she listened to the music, she stared mindlessly ahead, waiting for the cars to start moving forward.

The music made the wait more pleasant, so she didn't rehash the stress of being in a hurry.

Suddenly, however, during the second song, the relaxing tunes abruptly changed to the melody from her phone, set as the cue for an incoming call, which momentarily filled the car.

Surprised, Susan twitched in her seat which caused her heart to accelerate through a sudden feeling of anger.

She immediately pressed the green button, confirming that the call had been accepted, without checking the number.

As soon as possible, she wanted to switch o the loud and unpleasant sound, that made her head hurt.

"Hallo!" She called out into the receiver.

"Oh, Susan...?" A frightened, feminine voice that Susan didn't recognise at first rang out. "...Am I disturbing you?"

"Yes, no, sorry, who is this?" Susan was confused.

"It's me, Nattaly..." The woman replied. "...You said to call you, if I wanted to meet up."

Susan immediately felt her nervousness pass.

She had hoped to hear from Nattaly, but she didn't expect her to do it so quickly.

"Yes Nattaly, I'm sorry, I'm just coming back from the hospital and I'm cranky, because of the traffic. - Susan explained.

"I understand, it`s all good..." Nattaly replied. "...I'm still in town, do you fancy coming with me for some drinks?"

Susan instantly analysed the current situation in her head.

It's twenty minutes to five, I can spare an hour for her, at the most, I'll come back a bit later and say there was traffic. She concluded.

"Of course…" She replied after a while. "...Where are you now? Can we meet at the Café Orbi in five minutes? I'm not far away."

"Okay then, see you there." Nattaly replied and hung up.

In the car the quiet music sounded again.

Susan looked in the rear-view mirror, then carefully reversed the vehicle and turned into a small side street on the left.

From here, she was not far from the café and in fact, thanks to Nattaly, she remembered that she could have avoided the traffic jam before, using the side streets just for that.

"Better late than never." She said to herself already driving leisurely. As she approached the place, she felt excitement at the thought of meeting her old rival.

She couldn't wait to hear her talk about her failures at university and how, in the end, she ended up back in North Hill, with a young child.

Susan wanted to hear Nattaly lament, describing her life as one big string of failures with an unwanted pregnancy, interrupted studies, a wasted future and unfulfilled dreams.

She relished this thought at the time, driving to the meeting. But her good mood, was soon to turn unexpectedly into a huge disappointment.

What she hadn't anticipated was, for the next half hour of her meeting with Nattaly, she would have to sit, put on a good face and listen to her boasting about her wealth, thus bringing Susan, to an internal boiling point. After this conversation, only one question would remain in Susan's mind when it came to Nattaly's private life:

How the hell did this whore come into such money?

21

That day has come.

'A man is great not by what he possesses, but by what he is; not by what he has, but by what he shares with others.'

Eight months earlier,

25 April 2008, London, Canary Wharf, office of the agency "BnBL", 09:55am.

Lucy Clarke, the secretary, had been standing at the agency's door for almost an hour.

She was sure she had arrived on time, as there was no mention on Saturday that the opening hours were due to change on Monday.

On weekdays it was nine o'clock in the morning, they always arrived at work at this time.

Most of the time it was George arriving first to open their office.

Apart from him only Matthiew, who never turned up for the early schedule but usually in the afternoon or not at all, had the keys to the building. Lucy tried to call George several times, but the boss's phone did not answer, invariably remaining switched off.

By this time, the secretary began to sense that something very bad might have happened, because it was completely unlike George.

He was never late and always answered staff calls, even on his days off. Lucy didn't have Matthiew's number, so she couldn't try to find out from the other boss what was going on.

Then she thought she had two choices - keep waiting or go home.

She concluded that she couldn't just go, so she remained at the door.

She checked her phone again, nervously.

It's coming up to ten o'clock, someone's going to show up any time now. She thought.

She was right, no more ten minutes later, Jack Johnson, one of the estate agents, emerged from around the corner.

The time now was 10:05am.

"Hey Lucy...!" He called out as he ran across the street, in a slightly stunned voice, he was clearly in a hurry. "...Am I late?" he asked coming closer, at the same time wrinkling his eyebrows in confusion.

He clearly looked surprised that Lucy was still standing outside the building and the office was still closed.

"Actually, yes and no, I don't know." She replied unclearly.

"What are you doing here? Where is George?"

"Well, I don't know, I've called him a couple of times, but his phone is switched off, only voice mail answers all the time."

Jack furrowed his eyebrows even more; he knew straight away that George was not acting like this, never.

They had been working together for two years, and this was the first time no one knew where he was or why he was late.

"That is odd..." He said thoughtfully. "...Have you called ginger?"

"I don't have his number, obviously he can`t bother to let us know what is going on."

Naturally, they were talking about Matthiew, who had been jokingly nicknamed 'ginger' among the staff because of the colour of his hair. However, no one had the courage to tell him this directly and he was only called this in his absence.

Some employees preferred the nickname "lunch box", due to Matthiew's being considerably overweight.

Sometimes they even called him "fat bastard" but it was simply too rude a term, exceeding the limits of good humour and manners. Therefore, they were limited to these, the first two nicknames.

"I've got his number..." Jack said and pulled his phone out of his pocket.   "

"...Knowing him, he probably got drunk last night, I won't be surprised if he doesn't pick up at all." He added, winking at Lucy.

The girl smiled at him.

However, to Jack's surprise, Matthiew picked up, and after just the second beep.

Which made the man a little confused.

"This is Matthiew Braddock; how may I help?" he said in a serious, formal tone.

His voice was clear and sober, it meant he must have been up for a long time.

"Hallo, boss..." Started a little surprised Jack, but quickly corrected himself. "...This is Jack Johnson, I'm outside the agency but there's no sign of George anywhere, I'd like to know what time we open today?"

"Oh, it's you, Jack."

The man heard in the receiver, that his boss was in some crowded place, and the noises were all around him.

Jack thought he might be somewhere on public transport, but at the same time he knew this was unlikely, as Matthiew very rarely used it, and certainly not on weekdays.

As they were close to the agency, they had their own parking spaces reserved, so, like George, he moved by car on those days.

"I'm sorry, I forgot to call you." Matthiew said suddenly.

These words from his mouth, sounded, to say the least, weird.

Because, he had never called any of the employees before and most of all, never apologised to anyone.

Jack felt completely thrown off guard, he certainly hadn't expected to hear an apology from his arrogant boss.

At that moment he thought something was very wrong here, but he didn't yet know what it was.

Either way, Matthiew knew something and kept that information to himself, for now.

Jack looked at Lucy, with puzzlement and confusion.

The secretary waited patiently, watching him curiously as he continued talking to their boss. - Is something wrong, boss?

"This is not a phone conversation..." Matthiew replied briefly, then, quickly changed the subject, so as not to give Jack a chance to ask too many questions.

"...Are you alone, in front of the agency?" He asked.

"Lucy is here with me."

"Okay then, listen to me carefully now, I want you to do something for me."

"Of course."

"I want you to inform everyone, that tomorrow at 10am in the office, we have a team meeting, everyone's presence is compulsory, whoever does not turn up can immediately say goodbye to their employment with me, repeat everything exactly as I said, word for word, understood?"

Jack listened to him with his mouth open.

Lucy, standing next to him, didn't take her eyes off the estate agent, curious as to what Matthiew had just said.

"Okay boss, I'll get right on it…" Jack replied. "…What about work today?"

"Take the day off, we won't be opening the office...." Said Matthiew. "…I'll be in touch with you, see you later."

As Matthiew hung up, Jack stood still for a moment with the phone pressed to his ear, his mouth still open in a confused expression.

His boss abruptly ended the call, giving him no opportunity to add anything more.

He put the phone back in his pocket and turned his gaze to Lucy, who stood impatiently, waiting for some information.

When she saw that they had finished talking, she immediately asked:

"Well, what is it?"

"Well, nothing...." Jack replied, discouraged. "…We can go home. Lucy was irritated by this answer, felt unsatisfied and wanted to know more.

"But what did he say? What do you mean go home? What's going on?" She bombarded him with questions.

"Lucy, I know as much as you do, he hasn't given me any details, except that we're all supposed to be here tomorrow for a gathering, at ten o'clock in the morning..." he replied. "…I must tell the others." He added, already more to himself than his colleague.

Lucy continued to look at him with concern, full of questions and doubts.

She was worried about George.

"Where is George?" She finally asked.

"Really, I have no idea Lucy, but my gut tells me that something stinks here, we won't know anything until tomorrow, we must wait..." He replied. "...Is there anyone else coming here today?"

"I think Terry's supposed to start at eleven." She replied.

"I must call him and tell him not to bother."

"Then why don't we go and sit down somewhere? We'll have a coffee and call everyone," the secretary suggested.

"Good idea, I was in such a hurry today that I didn't even get a chance to have a coffee and now, it turns out, we must keep ourselves busy all day." "I didn't expect that either, but what can we do? Let's leave."

Across the street was the "Costa" café, which they chose as their next stop, so they both set o for the pedestrian crossing.

Both Lucy and Jack were feeling, uneasy about the situation.

They wondered where George was, and the lack of any information only added to their fear.

Nevertheless, they were aware that whatever had happened, it could not be a harbinger of good things to come.

The whole "BnBL" team sincerely sympathised with the good-natured boss, for some he was even like a father and an example to follow. This could not be said about the attitude of the employees in their relationship with Matthiew, because they simply had to put up with him. They all realised what kind of person he was and feared a situation where Matthiew would become their immediate superior.

The agency staff also knew that only George could maintain order and harmony in the business at a time when Matthiew was bringing chaos. Unfortunately, Lucy and Jack's fear and bad feeling, were to prove justified, the following day.

But neither of them had yet guessed that the day Matthiew had long looked forward to had just arrived.

The day when George would leave, and he would head the agency.

The next day, 10:07am.

All the staff arrived at the office before ten in the morning, not wanting to risk losing their jobs, just as Matthiew had threatened.

The agency employed a total of six people of which, only two had a full-time contract.

The team included two secretaries, Lucy Clarke and Katy Taylor who worked in shifts.

In addition to them there were four estate agents in the office, Jack Johnson and Andrew Harris also working half-time, rotating every three days of the week.

And Terry Smith and Ralph Williams, who, because they had the most work experience, were employed on a full-time basis.

Lucy and Jack arrived at the office as early as 09:20, immediately followed by the rest of the staff , so that at ten o'clock the team was almost complete.

The only one missing was Matthiew, who had told them to assemble punctually, but was obviously late himself.

It was not difficult to guess that this was due to Matthiew's lack of respect and competence towards the people who worked for him.

It didn't even cross anyone's mind that perhaps some fortuitous accident might have stopped the boss.

Instead, it was assumed that he was doing it on purpose, because that was exactly what suited his character.

Employees waited patiently outside the agency, passing the time with speculative conversation.

Some were sipping coffee from takeaway paper cups, smoking cigarettes in the process.

The main topic of conversation was, of course, George.

All in unison expressed deep concern at his sudden disappearance the previous day and guesses were made as to what might have happened to him.

Mere curiosity gave way to concern for his fate, an able boss and good friend.

He had not turned up for the past twenty-four hours and his phone, remained silent as if spellbound.

Unfortunately, this left the group with little choice but to slowly consider the thought of the worst-case scenario, while hoping that everything would turn out alright after all.

Time passed slowly in stressful anticipation when 10:10am appeared on the clock.

At that point, as it was unanimously agreed that Matthiew needed to be called, they saw his car approaching.

The boss stopped the vehicle on the opposite side of the street, in a specially reserved parking space, and then slowly and unhurriedly began to get out of it.

Everyone was already very much annoyed and impatient after waiting for him.

As they watched him walk calmly towards them, it added fuel to the fire.

"This guy has time for everything." Someone spoke up.

The moment he was close enough, he could be seen embracing the small group of people with his eyes, checking quickly that no one was missing.

They're lucky, they all came. The boss thought.

"Sorry I'm late." Matthiew declared.

Again, he wasn't fooling anyone, they all knew very well that these were just empty words.

They knew him well enough to know that he really didn't give a damn about keeping them waiting.

"Feel free to come inside." He added and walked to the door, holding the keys in his hand.

He opened the lock and was the first to go inside then, stood at the door and waited until everyone had entered the office, as the shepherd counted his sheep.

Once he had counted a team of six agency staff, he closed the door behind them and moved inside.

The office of "Bradley and Brad Lettings" was small, but modernly furnished and spacious enough so that everyone could move around freely.

"Well..." Matthiew said loudly. "...Let everyone take a seat. After he had said this, some of the employees pulled out chairs from behind their desks and sat down on them, while others simply sat down on their desks.

With every passing minute, one could literally feel the tension rising in the room, as people looked at each other nervously in anticipation of what the boss was about to tell them.

The uneasy atmosphere seemed to particularly affect the two ladies Lucy and Katy, who, perhaps most of all, were worried about George Bradley at that moment.

Matthiew, too, sat high up on his desk to be the centre of attention. "Thank you all for coming..." He started his speech, and all eyes landed on him. "...Because there is no easy way to say what I must tell you now, it is best if I say it straight away, without unnecessary digression..." He continued.

After this introduction, the employees, again exchanged anxious glances.

"... Well, my friend and business partner and your boss, George Bradley, suffered a serious heart attack on Sunday night, and unfortunately, he is no longer with us."

For the time being, there was still complete silence in the office, with everyone staring at Matthiew without saying a word, as if the significance of what he had just said had not been immediately grasped or allowed to sink in.

It was only when a few seconds had passed that the women began to sob loudly.

"What exactly had happened?" Andrew Harris, one of the agents, finally asked.

"As far as I know it was in the middle of the night, he called the emergency services to summon an ambulance for himself claiming he had suffered a heart attack...." responded Matthiew... "Medics, on arrival at his flat, took him to an ambulance where, on the way to hospital, he suffered a cardiac arrest, subsequent attempts at resuscitation were unsuccessful, the official time of death was at 6am on Monday morning..." he explained, then added. "...As I am, or rather I was, George's, first emergency contact, I was informed of this, at seven o'clock in the morning, I naturally went to the hospital where I completed all the paperwork involved, which is why I did not arrive at the office yesterday." He added.

Jack Johnson and Lucy Clarke looked at each other.

This explained where Matthiew had been at the time Jack called him, it was the hospital and not public transport.

The rest of the staff listened intently, but he had nothing more to say on the subject.

Lucy and Katy burst into tears and the others, lowered their heads sadly.

Only Matthiew Braddock sat motionless, showing no signs of empathy. A discerning eye could see that, in truth, George's death did not make the slightest impression on him, and the people in the office with him at the time also recognised this.

This was to be expected of Matthiew, everything in his current behaviour was to be expected of him.

Yet no one expected him to be so callous as to not show even the slightest regret at the loss of his partner.

A person he had known for many years and who considered him, after all, a friend.

The staff sat in silence; nobody really knew what to say.

They were overwhelmed by immense sadness and a feeling of sudden emptiness at the loss of George.

"The funeral will take place in two days..." Matthiew broke the silence. "...Until then, the office will remain closed, I will let you know exactly where and when the funeral ceremony will take place as well as when we will return to work, that's all for today, thank you all again for coming, you can go home." He added in conclusion.

Those gathered began slowly, rising from their seats and heading towards the exit.

Lucy and Katy walked side by side, holding each other's shoulders, all the while sobbing and wiping away the tears running down their cheeks. Once the last person was out the door, they realised Matthiew had been left alone inside and closed the door behind them.

Some turned around surprised that he had not gone outside with them. But the others preferred that he stayed inside the building, because they knew he did not share their feelings.

It was better for them to leave his empty words about how much he regretted George's death to himself now.

It wasn't the right time to listen to his outright lies, no one felt like it at the time.

So, it suited everyone that he left them alone and in peace they could, mourn George.

Once they had left, Matthiew stood by the door for a moment longer, then turned towards the office.

He ran his satisfied gaze over it slowly and a big smile appeared on his face, stretching almost from ear to ear.

"Yes... well now, I'm the boss here." He said to himself contentedly, then set o for the office that until two days ago had belonged to George.

He walked through it with a slow step, savouring every second. When he reached his desk, he settled himself comfortably in George's chair, then put his feet high on the table top.

"What do you think of that now, old geezer? Now this is my place!" he said loudly.

Even so, at the same time he was constantly aware that this was not quite the case yet.

For there was Nattaly, George's daughter, with whom Matthiew, had no contact.

George had never trusted his partner enough to give him his daughter's phone number.

Especially as she, clearly, did not wish it.

However, this situation gave him the perfect excuse to talk to her.

And in time also to try to pull her to his side.

His intuition, all the time, told him that in the end he would be able to establish a thread of understanding and convince her to co-operate. In the depths of his soul, he even felt that Nattaly was a bit like himself, as far as certain character traits were concerned.

"Well, yes, I absolutely must get her phone number, but how...?" He began to ponder. "...George's phone, it was left in his flat, I won't get there without his lawyer's permission." He said to himself.

He proceeded to search through George's desk, drawer by drawer.

He checked each sheet of paper for a clue.

It wasn't until he opened the last drawer at the bottom of the desk and started shuffling through it that a small notebook appeared to his eyes. Upon opening it, it was apparent that old-fashioned George had made various notes in there so as not to overload his memory, there were also phone numbers.

He probably thought that no one would find it here, or had forgotten, in fact it doesn't matter. He stated contentedly.

Some of the numbers were written in red pen and the notebook itself, was almost at the bottom of the drawer.

Matthiew took it in his hand, then began to look through it carefully, page by page.

Only halfway to the end did he find a piece of paper tucked inside, neatly folded into a cube.

He straightened it out slowly and realised that there were phone numbers printed on it, with the date "23 March 2004" written at the top. Indeed, it was a list that had been supplied to George, by Lucy, having previously obtained it from the telecoms.

Matthiew quickly ran his eyes over it.

Then, after a moment, he was delighted to see that next to one of the numbers marked in red marker, George had written "Nattaly" in pen.

"Gotcha! He he he... This must be my lucky day." He said to himself, smiling mockingly.

For a moment he still considered whether to make a phone call to her straight away or hold off until the evening.

In the end, he decided that there was no need to be in such a hurry. So, he folded the piece of paper back four times into a small square and then, just to be safe, stuck it in an inside pocket in his jacket.

He closed the drawers and leaned back comfortably in George's chair.

Well, it needs to be celebrated He thought contentedly.

A few seconds later he stood up, walked past the desk and headed for the door to the room, on his way out, he deliberately left it open behind him. He made this gesture on purpose because he recalled George's words when he called out after him and always told him to close the door. In Matthiew's mind it was supposed to be a symbol of the fact that he was now the one giving the orders and the days of obedience were becoming a thing of the past.

He stopped in the main office with a broad smile on his face.

"Yes, this is going to be a good day." He said to himself.

Without wasting any more time, he walked out into the streets and closed the doors of the agency.

He looked around, wondering what to do next.

The weather was nice, but it was still very early in the day.

Even so, he decided that he would call his two best mates, invite them to the pub and together they would start celebrating his promotion, disregarding the fact that his watch only showed eleven fifteen. This was no problem at all, as most of his friends were unemployed men living on benefits who enjoyed alcohol and drugs.

Therefore, getting his companions together to drink alcohol first thing in the morning was not complicated.

Matthiew was in a great mood and, disregarding the small state of his bank account, he did not bother about having a libation tonight if his colleagues happened to be without money.

From now on, everything was going to change, including the flow of funds through his bank account.

I'll have a couple of large drinks and call Nattaly when my personal charm turns on, she won't be able to refuse me anything. He thought delusional as ever, he was overestimating his abilities.

Speaking of 'personal charm,' he imagined himself as James Bond, gallant and handsome, seducing beautiful women.

But under the influence of alcohol or other drugs, he looked like a horny virgin drooling over every member of the opposite sex.

Fortunately for him, alcohol effectively obscured this image, so he could continue to lie to himself.

As some say, "ignorance is bliss," it fit here like a glove.

Less than an hour later, Matthiew was already in "Peckham," South London.

He had previously arranged to meet two colleagues there, Harry Green and Simon Edwards,

in a pub called "The Kentish Drovers" and was now waiting for them to arrive.

It was his favourite area in the city.

Because in those years, in such a notorious area of London, access to drugs or prostitution was as easy as buy cigarettes, which meant that he could have anything he happened to want; if he could pay for it, of course.

After consuming more alcohol, he usually became very unpredictable.

As a result, he never knew what his drunken mind would demand of him. Especially as a rule, he never shied away from any kind of stimulants and, he was not used to deny himself anything in life.

Therefore, he preferred to have dealers and pimps at hand in case he felt like doing something different.

This was very convenient, especially for such a vain person.

In this district, he was practically surrounded by people who, for the right money, are ready to give him practically anything he wants.

On that day, he was going to celebrate the death of George, the only person who could command him and limit his plans.

He was immensely pleased that his partner was no longer stepping foot in this world so, he was going to get drunk, and he had to be sure that he would not lack anything.

The sun hung high in the sky and the temperature remained pleasant. It was past twelve, when Matthiew stopped for a moment outside the pub to finish smoking his cigarette, still waiting for his companions for today's celebration.

He took a drag on his cigarette and looked at the name of the pub that hung above the entrance.

I'm not going to get out of here on my own legs. He thought and smiled under his breath.

Excellent well-being maintained a good mood.

He felt that now everything would work out as he wanted, exactly as he wanted, almost one hundred percent certain that now, after George's death, nothing would stand in his way of achieving his dream fortune, thanks to the agency.

There was still Nattaly, but Matthiew had a plan for everything. As a first step, he assumed that he should start as soon as possible by opening, a new office in North Hill.

He had been interested in this locality for a very long time, but George had always categorically refused and never wanted to agree to it.

In addition, he knew that George, apart from his daughter, had no relatives to whom he could entrust his share of the agency.

Therefore, it was obvious that it would be Nattaly who will take over George's place in the agency by inheritance, if of course he had managed to draw up a will beforehand.

However, he could be sure that George had made provision for such an eventuality.

Because he had always been aware that he would never allow Matthiew to become the sole majority owner, of his agency.

So, he had also prepared himself for such an eventuality, in which case his aim would become, precisely, to convince Nattaly to cooperate. Thanks to the fact that he already knew her, he knew that she was very smart, and it would not be easy to pull her over to his side, but he downplayed this.

He knew how to manipulate people professionally and thought she would soften once he made her realise how much money she could earn if she agreed to help him.

He wanted to make her start imagining, large sums of money.

"Anyone can be bought; all I need is the right price." He stated.

From his calculations, it then appeared that the earnings could be counted in as much as six figures for the next couple of years.

And what number appears at the beginning of that number will only depend on how his plan, which he has been laying out in his head to perfection, for the past two years, goes.

And on whether Nattaly will want to join him.

If she did, the rest would go easily. He thought.

But at the very beginning, he still had to complete the negotiations for the sale, of a beautiful house in North Hill, to a rich couple from Ethiopia. In truth, the conversation had already started almost four years ago, but the couple, who had initially shown considerable interest, were then still looking for a house in other parts of England.

The couple eventually returned to "Bradley and Brad Lettings," where the conversation was resumed in the same place, where it had previously ended.

This meant that this time they were almost certainly determined to purchase, the property previously discussed.

Matthiew had already seen at his first meeting with Angelina and Ain Hailu how much they liked the villa in North Hill, he had then groomed them with his innate flair, and although at one point he thought he was keeping them on the hook they, defiantly, decided to "think about it some more." There was nothing surprising about this, as investing in a property, worth over £1 million, required time and careful thought.

In total, over the course of two meetings, Matthiew tried every way possible to apply as much pressure as possible to get them to agree to the deal. He was keen to sell this house, in this location, to these very people and it wasn't just about making good money.

For in this exceptional case, he was planning much more than just to make a sale, and his intentions at the time, looked far into the future.

At the same time, he was also already thinking how to repurchase this villa back, in the relatively near future.

His intention was, to get the same house back at a much lower price than the original.

In this way, he wanted to keep a good portion of the cash and once again take possession of the place, which he could put back on the agency's books.

And he knew exactly how he was going to do it.

He was confident that it could be done, if only Nattaly would help him. Since meeting her for the first time, four years ago, he had managed to forget how George had told him that Nattaly's name was a derivative of her mother, Noelle Kemp, the woman from whom he had separated.

George's daughter had been referred to exclusively as Nattaly for the past four years, so it took on and stayed that way.

Over time, Matthiew stopped wondering if the girl had a different name.

At some point, he had forgotten all about it.

Now he kept her phone number, safely in the inside pocket of his jacket. Soon, he was going to call and inform her of her father's death and the planned date for the funeral ceremony.

He had no doubt that Nattaly would come to her father's funeral. "When she gets here, we'll talk face to face, I'll have a chance to start implementing the plan, I'll explain everything and persuade her...." He said to himself while standing outside the pub. "...But all in good time, it's time to party!" He added exultantly when he saw his friends, Harry and Simon, finally approaching.

22

Christmas with a psychic.

'Faith and the mind are like two wings on which the human spirit floats towards the contemplation of truth.'

Fourteen years later,

25 December 2018, London, Camberwell Green, Rachel and Danny Davis's flat, 04:30pm.

The Christmas period was going quietly.

As she does every year, on the twenty-fourth of December, Rachel threw a small party for friends and family.

We invited a total of ten people, which for our living conditions was, a reasonable number of guests.

A party without children, heavily spiked with alcohol.

Rachel's sister Emily came with her husband Christopher, leaving Rachel's nephews at home for the time with a babysitter.

Connor and a couple of other good friends were also there.

Everyone had a great time, so it was safe to say the party was a success.

I felt I was in my element.

Admittedly, after my last encounter with Connor at the pool bar, when I went way overboard with the alcohol, I tried to limit my drinking habit intake a bit more.

But at the same time, I didn't try to pretend to take a page from it completely.

The Christmas party was the perfect opportunity for me to feel at ease among the guests, where no one looked at me with disapproval as I sipped another drink.

There were no unpleasant situations, and all those invited went peacefully to their homes just after ten o'clock in the evening.

The next morning, Rachel and I exchanged gifts and relaxed after last night's party, sitting on the sofa, and watching some film on the TV.

She got me an elegant, albeit, not super expensive, watch, and I bought, as a gift for my wife, gold earrings with her favourite gemstone - a small diamond and a beautiful red ruby.

I was a little surprised when she suddenly got up from the sofa, instead of relaxing with me, as we were in the habit of doing every year.

She set about clearing the flat of the remnants of the party.

I thought it was a bit strange, when she so unexpectedly started to bother about it.

Since it wasn't a mess and she'd never done it before, immediately on the first day of Christmas.

Especially since we had spent an hour together the night before, tidying up after our guests, so the next day we could spend lazing around.

This year, Rachel behaved a little differently than usual.

But I thought, she might be bored a little.

If she wants to clean everything thoroughly by all means do it, she doesn't have to sit around all day if she doesn't want to. I thought to myself. I could guess that she was doing this because she was expecting another visitor that day.

However, I didn't feel like thinking about it any further and bet that simply, she wanted to get on with something.

Still, I felt silly sitting around doing nothing while she was working. *Maybe it would be better to get it over with?* I thought and rose from the sofa to join her.

Of course, I could help with the cleaning, but I was terribly reluctant to do it at the time.

A little while later, I picked up the most visible mess, a couple of empty beer bottles and other drinks, sweet papers and so on.

Once I decided that I had done enough, I decided to end my participation in the action entitled "Cleaning the flat."

So, I headed to the kitchen to get the beer out of the fridge, then returned to the sofa in front of the TV.

Rachel, meanwhile, was doing something upstairs.

Being temporarily alone in the living room, I decided it would be useful to check the stock in our home bar.

I was then pleased to find that there was still quite a lot of alcohol left over from the night before.

It was customary for guests to bring a bottle of some kind of liquor as a gift.

In this way, all sorts of different coloured, spirits accumulated.

By putting some of the "gifts" in the bar and some in the fridge, also what Rachel and I had bought for refreshments, we ended up with more than everyone needed the night before.

Therefore, there was quite a stockpile.

I knew Rachel was looking at me unflatteringly as I sipped my beer. She resented me for it, and not at all surprisingly, but I still couldn't help myself, at the time.

I slowly started to agree with her when she said that my drinking problem was getting serious.

For this reason, I promised her that from next year, I would start attending Alcoholics Anonymous meetings.

My psychologist also advised me to do the same.

But it was one of those situations where it's easier to say something than to do it.

The professionals' opinions of me, were not favourable, which seriously jeopardised my career.

I feared that this was the beginning of the end of my police work. In particular, I was diagnosed with post-traumatic stress disorder and a developing alcohol dependency.

Everything that, in this situation, ruled out my return to duty temporarily or perhaps even permanently.

It became an increasingly real problem, and I was aware of all this. When I sometimes wondered what my future career in the police force would look like, I couldn't imagine it, which made me fall into extreme depression.

I would like to return to the service, but at the same time, I knew that it was more likely that I might be forced to take early retirement due to my mental state.

Even though, deep in my heart, I did not want to leave the service yet, common sense told me that I had to take such a circumstance into account.

Or maybe even, start preparing for it.

I thought about it many times.

I was 51 years old and no longer a young officer.

Therefore, such an eventuality as retirement was the natural course of things, and probably, for many people, it might seem like a good option. But for me, I couldn't imagine what I could do if I had so much free time to spare? Especially since, even then, I was already having problems with it. Time, which was running out so quickly, was increasingly playing against me.

But there was nothing I could do about it, so I tried not to think too often at the same time to save myself additional worries.

Things will be what they need to be. Soothed the troubled conscience of my mind.

It was past four o'clock when I unexpectedly heard a knock on the door. It was surprising, to say the least, as on the first day of Christmas, everyone was usually staying in their homes.

Therefore, the likelihood of someone visiting us that day was close to zero, and yet there they were.

I had no idea who would want to visit us that late afternoon.

Rachel was closer to the door, so it was she who went over to open it.

A moment later, I heard words coming from outside the hallway. As I leaned back on the sofa to see who had come in, I saw Connor and behind him was some older, short woman who I had seen in my life. Although I felt intrigued by the unexpected arrival of this strange-looking couple, I was in no mood to get up from the couch to join them. Instead, I momentarily ignored them and turned my gaze back to the TV, waiting for events to unfold.

When the three of them came into the living room a few seconds later, Rachel stepped in front of me, at the same time blocking the screen. "Danny..." She began to speak to me, slowly and calmly. "...I'd like to introduce you to someone."

At this point, an older woman, unfamiliar to me, approached me and held out her hand to greet me. I reciprocated the polite gesture.

"Good afternoon, Mr Davis..." She said, in a slightly husky voice. "...My name is Sarah White; I am a medium." She added, smiling at me in a friendly manner.

I looked at her confused, then turned my gaze to Rachel and Connor. "This can't be happening for real." My instincts commented on the situation.

"Excuse me, who are you? A clairvoyant?" I repeated in disbelief. "No Mr Davis, I'm a medium. I've been talking to your wife and a friend and the three of us have concluded that you need a guide to the spirit world." She said.

"A guide, to the spirit world...?" I repeated after her once again, not believing what I was hearing. "...I am terribly sorry, but is this some kind of grim joke?" I asked directing my gaze at Rachel.

She sat down next to me and put her arm around me, hugging me close. "Don't fret darling, it's only for your own good." She whispered into my ear, soothingly.

"We didn't want to tell you because we know how sceptical you are when it comes to this sort of thing." Connor interjected.

He was right.

In fact, I couldn't find an explanation for a lot of the circumstances that happened over the course of a few weeks.

But certainly, it would never have occurred to me to meet a woman who claimed to talk to ghosts.

It was ridiculous to me.

I looked at the unknown woman who was facing me and, for some reason that was only obvious to herself, she stood still with her eyes closed. Her head had tilted slightly downwards, and her face looked different. It was now as if she was more drawn and stiffer. Also her closed eyes did not move under her eyelids, while breathing slowly and deeply, as if she was putting herself into some kind of trance.

She looked so eerie that I felt shivers run over my skin.

"I feel the presence of a child, Mr Davis. It is close by and draws strength from your life aura..." She spoke up after a moment, remaining in the position she had assumed earlier, she added: "...There is also another soul, that of an elderly person, both of whom are lost and are looking to you for help."

I furrowed my eyebrows nervously and looked around me.

Then, I cast an angry glance towards Connor and Rachel.

"Can I please know, what you guys have been telling this lady?" I asked both.

But when I saw the expression of genuine embarrassment on their faces, I quickly realised that I was wrong to suspect them of something.

"They didn't say anything, no details, especially the fact that I talked about the circumstances when I was haunted by little Denise's soul... - My instincts were corrected, at which I became even more enraged." ...*If neither Connor nor Rachel told her about Denise, before they came here, then how is she now saying that she feels the presence of some child? And who is this other character I first hear about?* My mind was working things out.

"I swear to you Danny, this lady doesn't know anything, I didn't say anything, you can believe me," Connor spoke up.

"Me neither. - Rachel added.

I had no reason not to trust them.

For as long as I could remember, they had both done everything in their power to help me in some way, and I felt that I should be grateful to them for that.

"It's true Mr Davis, these people contacted me saying only that you needed assistance with events that might be paranormal and hard for you to interpret, nothing, other than that, I wasn't given any details as to what this assistance would consist of..." the woman explained, already looking at me normally. "...Now, you have two options to choose from, Mr Davis. The first is that you can immediately refuse my services, which means that I should leave. The second option is that we can work together to find out why the souls of the dead attach themselves to you..." She said patiently. "...I can leave Mr Davis, but they will remain, and I can swear to you that you will regret not wanting to try to find out more."

Frankly, I was shocked by this speech, and faced with a difficult decision. Either to go along with the proposal against everything I believed in or to stay by my beliefs and send her away?

I wondered what I should do.

However, I had to admit that Rachel and Connor had put me up against the wall.

I couldn't just say no and ask her out of the flat because she was very convincing, and I guessed how much effort and hope had gone into this meeting, checkmate.

On top of that, the female medium spoke in a way I couldn't ignore. Throughout the entire conversation so far, my instincts had not once alerted me to the fact that some kind of scam was taking place here, which was an extraordinary, positive sign.

"Okay, I agree...." I replied after a while. "...We can try."

The woman smiled at me in agreement, and on Connor's and Rachel's faces, I saw an emerging feeling of relief that took the place of uncertainty. I was probably the only person in the room at that moment who couldn't say they were somehow particularly happy.

It was supposed to be a quiet, festive day and it looked like I was in for a long evening.

Sara White, a female medium or so-called guide to the world of the dead, suggested that we go to some room with a table so that everyone could sit facing each other.

So, we chose for this purpose, the kitchen.

When we entered the room, the woman medium placed two candles on the table and lit them.

Then, the first task we were to perform, after taking our seats, was to form a circle by grabbing our hands.

In the end, Connor, Sarah and I took part, as Rachel was afraid to join us though.

Therefore, she decided to sit on a chair in the corner of the kitchen and watch everything from afar.

For a split second, I saw the look of fear appear on my wife's face, and I felt sorry that she had to go through this because of me.

But when Sarah communicated that Rachel did not have to participate, she was visibly relieved to sit a little further away from the table. At that point, the woman stated that we were ready to begin and in turn, advised us to hold hands.

I felt a little strange holding a friend's hand as I never done this before, but I quickly dismissed the feeling of slight embarrassment, especially when I realised that Connor was not making a fuss about it.

It was only 05:40 pm, but due to the wintry season, it was already getting dark outside, which naturally meant that the kitchen was in semi-darkness, lit only by two, medium-sized, candles.

At the time, I thought it made for quite an interesting atmosphere. The three of us holding hands at the table, the spirit guide leading us with closed eyes moving her mouth from which no words came out, in the darkness, illuminated only by two small wicks burning side by side. This made quite an impression on me and slowly I began to get more and more into the atmosphere.

I glanced over at Rachel, who also looked very curious, as did Connor.

We were all waiting to see what would happen next.

"At the outset, I must inform you that I cannot guarantee that we will directly contact the person I am trying to bond with..." She said suddenly. "...Sometimes it happens that the soul does not know how to do it or simply, they're too weak, at the time when I make my body available to them, I also transmit life energy, it becomes a kind of portal for the dead to the world of the living, then, I try to evoke in thought and word the soul that is closest to me, in this case it will be the form of a child that I sensed earlier just after I arrived, but there was another energy at that time, there are cases when another soul takes advantage of the moment I open up, and then the moment begins when the energies compete to take over my body and return to the world of the living, even for only a brief moment to say something else, the stronger energy wins, so remember, whatever happens, do not be afraid and do not, under any circumstances, break the circle." She added, in a serious tone.

Her gaze almost pierced through me and Connor, we just nodded our heads as a sign that we understood everything and would comply with the rules.

Rachel sat quietly, like a mouse.

The female medium closed her eyes and lowered her head, while breathing slowly and evenly. She sat in this position without moving for a few seconds and then spoke.

"I want to speak to the child who is in this house..." She said aloud. "...I have seen you before, and I know you are here. I give you permission to use my body now and introduce yourself. You have permission to use my energy. - She added and fell silent, waiting.

I decided it was best not to tell her that I was almost 100 per cent sure that the soul that was here was named Denise.

I kept it to myself, while using this knowledge as a small test to see if, surely, we were not dealing with an imposter.

If she really is honest, she shouldn't have much problem finding out for herself. My instincts were telling me.

"She's here, I can feel her..." She said suddenly, at the same time she slowly raised her head. "...Girl can't make contact; I can sense her fear..." She spoke taking short pauses. "...She is afraid of something, she is anxious, I can hear her, she is saying something, what are you afraid of child? Talk to me, follow my voice, yes, I can hear you, what's your name? Her name is Denise..." Saying this she turned her face towards me without opening her eyes.

In that moment I felt her start to squeeze my hand tighter, Connor's probably the same.

I must admit that although my hands are large and hardened and I am not an overly delicate man who is easily hurt, I felt the strength of an inconspicuous woman at that moment, which made me squirm slightly. - Damn it, I must endure, or else I will show embarrassment. - I was motivated by my mind.

So, I sat firmly in my seat, struggling against the unbearably imprisoned hand that was almost crushed by the lady.

"...Follow my voice, child, don't be afraid, use my energy..." She continued. "...There is also this other soul with us, it is approaching, whatever happens, don't let go..." She started to speak to us, but she didn't manage to finish her sentence.

Because at that moment, her body suddenly convulsed violently and momentarily, she straightened up stiffly on the chair by pushing her body forward firmly, raising her head at the same time, she turning her face upwards.

It looked unnatural and grotesque to say the least, as if she wanted, immediately, to see something located on the ceiling.

She continued to hold my hand tightly, and I felt her body start to convulse in a strong convulsion.

In the first few seconds, I was very frightened. I wasn't sure if I should react in any way, as the whole situation was extremely surreal.

However, the words of the clairvoyant lady were going through my mind, to remain calm at all costs so, so I did.

Instead, I thought, I had never in my life seen anyone normal make such movements as this woman was making now.

It was encountered at most in the circus or at some gymnastic performance.

When I looked at Connor in horror, he did not take his eyes off the lady with his mouth wide open.

Rachel, too, was observing the incident, eyes bulging, from her seat in the concourse, covering her mouth with her hand.

While the woman sat in position for a few seconds in silence, breathing deeply with her face upwards.

She continued like this for a moment then, remaining motionless, she spoke: "...JOOOHN...."

The tone of the medium's woman's voice became thick now and sounded serious, at the same time it seemed to come as if from some depth of something like a cave.

It was no longer her voice, it clearly belonged to a man.

I thought it was probably the other person the lady had mentioned before, trying to speak to us.

Despite the not inconsiderable stupor I was in, I found that communication came with great difficulty, because the first word sounded as if it had been spoken with great effort.

"JOHN...MCKANE... HELP..." She spoke slowly, in single words. We looked at the woman and waited patiently, not even for a moment, letting go of each other's hands.

We stayed in a circle, just as she had advised us at the beginning. At the same time, we looked at each other and silently exchanged ideas about what "John," might be about, but neither of us had any idea at the time who he might be.

Personally, I didn't know anyone named John, but it didn't really matter at the time.

I'll try to find out later. I thought.

"HELP...JOHN...HELP...DENICE...."

A male voice spoke as if at random, but the moment I heard the name, I trembled, and goosebumps appeared on my body.

The three of us looked at each other in disbelief.

I saw tears appear in Rachel's eyes, from behind which my wife's piercing gaze emerged.

It was then that I felt that I was finding it increasingly difficult to control the emotions that swept over me in their entirety and intensely affected my body.

When we turned our gaze back to the female medium, she was breathing deeply in silence.

After a moment, in one swift movement, she abruptly lowered her head as if lifeless.

It looked very disturbing, and I had the impression that she had lost consciousness.

This was a completely new experience for us, so neither of us knew how we should behave.

If we should have reacted in some way?

But we had promised not to move, so all we could do was wait.

"Are you alright?" I finally asked uncertainly, pulling her gently by the hand.

Her body moved inertly; she was unconscious.

I was already opening my mouth to speak to her again, when she took in air vigorously, at the same time giving us a sign that she had returned to reality.

This whole situation could not have lasted more than a few seconds.

Once she regained consciousness, she seemed very tired and confused.

She ran over us slowly with her eyes still dazed.

"Did, did we make contact?" she asked already in her feminine voice.

"Yes, I think we have." Connor replied.

"With the baby?" She wanted to know.

"A man spoke up…" I replied. "…He said a few words at a time.

Help, John McKane and Denice." Quoted Connor.

I understand, it seems someone else answered, but he quickly moved away, I felt his presence, but I felt the presence of the girl too, she was talking to me, I could hear her, she didn't know how she was supposed to contact us.

What she was saying was confirmed, but not completely, because the name "Denice" was mentioned.

That is, a name she could not have known even if, she tried to insinuate it all.

"Okay, there's another method I want to use today..." She announced. "...Please turn on the light." She instructed Rachel then blew out both candles.

Thus, ending the seance, then she let us know to let go of our hands. Then she went into the living room to get her things, leaving us alone in the kitchen for a while, I didn't know what to think about it all.

"What a situation." Connor commented briefly.

Apart from him, neither Rachel nor I had anything else to add, still analysing in our heads what we had just witnessed.

I thought it best to analyse everything thoroughly once we were left alone. Not knowing what additional attractions the clairvoyant woman had lined up for us this evening or how long it would all last.

As far as I was concerned, it could have already ended at that moment, just after the first adventure with the circle and the candles.

But apparently, there was to be something more.

When the woman returned, she was carrying something in her hand that, at first glance, looked like a folded chessboard.

Only when, she came closer could I read that the object said, "Ouija Board".

I had heard of this supposedly satanic spirit calling boards before but had never encountered one.

Having laid the board out on the kitchen table, the female medium sat down, a serious look on her face.

"I'm guessing you have some idea what this is?" she asked.

"Of course..." Connor replied. "...So-called, ouija board."

"That's right."

"I'm sorry to interrupt..." Rachel said. "...But it's a toy after all? I've seen those in children's shops."

"It's not a toy, Mrs Davis, and I think it's human folly that they are so readily available, it's just asking for trouble in its purest form, and I would even say that in the spirit world, it is generally believed that these items are sold on purpose, through the evil intentions of people who profess Satanism and have the task of bringing down as many demons as possible who serve the devil's powers." She added, pointing her finger at the board.

At this point, I thought that this was probably a slight exaggeration.

It was slowly starting to become too much for me.

However, I could not negate her words, as she had recently proven her credibility.

Nevertheless, there were still two explanations that could be considered and considered true.

The first was that she is a great actress who is additionally excellent at manipulating and changing her voice, or that her body really was embraced by an alien soul that we could not see at the time.

Either way, there was something compelling about it all, which is why we had to see it through to the end. - So, how does it work? - I asked.

"Basically, it's very simple, Mr Davis, each of you put two fingers of your right hand on the pointer, make circles around the board with it three times, then walk it to the centre and ask questions." She explained.

"The pointer itself should guide us with numbers and figures, answering our questions." Connor added.

"That's right, by making a circle three times on the board we open a portal between the world of the living and the dead." She said.

"How can you be sure it's neither of us pushing the pointer?" I asked again. "The trick is not to exert any pressure with the fingers held on the pointer, they are only supposed to rest gently on it, besides, none of us gain anything by making silly jokes, the situation is simple, if the pointer shows us the answer, then we will learn something, if not then we won't." She opined.

It made sense to me.

Connor certainly, wouldn't want to make fun of me to prove something. He acknowledged my instincts.

I was even less likely to do so.

So, even if Sarah tried to do something like that then, both Connor and I would know exactly that she was the one pushing the indicator by force.

"All right, all clear." I said.

"Shall we get started?" Connor asked.

"In a moment, you still need to know the most important thing and I stress this very clearly, remember, this is not a toy..." She pointed again to the board. "...And under no circumstances are we allowed to take our fingers off the pointer, we will only be able to do this when the session is over and we hover over the word "Goodbye", because if we make contact, thereby opening a portal, then if at some point one of us suddenly takes our fingers o the pointer this portal will close, this could mean that if anything has passed through it into our world, it will stay here, it could be a soul or a demon that will take up permanent residence in this flat, or worse, it could attach itself to one of us, then it could do you or me a lot of harm, it's very dangerous, so please don't underestimate my words and adhere to them, really, I know what I'm talking about." She said in a serious tone.

It gets better and better. Commented my mind.

But I didn't have the slightest desire to make jokes, and, to be honest, it didn't amuse me at all.

I looked at Connor, who, despite his interest in the subject, had gone so pale face that I thought he resembled a ghost himself at the time. Rachel also looked frightened and silently did not pull her hand away, with which she kept covering her mouth and her eyes, invariably huge. The situation was becoming increasingly tense, which was affecting me in a way I had never experienced before or subsequently.

In short, I was genuinely frightened looking at a board that should have been, in my mind, just an innocent toy.

And it was a completely different kind of fear. If I had to compare it to something, I would probably describe it as a fear of something you can't see, which could prove to be extremely dangerous.

Like putting your hand into a hole in a tree that is almost certainly filled with venomous insects.

This was the impression I got when the female medium described what was on the table in front of me at the time, and what the consequences might be if the board was used incorrectly.

It all worked on my imagination, negatively.

Well, let whatever happens happen. I thought.

The woman put two fingers of her right hand on the pointer that lay in the middle of the board. I followed her lead and did the same, after a while Connor joined us as well.

"Alright, we can get started." She said and started pushing the pointer so that it made the first circle after that the next and the next.

I just kept my fingers in place and didn't add any energy from myself to help circle the three circles, I had a feeling Connor did the same. After completing the first stage of the game, the woman stopped the pointer in the middle of the board, along with our hands resting on it.

She asked the first question out loud:

"Is, is the soul of Denise here with us?"

We sat, nervously watching the indicator.

A few seconds passed waiting in uncertainty as to whether anything would happen, the indicator, however, stood still.

"Is John McKane with us...?" She continued to ask.

Time passed, but the indicator didn't budge.

"I want to speak to Denice..." She tried. "...Child, are you still with us?"

More minutes passed, with no results.

It was then that I began to doubt whether this whole experiment would prove fruitful.

However, left with no other choice, I continued to wait patiently until the end.

"I feel your presence, speak to us, are you here child?" She said again.

Then the thought struck me that it was a little strange that she had just said this.

Admittedly, it could have been pure coincidence, but at the same moment, I also began to feel the familiar sensation that she was just near us. The feeling of being watched, which had plagued me since the shooting, returned.

I knew this sensation all too well, as it had already started the first night when I saw Denise after waking up in my and Rachel's bedroom, as she was then standing at the foot of our bed.

Then it attached itself to me, almost twenty-four hours a day, day and night.

Before I knew it, the days turned into weeks and, in time, months. And I could not get peace from the tiring feeling.

I lost myself for a moment in my own thoughts, recalling all these situations, which made me stop watching the pointer.

But when I noticed out of the corner of my eye that it started to move slowly, I was quickly brought back down to earth.

I lifted my gaze to Connor, who had the same surprised expression on his face as I did.

I could see that he was clearly in shock, so I could immediately rule out that he was helping the pointer move.

I then looked at the female medium, who, in turn, had her eyes tightly closed.

This made me realise that there couldn't even be any way she could guide the pointer to any letters or numbers, completely unable to see the board. I preferred to make sure that nothing was pre-meditated and that they weren't trying to play a joke on me because I still had a little doubt the whole time.

Connor and I looked at the pointer, which was moving towards the top left corner of the board.

We had to almost catch it up with our fingers so that it didn't slip out from underneath, as it moved suddenly and expectantly at quite a fast pace, until it finally stopped in the left-hand corner marking the word – "Yes."

"It shows the Yes." Connor informed the woman since her eyes was closed.

"How old are you?" she asked immediately.

The pointer stood for a moment longer on the word "Yes" then began to vibrate again, gently at first, to eventually take the direction confidently.

This time, it decisively points the numbers, 1 and 0.

"Ten," Connor said.

My heart sped up again as Denise was ten years old at the time, of her tragic death.

At the time, everything pointed to the fact that this time, she was the one communicating with us through this mysterious board.

On the one hand, part of me wanted it to be so.

However, at the same time, I feared what she might want to communicate with me.

I was troubled by the suspicion that her tormented soul was blaming me for her death, just as I felt responsible for it, which is why she was stalking me. In my heart, I knew there was nothing I could have done to prevent that situation, but I couldn't just let go of my remorse.

"I made eye contact with Rachel and, moving my lips without making a sound, I whispered," Denise.

Rachel was often able to read lips and this time I could also see that she understood what I was trying to communicate to her, because tears appeared in her eyes.

"Tell us, what is your name?" The clairvoyant lady continued.

At that moment, I was sure she was going to start spelling the name "Denise."

But, to my surprise, this was not the case.

The pointer once again moved confidently, but instead of going to the letter "D," it ticked "H" and then, one by one, the next digits, which all together formed the word "Help".

After that, my heart broke.

It was like a punch aimed below the belt.

I was overwhelmed by nervousness combined with despair and helplessness.

As a result, tears spontaneously ran down my cheeks.

"I could not help her..." I whispered, humbly lowering my head. ...She continues to beg me for help and I, can't do anything.

I had to say it, I just had to.

I unconditionally had to get it out of my system finally and once and for all, admit it in front of everyone.

At these words, Connor looked at me with a sad expression on his face, Rachel also looked in our direction, depressed by this confession. Nevertheless, no matter how painful the moment was for us at the time, it was the kind of breakthrough I needed.

Sooner or later, it had to happen.

When I think about it now, I can say with certainty that it was almost the perfect moment.

Only the female medium sat unmoved.

"It's not what you think, Mr Davis..." she spoke up suddenly. "...She's not asking you to help her at all. It's about something completely different, unfortunately, I don't know what it is yet..." She added in a calm tone.

After this statement I was completely confused.

"What do you mean, she's not asking me for help...?" my mind began to wonder feverishly. ...If not her then who? After all, clearly everything revolves around that word "help..."

The blood in the veins at my temples began to pulsate intensely which made my head hurt, especially on the right side where the already healed gunshot wound was located.

...I don't understand any of this, so why the dreams? Why does she appear late at night in my bedroom? Why does my emergency phone ring, all by itself? Why are things shifting? Why do I feel her

370

presence? What does she want from me? A restless mind bombarded with questions. I had many questions and not a single answer, hardly any comfort in such circumstances.

Before, at least, I had an explanation.

The justification that this was all happening because Denise's lost soul wanted compensation or help was far better than none.

But now it turned out that I had been wrong all along, and, in fact, I could no longer be sure of anything.

All this made me feel completely helpless, not to say defenceless. Everything spoke for the fact that the situation in which I found myself had outgrown me several times over, and only one fundamental question remained in my mind:

What, exactly, could she want from me?

"...Don't worry Mr Davis, I will soon explain everything to you." Added Sarah.

I needed some kind of explanation more than ever before.

At this point, I was completely exhausted, both mentally and physically, and I could not believe anything she told me.

The memories of that evening, which effectively and once and for all buried all my previous logic and outlook on the world, were going to stay with me forever.

However, before there could be any conclusion to all this, Sarah White wanted to ask a few more questions of the unseen guests.

We spent another twenty minutes at the board without receiving any more answers.

Then, I was relieved when the female medium decided it was time to end it.

It was past nine twenty when we collectively escorted the pointer to the word "Goodbye."

At that point, the guide stated that it was safe for us to take our hands off now.

Without knowing how more than three hours had passed, so when we had finally finished the session, everyone could finally breathe a sigh of relief and relax for a while.

Therefore, immediately afterwards, we spent the next few minutes remaining at the kitchen table, completely silent.

From the very beginning, no one quite knew what to expect that evening. But when we got to the end, I could honestly say that it was indeed an interesting experience, and I did not regret taking part.

We contacted the world of the dead, which helped me personally immensely in my future endeavours.

"Maybe, we should go to the living room?" Rachel suggested in a low voice, thus breaking the silence in the room.

Then she got up from her chair and, without waiting for anyone, made her way to the sitting room, leaving us behind.

"Let's go then." I added and pushed back my chair, getting up from the table at the same time, Connor did the same.

Finally, the bright-eyed woman joined us, and we all followed Rachel into the lounge room to rest more comfortably there.

I don't know about the others, but I felt completely exhausted.

I only guessed that only Sarah, our guide, felt worse than me.

The woman looked very tired at the time.

Connor and I left the kitchen.

Sarah stayed behind us to assemble her ouija board, then tucked it under her arm and set o after us, leaving the candles on the table as they had stood before, extinguished.

Once we were all comfortably seated on the sofas, it was time to take stock of the evening.

"Mr Davis..." She turned to me.

As soon as she started talking, Connor and Rachel immediately turned their heads, curious as to what she was going to tell me.

"... There is something I can't understand here..." she said, clearly thoughtful and tired at the same time. "...For some reason, you are attracting the souls of the dead to you, Mr Davis. I don't know what they expect from you or what they might want..." She collected her thoughts. ...However, I am one hundred per cent sure that the souls of the girl and the man who made their presence felt this evening want to tell you something, but unfortunately, I do not know why they chose you...

Well, that's brilliant, that's all I needed. I summed up my mind, irritated. Honestly, I didn't feel the slightest bit better at this news, but I agreed with it on this point.

Because sometime before, I had already begun to realise that this must be the explanation for these events.

Which, however, did not bring me one bit closer to understanding the situation completely.

Nevertheless, I needed to hear it from the mouth of a stranger, because I could not accept this fact myself.

Finally, at least I could come to terms with it.

"...But do not be afraid, I have not sensed any negative energies, you are not in danger of anything bad coming from them, they are just trying to make their presence known to you, quite clumsily, which can sometimes look scary, but these are the inherent feelings that come with dealing with the paranormal world, I can assure you that we are not dealing with a demon here, but with friendly souls, there is really nothing to be afraid of." She added in conclusion.

If she could see, even one of my nightmares, she wouldn't say there's nothing to be afraid of. My instincts suggested ironically.

I looked at Rachel, her eyebrows furrowed as a sign that something was wrong with her.

"I'm sorry, so you're saying there are a few souls stalking my husband?" she asked.

"Stalking is such a strong word, but yes, there is a man named John and a girl, Denise." She replied.

"But we don't know any John." Rachel replied and looked at me questioningly.

I nodded affirmatively, albeit, without conviction.

"In truth, I couldn't name a person close to me by that name, but the name McKane itself, was not entirely unfamiliar."

"You probably meant to say, we didn't know, because the guy is dead." Connor added.

"Well, yes, but that doesn't change the fact." Rachel was annoyed. "Okay, that's right..." The medium interjected. "...As I said, for some mysterious reason, this man is also trying to contact your husband." That's when I decided to end this meeting to really relax, I didn't have the strength to continue this, so I said:

"It's getting late."

I wanted to let everyone know that it was high time to go.

Rachel immediately picked up on what I meant.

"You're right, I think it's time for a rest." She said.

It was past 09:30 pm, and it didn't take long to convince anyone that it was getting late. Everyone clearly already felt like going to their house.

I went along with Rachel to escort the guests to the exit.

At the door, I thanked Sarah White for coming and for her help, then shook Connor's hand goodbye.

Rachel exchanged a friendly kiss on the cheek with Connor and thanked the woman. When they went outside, we were able to close the door behind them.

At last, we were left alone.

"What an evening." Said Rachel to me with relief, letting the air out, in her characteristic way.

"That's right, I'm exhausted."

"Me too. Would you like a cup of tea? Because I'd love to."

"Yes please." I replied, and we both went back into the depths of the flat.

Rachel headed into the kitchen and I, into the living room.

I was troubled by the name "McKane," my mind reminding me that I had come across it in articles I had read about North Hill.

McKane... Susan McKane? Are these two people related? my instincts prompted me.

I had to check it immediately.

I pulled out my phone and was already about to type the phrase into the search engine, but I didn't make it because not even five seconds had passed and, in that time, I hadn't yet reached the couch, when my wife called out to me.

"Danny, can you come over here for a minute?"

I immediately, but reluctantly, made my way to the kitchen at her request. When I got there, Rachel was standing stiffly by the door, so I walked over to her and stopped next to her.

I didn't even need to ask what it was about, as I saw from the spot the reason she had called me to her.

"I thought she had put them out." She said pointing her finger to the candles Sarah had left on the table.

"Because she did." I replied.

In that moment, Rachel experienced for the first time what I have had to deal with over the last few weeks.

"But they are lit." She added in a puzzled voice.

"That's right, welcome to my world." I replied calmly.

At that point, I felt that I was no longer impressed by such phenomena, but Rachel was genuinely surprised.

The two previously extinguished candles, which had been left alone on the table after our session, now flared up with the distinct radiance of their flames.

Rachel stared at them in a stupor; I knew she couldn't believe what she was seeing.

I suspected, however, that on that day, she had finally realised the foibles I had to deal with on a daily basis.

www.ingramcontent.com/pod-product-compliance
Lightning Source LLC
Chambersburg PA
CBHW030355030726
47497CB00002B/353